SKY ZONE

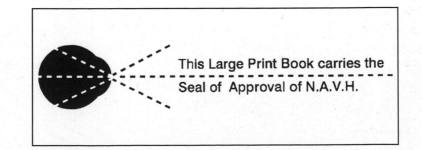

This Large Print Book carries the
Seal of Approval of N.A.V.H.

THE CRITTENDON FILES

SKY ZONE

CRESTON MAPES

THORNDIKE PRESS

A part of Gale, Cengage Learning

Farmington Hills, Mich • San Francisco • New York • Waterville, Maine
Meriden, Conn • Mason, Ohio • Chicago

GALE
CENGAGE Learning®

LIBRARY OF CONGRESS CATALOGING-IN-PUBLICATION DATA

Mapes, Creston, 1961–
    Sky zone : the Crittendon files / by Creston Mapes. — Large print edition.
      pages ; cm. — (Thorndike Press large print Christian mystery)
    ISBN 978-1-4104-7230-4 (hardcover) — ISBN 1-4104-7230-2 (hardcover)
    1. Reporters—Fiction. 2. Terrorists—Fiction. 3. Large type books. I. Title.
    PS3613.A63S58 2015
    813'.6—dc23   2014041098

Published in 2015 by arrangement with David C Cook

Printed in Mexico
1 2 3 4 5 6 7 19 18 17 16 15

For Mindy and Bernard,
With thanks, love, and admiration

ACKNOWLEDGMENTS

Special thanks to:

Patty, Abigail, Hannah, Esther, and CP for
your support and encouragement.
Anita Mapes for your creativity and
generosity.
Steve Vibert, Buck Alford, and Frank
Donchess for your timeless friendship.
Natasha Kern and Mark Sweeney for
believing in my writing.
LB Norton and Julee Schwarzburg for
making me a better author.
Jerry Jenkins and Nora St. Laurent for
your enthusiasm.
Joseph Cheeley III for expert legal insights.
Christie Cooksey for your keen eye and
friendship.
Jeane Wynn for your hard work on my
behalf.
Jason Chatraw for your guidance, expertise,
and friendship.

The team at DCC, with a special bow to Karen Stoller,
Amy Konyndyk, and Caitlyn Carlson for your keen eye, creativity, and tirelessness.
The gang at Starbucks for a fine place to write.
My readers for encouraging me to keep at it.

I have told you these things so that you won't abandon your faith.
For you will be expelled from the synagogues, and the time is coming when those who kill you will think they are doing a holy service for God.
This is because they have never known the Father or me.
Yes, I'm telling you these things now, so that when they happen, you will remember my warning.

— John 16:1–4

1

Festival Arena, October 6

A breeze scattered leaves across the familiar winding blacktop driveway that led Jack Crittendon to the back of the gleaming steel-and-glass Columbus Festival Arena. At 4:30 p.m. the massive parking lot was a ghost town, but soon it would be teeming with cars, school buses, campers, and Greyhounds. People would be coming from across the region to catch a glimpse of controversial senator and independent presidential hopeful Martin Sterling as he stumped through the swing state of Ohio with hopes of making it on the November ballot next year.

Eight months ago Jack would have been covering the event as a reporter for the *Trenton City Dispatch*. But after the debacle that sent four top *Dispatch* employees to prison for their involvement with the felonious Demler-Vargus Corporation, the newspaper

11

had folded and left him out of work. Things had been unraveling ever since.

He slowed at the guardhouse, where the slouching guy inside squinted to check the parking sticker on Jack's windshield. The gate lifted, and Jack zipped through. He curved around to the enormous loading docks in back of the arena, where on concert days roadies loaded and unloaded stage equipment and where the stars lived in their decked-out tour buses for the brief time they were in town.

Although Jack was thankful for the part-time job he'd found working for EventPros, the firm that provided security and guest services for events at the twelve-thousand-seat venue in downtown Columbus, something had to change. He had to find a full-time job in journalism or PR or anything that had to do with writing. Thus far, endless hours of research, filling out applications, and sending résumés had turned up zero, and he was feeling the strain at home.

Jack's wife, Pam, had been forced to give up her cherished role as stay-at-home mom to go back to work. She would have returned to the classroom, but her teaching certificate had lapsed. Plus, she wanted to spend her evenings with the girls, not grading papers and creating lesson plans. So she ended up taking a job as an administrative assistant at a local orthodontist's office.

Jack swung the Jetta into the dark parking deck, backed into his normal spot, and checked the time. He still had a few minutes. He dug around in the glove compartment for some mints and thought about texting Pam to let her know he'd arrived. They'd had to pay three more bills from their dwindling savings account, and it had caused major havoc between them on his way out the door. He felt as though she resented him for failing to provide, and he really didn't feel like talking with her.

But since she was eight months pregnant with Crittendon number three, he checked his phone to make sure he hadn't heard from her. No texts or missed calls. He leaned back and closed his eyes. It was a relief to get away for a few hours. Although he was grateful for Pam's mother, Margaret, who'd come to live with them after her husband died last winter, her constant presence in the midst of their deepening financial woes was stifling.

Jack stuffed a handful of mints into his pocket, locked the car, and headed for the staging area in the bowels of the arena. On his way, he double-checked his uniform: black lanyard with ID badge, flashlight on belt, khaki cargo pants, black Reebok high-tops, black EventPros golf shirt, and orange EventPros windbreaker. All set.

"Hey, Jack." His elderly coworker Edgar, seated behind a table stacked with pagers and walkie-talkies, ran a trembling finger across a page, found Jack's name, and signed him in. "You'll be on the floor. Section A-2. Take a radio."

Good. He liked being close to the action.

He grabbed the agenda for the evening and scanned the busy room. People aged seventeen to seventy worked for EventPros. Many of the retired ones like Edgar treated the job as a hobby. It gave them a chance to get out of the house, earn some gas money, and see all the big stars — from Justin Bieber and Keith Urban to Green Day, James Taylor, and Carrie Underwood.

Jack grabbed a walkie-talkie and untangled a headset from a knotted pile. Many of his colleagues, all dressed in similar uniforms, were sitting as long as possible before they would be required to stand for their four-to six-hour shifts.

He spotted the colorful self-proclaimed "survivalist" Brian Shakespeare sitting at a table with two other friends and headed over.

"Gentlemen." Jack exchanged fist bumps,

14

then clipped the radio to his belt and got the headset and mic adjusted.

"You hear who's gonna be here tonight?" said Shakespeare, who once claimed he was related to the famous English writer.

"Besides Senator Sterling?" Jack said.

"Everett Lester," Sid Turk, an overweight, blond kid with oily skin, chimed in through a mouthful of Whopper.

"You're kidding me," Jack said.

They all shook their heads.

"Since when? Pam loves him."

"It was a last-minute deal," Shakespeare said. "I heard it on the news on the way over. Clarissa's trying to keep it hush-hush, but Chico heard it too. It's gotta be goin' viral by now."

"Gonna be a full house for sure," said Chico Gutierrez, a rail of a kid with straight black hair. "Anytime you can see Everett Lester for free, you're gonna pack the joint."

Jack tested his radio by clicking his Talk button and listening for the static in his headset. The radios, headsets, and pagers were beat up and needed to be replaced.

"Lester's a pansy," Shakespeare said. "He was better before his big conversion."

"Come on, dude. You gotta like some of his new stuff," Jack said.

"I'm just saying his music was better

15

before. It's just a fact. He's not the same without the original band."

"Oh, dude, Death Stroke rocked so bigtime," Sid said. "Even I know that, and I was in diapers when they were in their heyday."

"That they did," said Shakespeare, whose once-booming swimming-pool business drowned when the market plunged in 2008. He and Jack worked almost every event because they both had marriages, mortgages, kids, and cars, as well as a long list of bills to pay.

"Are we gonna have enough staff?" Jack scanned the room again.

"Are you kidding me?" Shakespeare said. "This was supposed to be a spur-of-the-moment whistle-stop. Two to four thousand people, tops. But with Lester here? We're gonna be turning people away — you watch. Clarissa's got calls out for all hands on deck, but we'll be short. What else is new?"

Tab Deacon blew into the staging area with a gust of wind, his walkie-talkie glued to his mouth, and a chronic limp. That was Tab — always a flair for the dramatic. He dashed up to Clarissa and whispered in her ear at length. The pointy-nosed, gum-chewing Clarissa Dracone, head manager of EventPros, pulled back and scowled.

16

Jack found it odd he hadn't picked up Tab's voice on his headset, but he knew upper management had other channels they used to address sensitive issues.

He watched the two face off. At six foot four, Tab stared down at Clarissa with creased brow and a face full of fret. She glared up at him in her baggy orange windbreaker, her lipstick suddenly looking starkly red against her pale white face.

In an instant she snapped out of it and whipped into action, tapping one, two, three of the nearby supervisors and waving them into her office with walkie-talkie in hand. She quickly shuffled in behind them, practically stepping on Tab's heel, and slammed the door.

"Hmm." Shakespeare switched from channel to channel on his radio, trying to pick them up. "Very interesting."

Jack did the same but got nothing.

"Wonder what's up?" Sid wiped his runny nose with a worn-out napkin. "Are you guys getting anything?" He and Chico only had pagers.

Shakespeare shook his head. "Never seen anything like that before. I'll be right back."

A twitch of anxiety turned at the pit of Jack's stomach, but nothing ever worried Shakespeare. He was a former marine who looked you dead in the eye, told you exactly what he thought, and never backed down. Jack once saw him manhandle five drugged-out freaks at a Kid Rock show who'd gotten way too violent in the mosh pit. Shakespeare had zero tolerance for thugs. He once called himself a "righteous patriot," and it fit.

As Jack watched, Shakespeare tapped once at the office door and barged in. From his vantage point in the hallway, Jack saw Clarissa and the others turn toward his friend, each face pale with alarm.

Shakespeare said something. Clarissa spoke right back and waved him in.

Shakespeare spoke again, throwing a thumb back toward the staging area.

Clarissa threw up her hands, turned, and glared at Jack.

At first he thought he was just standing where her eyes happened to fall, but then he realized she was staring at him. His face flushed.

Shakespeare turned to Jack and waved him into the office.

Although Shakespeare wasn't a supervisor, Clarissa knew he was her toughest, most street-smart team member — and apparently he wanted Jack in there with him.

"Uh-oh," said Chico, his black eyebrows raised.

"Dude, let us know what's goin' on," Sid said.

"Will do." Jack took a deep breath and headed for the office. He walked past other EventPros who hadn't noticed the developing situation.

He approached the door with a silent prayer to stay cool and stuck his head through the doorway. "Hey, folks. What's going on?"

The room was silent.

Somber faces looked back at him.

"Get in and close the door," Clarissa said. "We've got a national security threat."

2

Shakespeare's house, three months earlier
At five months pregnant, Pamela Crittendon was feeling sluggish and cumbersome, but much better than she had felt during her first trimester. However, she did question why on earth they were eating outside in July when it was ninety-two degrees. This Brian Shakespeare, Jack's friend from work, was one strange bird.

Pamela tried to cool herself with the oriental fan she'd been carrying around for months. It had been kind of Shakespeare and his wife, Sheena, to ask their family to dinner. They'd even invited Pamela's mother, who was presently walking with Shakespeare through the rows of his huge garden.

Jack was helping Bobby, one of Shakespeare's boys, get the John Deere toy tractor going. Shakespeare ran back and forth between pointing out his prized vegetables to Margaret and checking the meat on the sizzling grill. His own five children — including four boys (two with special needs) and a little girl — were everywhere, ecstatic to have guests in what Pamela was gradually realizing was their own crazy little compound. Her own children, ten-year-old Rebecca and eight-year-old Faye, were laughing and playing with them like old friends.

"You control individuals with guns and weapons, like Hitler did, but you control populations with *food.*" Shakespeare, wearing a brown denim apron, was on one knee, pulling weeds and lecturing to anyone within earshot. "The lettuce you see at Kroger, it's coming from hundreds of miles away. There's only a three-day supply in stores. What happens when the economy tanks or there's a fuel shortage? I'm telling you, Margaret, you need to get on Jack's case. He's totally unprepared. I've been telling him this ever since we met."

Margaret glanced over at Pamela as if she'd seen a ghost. Unfortunately, her mother was buying into Shakespeare's gloom-and-doom theory. That was all they needed, with all the other stress at home.

"When everything collapses — and it's only a matter of time — food will be king.

If food is cut off, you've got chaos. Societal bedlam. Pillaging. Theft. Gangs of looters. What do you do then?"

Shakespeare grunted as he got up and moved on. Margaret stumbled in an effort to keep up with him, grabbing the crook of his arm.

"See those blue tarps along the border? That's our SPR — strategic petroleum reserve. Ten barrels of petroleum."

Shakespeare spoke in a deep, authoritative tone. The man had massive shoulders and a chest the size of a barrel. And, Pamela acknowledged to herself, with his curly black hair and large dark eyes, he was quite handsome in a rugged, outback sort of way.

"In the shed we've got a dozen five-gallon metal tanks full of fuel, a riding mower, and seven bikes. What's Jack gonna do when there's no gas at the pumps?"

Shakespeare excused himself to turn the meat. The aroma drifting over from the grill smelled scrumptious.

The spacious backyard was enclosed by a five-foot-high wall of cut firewood, which formed a homemade fence about four hundred feet long. Earlier, Shakespeare had shown them his "H_2O stash" in the crawl space beneath the house, which included numerous water storage tanks, each filled with a hundred and fifty gallons of potable water.

A clanging bell.

"Chow time!" Shakespeare rang a bell on a post next to the grill. "Grab a plate from the porch. We've got dogs, burgers, and steaks. Take plenty."

Sheena directed the guests to a spread that included potato salad, squash casserole, deviled eggs, chips, slaw, watermelon, cookies, and more.

"The eggs are from our own hens." Shakespeare nodded toward another small shed at the corner of the property as he set the platter of meat down. Pamela wondered what the neighbors thought of Shakespeare's survival camp.

The kids, red faced and sweaty, gathered with their plates on the porch steps while the adults sat down at a long picnic table in the direct sunlight. Eventually it seemed to dawn on Sheena that Pamela might be uncomfortable in the sun, and she dug out an old checkered patio umbrella, which she shoved into Shakespeare's chest and asked him to set up.

"So just what is it that you think is going to cause these food and gas shortages?" Margaret had chosen a spot right next to Shakespeare. He couldn't know that he was poisoning the mind of one of the most paranoid human beings on the planet.

Shakespeare smirked and took an enormous bite of his burger. "Let me ask you this, Margaret," he said through his mouthful. "How long do you think our country can keep printing new money to throw after bailouts? How much longer will China wait before they call us on our debt? Hasn't Jack told you anything I've taught him?" He looked at Jack, shook his head, and took another bite.

"Economic collapse?" Margaret said.

Shakespeare's eyes darted from one food item to the next on the massive spread before them. "That or terrorist attacks, whichever comes first. Pick your poison. They could knock out the Internet, poison our food and water systems, cripple our fuel resources, hit us with WMDs . . ."

"Brian, please, can we not get into this?" Sheena said.

"What?" Shakespeare stared at his wife. "Margaret wants to know. And Pam should know too. It's reality. Biological weapons, dirty bombs — the threat is real. They could spread a virus or attack the Internet with an EMP. It doesn't matter how it happens, the fact is, it's coming — and ninety-nine out of a hundred Americans aren't prepared."

Jack gave Pamela a look that said he was glad she was finally hearing it from the horse's mouth. Pamela wished Margaret wasn't there; she would be up all night worrying about it. Fortunately, Rebecca and Faye were clueless as they giggled and spit watermelon seeds with Shakespeare's kids.

"But how real is the threat of terrorism here in America?" Margaret said. "Things seem safe . . ."

Shakespeare threw his head back and laughed. "That's precisely what they want you to think. The terrorists have training camps embedded across the US. It's only a matter of time." His eyes narrowed. "These people hate the West. They despise Jews and Christians. They think they're obeying their 'god' and earning an afterlife in paradise by killing us."

Margaret had barely eaten a bite. She looked away, out toward the garden, then at Jack. "What are you doing about this?" There was a tinge of anger in her voice, and she waved a hand toward Rebecca and Faye. "How are you preparing so they can survive?"

Jack's face flushed. Pamela was about to stop her mom when Sheena intervened.

"Don't even start." She closed her eyes and shook her head. "Once you do, it becomes an obsession. You can never get prepared enough. You can never *do* enough. You can never *have* enough."

Shakespeare rolled his eyes.

"Look at us. Look at our kids. Look at the way we live." Sheena threw her hands up. "This is *not* normal. We're like our own secret little militia. We've been living like this for so long, I don't know any other way. We've lost touch with reality."

"No, you live *in* reality." Shakespeare jabbed a finger at her. "It's everyone else who's been hypnotized by the liberal media into thinking everything's fine. One of these days when we're hunkered down in the winter, staying warm by the wood-burning stove, generators giving us power, eating fine, and safe because we're armed to the teeth — you'll thank me."

An awkward silence hung over the group. Margaret stared at Shakespeare with her mouth agape.

Pamela changed the subject. "This is the best burger I've ever had. Where do you get your beef?"

"It's venison," Shakespeare said proudly as Pamela immediately stopped chewing. "Made the hot dogs myself. Jack, remind me to give you some of my jerky when I show you the food-storage supply."

Pamela forced down a long drink of water and vowed not to eat another bite.

"I've actually been thinking about storing a little food," Jack said. "Nothing elaborate. Just enough to get us through an emergency."

"Well, I should say so," Margaret said. "You've got the girls to think about."

Pamela didn't disagree with having a few extra canned goods in the pantry. But she would absolutely not let Jack get excessive about it.

"Basic starter, get twenty pounds of rice and twenty pounds of pinto beans," Shakespeare said. "You gotta have a way to cook it; I'll show you in a minute. You'll need multivitamins, plenty of water, flashlights, batteries, at least one generator, gas, weapons, ammo . . . I'll give you some websites before you leave."

Sheena shook her head, stood, and gathered some trash. "Don't start, Jack. Honestly, if I had to do it over, I would do absolutely nothing —"

"Oh yeah, and when the mud hits the fan, the kids starve and we're all dead meat. That sounds like a great plan, Sheena," said Shakespeare.

"I don't even care anymore." Sheena's voice broke. "Let it come. We'll die with

27

everyone else. What are the chances of that, though? I'd rather *live* while we're *alive* than live like we're dying! It's gone too far, Brian. I'm sure Jack and Pam can see that." She marched into the house.

With his big elbows on the table, Shakespeare examined Jack, then Pamela, then Margaret. He spoke in a low, even tone. "Look, I've done my research. This country is gonna get hit, big-time. People are going to *panic* because they are absolutely unprepared. Looters will take over the streets. It is not going to be pretty. If I know this is coming, why would I not prepare?"

"Where do you get your news?" Jack said. "Where do you find out about this stuff?"

"There are tons of sources online. I'll show you," Shakespeare said.

"I want those links," Margaret said.

It amused Pamela that her mom had become so tech savvy since she'd been living with them — but this was an invitation to disaster.

"Currency is another issue," Shakespeare said. "Look at its value — it's plummeting. This country is broke."

"I know, I know — 'cash is trash.' " Jack mimicked the expression he'd told Pamela that Shakespeare uttered so often.

"That's it. I've told you, you need to get

into the metals, real silver and gold. When the mud hits the fan, it'll save you."

"Dude, I wouldn't even know where to start," Jack said.

Shakespeare grimaced as if he'd told Jack this a thousand times. "I can hook you up. Start by buying a sleeve of twenty silver one-ounce coins, and if you can, an ounce of gold. Add to it as you can. It'll add up fast."

"I want to get some," Margaret said.

"Well, it sounds like you're the one I need to be harping on, Margaret." Shakespeare eyed each of them. "People who went into the Great Depression with just ten percent of their investments in gold came out rich. You need gold and silver to barter with." He looked at Pamela. "I've been nagging your husband about this for months."

Pamela's mind spun, thinking of how ill prepared they were, especially with the baby coming in four months. Should they try to do a little of everything — or nothing at all?

3

Festival Arena, October 6

"All we know at this point is that Homeland Security picked up some kind of algorithm, either over the Internet or the phone lines." Clarissa's brown eyes flicked back and forth, and veins arose from her scrunched forehead. "It mentioned the word *attack,* here, tonight."

"It named the arena specifically?" Shakespeare said.

Clarissa nodded. " 'Columbus Festival Arena' was picked up, as was Senator Sterling's name."

Jack didn't like the concern etched in Shakespeare's scowl, and it made him tip off balance, light-headed for a second.

"Who's behind it?" said Steve Basheer, their tall, fiftysomething supervisor.

"No idea," Tab said. "At this point it doesn't matter. We need to do everything in our power to protect the guests coming to this venue tonight."

"Tab, have Charlie do a complete sweep of the building, top to bottom," Clarissa ordered.

Electricity sizzled in the air as Tab made the call on his radio.

They searched one another's faces. Jack was thinking terrorists, or homegrown nut jobs. He was sure Shakespeare would have his own theory.

"You *are* going to announce it to the team." Shakespeare eyed Clarissa.

"Yeah . . . of course," she said tentatively, her head dropping. "Ideally I'd like to have more intel." She straightened her posture and put a fist to her lips. "Tab, you need to track down Hedgwick at the Columbus PD and get as much police backup as they'll give us — I mean busloads."

"We need to contact Sterling," Shakespeare said.

"I've got a call in to him. I'm thinking he might cancel."

"He won't cancel." Shakespeare pursed his lips. "His whole platform is built on anti-terror, building our defense back up — higher than it's ever been. He's pushing for that billion-dollar surveillance system —"

"Cameras on every major building and interstate in the country," Steve said.

31

Shakespeare nodded. "He wants to hunt down every homegrown terrorist group on US soil and punish them, severely. That might be what this is about."

"Assassination attempt?" Steve said.

Shakespeare shrugged. "Who knows? I'm sure terrorists don't want him on the ballot. Whatever the case, I'm thinking Sterling might have the clout to get a special-ops team in here."

Tab squirmed. "The army?"

"They're trained for this," Shakespeare said. "All we are is a bunch of suburbanites with flashlights."

"Oh, come on," Tab complained.

"He's right," Clarissa said. "I'll put in the request as soon as Sterling contacts me."

Suddenly Jack and Pam's financial woes meant nothing. Their differences had been pure stupidity. He regretted that he'd been so negative toward her.

The baby was due in a month. What would Pam do if something happened to Jack and she was left with three kids to support? Things had been so tight that Jack had been forced to reduce the death benefit on his life insurance to lower the cost of his payments. The current benefit was so low it would barely get him in the ground, let alone provide any extra funds for Pam and the kids. And he hadn't told her he'd changed it, because he fully intended to raise it again when he landed a decent job.

All the more reason he needed to make sure that he and everyone else in that building remained safe and secure.

"Hold up." Tab shot up a hand. "I've got Keefer on the phone. He's heard from Homeland."

Everyone inched closer to the speakerphone as Tab pushed a button, hung up the phone, and adjusted the volume.

"Clarissa, can you hear me?" said Keefer O'Dell, the president of EventPros, based in Cleveland.

"I can, Keefer. I'm here with some of my team."

"Okay." Long pause from Keefer's end. "The latest intel from Homeland Security is that fifteen to twenty hostiles are planning some kind of takeover during Martin Sterling's visit to our venue."

Eyes searched eyes. Some heads dropped.

Jack felt sick to his stomach.

"We've contacted Sterling and advised him to postpone, but he's a tough nut," Keefer said. "You know his stance on terrorism. He's still deciding. We're trying to get more intel. We've also told Everett Lester and his people that we think they should postpone. Ultimately it's up to him and Sterling and the arena if they are going to go on with the event or not."

"We can't just shut it down based on this threat?" Tab said.

Clarissa gave him a nasty look and shook her head at him.

"Who said that?" Keefer barked.

"It was me . . . Tab Deacon." His face was instantly pink.

"Deacon, you should know by now what service we provide. We're just a contractor in that venue to welcome guests, make sure they have a good time, and keep them safe. Only the arena's CEO can call off an event. So until I hear from Reese Jenkins, we're full speed ahead."

"Yes . . . yes, sir, you're right. I apologize." Tab twiddled his fingers and stared down at the floor as if Keefer were standing there in person, burning holes into him with glaring eyes.

"Clarissa, tell your people to keep their eyes and ears peeled and to contact you if they see anything suspicious. You should have Hedgwick and the Columbus PD in your office so they can respond in real time. I'm on my way down, but it'll take me a while. Any questions?"

Tab stood like a soldier, hands clasped

behind his back, shaking his head no.

"Sir, this is Brian Shakespeare. As you know, our team is not prepared in any way, shape, or form for combat with hostiles."

"Shakespeare? The marine?" Keefer said.

"Yes, sir."

"I'm glad you're on duty. And you're right. Look . . . the main thing is, if our people do see anything suspicious — anything at all — we evacuate the building. Pronto. Have all your people know precisely where their exits are tonight. Tell them to remain calm and guide people to the exits in an orderly fashion. Clarissa, don't hesitate to evacuate."

Shakespeare rolled his eyes.

"Mr. O'Dell, do we know anything more about the threat? This is Gordy Cavelli, by the way." Gordy was a slight guy, about thirty-five, with ruddy cheeks.

"Gordy, I've told you all we have," Keefer said. "But Homeland is good, very good. They're on this, and they'll have more for us, I'm confident. And I'll let your team know the second I do. There's a good chance this is not real. It could be anything: kids pulling a prank, wannabe terrorists. It happens all the time."

"This is Shakespeare again. What about getting a special-ops team in here?"

"If Reese Jenkins wants to request that, he can. Same with Martin Sterling. I'll be there as soon as I can. I've got another call coming in. Over and out for now."

"Bring it in, everybody," Clarissa called out from the top of the steps in the staging area. "Bring it in and quiet down."

Dozens of bright orange coats closed in around her for the usual pre-event talk. But this one was anything but usual. Jack was on edge. He hadn't had a second to contact Pam and was debating whether he should even tell her what was going on.

"Quiet, people," Tab said, towering over Clarissa, who stood next to him.

"Tonight we have the campaign rally with Martin Sterling and Everett Lester," Clarissa announced. There were cheers, hoots, and clapping. "Quiet . . . listen up." She spoke loudly enough to be heard by the EventPros thirty feet back, but her voice wasn't as confident as usual. Jack sensed fear in her eyes and voice.

"The event is general admission, so no tickets. That's good, makes our job simpler. There are passes." She held up a printout showing three different-colored badges guests could be wearing. "This one is all-access — the God badge — they can go anywhere, anytime; this next one is back-stage, but preshow only; and this third one is for the meet and greet afterward — that'll be upstairs, club level with Sterling. I'll need some of you to stay late for that."

Jack listened anxiously, wondering how Clarissa would communicate the threat and how his colleagues would respond.

"We've got chairs on the floor, the same as a concert setup, but we are in the round tonight with the circular stage in the center of the bowl. Doors open at six thirty. Everett Lester is due on at seven thirty and will go just thirty minutes."

Again, catcalls and laughter.

"Quiet down. I understand Mr. Lester's visit has hit the airwaves. We originally staffed tonight for about three to four thousand people, but we're going to have way more than that. We'll fill in the bowl first, then the mezzanine. We'll open the club level only to people with club level passes." She examined her notes. "Fifteen-minute intermission between Lester and Martin Sterling. Sterling is scheduled to go from eight fifteen to nine thirty. Now, before I have supervisors call your people, I need to make an announcement."

Clarissa dropped her head and waited.

Slowly the room fell silent.

Her head lifted. Her shoulders went back. "What I'm about to tell you, you are not to discuss with any of our guests. I realize word is going to get out, but we have no comment on it. I need your full and sober professionalism on the job tonight."

Jack had never heard it get so quiet so fast in there.

"I don't know how to put it gently. Homeland Security has picked up the threat of a possible attack here at the arena tonight."

Instant commotion arose across the crowded room.

"Quiet, please," Clarissa said.

"Quiet, guys!" Tab yelled.

"Senator Sterling's name was mentioned. The arena was mentioned. Homeland says fifteen to twenty hostiles may try some kind of takeover or attack. That's all we know at this point."

Loud talking. Movement. People on cell phones. One older blonde EventPro turned and busted out the double doors. She was quickly followed by a teenage employee and two more female staff.

"People . . . people, please." Clarissa held up a hand. "Just hold on and give me a chance to talk. We are not going to make you work this event. Let me finish explaining the situation, then we'll see —"

"Why don't we just cancel and get out of here?" a male voice called. His question was met by shouts of support.

Clarissa nodded. "It might be canceled. That has to come from Mr. Jenkins, the CEO of the arena, or from Sterling's team. Now listen, please." It was loud. EventPros were texting and talking.

"We do not know that an attack will happen. This could well be some sort of prank. We will have plenty of police here, and possibly special ops."

It dawned on Jack that every person in that room could walk out right then. Most of them were part-time. But for Clarissa, this was her career. She needed them. She might even doubt their safety and well-being, but this was her job, and she could not abandon ship if she intended to keep it. Tension electrified the room.

"This is all being figured out as we go," she said. Would things unravel completely right then? On her toes, Clarissa yelled to be heard over the clamor. "Your job tonight is to take your positions as usual, be friendly, greet people, and be *keenly observant.* I need you to check your exits when you get to your posts; know where every nearby exit is. I need you to let your supervisor know if you see *anything* suspicious — a backpack, a bag, a package sitting unattended. We will have team members outside doing quick bag checks. Keep your eyes open for suspicious people with bulky jackets who might be hiding things underneath . . ."

Two male EventPros ducked out; one Jack knew well.

"We will have at least five floaters checking restrooms and empty club rooms, patrolling, watching, checking in on you." As Clarissa examined her notes with trembling hands, the EventPros surrounding Jack talked in hushed voices and wore somber expressions. Many were texting as they spoke to coworkers.

Clarissa looked up. "There is a chance we might need to evacuate the building. If that happens, people with radios need to inform people with pagers. Then we need to be calm." One more EventPro exited the building as she spoke. "I repeat, remain calm and get people out of the building in an orderly fashion. That is our job, people. If you don't think you can do that in a professional manner, now is the time to clock out. Edgar? Where's Edgar?"

Edgar raised a hand. He'd already grabbed his clipboard and was checking out the people who'd left.

"Thank you, Edgar," Clarissa said as

several more EventPros exited through the double doors.

"I want to thank you for being here tonight. When we know more, we will let you know. The key tonight is going to be flexibility. Be ready to move around, to go where we tell you and do what we ask." She looked at her watch. "We need to get to our positions and check our exits. Supervisors, call your people . . ."

4

Shakespeare's house, three months earlier
Shakespeare didn't have the air-conditioning on in the house, and Pamela was hot and weary on her feet. Her ankles were swollen, and her knees and hips ached as she helped Sheena clean up the kitchen.

"You're hot, aren't you? I'm sorry." Sheena scrubbed a pot. "Brian won't have the AC on, almost never. You hear that rumbling noise? Attic fans. He says they cool the house just fine." Sheena's dejected face glimmered with sweat. "I'm dreading winter. He only sets the heat to come on if it hits fifty-five degrees in here. Tells the kids to bundle up."

The house was a sight. The kitchen overlooked the family room, which featured a cast-iron stove and old-fashioned oak furniture, including a gliding rocker and matching footstool with bright blue cushions. The walls were bare except for a few faded paintings of hunters and hound dogs that hung crooked in dark wood frames.

"For a long time I believed him," Sheena said. "I thought he was the smartest man alive — that economic collapse was right at our doorstep. I pictured us being the only ones prepared." She stopped scrubbing and stared out the window above the sink. "Huh. That was eighteen years ago."

"It could happen, I suppose," Pamela said as she dried the cookware Sheena had washed.

The sliding door opened, and Shakespeare and Jack came in carrying a bunch of trash, which they deposited in a large trash can.

"Time for the inside tour," Shakespeare announced. "Come on, Pam."

Jack smiled and raised his eyebrows as he followed Shakespeare through a maze of bookshelves leading to the adjoining living room. That was where Sheena home-schooled all five children. There were books everywhere, overflowing from the shelves and stacked in piles on the floor. There was barely a path to walk by the cheap-looking black computer, old printer, chalkboard, encyclopedias, and tables and chairs.

"I'll be there in a minute," Pamela said and turned back to Sheena. "Was Brian like this when you got married?" she asked.

Sheena sighed. "We were so in love." She shook her head. "I knew the type of man he was. He liked guns and knives and hunting. But this whole thing? It's become an addiction. He eats, drinks, and sleeps it. Do you know, he thinks the 9/11 attacks were a government plot?"

"What?"

She nodded and wiped her nose with the back of her wrist. "Yeah. He thinks it was a 'controlled demolition.' Says there's no way the fuel from those planes could have melted the steel to make the Twin Towers collapse. He's watched a million videos and listened to recordings that he claims prove there were other explosives involved." Sheena looked to make sure no one else was around and whispered, "He thinks the government wants to control our lives."

All Pamela could think was, *What on earth are we doing here? Why is Jack friends with this guy?*

Sheena went back to scrubbing. "Go see the garage. That'll confirm that we're absolute lunatics."

Pamela finished drying a casserole dish and set down the towel. "I will take a look," she said awkwardly. "It certainly is . . . interesting . . ."

"You're polite, Pam. Just don't fall for it."

44

5

Festival Arena, October 6

After his regimented days as a marine and sharpshooter, Shakespeare had very few worries in civilian life; compared to war, it was a stroll in the park. But this was different. He hadn't felt all his senses revving like this since he and a ragtag team of ground forces by the call name Red Horse led an assault to expel Iraqis from Kuwait during Desert Storm.

As supervisors called the team members who would be working with them that night and then headed off to gather in various parts of the arena, Shakespeare listened for his name. When the last group had left, he approached Clarissa.

"I didn't get called," he said.

"I know. Martin Sterling will be here any minute. I want you to choose whoever you want to partner with, go to the ops tunnel, and meet up with Sterling's party. His handler, Jenny King, is expecting you. He'll have his own security detail, but you'll have full access. They'll be counting on you to know your way around the building."

"Okay." Shakespeare took in a deep breath and exhaled silently. "What about police backup?"

"On their way, supposedly."

Shakespeare started toward the steps that would take him up to the main concourse.

"Who do you want to help you?" Clarissa held up the clipboard. "I need to know who's where."

"Jack Crittendon."

Clarissa shook her head. "Sorry, I'm assigning him to Everett Lester."

This was not going right. Jack and the other EventPros staff weren't trained for terror. "Are we getting a special-ops team in here or what?"

"Look, I want the police and army and whoever else here as much as you do. The requests have been made. But until then we have to go on as if they're not coming. Now who do you want with you?"

Shakespeare shrugged. "Chico, I guess."

She scanned her clipboard. "What's his last name?"

"Gutierrez."

"Okay, I'll radio his supervisor and have

46

him meet you in the ops tunnel."

Shakespeare started off.

"Sterling doesn't leave your side," Clarissa called. "You got me?"

"Got you."

Jack's breathing was shallow as he hurried down the steep concrete steps within the vast arena, from row Z at the top to row AA at the floor. It always amazed him how quiet the bowl could be before fans arrived. Soon doors would open, and thousands of people would fill in the seats like ants on crumbs.

The air was filled with a smoky-looking haze, and an enormous red-white-and-blue banner stretched across the stage: *Sterling for President — Sterling for America!*

Once to the floor, Jack walked to the circular stage, which featured a large drum kit, main microphone and stool, several backup microphones, and six guitars lined up offstage — likely for Everett Lester and whoever would be playing with him that night. Pam would be so jealous.

Near the stage, four very large colleagues milled around where they would form a human barrier later in the evening. It was cold down there because the arena's wood floor covered up the home ice for the Columbus

Spoilers, who had lost in overtime the night before.

"Base to Charlie," Jack's radio chirped. "What's your twenty?"

Static.

"This is Charlie. All clear from floor up to club level. Over."

"Roger that," Clarissa said. "Keep going all the way up to the Sky Zone, Charlie. Let us know it's clear."

Jack made his way toward the ops tunnel, acknowledging his orange-clad coworkers stationed at various floor entry points along the way. Doors hadn't opened yet, so some colleagues were sitting, some were standing, many were texting — probably to let loved ones know of the threat. About fifteen EventPros had gone home, and Jack second-guessed himself. Should he have been one of them? Pam would definitely say yes.

He scanned the arena for any sign of police or special-ops people, but all he saw were the regular few Columbus police officers who stood at different spots along the perimeter of the main concourse.

About thirty feet above the main seating in the big bowl was an additional narrow strip of seats that ran the entire circumference. This was the mezzanine section, the cheapest seats in the house, but still good.

Now it was dotted with several colleagues, either sitting or wandering the aisles. Tonight the upper level was adorned with half-moon-shaped red-white-and-blue flags positioned every thirty feet.

Partitioned off from the mezzanine section was the club level. EventPros who worked there had to wear coats and ties because it was a higher-priced VIP section. Its concourse featured plush carpeting, recessed lighting, polished wood floors, bars and restaurants that overlooked the arena, corporate club suites, and elegantly framed photographs of famous entertainers who had performed here at the arena. Jack had worked there several times but didn't get to see the events as much as when he was ushering in the bowl.

Above the club level, a large black curtain ran the entire circumference of the arena; it blew and waved from the air being circulated near the top of the building. Above the curtain, about six stories above the floor up in no-man's-land, were press boxes for radio announcers and hockey officials. Jack could see several people stirring up there now. Were they aware of the threat?

Something orange above the announcer boxes caught his eye. It was Charlie, way up at the top of the venue in the area known as the Sky Zone. He was clutching a black railing that circled the rim of the facility. From there, two black catwalks ran across the top of the arena about seven or eight stories off the ground. Jack would never want to go up there; he didn't like heights.

He passed through large strips of plastic curtains and found Sid waiting for him in the ops tunnel next to the huge doors and docks where roadies loaded and unloaded stage equipment.

"Dude, this is nuts," Sid said.

"Is Lester here yet?"

"En route. From what I hear, the show's going on. I wish they'd just cancel. I mean, why would you take the chance?"

"I agree," Jack said. "But I guess if we stopped every event where there was a threat, the country would eventually be crippled."

"I guess," Sid said. "I called my girlfriend. There's nothing about it on the news yet."

"Base to Charlie." Clarissa's voice filled Jack's headset. "Have you finished your sweep?"

There was no immediate response.

Jack said to Sid, "Look at it this way — we're about to meet a rock legend."

They both chuckled.

Years ago, when Everett Lester's personal

psychic turned up murdered, he was charged for the crime. That was when Everett started getting letters from a girl in Topeka, Kansas, named Karen Bayliss. The message of her letters eventually penetrated his heart, and he became a Christian. Against all odds, he was acquitted of the psychic's murder, ended up marrying Karen, and now used his raspy Springsteen-like voice to stir millions of fans with the gospel.

"My wife's not going to believe we get to hang with Everett Lester," Jack said. "She's going to want to know every detail."

"They adopted a kid, didn't they? I wonder if he'll be with them."

Jack nodded. "Cole. I think he's like ten or twelve."

"You're going to have to at least get a picture to show your wife," Sid said.

Jack squinted. "We're not supposed to."

"Oh, *phht.* We'll get you a picture."

"Base to Charlie, base to Charlie." Clarissa's voice filled Jack's headset again. "What is your twenty, Charlie? I repeat, what is your twenty?"

A loud buzz shrieked inside the guardhouse next to the back door, startling Jack. He watched as the gray-haired security guard popped to his feet, eyed one of the many video screens on a panel above his desk, and spoke into an intercom. The guard pressed a button, walked around the corner, and opened the back door.

An entourage of young men and women filed in. Then a healthy-looking Everett Lester entered with a smile and a handshake for the guard, followed by his wife and a boy with curly brown hair and freckles.

"Here we go." Sid bounced on his toes.

"Larger than life," Jack said. "They'll come through this door. You ready?"

Jack's earpiece flooded with static. "This is base to Charlie, base to Charlie," Clarissa barked. "What is your twenty, Charlie? I repeat, what is your twenty? Has anybody seen Charlie Clearwater?"

"This is Tab. Last I heard his sweep was clear through club level. Over."

Jack pressed the Talk button on his headset. "This is Jack to base. I saw Charlie along the railing up in the Sky Zone a few minutes ago, after he'd swept the club level. Over."

"Steve? Where is Steve Basheer?" Clarissa said.

"This is Steve, over."

"I need you to go up to the Sky Zone and check on Charlie. He's not answering his radio."

"Ten-four. I'll let you know when I get up there. Over."

6

Shakespeare's house, three months earlier
Pamela tiptoed through Sheena's jumbled homeschool room with its heavy fingerprints on the walls and followed the men's voices to the garage. It was dark and hot. Low-hanging fluorescent lights glowed above a massive tool bench. Various storage boxes and equipment dotted the cluttered room, which was obviously not used for parking cars.

Shakespeare and Jack were standing next to a six-foot-tall metal storage cabinet. "So we cycle these foods into the house for consumption, then buy more for storage here," Shakespeare was saying. "Come on in, Pam."

The cabinet was packed with containers of peanut butter, salt, coffee, spaghetti sauce, pepper rings, salsa, olive oil, tuna, evaporated milk, jam, soup, and more.

"Over here we have our three-gallon bins."

Shakespeare opened a white plastic container. "We've got our beans, black-eyed peas, rice, yeast, potatoes, pasta . . ." He explained that he kept dry ice in some of the containers to freeze out any bugs. He opened another, revealing cornmeal, nuts, garlic, cornstarch, and vacuum-packed dry fruits.

Before Pamela had time to process it all, Shakespeare had moved on to an apparatus next to the tool bench that looked like a moonshine still.

"When the water gets poisoned or stops coming, for whatever reason, this little baby gives us water to drink and cook with," he said. "Found it at a garage sale."

"What is it, a purifier?" asked Jack.

"Distiller." Shakespeare flipped open a metal lid. "Pour the water in here, it boils, runs across these coils, and comes right out the tap. Good to go. Over here are my kerosene heaters, jugs of kerosene, portable gas cooktops, propane . . . Gotta be careful with propane. If it leaks, it sinks to the bottom of the room, and if there's any sort of spark — kablooey."

"What are these?" Jack held up two metal rods.

"Parts of cooking kits I'm fixing. You guys got a freezer?"

Jack shook his head, and Pamela felt an increasing sense of inadequacy.

Shakespeare lifted the top of a large white freezer, and a cloud of frosty air rolled upward. "Look here," he said. "You're gonna need protein, Jack. We got plenty of deer meat and chicken . . ." There were containers of eggs and large blocks of cheese.

"What if the power goes out?" Pamela said.

Shakespeare dropped the lid of the freezer, walked several steps, and kicked a bulky red machine on the ground. "Four thousand watts."

"Generator?" Jack said.

Shakespeare nodded. "There's a backup in the shed. This'll keep both freezers going and a small section of the house. 'Course, we're gonna have to be careful. We wouldn't want the neighbors or bands of ruffians to know we have power. We've got heavy window shades to block out the light."

"Why wasn't I included on this tour?" Margaret stumbled into the garage, looking around in awe, as if she'd just discovered the Batcave.

"Hey, Mom." Pamela wished she hadn't found them.

"I wondered where you went," Shakespeare said.

"I was helping the kids with that darn tractor. Then Faye fell, and I had to tend to that."

"Is she okay?" Jack said.

"She's fine. Brian's kids got out their first-aid kit and did 'triage.' They were glad to have a patient. It's just a little strawberry."

"Over here we have ammo." Shakespeare drummed the top of two large metal coffee cans; there were seven in all. "Weapons are in safekeeping."

"What kind of weapons?" Margaret said.

Shakespeare chuckled. "Let's just say we have arms for any occasion."

Ever since Pamela's former classmate Granger Meade had broken into their home a couple of years ago, she and Jack had been back and forth about whether they should own a gun. When Granger got out of prison, Jack had carried a gun strapped to his ankle for a time.

"Do you have guns, Jack?" Margaret said.

He glanced at Shakespeare. "We have *a* gun. It's under lock and key."

"Good," Margaret said. "And I want to get one for myself, too. Will you take me to the gun range if I do, Jack?"

"You can get them through the mail these days. Order online. It's a breeze," Shakespeare said.

"Really? That's legal?" Margaret said.

"As long as it's a dealer with a federal firearms license, absolutely." Shakespeare was fiddling with something near the ammo, his back to them, then turned around suddenly. "And don't forget your gas masks!"

Pamela and Margaret screamed. Even Jack jumped back and laughed nervously.

Shakespeare breathed in and out, sounding like an astronaut through the black, heavy-duty gas mask. "These are a necessity. One for every family member. They come in kids' sizes." He ripped the gas mask off. "Seriously. They could hit us with nukes, crop dusters, dirty bombs. There's no other protection." He shook the gas mask. "But get good ones. The cheap ones aren't worth zip. You gotta spend money to get the best. I'll send you the links." Shakespeare tossed the gas mask aside. "There you have it. You now know about sixty-five percent of my secrets."

"I am so ill prepared," Margaret said. "Jack? We need to get busy, for the sake of the girls . . ."

"I've been thinking about it. Pam and I need to talk," Jack said.

"You need to do more than talk," Margaret said.

Pamela was restless and ready to get home. She was hot and overwhelmed. She was glad she'd seen Shakespeare's stash, but she didn't want to think about it anymore. "We should round the kids up," she said.

"Okay." Jack got the hint and started out of the garage.

"I mean it, Jack. This is paramount," Margaret said. "Before I . . . you know . . . before my time comes, I want to know you're prepared."

Shakespeare turned the lights out, and they followed him back through the schoolroom and the kitchen, and out the sliding door to the back porch, where Sheena sat thumbing at her phone.

"Oh, one last thing." Shakespeare stopped and turned toward them. "Everyone needs a Get Home Bag."

Sheena shook her head and continued tapping away at her phone.

"What's that?" Margaret said.

"Don't ask," Sheena said.

Jack told Rebecca and Faye it was time to go.

"It's a bag of necessities you keep in your car in case the mud hits the fan while you're away from home. It's got everything you need to get you home — then you decide whether you're going to bug out or hunker down. I can show you mine."

"Oh yes." Margaret began to follow Shakespeare, but Pamela cut her off.

"Mom, we've got to go. I'm wiped out. Maybe next time, Brian."

"Oh . . . sure, sure." He leaned closer to Margaret and lowered his voice. "It's all about the basics: food, clothing, and shelter. It's got a miniature tent, poncho, flashlight, knife, matches and tinder, filtered water bottle —"

"Will you write this down?" Margaret started digging in her purse.

"I'll give Jack the websites. Mine has a folding shovel, rope, protein bars, instant coffee. Let's see . . . extra socks, first aid, duct tape, weapon and extra ammo —"

"I have email," Margaret said. "Send these things directly to me. If you send them to Jack, I'll never see them."

Rebecca and Faye arrived on the back porch sweaty, pink faced, and even dirty, which was totally out of character for them. Jack made sure they gave a proper thank-you to Sheena. All of Shakespeare's kids gathered around too.

"What does 'bug out' mean?" Margaret said.

Pamela couldn't help listening.

"Take off, get out of town, get to your SRL — survival retreat location," Shakespeare said. "It's where you go in a yellow or red event when there's gonna be a complete breakdown of society with people starving and panicking, looting house to house. It's when home base is no longer any good. You've got to bug out because every house, barn, store, and building will be searched for food and supplies."

"But where would you go?" Margaret pleaded.

"You've got to have a plan." Shakespeare looked at Jack.

Shakespeare's oldest son, Bobby, spoke up. "Your survival retreat location should be at least one full tank of gas away from home."

"And . . ." Shakespeare waited.

"And it should be at least forty miles from the nearest city," Bobby said proudly.

"That's right." Shakespeare rubbed Bobby's curly, black hair. "And at least forty miles from the nearest major highway."

"Mom, time to go. Say good-bye." Pamela was frustrated that Shakespeare would load her mom down with such fears. And it was scaring her, too.

Pamela and Jack had no petroleum or water reserves, they had no freezers or generators, they had no survival foods or gas masks, they had no Get Home Bag or survival retreat location. And the thought of looters going house to house downright freaked her out.

But what they did have was today and each other. They had the miracle of life growing inside her. They had a promise from God that he would never leave them or forsake them. For the moment, those things were going to have to be enough.

7

Shakespeare and Chico were practically running down the white hallway below the arena, trying to keep up with Jenny King, the bossy, young handler of Ohio senator and independent presidential candidate Martin Sterling. She resisted their help, insisting she'd been there many times before.

"Miss King," Shakespeare said. "We need to turn at this next hallway. You're set up in room 3-A."

King, wearing a tapered gray pinstriped suit, didn't slow a beat but continued taking mammoth strides in her black stilettos, her jet-black hair bouncing at her shoulders.

They flew into 3-A, where she whizzed from table to table, checking beverages and ice, lifting the lid on each steaming silver tray, as if making sure the massive amounts of food prepared by the in-house caterers looked reasonably warm and edible.

"Jenny to Stagecoach." She checked her sleek watch and looked up at the ceiling as she spoke into her big gray radio. "The senator is good to go for room 3-A, that's 3-A. Have his security detail escort him in. Over."

"Ten-four. It's going to be just a few more minutes, Miss King," said a male voice from the other end of the radio. Shakespeare assumed the reply came from inside Sterling's tour bus, which was parked at the loading docks.

Jenny sized up Chico, then eyeballed Shakespeare, placing an index finger on her pointy chin. She smelled like a bouquet of expensive flowers. "You don't have to be here," she said.

Shakespeare took a deep breath and made himself pause before saying something he shouldn't. "You are aware of the threat."

She closed her eyes and nodded, as if dealing with a five-year-old. "We get threats all the time." She squinted at his name tag. "Really? I suppose you're related."

"Actually, I am."

She rolled her eyes. "We're going to be fine in here. You gentlemen can go tell your boss to station you someplace else."

"Her name is Clarissa Dracone," Shakespeare said. "She just wants to make sure you have someone familiar with the building —"

Jenny nodded, looking annoyed. "I've done the Sean Hannity Freedom Concert here five years in a row. We know the building, we know what we're doing. Really, your time would be better spent elsewhere."

Shakespeare looked at Chico and shrugged. "I'm going to have you take that up with her. And she's a busy lady right now. Until we get the order from her, I'm afraid we're here."

"I know Clarissa." Jenny whipped around, looking at the catering tables as if she'd already forgotten the conversation. "She's probably fit to be tied right about now. Just stay out of the way until I find a good time to talk to her."

There was a commotion in the hallway.

"Station yourself in that corner," Shakespeare whispered to Chico. "I want to know anything they mention about the threat. Page me if you need me. I'll be floating."

"Didn't Clarissa want us both here?" Chico's dark eyes were huge.

"Don't worry. When Sterling gets here, I'll be here."

Shakespeare stepped into the hallway. Coming toward him was an entourage of people led by Jack and Sid. Shakespeare felt a tinge of pride and nostalgia when he saw Everett Lester and his wife. Their handsome son was with them too. He had long brown hair and, even though he was adopted, looked exactly like his dad, minus the tattoos that crept up and down Everett's forearms and neck.

Shakespeare backed up against the wall. "Jack, how goes it?"

"All good so far," Jack said with a mixture of confidence and nerves. "You?"

"Nothing new. Where you headed?"

"5-A," Jack said. "We're gonna be neighbors."

"Sounds good." Shakespeare acknowledged the guests. "Hello, Mr. Lester, Mrs. Lester. Good to have you here this evening."

"Thanks. It's good to be here . . . we think." Everett chuckled. "I'm sure you guys have everything under control, right?"

Shakespeare could only think of the lack of police support he'd seen so far, but he gave Everett and Karen a thumbs-up and said, "Absolutely."

Shakespeare's radio sounded in his earpiece.

"Okay, all EventPros, listen up. We have a SWAT team arriving by bus at the cargo entrance." Clarissa sounded relieved. "They are in dark blue and black from head to toe. Each of them is wearing a dark helmet and shield. They are armed with nine-millimeter submachine guns and Glock handguns. Several have sophisticated rifles."

Probably M14s, Shakespeare thought. His best friend during Desert Storm and one of the weapons in his Get Home Bag.

"So far, that is all of the excess staff we have on duty," she continued. "We hope more are coming. But in the meantime, these are the only people besides EventPros and arena staff that you should see in uniform."

"How many are there? Over. Sorry . . . this is Shakespeare."

"Eight to twelve," Clarissa said. "I'm not sure where they'll be stationed yet. That's up to their commander."

"This is Steve Basheer to base."

"Go, Steve," Clarissa said.

"I'm at the club level. Nothing doing here. I have not seen Charlie. Have we heard from him?"

"Not yet." Clarissa paused. Static. "Charlie Clearwater, if you can hear this, please respond. Steve, keep going up to the press boxes, then the Sky Zone. Let us know ASAP."

"Ten-four," Steve said.

Charlie could be silent for any number of reasons — bad radio or batteries, out of range, heart issues . . . He had to be in his midsixties.

But Shakespeare didn't like it.

He glanced at his watch. The doors would be opening soon. He had all that artillery at home. But it was too late to call Sheena and ask her to lug it down here. She would never get near the place, anyway. If it came to it, the Get Home Bag in his truck was going to have to do.

It was time for a ceasefire in the war at home. He needed to let Sheena know what was going on. He got out his phone and quickly typed a text message to her.

Hey. Terror threat at arena. SWAT here. Watch news. Let me know of anything else going on. Thx.

8

Downtown Columbus, two months earlier
Lunch with Derrick Whittaker, Jack's best friend and former colleague from the *Trenton City Dispatch,* was just what Jack had needed. They met in downtown Columbus at Katz's, a dark deli that smelled like kosher pickles and served mouthwatering corned beef piled high on rye with homemade potato chips. It was close to the city newspaper where Derrick had landed a job as a reporter after the debacle at the *Dispatch.*

"I've mentioned you to each of these guys. You need to call them." Derrick pushed a napkin toward Jack. On it he'd scribbled the names of three editors from his new employer, the *Columbus Gazette.* "Ask if you can come up for five minutes to say hi, and bring your portfolio. You need to meet face-to-face. They'll love you. We need you. We're so short, it isn't even funny."

"What do they have you working on these days?" Jack said.

"Dude, don't you read my paper? They've got me covering the senator," said Derrick, pushing his retro black glasses up on his nose.

"Martin Sterling? Get out," Jack said.

"No joke." Derrick squeezed a glob of ketchup into his basket. "It's a total blast. I'm on the campaign trail. We've been to Rochester, Philly, Chicago . . . Can you believe it? That's why it's taken me so long to hook up with you. Me and old Martin are like this." He crossed two fingers.

Although Jack had at least five years more journalism experience than Derrick, the *Gazette* hadn't looked twice at him. He guessed it was because he had more experience and they probably thought he would be too expensive.

"Have you been able to get to know Sterling?" Jack said.

"Oh yeah. We stay at the same hotels, cover all his rallies —"

"Who's we?"

"Me and Daniel Woodhouse, photographer. Remember, from the *Dispatch*?"

"Yeah. Good shooter."

"Dude, you look down," Derrick said.

"Just frustrated." Jack shook his head.

70

Here he was, basically out of work, eating the cheapest thing on the menu, working nights as an usher. "I've got to find a decent job. Pam and I are running on empty. She's working all the time and isn't happy about it."

"Dude, I'm treating today."

"No, you're not. Thanks anyway. Come on, tell me more about Sterling. He's going independent, isn't he? You think he's got a chance?"

"Heck, yeah. Are you kidding me? He's a smart guy. He's got specific ideas on how to get us out of this economic rut. I think he's gonna kill it in the debates."

"Will you cover those?"

"Oh yeah. The first one's at Lee University, down in Tennessee. Then San Antonio . . . and someplace else. He'll be stumping in Ohio big-time over the next year. It's one of the top three swing states."

"He's pretty rad on the whole terrorism thing."

Derrick stopped eating and leaned across the booth. "We need that, dude. It's a true threat. Nobody realizes how serious it is. These extremists are infiltrating the country. Sterling knows what he's talking about. The guy is ruthless, too."

"He wants to put an end to mosques being built on US soil."

Derrick's eyes opened wide. "That's just the one everyone knows about. He also wants to quadruple spending on the National Counterterrorism Center in Virginia. He wants to partner with a bunch of top intelligence agencies to neutralize terrorist cells and operatives in the US. He wants to get on top of cyberthreats. Do you realize President Brumby finances the Iraqis and others under the table, which nobody seems to care about? Sterling's going to stop all that nonsense."

"Sounds like he's made you a believer."

"He has." Derrick looked around and lowered his voice. "We've got to crack down now, before it's too late. Otherwise our kids are going to be living in a war zone — right here on our streets."

Jack told Derrick about Brian Shakespeare and his extreme preparations in anticipation of a catastrophe.

"Dude, he's a prepper. There are a lot of them out there — and they might not be too far off," Derrick said. "I know Zenia and me aren't prepared for anything like that. I'm just a city boy."

"Me, too, but my mother-in-law's a different story."

"Margaret? She still living with you guys?"

Jack gave a slow nod.

Derrick laughed. "Man, it's been a long time, hasn't it?"

"More than six months."

"Ouch."

"Actually, it's a good thing. With Pam back to work, Margaret can take care of the girls after school. But we made the mistake of taking her to a picnic at Shakespeare's place, and she's been stockpiling food and supplies ever since."

Derrick's roaring laughter was contagious, and it felt good for Jack to join in.

"And she's fallen in love with Sterling," Jack said. "Overnight she's turned into a political activist."

"Well, Sterling sure beats the alternative," Derrick said. "I don't think we can endure four more years of what we got."

"I agree with that. But, dude, Sterling wants to arm teachers. What do you think about that?"

"I . . . I just don't know what I think about that. I'm telling you, he's rad. Zenia thinks it's nuts."

"Wait till you have kids," Jack said.

"Oh, I can imagine."

"Let's change the subject. How is Zenia, anyway? How's married life?"

Derrick shook his head and smiled. He

73

was wearing his afro about two inches long and had put on a few pounds since his wedding in the spring, when Jack served as his best man. "Better than I ever imagined. We're having a lot of fun."

"She still working for parks and rec?"

"Yep. Trenton City's been good to her."

"You guys must be doing okay financially."

"We're socking some funds away. Spending a lot too. She thinks she's ready to have a baby, but I'm not there yet. When's Pam due again?"

"Three months, if you can believe that."

"Wow, that'll be here in a blink."

"That's why I need to find a decent job," Jack said. "We've gone through almost all our savings."

"You should be glad she found work."

"I know, but it's the last thing she wants to do. Rebecca and Faye are used to having her home. She wants to be a full-time mom."

"Hey, you do what you gotta do, right?"

"Yeah." Jack paused. "Rebecca and Faye just seem to have such a good foundation. I know a lot of it has to do with Pam being there for them."

"We all go through seasons, Jack. This isn't going to be forever. You're going to find something."

Jack studied the names Derrick had scribbled on the napkin. "Don't be surprised when you see me in the newsroom peddling my goods."

Derrick laughed heartily. "We're going to get you a job at the *Gazette* if it's the last thing we do."

For the first time in months, Jack felt a surge of optimism. "Thanks, man. I appreciate you," he said.

Derrick leveled his gaze at Jack. "No, I appreciate you. You've been a role model for me. Don't give up now, man. You've always had a powerful faith. Cling to it. And while I've got you all serious . . ." He snatched the check and laughed the contagious laugh that made Jack feel so good.

9

Festival Arena, October 6

"My wife is a huge fan of yours." Jack's heart beat like that of a boy meeting his favorite baseball star as he got Everett Lester and his larger-than-life entourage settled into room 5-A in the bowels of Columbus Festival Arena.

"Will your wife be here tonight?" Everett grabbed two bottles of water from the ice bucket and handed one to Karen.

"No, she won't," Jack said. "She's eight months pregnant with our third child." Jack knew from reading about Everett and Karen that they'd not been able to have children, so he wanted to be sensitive in his response. "Plus, we didn't know you were going to be here. I think if she'd known, she probably would have taken her chances."

Everett and Karen laughed, and Jack joined them.

"Do you know if it's a boy or a girl?" Karen asked.

"No. Pam didn't know with our two girls and didn't want to know this time either. She says the anticipation helps her get through it."

Karen smiled brilliantly and addressed Everett. "You should give him something to take to his wife."

"Good idea —"

"I'm sorry, can I interrupt?" Gray Harris, Everett's longtime road manager, placed a hand on the sleeve of the musician's denim jacket.

"Sure. Excuse me a second." Everett and Gray walked to the corner of the room.

Jack noticed Sid standing at attention next to the mini hot dogs — with a mouthful. Jack scowled at him and pointed to his own mouth. Sid's eyebrows jumped, and his big cheeks turned pink.

"It's a little bit scary, about the threat." Karen crossed her arms, her dazzling gray-green eyes looking into Jack's as if awaiting his opinion.

"It is. But I understand SWAT's here now. That's good, anyway," Jack said. "And we're supposed to get more police in here soon."

"I'm kind of hoping they just cancel it, for safety's sake."

Everett and Gray were talking softly but

intensely.

"All EventPros, this is Clarissa," came the voice in Jack's headset. "Good news. Hedgwick and a team from the Columbus PD are en route. We're expecting them to arrive at the loading docks within thirty minutes. Do what they say. If you come across any trouble, turn it over to them and get out of the way. Over and out."

Jack shared the news with Karen, then took a deep breath and exhaled, somewhat relieved. As he stepped over and whispered the news to Sid, his phone vibrated. He quickly made his way into the long hallway and found a text from Pam.

I have a surprise for you!

Before he could reply, Clarissa's voice came over his headset again. "All Event-Pros: Doors open in ten minutes, ten minutes. Remember, everyone's eyes are peeled. If you haven't checked to know precisely where your exits are, do it now. Contact your supervisors about anything suspicious. Over and out."

Once again Jack struggled with whether to let Pam know about the threat. But why worry her? If things heated up, he could contact her then. Until then, it was only words. He silently prayed that's all it would remain.

Way down the hall, around the corner, came a bicycle ridden by a teenage boy wearing a black ski cap, floppy flannel shirt, and fingerless gloves. He called out to Jack as he approached. "Lookin' for 5-A. Know where it's at?"

"Right here. What can I do for you?" Jack said.

The kid started his dismount, standing on one pedal, gliding, then jumping off and trotting up to Jack. "Got a delivery." He bent over a basket behind his seat and came up with a dozen red roses. Ignoring Jack, he knocked on the door.

"Hey, hold up . . ."

As the kid opened the door, all heads snapped toward him. There was tension in the air, all right.

Jack followed the delivery boy in, embarrassed, feeling as if he'd been run over.

But Karen just smiled, took the flowers, and, on tiptoes, kissed Everett.

Everyone else in the room had gone back to what they were doing, and no one besides Sid and Jack seemed to raise an eyebrow.

Everett shrugged at Jack. "It's a tradition."

"Roses play a big part in our past." Karen smelled them with a shy grin. "I think tonight these might go home with you — for your wife."

"Oh my gosh, she would die," Jack said.

"I'll put them in water, and they'll be right here. I'll have Ev write a note." Karen looked up just as Cole was walking out the door. "Cole?"

The boy stopped, turned toward his mom, and raised his dark eyebrows.

"Where're you going?" Karen said.

"Vending machine." He sounded a tad annoyed, probably because most everyone in the room was watching.

"What do you need that we don't have here?" she said.

"Gum."

"Do you know where it is?"

"We passed it coming in. I'll be right back."

She looked at Jack. "You think it's okay?"

"Mom!" Cole said.

"It's not far, and the doors haven't opened yet. I can walk him down there if you want," Jack said.

"No, it's okay." She looked at Cole. "Go ahead, but hurry right back."

Cole scampered off.

"We told him there was a remote threat," she said.

"I'll peek after him, just in case."

She thanked Jack, and he headed out the door.

"Dude!" called a voice from the end of the hallway.

Jack turned to see Derrick flashing the press credentials that hung around his neck to another EventPro, who was seated on a metal folding chair. With Derrick was a younger black guy Jack recognized from the *Dispatch*, who was lugging a heavy camera bag over each shoulder.

"I wondered if you'd be here," Jack called.

"I'm his shadow. Of course I'm gonna be here." Derrick walked toward Jack in his no-hurry swagger, looking good in a dark-green jacket and gray slim-fit cords. His leather satchel swung on his shoulder. "You remember Daniel Woodhouse?"

"Yeah." Jack reached out and shook hands. "Good to see you."

"You, too," Daniel said.

"This campaign's wearing me out," Derrick said. "Zenia's fit to be tied 'cause I'm gone all the time. Can't imagine what it'll be like a year from now. Sheesh."

"Glamour's gone?"

"It's going. I mean, it's exciting, but it's a ton of hours."

"What've you heard about this threat?" Jack said.

"No one's talking. Who can I talk to? And I don't mean that barracuda boss of yours. What's her name, Dracula?"

"Dracone." Jack chuckled. "Clarissa Dracone. She's the one, but she won't talk. You got a pen?"

Derrick got his phone out and thumbed the screen. "Go."

"Keefer O'Dell is Clarissa's boss — he's the president of EventPros. He's on his way down from Cleveland now. But Reese Jenkins is top of the order. He's the CEO of the arena. I'm not sure if he's here or not."

Derrick punched in their names.

Jack scanned the hall. "I better get going. Clarissa doesn't like us talking to the press."

"I hear Everett Lester's here," Daniel said.

Jack nodded toward room 5-A. "Right through that door."

"Dude, that is *sick*," Derrick said. "Can you get us in there?"

Jack searched the hall again, wondering what was taking Cole so long. "No way . . . not right now."

The door to Sterling's room opened down the hall, and out came Shakespeare and a sharp girl Jack recognized as one of Sterling's assistants. She wore a well pressed gray pinstriped suit and had a large gray radio in her hand. It looked a lot nicer than those the EventPros were issued. Shakespeare and the girl were followed by three security guys in dark suits, with Sterling right in the middle of them. Chico brought up the rear.

Shakespeare gave a nod to Jack as they headed toward him. "We're coming over to your place."

The long-legged girl in the suit took the lead, strutting down the hall as if she was leading a fire drill. "Hello, Derrick, Daniel . . . Excuse us." She reached in front of Jack and opened the door to room 5-A.

"Jenny, can I come in?" Derrick said.

She looked back at him as if she'd smelled a skunk. "Later, maybe."

Shakespeare started in, and Jenny held up a hand like a traffic cop. "Okay, Shakespeare can come in, but no other arena staff. No press." She looked at Jack. "You, wait right here. We're expecting Reese Jenkins, Clarissa Dracone, and the head of SWAT." She craned her neck. "Ah, there's Mr. Jenkins now . . . good. Derrick, we'll give you an update in a few minutes. Hang tight." She entered the room, and the door closed behind her.

Jenkins, CEO of the arena, was lanky, tan, and distinguished. A short, plump woman with black glasses and a briefcase walked beside him. They barely acknowledged Jack as they made their way into the last-minute powwow.

Karen stepped out of the room, looking a bit pale. "Where's Cole?"

Jack had forgotten. He looked down the empty hallway and was overtaken by a pang of anxiety. "I'll go check on him."

"How long can it possibly take to get a pack of gum?"

10

"Senator Sterling, can I talk to you for one minute?" Derrick wiped the August sweat from his forehead as he followed the senator and his bulky security guard through a maze of desks and file cabinets toward his cramped office in the Hart Building in downtown Washington, DC.

At the doorway Sterling turned to face Derrick; the security guard awkwardly ducked out of the way, straightening himself in a military stance off to the side.

"Good grief, Whittaker, you'd think the AC wasn't working in here the way you're sweating," Sterling said.

Derrick followed the security guard's eyes down to his own armpits, where his neatly pressed light-blue dress shirt was soaked with two huge dark blotches of perspiration. "I know, sir. I'm not used to this humidity. It's hotter here than it is at home."

85

"Well, come in a minute." Sterling went into his office. "Sit down, get cooled off. We Buckeyes have got to stick together."

"Thank you, Senator." The only chair besides Sterling's had stacks of papers in it.

"Just set that stuff on the floor." Sterling dropped his notebook atop reams of paperwork spread across his desk like a mountain range. He tossed his dark suit coat onto a small table stacked with books and journals, went around, and dropped into his big leather chair. "Do you know how much reading this job entails? I could read sunup to sundown and never get to half of it."

"I believe it, sir." Derrick plunked into the chair, wiped the sweat from his upper lip, and flipped to the questions he'd jotted down during Sterling's speech to the Senate an hour earlier. It wasn't only the humidity that was getting to him; he still got nervous around Sterling, probably because the man could very well be the next president of the United States.

"A lot of senators don't read a tenth of it. You believe that?" Sterling swiveled around to his computer screen and moved the mouse. "Some have their aides do it . . . Oh, for goodness' sake. Seventy-four new emails in the last ninety minutes. And I guarantee you, half of it's hate mail." He shoved the mouse, turned the chair toward Derrick, and leaned way back, clasping his hands behind his head.

In the glow from his computer screen, Sterling's thick hair, combed over in front, had the color and texture of steel wool. Although he wore an expensive suit, his wide red tie was crooked and his gray shirt wrinkled. Derrick even noticed some grayish beard stubble beneath the sides of his sharp jaw. As Sterling rolled up his sleeves, revealing dark hairy wrists, Derrick got the impression that the man's life outside the office mirrored the mess on his desk.

"You've got to keep focused on your top priorities in this work and forget the small stuff." Sterling tossed both hands into the air. "Let it roll right off. Otherwise you'll never get anything accomplished."

"Speaking of priorities, sir, I want to ask you about the proposed initiative you just talked about in Senate chambers — to get the country up to speed on the threat of an electromagnetic pulse attack."

Sterling opened his hands like a bomb exploding. "We're totally unprepared for an EMP. Our power grid is vulnerable at best. Such an attack would bring the US to a standstill. It would permanently disable electronic devices. You've seen the show

Revolution, where the power goes out?"

Derrick nodded.

"That's what we're talking about. ATMs stop working. Water and sewer systems shut down. Transportation comes to a halt. We'd be in the Dark Ages —"

"You mentioned this threat is real, right now. It could happen . . ."

"A short-range ballistic missile carrying an EMP device could destroy our critical infrastructure *today.*" Sterling snapped his fingers.

"Who would this come from?"

"Any rogue nation could create a radio-frequency device that could cause an EMP that would disrupt critical systems. Heck, Iran and North Korea have ballistic missile capabilities. We are not ready! This is the platform I'm running on, Whittaker. President Brumby is burying his head in the sand. His job is to protect the people of this country. The job ain't gettin' done!"

Derrick had heard all of this in Sterling's speeches. "What I want to know, Senator, is what it would cost to develop the system you talked about that would combat these vulnerabilities."

Sterling shook his head. "Millions, maybe billions. But you see, herein lies the difference between the president and me. For me, this is a hands-down, red-alert top priority. For him" — he slashed his hand low — "it's not even on the radar. Our nation's defense is this administration's lowest budget priority among the major responsibilities of the federal government. His proposed plan would *shrink* our defense budget even more than he has already, not just slow its rate of growth as he claims. Heck, everybody knows he's financing terrorist sympathizers."

"Where would the money come from to pay for the defense against EMPs?"

"It's back to my mantra. Cut. Government. Spending! We are gonna be ruthless when it comes to this. I truly believe government is four to five times larger than it should be. Some of those funds we save by reducing big government will go toward EMP defense, the National Counterterrorism Center, new defenses against cyberthreats —"

"Okay, fine. I get that," Derrick said.

"Good." Sterling leaned on his desk. "You cooled down?"

Derrick chuckled. "Yes, I am. Thanks for letting me come in."

Sterling rose. "Anything else?"

"One thing I'm curious about." Derrick pointed to Sterling's computer. "The hate mail. I can guess what it's about, but I'd like to hear from you. And who does it come from?"

"Off the record?"

Ugh. Derrick hated when politicians did that. "I guess so . . ."

Sterling walked around his desk to the door and closed it. "*Off* the record — it's from liberals and leftist advocates who are blind to the fact that this country is going straight to hell in a handbasket. They're opposed to my strict stance on illegals. They're opposed to my plan to root out terrorists, homegrown and foreign, and cut them off at the knees —"

"They think you're profiling —"

He threw his hands up. "Call it whatever you want! The fact is, if America doesn't do something — and I mean something *radical* — this country will never be the same. I hope it's not too late already. Four more years under this president will sink the ship, I can assure you of that."

"Can I just read something? I'd like to get your feedback on this — on the record."

Sterling waved his hand, walked to the window, and stared out.

Derrick found the printout he'd tucked into his notebook. "Some of your opponents believe you're advocating what they call 'religious and racial profiling.' They say, and I quote, 'Profiling violates our country's fundamental promise of affording every citizen equal justice under the law. Biased policing makes us less safe because it wastes resources and misleads law enforcement authorities away from focusing on real threats.' "

"That is the biggest load of you-know-what I've ever heard, and yes, that's the type of people from whom the hate mail flows in."

"Let me just add this," Derrick said. "It says, 'Since the terrorist attacks of 9/11, religious and racial profiling has namely victimized Muslims, Arabs, Middle Easterners, and South Asians, all of whom have endured disproportionate scrutiny from law enforcement.' "

"See, Whittaker, what those people don't want to admit, for whatever reason, is that there is a very real terror threat in America. Within the last year we've been made aware of increased incidents involving the stockpiling of explosives, the surveillance of targets, and an increasing number of significant plots and attack plans. Some of these come from —"

"Are we on the record?"

"Yes. Some of these initiatives come from

homegrown terrorists, common criminals who set out on a path of radicalization toward jihadism. Many others come from people who've come to the US for the sole purpose of causing havoc and ruining the freedom we have in the West. I don't care which they are; under my presidential leadership they will be ferreted out and brought to the severest justice. Call it whatever you want. Someone's got to do something. My administration will do whatever it takes."

"So —"

"If people have a problem with that" — Sterling raised his voice — "they shouldn't put me on the ballot for president. But if they have a problem with bombs going off in our subways, I'm their man. They need to support me and encourage all their friends to do the same."

Derrick scribbled furiously as Sterling walked around his desk to the door.

"I guess the next time we'll see each other will be back in Columbus, eh?" the senator said. "I'm anxious to get home. See the family. Who knows, in another fifteen months we may be living over on Pennsylvania Avenue."

"Hold on a sec, sir." Derrick continued to write. When he finally had it all down, he

eyed the senator. "Are you conc____
your safety at all? I noticed you ha____
guards."

"Back off the record?" Sterling said.

"Okay." Derrick gathered his things and went to the door.

"I feel like this is my calling. I truly believe my becoming president will be the best thing for this country. We're at a turning point. It's a crucible of sorts. Someone's got to take the reins. And, yes, with that are going to be threats. I'm not afraid." He shook his head. "I've never been afraid to die, especially not for my country."

"You never had your own security detail before . . ."

"I've had to hire my own! You wouldn't believe the threats. But that's a story for another day. I've got to get busy." Sterling opened the office door and stepped out. "Needless to say, I'm becoming close friends with old Parker out here." Parker, the hefty security guard, nodded while staring straight ahead.

Derrick smiled and headed out. "I'll see you back in Ohio, sir."

"What was it the chaplain said at the prayer breakfast this morning?" Sterling said. "Don't say, 'Today or tomorrow I'll go to this city or that — for you don't even ιow what will happen tomorrow.' "

That was odd, Derrick thought. He never knew Sterling to be a religious man. In fact, behind closed doors with his cronies, the senator's language could be vividly R-rated. But then again, when you had enemies like he did, foxhole religion might not be so out of the question.

11

Shakespeare stood with his hands clasped behind his back in the far corner of the buzzing room, glad to be able to hear firsthand what was going on with the arena brain trust. All the key players were there, from Martin Sterling and Everett Lester to Reese Jenkins, Clarissa Dracone, and the head of the SWAT team.

Jenkins straightened his tie, took a swig of water, and raised a hand with a thick gold ring on his finger. "Ladies and gentlemen, your attention please."

The room immediately went silent, and all eyes turned to the arena CEO.

"By now we've all been made aware of the threat," Jenkins said. "The very latest intel from Homeland mentions fifteen insurgents planning some kind of attack or takeover here tonight. Senator Sterling has been mentioned as a target."

Sterling cleared his throat and held his head high.

"From what I am told, there is a 38.8 percent chance this could really happen." Jenkins nodded to a husky, sour-faced man, fully armed and shielded from head to toe in navy fatigues and combat gear. "Lieutenant Wolfski here has a top-notch SWAT crew spread out across the arena. Columbus PD will be here shortly with at least twenty more officers with shields and combat gear." Jenkins put his hands on his waist and strolled several steps. "Senator Sterling wants the show to go on. Mr. Lester, I believe, is awaiting a consensus from all of us —"

"Can I just say a few words?" Sterling gripped Jenkins's shoulder.

"Please." Jenkins swept a hand toward the others. "Go right ahead."

The senator slowly ran a thumb across his lips before speaking. "Folks, since I began my campaign, we have had threats — all kinds of threats." He paused. "Why is this happening almost everywhere we go? Why?"

Sterling walked several steps, intently examining each face in the room. Then he spoke almost in a whisper. "Freedom. It's why we're here tonight. I can guarantee you that the thousands of people lined up outside this building want this event to go on." His volume increased with each word. "That's why they're here. That's what our ticket is about — stopping these evil lunatics from scaring us to death, from threatening our liberties and stealing our American way of life."

Jenny King's broad shoulders straightened, and her chin went up proudly.

Static blurted in Shakespeare's earpiece. "This is Steve Basheer to base, over."

Clarissa blinked, looked down at her radio, and adjusted the dials.

"Go ahead, Steve," Tab said from base.

"I'm just getting up to the Sky Zone . . ."

There was a clattering sound. Clarissa's head jerked up, and her eyes burned into Shakespeare's.

"Steve?" Tab said. "Steve Basheer, go ahead from the Sky Zone."

Nothing.

That was it.

Something was wrong up there.

Clarissa turned her back on the group in the room and walked to the corner opposite Shakespeare. "Base, this is Clarissa. What about Charlie? Any word? Has he turned up? Over."

"Negative. Over."

Sterling continued his speech, but Shakespeare was listening to Tab in his earpiece, pleading for Steve Basheer to answer his radio but getting nothing.

Clarissa checked her watch and weaved her way to the front of the room next to Jenkins. She whispered in his ear, and he looked down at her, his face darkening.

He spoke up. "Excuse me, Senator. We have a development."

All heads turned to the CEO of the arena.

"One of our security people is . . . he's not been heard from in a few minutes."

The room fell even more quiet.

"We sent a man up to find him at the top of the arena, what's known as the Sky Zone." Jenkins turned to Clarissa, then back to those in the room. "The man we sent up made it to the Sky Zone, but we've lost contact with him."

If this had been a normal group of spectators, gasps would have rung out. But these were professionals, security guards, SWAT. People stared straight ahead, jaws clenched.

Just then Karen entered the room with a sheepish look, followed by Cole. They made their way to Everett and stood next to him.

"Sir, doors are scheduled to open in exactly three minutes," said Clarissa. "As the senator said, we have a huge crowd outside. Many, many more than expected.

We could have ten or twelve thousand here tonight — many women and children, many elderly. We need to make a decision. I'm 95 percent sure that I can speak for my boss, Keefer O'Dell, who's en route from Cleveland, when I say we should not let one guest inside this building when there are one, possibly two EventPros missing."

Jenkins pursed his lips and nodded respectfully.

Sterling rolled his eyes as Jenny King whispered in his ear. The senator ripped his coat off and stuffed it in Jenny's arms.

"From what I'm told, the man missing is elderly, with a history of heart issues," Sterling said. "Let's not jump to conclusions and go into panic mode without concrete reason to think something is amiss."

"Sir, with all due respect, if I may . . ." Shakespeare couldn't keep quiet a second longer.

Sterling scowled. "And you are?"

Clarissa spoke up. "This is Brian Shakespeare, former US marine, sharpshooter, and Desert Storm veteran."

Shakespeare was pleasantly surprised by Clarissa's accolades.

Sterling raised his eyebrows.

"Go ahead, Brian," Everett said. "Give us

your take."

"Why risk it?" Shakespeare's hands remained behind his back. "I mean, I'm with you, Senator. No one's more against terror on our soil than I am —"

"If that's true, you would agree this event must go on!" Sterling said.

"Sir, in my eyes, the only real defense we have in this building right now is Lieutenant Wolfski's SWAT team. It's just not enough —"

"More are on the way," Sterling argued. "Plus, we have your team."

Shakespeare chuckled. "Sir, again with respect, the EventPros staff is unarmed and untrained in the type of event we're talking about. Why not at least wait until Columbus PD arrives before opening the doors? And also, find our two people. I'm not saying cancel the event, but get more armed people in place and make sure our people are okay."

"I agree," Everett said. Karen looped her arms around him and nodded.

Clarissa's shoulders slumped in relief.

Jenkins nodded, looked at Clarissa, and tapped his watch.

The SWAT leader looked at Sterling as if awaiting the final verdict.

Sterling rubbed his forehead and leaned backward as if in pain. "You people forget we are the ones footing the bill for this venue."

Jenny whispered something to Sterling.

"Oh, all right, all right," he conceded. "Delay it fifteen minutes. But we're opening at six forty-five. Not a minute later."

"Thank you, Senator." Clarissa hustled for the door.

Jenkins called to her. "Let me know the minute O'Dell gets here."

"Yes, sir." Clarissa ran out.

Everyone in the room seemed to breathe a collective sigh of relief.

"Urgent, urgent. This is Clarissa to base and all EventPros."

Shakespeare listened intently on his radio for her announcement while looking at his watch, then his cell phone. Both read 6:33 p.m.

"Doors are being postponed fifteen minutes," Clarissa said.

Several shots of static sounded.

"I repeat, doors are delayed fifteen minutes!" Clarissa spoke as if a volcano were erupting. "Doors will now open at six forty-five — I repeat, six forty-five. But even then, *wait for my go-ahead.*"

Bursts of static continued to interrupt her.

"Who is talking while I'm talking?" she demanded.

"Clarissa, this is Tab." There was commotion in the background.

Shakespeare knew immediately what was happening.

His countenance fell.

"We opened the doors already!" Tab yelled over what Shakespeare envisioned was a stampede in the lobby. "We opened at six thirty on the nose. Didn't you hear the call?"

Shakespeare closed his eyes and waited for the bomb to drop.

"No! Close them down!" Clarissa screamed. "Shut them all down. Now, now, now!"

12

The Crittendons' house, three weeks earlier
Pamela pulled her car into the garage, turned it off, and sat there dazed. Resting both hands on her hard tummy, she longed for a quiet moment to herself, to switch hats from administrative assistant to mommy and wife. But she knew Rebecca and Faye would be out to greet her any second.

If no one was home, she would sit there and cry her eyes out.

This was not the way it was supposed to be — not what God intended. She was seven months pregnant, much heavier than she'd been with either of the girls. Her feet were killing her. She was so tired . . . so very tired.

Back when the girls were born, Jack had a good job and she'd had the luxury of staying home. Her only job during those pregnancies had been to remain healthy and rested. She walked three miles a day, did exercise videos, and gladly did the cooking and laundry and kept the house clean. Now Jack did most of those things, and the backwardness of it was tearing her down — physically, emotionally, spiritually.

"Mommy!" Faye was the first one out the door, followed by Rebecca. They dashed around to her car door and reached in for hugs as they jabbered away about school. Pamela smiled and kissed them and gave them all the joy she could muster while her mom stood leaning in the doorway. The girls carried Pamela's purse and laptop into the house.

"Where have you been?" Margaret said. "I didn't even see you leave."

Pamela stared at her, waiting for her to come to her senses. But Margaret just looked at her, waiting for an answer.

"Mom, really? Think about it."

"Oh, for Pete's sake." Margaret snapped her fingers. "Work. I knew that. How was it today? I bet you're dead tired."

And *she* was retrieving the girls from the bus stop? Watching them after school while Jack worked on the job search?

"Same old thing." Pamela got her coat off, ran to the bathroom, then made her way to the pantry to get a snack for the girls.

"Come see what came in the mail today,"

Margaret called from the dining room.

"Just a minute." Pamela set the girls up at the kitchen table with chocolate graham crackers and milk.

"I ordered this through one of the websites Shakespeare recommended." Margaret entered the kitchen carrying a package the size of a shoebox.

Pamela could only imagine what she'd bought now. Margaret had already filled two huge plastic bins with dry food and rations.

"It's a water filter." Margaret put on the reading glasses hanging from her neck and read the box. "With the Max Two-Zero portable filter, turbid and heavily biologically contaminated water can be transformed into safe drinking water. Self-disinfecting. Chemical-free. Da da, da da, da da . . . Ideal for expeditions, extended journeys, civil-defense usage, and disaster-relief operations."

Pamela stared at the box, dumbfounded. "That's great, Mom."

"That's going to save our lives when the big one hits," Faye said with her mouth full.

The girls looked at each other and giggled.

"Don't tell me you've been talking to the girls about that stuff," Pamela said.

"Only making them aware of the possibilities, so they won't go into shock when it happens. We've all got to prepare mentally for anything."

"Okay, girls, that is all in-family talk. Not a word about any of that to your friends."

"Oops!" Faye put a hand over her mouth and continued in a muffled voice. "I told Rachel and Larissa."

Pamela rolled her eyes. She just didn't have the energy to address it any further. "Well, no more," she said. "Where's Daddy?" Jack usually greeted her when she got home.

"He's been shut in his office for the last hour. On the phone," Margaret said. "I'm hoping it's a hot job lead."

If only! If Jack got a job, Pamela would turn in her notice in a heartbeat — the very next day! Not that she wasn't grateful or dedicated, but she would be going on maternity leave anyway. Whoever replaced her could have the job as far as she was concerned.

She went back to the den, knocked, then opened the door and started to say hello.

"Hold on —" Jack said, but he wasn't on the phone. His head was buried in his hands at the desk.

"Sorry." Pamela's heart stopped. Was he crying? She closed the door and stood in the hallway, frozen.

"What is it?" Margaret came up behind her. "Did he get something?"

Pamela's face flushed. Every time Pamela turned around, her mother was there.

"He didn't get the job?" Margaret pried.

"Mom, I don't know! He wants to be alone. Please, just give us a little space."

"Well, excuse me." Margaret walked away curtly.

Pamela immediately regretted losing her patience.

There had been a lot of regrets lately. Words that shouldn't have been spoken. Frustration. Stress.

What was wrong with Jack?

The door opened, and Jack looked at Pamela, his eyes red. "Can you talk for a minute?"

"Of course." She went in and sat on the ottoman.

"How was your day?" he said. "How are you feeling?"

"Fine. What's wrong, honey?"

He plunked down in the chair, his head dropping to his chest. "I've been on the phone with the bank. We missed our house payment last month. I didn't tell you because I thought there was a grace period, and I was due to get a check from Event-Pros."

"Okay . . ."

"The grace period was only five days. We're late."

"Jack." She got on her knees and slid over to him, putting her arms around his waist. "Honey, it's okay —"

"It's not okay! It's not okay on many fronts. It's not okay with the bank. It's not okay for our credit. And it's not okay for me to keep letting you down. Look at you. You're seven months pregnant. You should be *home*!"

He drew her in and tried to suppress the sobs.

She tried to comfort him. "Listen, honey —"

"Why is God doing this? It's been months! What did I do that was so wrong? Why haven't I gotten a job yet?"

She'd asked the same questions a million times.

"I don't know." She held him tight, their heads next to each other. "I just don't know."

"I feel so bad, having you head off to work each day, all day long . . ."

"Honey, it's not like you're sitting around eating popcorn and watching movies. You're working at the arena, applying for jobs all day, keeping the house up, getting me and the girls off in the morning . . . putting up with my mother." Pamela laughed and squeezed Jack tighter, forcing him to chuckle.

"She's been a big help." He pulled back to look at her.

She wiped his tears away with her thumbs. "I bet she would help us, you know, lend us a little bit —"

He shook his head. "No way. I don't want to owe her."

"She's mentioned it to me before."

"I thought we were okay," he said. "I had everything budgeted. The check just didn't show up in time. I feel like such a failure. And I feel sorry for you. I want a job so bad. I'd take anything."

"Something will come, honey. We've got to just keep praying. Keep doing what you're doing. I bet you're going to get the best job you've ever had."

"Thanksgiving's coming. Christmas. How are we gonna pay for gifts?"

"Jack, look at me. We have each other. We have the girls and our parents. We're healthy. I don't care where we live. We can move to a smaller house for all I care."

"But you're unhappy because you're working, and I don't blame you."

"I've got maternity leave coming."

"Then what? Twelve weeks? You're not going to want to go back." He held her face in his hands. "You're not going to be able to go back."

He was dead-on. The thought of leaving her twelve-week-old baby all day, five days a week . . . She couldn't even go there.

"You'll have something by then," she said. "I know you will." She squeezed his hands. "In the meantime, let Mom pay the mortgage, just once."

"I'm due to get that check. It should've been here."

She nodded. "When it finally comes, you pay her back. Simple as that."

"I just can't believe we're in this place. We had over thirty-five thousand dollars saved up."

"Yeah, and we used it on life. It's not like we've been living extravagantly. God knows where we are. He knows we've honored him with our tithe. He's going to take care of us."

"That money was for college, weddings . . . retirement."

"We'll catch up, honey. The important thing is, we're going to have a baby, a healthy baby. Right? And we've got insurance through my work. Think if we didn't have that."

110

She put her hands around his back and snuggled close.

They stayed like that for quite some time.

To lighten things up, she told him how her mother had said she hadn't noticed Pam leave for the day.

After a moment, Jack chuckled into Pamela's shoulder.

Since she had him on a roll, she then told him how proud her mother was of the lifesaving water filter that had arrived in the mail.

He outright laughed at that.

Then he told her how much he loved her.

She knew he meant it.

And that felt like gold.

13

Festival Arena, October 6

Clarissa dashed up the concrete steps marked Employees Only. Derrick and his photographer followed twenty feet behind. All Derrick could think about was letting Zenia know what was happening. But he hadn't had a second.

Clarissa threw open the door leading to the main concourse of the arena. Derrick and Daniel followed. Pure bedlam. They stood frozen as masses of people rushed by them in every direction — to concession stands, to restrooms, and into the bowl of the arena.

"It's too late to get them out," Derrick said.

"Unless they make an announcement and force them out," Daniel said.

"Let's follow Clarissa." Derrick headed toward the enormous glass front of the arena, with Daniel and his equipment in tow.

"Get shots of this!" Derrick called over the noise, pointing toward the commotion at the large bank of front doors.

At Clarissa's order, EventPros had shut all of the doors in midflow, and the people outside were shaking fists, scowling, and pounding at the glass. A young EventPro stood with her back to the doors, her face contorted in panic. Many of the people who'd made it inside looked scared, determined to get away from the chaos at the front doors. Some flashed nervous smiles as they latched hands with loved ones and forged ahead into the arena.

Clarissa huddled up with a group of supervisors by the long, curved customer-service desk. The TV screen above them showed the massive crowd packed like a soccer-riot mob outside the lobby. It was a sea of people — leaning, swaying, pushing. The way they were pressing and pounding at the front doors made Derrick sick to his stomach. He supposed the people complaining angrily outside viewed the locked doors as some sort of liberal plot to suppress their freedom of speech or to ruin the independent candidate's evening.

Daniel was standing on a chair behind a

display table, holding his Nikon high and firing flash after flash. Derrick signaled to him that he was heading toward Clarissa's group. The crowd was so thick, he had to weave and force his way within earshot of her team.

"I can barely hear you." Clarissa pinched her mic right up against her lips. "No, we need them up here, now! And six forty-five is out of the question until we get control of things. Over."

She let the mic drop to her chest and addressed her team. "SWAT's on the way up. We've got to get this crowd spread out. Have your people motion the crowd *inside* the bowl. *Inside* the bowl. That's all we can do. Get people into the bowl and get them seated as fast as possible."

Derrick could only imagine how the mob outside would react when they saw the SWAT guys with their guns, helmets, and shields.

"What about Charlie and Steve?" said Gordy Cavelli.

"Still nothing," Clarissa said. "Two SWAT are on their way up to the Sky Zone. You'll hear as soon as I do. Now let's get busy."

The supervisors began to disperse, but Clarissa called, "Wait!"

She cupped a hand over her earpiece and

held up a finger, listening intently.

"Three more team members have left." She shrugged, relaying the information coming in her earpiece. "SWAT wants us to take Sterling to suite 227 on the club level . . . Once that happens, they want Lester to go to suite 213, club level . . . Wait a minute." She squinted and put her mic to her lips. "Why would we do that? They're safer in the bunker. I repeat, *they are safer in the bunker.* Over."

Clarissa squeezed the back of her neck and dropped her head, awaiting a response. She shook her head and spoke into her mic. "This whole thing should've been called off —" She blinked several times, as if getting shot at with verbal gunfire. "Yes . . . yes, sir . . . understood. Over."

Her mouth sealed to a slit, and she looked soberly at her people, her chin jutting out. "Okay. SWAT wants Sterling and Lester up high. They intend to keep that level closed so they can isolate them. They don't like all the possible entry points in the bunker. Also . . . the squad from Columbus PD is having a difficult time getting here."

Several of the supervisors shook their heads, concern brimming in their eyes.

"Apparently traffic is at a standstill, and they're caught in a bottleneck before the bridge at Overbrook Parkway. Word's gotten out that Lester's here. And who knows what else is being said on the news." Clarissa cupped her mouth, turned, and glared at Derrick as if he'd caused all of her problems.

He just shrugged and held up his hands.

She looked around the packed lobby with weary eyes. "I don't know if we're going to be able to fit all these people in the bowl without opening the club level . . ." She threw her hands out as if shooing a cat. "That's it. Go. Do your best."

Shakespeare never shied away from a fight, but the team he was playing for this night was unraveling before his eyes. He felt as if they were fifty-point underdogs, with the odds worsening with each passing second.

As long as he could remember, people had relied on him to know a little about everything, to give good advice, to be prepared, to have the answers, to be brave, to know how to fight — and win.

It wasn't going to be any different tonight; he could feel it.

The cold truth was, Charlie and Steve had probably been overtaken by terrorists up in the Sky Zone, maybe even killed on the spot. More than a thousand civilians had been let inside the building, basically to go

116

wherever they wanted. The thought was crystallizing in Shakespeare's mind that his leadership in the next few hours might well mean the difference between life and death for a good number of people. It was time to make the mind-set change from EventPro to soldier.

He approached Chico. "I'm gonna disappear for five minutes. Stall till I get back."

"You can't leave, man!" Chico's black eyes about popped out of his head. "We're about to take them upstairs! Can't it wait?"

"No. I've got to get some things out of my car. Don't worry. It's right on the parking deck. It'll take no time."

"Please, Brian, don't leave. Get it later."

Shakespeare started for the door. "Stall them till I get back. Say I'm in the boys' room. They'll wait."

"Hey, you got a minute?" Jack got in step with Shakespeare as he stepped out the door. Clarissa was coming toward them down the hall at full steam.

"You guys heard Columbus PD is stuck in traffic?" she said, out of breath.

"This is serious, Clarissa," Shakespeare said. "I think the terrorists are in the building, in the Sky Zone."

"That's impossible," she said. "We did a

thorough bag check on everyone who came in."

Shakespeare closed his eyes and shook his head. "They've *been* here. Embedded. Overnight. Probably came in as civilians for the hockey game last night. No bag checks at hockey games."

"We did a full sweep last night after the game, just like always," she protested. "I was here."

"You know as well as I do that if someone wanted to spend the night in this building, they could. If these guys are pros, and this thing's been planned out, they could have been hanging from the ceiling like bats for all we know. There are plenty of places to hide. I say they're in here now, and we should evacuate."

Jack's mouth was agape. He swallowed visibly. "What are we gonna do?"

"Stay calm." Clarissa took in a deep breath. "You may have something. I'm gonna run your theory by Lieutenant Wolfski."

"We definitely have a situation," Shakespeare said. "I'm gonna go get some things from my car that will come in handy —"

"Oh no you're not." Clarissa shook her head. "There're no weapons allowed in this building — not on us, anyway. I want you

118

to get back in there and escort Sterling to the club level. That's an order."

Shakespeare clenched his jaw and paused a moment, composing his thoughts. "I don't mean any disrespect, Clarissa, but these are special circumstances, and I'm going to my car. If you don't want me to come back, tell me now." He started walking. "Otherwise, I'll see you back in here in five minutes, and we'll take care of business."

Not another word was spoken.

14

Offices of the **Columbus Gazette**, *ten days earlier*

Jack couldn't believe how nervous he was, sitting there in a chair by the bustling city desk in the newsroom of the *Columbus Gazette*. A week ago he'd called each of the editors whose names Derrick had given him, and now he was waiting for his appointment with Buck Stevens, the one who'd agreed to see him.

With his big leather portfolio on his lap, he gazed out at the maze of cubicles before him, a football field's worth of computers, scanners, printers, and reporters. The sound of keyboards clicking and people on telephones trying to get facts and quotes and scoops mesmerized him. He didn't even know if there was a job opening, but he wanted to work in that newsroom so badly, he could taste the newsprint.

Derrick had called Jack to let him know

he was in a studio somewhere in the building, overseeing a photo shoot with Ohio senator and presidential candidate Martin Sterling. They planned to meet up when Jack was finished with his interview.

Jack desperately needed the job, for Pam's sake if nothing else. She was almost eight months along, yet she was up and down all day long at the orthodontist's office, escorting patients, retrieving files, answering phones. He'd recently spent more than they could afford on some really cushy shoes for her, but even so, her ankles swelled up almost every night.

Please, Father, let this Buck Stevens find favor on me.

His phone vibrated. Probably Pam checking in on him.

Hey. You got a minute to meet me?

It was Shakespeare, not Pam.

Jack replied that he could meet in a while and reminded Shakespeare that today was his big interview downtown.

He unzipped the portfolio and double-checked that his résumé was on top and ready to present. He'd brought five copies just in case.

"Jack?" A gray-haired man, probably in

121

his early sixties, approached. He was holding a mug with a Denison University logo and wearing a white shirt, red suspenders, and khakis. He stuck his hand out. "Buck Stevens."

"Very good to meet you." Jack stood and shook the editor's hand. "Thanks for agreeing to see me today."

"Let's go back this way where we can talk." Buck headed off, looking behind him to make sure Jack was following. He had kind of a hunched back and a medium build. "Derrick's told us a lot about you. I actually remember your work from the *Dispatch.*"

The buzz of the newsroom gave Jack a euphoric feeling, almost as though he were floating as he walked. And he could actually smell the newsprint from the presses, which were in the same building.

They settled into a tiny conference room with a huge table and almost no room for the many large chairs that surrounded it. Buck motioned for Jack to sit.

"This election is knocking us on our rears, and it's still a year off," Buck said. "It's because Sterling is so darn popular. His numbers are soaring."

"So I've heard."

"Oh yeah. As of a few minutes ago, he's

atop *all* polls, including Republicans."

"That's amazing," Jack said, still nervous. "Would he be the first independent candidate elected president?"

"Actually George Washington was independent both of his terms," Buck said.

Why did I ask a question I didn't have the answer to? Isn't that one of those things you're never supposed to do?

"We're excited because this is an Ohio boy and he's got a real shot," Buck said. "This is no Ross Perot or Ralph Nader. The guy is a contender, and we're going to cover him like a pack of dogs. Your buddy Derrick's working it full-time, and we've got some others doing the same, in various capacities."

"Yes, he told me it had him running," Jack said.

"You and Derrick did quite a job on that Demler-Vargus exposé for the *Dispatch*. It was fine work. You certainly scooped us on that one."

"Thank you." Jack fingered his résumé, anxious to give it to Buck and start showing off his clips.

"I don't need to see your book." Buck nodded at the portfolio. "I've done my homework."

"Okay. I've got a résumé for you." Jack

123

tried to mask his enthusiasm.

Buck shook his head. "I've got your number. Listen, let me get right to this thing. We like your work. We like what kind of man you are. We like your experience. Derrick's filled us in, and as I said, I've done a good amount of homework."

This was sounding good. Really good.

"So we've been looking ahead to the election next November, trying to plan what it will mean to the paper as we head into the new year," Buck said. "It's quite possible — likely even — that our local boy will make it on the ticket and, ultimately, make it to the White House. Right now he's got a darn good shot, and we plan to cover him every step of the way."

It was sounding so good, Jack was already envisioning a dinner-out celebration with the family.

"So what we've determined is this. If Sterling continues to remain up in the polls for another month, until Thanksgiving, we will likely assign Derrick to cover a new Washington-slash-Sterling-slash-political beat that would keep him busy full-time. He'd be back and forth between here and DC and working on nothing local. In that case, we would need a reporter to take his place on his normal beat."

"I see." If there had been any doubt before about whom Jack was backing for president, it was gone now. Sterling was his man — and his meal ticket.

"I know what you're probably thinking, but bear with me," Buck said. "We wouldn't want you for that job."

Jack felt a tinge of despair.

"We've got a relatively new editor on staff who's missing her old beat as a reporter," Buck said. "So the plan would be to have Derrick cover Sterling full-time and move this editor back to a reporter slot. The upshot is, we need to replace the editor. That's where *you* would come in."

Even more pay! *Yes, the answer is yes!* Jack tried to contain his excitement. "That sounds interesting."

"I know there're quite a few 'ifs' involved, but when I realized you were available, I told our senior editor we needed to try to make a place for you. Your call came at just the right time."

That was God.

"Well, I'm interested." Jack realized he was smiling.

"We can talk about salary and benefits if and when it happens. Again, the target is Thanksgiving."

"Super," Jack said. But suddenly the

doubt that had built up like a massive dam over the last seven months got the best of him. "What if, by chance, Sterling's popularity should wane?"

"We can cross that bridge then." Buck stood. "I'm looking at this as a long-term relationship. If this doesn't pan out, there'll be other opportunities down the road. Let's commit to keeping in touch."

"Okay." Jack stood, debating whether to crack the joke that came to mind. *What the heck.* "I can call you every day, if you like."

"Jack, hold up!" The shout came from across the newsroom. It was Derrick, leading a group of dark-suited men and one woman.

"Mr. Stevens, thank you again," Jack said to Buck. "I'm going to say hello to Derrick."

"Fine. I'm going to scoot back to my office before I get swept up in all the hoopla." Buck waved at Derrick's group, then went the other way.

Derrick approached, leading Martin Sterling and his entourage, and Jack felt as if he were in a dream. The whole morning at the newspaper had been a dream — a very good dream from which he had no desire to wake up.

Sterling was flanked by two generic-looking security guards and his sharp young black-haired handler lady, who ran a finger down a clipboard, checked her watch, and whispered something to Sterling. A third security guy, portly and dark skinned, brought up the rear. He produced a toothpick from somewhere in his big mouth, swirled it on his tongue, and made it disappear again as he gazed about the newsroom, looking bored.

"Jack, I want you to meet the next president of the United States, Martin Sterling." Derrick smiled and gestured toward the senator. "Senator Sterling, this is my best friend, best man, and hopefully soon-to-be new reporter with the *Gazette,* Jack Crittendon."

Sterling had a viselike grip. "Pleasure to meet you, Jack. You two made quite a team on that Demler-Vargus fiasco. Woodward and Bernstein got nothing on you."

Jack chuckled. "Thank you, sir."

"We just did a photo shoot for the Sunday magazine," Derrick said.

"My mother-in-law is a huge fan of yours," Jack said to Sterling. "Wait till she hears that I met you."

"Jenny, do we have a photograph for Jack's mother-in-law?"

From beneath her clipboard Jenny produced an eight-by-ten glossy of Sterling wearing a bomber jacket with an American flag on the shoulder. She uncapped a Sharpie and handed them both to Sterling.

"What's her name?"

"Margaret," Jack said.

Sterling scribbled a brief message, signed with looping exaggeration, and handed the photo and marker back to Jenny, who blew on the signature and gave the photo to Jack.

"Thank you very much. She's going to collapse when she sees this," Jack said. "I mean it. Over the past few months she's become a diehard supporter, mainly because of your stance on national security and defense spending."

"We have a great deal of support from the elderly. More than the president does. That's clear. At least that's what the polls say. It's the young vote we must have."

Sterling looked at Derrick to say, *This is off the record,* then turned back to Jack.

"We don't think young people grasp what the country's in danger of losing. It's about freedom and heritage and legacy. But they're more concerned about taking pictures of themselves and posting them on Twitter and Facebook." He lowered his voice and inched closer to Jack. "They're so darn inward-focused . . . they're *asleep.* They have no concept of reality. Not in their wildest dreams do they realize how drastically things could change." He snapped his fingers. "Overnight."

"Senator." The young lady tapped her watch. "We do have a tight agenda. Best we keep moving."

Sterling shook his head and waved a hand. "Aw, don't get me started. Jack . . ." They shook hands. "Great to meet you. I assume I'll be seeing more of you, if and when you come on board here."

Jack smiled. "Yes, sir. I look forward to it. Good luck in the days ahead."

Derrick and he bumped fists, and the Sterling entourage continued through the newsroom like a dark cloud working its way across a white sky.

The new text waiting on his phone was another from Shakespeare. He was at the Sinclair, a tavern several doors down from the *Gazette*. With a bounce in his step, Jack made his way to the windy city street. He stood there for a moment, eyeballing the concrete landscape, high-rises, eateries, and businesses, and pictured himself working there.

He took in an enormous breath of cold air. He hadn't felt so excited in months.

Thank you. That was good. Please . . .

please let this happen.

He ducked into the dark bar, let his eyes adjust, and walked toward the back. It smelled like . . . fish. Shakespeare lifted a drink to get his attention.

"Hey, man." Jack slid in across from him. "What's going on?"

Shakespeare reeked of booze. His drink was dark gold with no ice — whiskey, Jack presumed.

Both elbows on the table, Shakespeare pursed his lips and swirled the drink. "Sheena's leaving."

Jack deflated.

A waitress appeared. Jack ordered a tonic and lime. Shakespeare ordered another short whiskey.

"Why?" Jack asked.

"I am a 'survivalist freak.' I have 'lost touch with reality.' " His head wobbled back and forth sarcastically with each word. "I have taken my 'threat addiction' too far. I have failed as a husband and father . . . You want me to keep going?"

"What about the kids?"

Shakespeare tossed his head back, draining the drink. "She says she's taking 'em." He wiped his mouth with the back of a wrist and nodded slowly.

"Does she want the house?"

"She doesn't care. Just wants out." His speech was slurred.

"Maybe it was just a bad day," Jack said. "Didn't she do this once before?"

"She's talked to a lawyer. She means it this time."

"Man . . ."

He lifted up and craned his neck toward the bar. "How long does it take to pour a whiskey?"

"So what're you gonna do?"

He looked down, shook his head, then tipped the empty glass way back again, loudly sucking at the last few drops. "Looks like I'm gonna be flyin' solo."

"Dude, I know a really good marriage counselor. She's helped a couple of my friends. One says she saved their marriage."

The waitress showed up, and Shakespeare eyed his drink as if she'd just arrived with a lobster dinner.

"Christian, I suppose." He didn't take his eyes off the drink.

"Yes."

He took a swig, puckered his lips, and let out an "Ahh," as if the drink was his lifeline.

"You're not driving home. I'll take you," Jack said.

"I'm not like you, Jack . . ." Shakespeare winced. "There's something different about

131

you. I've always admired it —"

"You need to make an appointment with this lady —"

"I mean it. You're a real Christian. You don't just hang out with other Christians. You're friends with everybody. You care about people. *Phhh* . . . what a concept." He took another swig. "Most of the Christians I know are self-righteous idiots. Think they're better than everyone else. Bunch of hypocrites. It's all just talk. I can't stand it."

"God knows our hearts, dude."

"Yeah." Shakespeare chuckled but didn't smile. "That's what I'm afraid of."

Jack got out his phone and searched for the counselor's name and number. He and Pam had actually discussed going to see her on several different occasions.

"Don't bother. She won't do it. She's done." Shakespeare looked at his watch. "Thanks anyway."

"What if you and I were to get together? Say once a week."

Shakespeare looked at Jack intently, his mouth sealed shut.

"Maybe Pam could even get together with Sheena. I could talk to her about it."

Shakespeare gave a half smile. "I take it you don't mean for drinks . . ."

15

Festival Arena, October 6

From a corner of the drafty room where Everett and Karen Lester talked quietly and their son read a book on the floor, Jack made a quick call to the house to fill Pam in on what was going on — but he got no answer.

How could that be? Unless they'd run out for dinner. But Pam hadn't felt like going anywhere, especially at night — in the cold.

What had she meant in her text about having a surprise for him?

Could she possibly be in labor — early? On the way to the hospital?

But no, she would want him there.

A wave of dread rolled over him.

Surely Margaret would let him know as soon as possible.

What about the girls? The hospital was no place for them.

He should've left when Clarissa gave the

option. Idiot. It was too late now; he was needed here. But if Pam really was in labor, he would have to go. But . . . just leave?

He thumbed to his favorites for Pam's cell number.

"Jack, we're switching things up." Clarissa strode into the room and got right in his face. "I want you and Sid to escort Lester and his people to suite 213 *now.* Use the service elevator."

He nodded, his mind racing.

She continued, "As soon as Shakespeare gets back, he will bring Sterling up. Lieutenant Wolfski thinks this is the best play right now."

"But if the bad guys are already in the building, shouldn't we stay put?" Jack said.

Her shoulders collapsed, and her head dropped in frustration. "Mr. O'Dell says we are to do everything SWAT tells us. That's the order from the top."

Wolfski was in the hallway, talking on his radio. Sterling was in a deep and private conversation with Jenny King.

"So let's roll." Clarissa turned to face Everett and Karen. "Mr. Lester, Jack and Sid are going to escort you and your party up to the club level now. We have a nice suite waiting for you."

"Clarissa." Jack couldn't hold it back any

longer. "Can I talk to you one minute?"

She scowled at him and asked the Lesters to excuse her. "What is it?"

"My wife's eight months pregnant. She's not answering the house phone. I was going to try her cell."

Clarissa rolled her eyes as her head tilted back, then evened her gaze at Jack and breathed out before speaking. "Just get them up there safely, make sure they're comfortable, then go outside the door and make your call." Her voice was amazingly calm. "If she's in labor, tell me. We'll figure something out."

Jack's whole body eased. "Thank you, Clarissa."

With renewed zeal he instructed Sid to follow behind the Lester party as he led them all out the door into the long concrete hallway. Stopping, Jack counted nine people in all, including Everett, Karen, Cole, Gray, and five security and staff members. The rest of Lester's entourage were backstage preparing for the show.

He glanced at his phone again. Nothing from Pam or Margaret.

"Okay, folks, just follow me." Jack began to walk at a good clip. "We'll have you up to your suite in no time."

■ ■ ■ ■

"Daniel!" Derrick yelled to his cameraman over the clamor of the crowd, jabbing a finger toward the helmet-clad SWAT soldiers jogging single file into the arena lobby, carrying shields and armed with clubs and heavy artillery.

With the fluidity of a cat, Daniel weaved his way through the crowd, shooting frame after frame of the SWAT officers as they stationed themselves along the front doors of the venue.

"This way, folks. This way. Keep moving," called one of the orange-jacketed EventPros, his hands held high in the air as he motioned for people to move deeper into the facility. Down the way, other EventPros stood at the open doors leading into the bowl, calling and waving their hands for guests to file into the seating area.

"Ladies and gentlemen, boys and girls, welcome to the spectacular Columbus Festival Arena!" a booming voice echoed over the PA system. "If you will, please make your way inside the event hall through the many sets of double doors. This is a general admission event and we have many guests to accommodate, so again, please make your way *inside* the event hall while the best seats are still available."

Derrick went with the flow through the first set of doors and, once inside, hopped out of line near the top of the steps, where he stood next to a large column to get a bird's-eye view. All around the oval-shaped arena, people were making their way down the long rows of steps, many filling in the seats around the stage.

His cell phone vibrated, and he glanced down to read a text from Daniel:

Where did you go?

He checked the sign above him and texted back that he was at the top of section 103. While he had his phone out he thought of calling Zenia, but it was too loud to hold a conversation, and he couldn't explain it in a text.

Daniel came through the doors wide-eyed, jockeying his way to Derrick. "Man, this is nuts. Those people outside are ticked off."

"It's gonna be an interesting night," Derrick said. "You have any reservations?"

"What do you mean?"

"It could get dangerous . . ."

Daniel shook his head. He had a shiny brown baby face with huge brown eyes, the whites of which were crystal clear. "This is what we do. I'm all in."

Derrick nodded, wishing he felt the same. Of course, he would have when he was young and single like Daniel, but now he was over thirty and married — both good excuses.

"You think anything's going on up there?" Daniel nodded up high, toward the top of the arena, where a black curtain gusted and a black railing ran the entire circumference of the venue.

Derrick exhaled aloud. "I hope not."

"You think we ought to catch back up with Sterling?"

"Yeah. We've seen what the public's seeing. Let's find out what's going on behind the scenes."

16

The Crittendons' house, three days earlier
"What was that?" Pamela asked.

Margaret clicked the mouse, quickly closing the screen she'd been viewing when Pamela came around the corner into the family room. "What?" She continued to look at the computer and clicked open something new on the screen. "Just checking the old email. Shakespeare's been sending me links. You don't know how survivor savvy I've become."

"That's what I'm afraid of. What was that video you were watching?"

"YouTube."

"Did Shakespeare send you that link?"

"No."

"What was it, Mom? It looked like a close-up of someone with a gun."

"He was sliding the rack on a nine-millimeter semiautomatic." Margaret pronounced every word like an expert at a gun show. "It interests me, that's all. Gee whiz, can't a girl have a little fun — and privacy?"

Ha. Privacy! It was something they'd had none of since Margaret moved in with them so many months ago.

Pamela was sorry the second she thought it.

"Mom, yes, you can have privacy. I just don't want you to get carried away with all that Shakespeare survivalist stuff. It's not healthy. I'm fine with your buying some extra food, ordering the water filter. But watching videos about guns?"

"It's not healthy to ignore the threat." Margaret continued to work the mouse, examining the screen.

"Yeah, well, if your little food stash gets any bigger, we're going to need to rent storage space."

"Very funny. You won't laugh when the stores are all closed and my little stash is what's feeding your girls — and the baby." She'd purchased dozens of jars of baby food.

"You heard what Sheena said. It's an obsession with Brian. And now look at them — they're totally unhappy."

"If you ask me, she's the one who's a little off-kilter," Margaret said. "I wonder if she isn't clinically depressed. It's no surprise he's found . . . other interests." She quietly murmured the last few words.

There were times Pamela had to count to ten to keep her mouth shut. She took out her frustration by fluffing and straightening the big pillows on the couch. Then she picked up crayons and coloring books the girls had left out, all the while trying to process the fact that her mother was watching YouTube videos of rednecks firing guns.

But then again, what difference did it really make? Her mother was old. She wasn't bothering anyone. She was harmless.

"Look at this. Even CNN is saying Sterling won Monday night's debate," Margaret said. "If *they're* saying it, you know he dominated."

Ever since Jack had gotten to meet Senator Sterling at Derrick's newspaper office a week ago, they'd all been following him on the news, cheering him on, knowing that if he remained strong in the polls through Thanksgiving, Jack would have a full-time job as an editor at the *Columbus Gazette.*

The thought of being able to stay home with the baby made Pamela's heart soar. She would be a full-time mommy again for Rebecca and Faye. Laundry and house-cleaning and grocery shopping had never looked so good. She would be able to nurse the baby, change her, put her down for naps — all day long.

It was funny, but the whole pregnancy Pamela had been referring to the baby as "she." That was probably because they were just so used to having girls. They certainly had all of the clothes and toys a girl would need. But what if it was a boy? She smiled. Jack would be ecstatic.

"Are you sure you don't want to take me to Festival Arena Friday night? I bet Jack could get us backstage," Margaret said.

This must've been the fourth time she'd mentioned it.

"I told you, he can't do stuff like that while he's working, Mom. They're strict."

"Oh, I know. I'm just teasing you. I would never ask you to go out at night in your condition."

Pamela had secretly contemplated surprising her mother and taking her and the girls to see Senator Sterling at the rally. It was free. She knew her mom would love it. And it could be an educational field trip for the girls.

But she was so tired at night after working all day. She knew she wouldn't feel up to it, especially making the long walk from the parking lot to the venue and back again late at night. Plus, it was getting colder, and it was getting dark so early. She just knew she wouldn't want to make the thirty-minute drive into the city. And what if, by chance, she went into labor? She just wanted to be close to home.

"Where are the girls, anyway?" Margaret said. "I haven't seen them all day."

Pamela's heart sank. She paused — longer than she meant to. "At piano lessons."

"Shouldn't they be home by now?"

Miscues like this came out of the blue. And they were happening more frequently. Pamela was learning to just get on the bus with her mother and ride.

"I'll get them in about thirty minutes. You can go with me if you want."

"I don't think so." Her mom had finished on the computer and was standing at the window, staring into the backyard. "What about Jack? What time does he get home?"

"He's running errands, remember?" Pamela said. "I need to start thinking about dinner."

Margaret turned around and faced Pamela with her arms crossed. "It's been eight months since I've had a drink."

Okay . . . shifting gears.

"Eight months — today?" Pamela said.

Her mom nodded. "I don't miss it. I really don't."

"You should be so proud, Mom. Eight months. Wow."

"My clothes don't smell anymore. My breath doesn't reek. And I've saved a whole bunch of money. What a monkey off my back. A big part of it's been the girls. Reading to them. Helping with homework. Just talking. It's been like therapy."

"They love having you here."

She smiled and nodded, but creases formed on her brow. Her head dropped.

Pamela went to her.

"I just hate getting old," Margaret whimpered. "I want to be able to take care of myself. I know I . . . I get a little off at times. It's scary."

Pamela rested a hand on her mother's shoulder. "I know, but you're doing great, Mom. You're in good shape. You're still very independent."

But Pamela did question — even doubt — whether her mother would be safe living alone again. Margaret was on the waiting list at an assisted-living home in Cleveland where several of her friends resided. But Pamela couldn't imagine leaving her up there alone.

"Okay." Margaret sniffed and threw her shoulders back. "Enough of this pity party. I've got things to do in the nursery." She headed for the stairs.

"Like what?"

The phone rang.

"I'm in the middle of building that mobile thing that hangs over the crib."

"Oh yeah." The phone wasn't in its cradle, so Pamela pressed the Page button.

"Speaking of the crib, that thing is a relic," Margaret said. "Are you sure you don't need something newer? They're probably much safer these days."

"No, Mom. It's fine." Pamela found the phone buried between the seat cushions on the couch and answered it.

"Hello, is this Mrs. Crittendon?"

"Who's calling?" Pamela said.

"My name is Alan Bingham, with Triple A Credit. I'm calling for Mr. Jack Crittendon. Is he in, please?"

"No, I'm sorry." Pamela spoke in as kind a tone as she could muster. "Can you take us off of your call list, please?"

"Oh, I apologize. I didn't communicate clearly. This is not any kind of telemarketing. I am *returning* Mr. Crittendon's call. He contacted me about having Triple A help consolidate his debts."

Pamela felt the wind go out of her. She sat down at the kitchen table.

"I can call back if he's not home . . ."

Margaret had paused at the steps, listening.

"Or you can just tell him Alan called from Triple A Credit."

Pamela mumbled something and turned the phone off in a daze.

"Who was that?" Margaret said.

"Someone for Jack . . ."

"Oh . . . okay." Margaret started up the steps.

"Mom, wait . . . can you come here? I need to talk to you."

17

Festival Arena, October 6

Shakespeare was huffing by the time he got back to room 5-A, lugging a heavy backpack over his shoulder. Clarissa's jaw clenched when she saw it, but she ignored it and quickly explained to him that she'd sent Jack upstairs with Lester's party.

"Once we hear they're situated, you're moving out with Sterling," she said. "I want you up there as fast as possible. I don't like this at all."

"What about doors?" Shakespeare looked at his watch.

"We moved it to seven o'clock. Sterling's furious."

"It's almost seven now."

"He wants those people in here," Clarissa said.

"That guy's got some screws missing. We need to *wait.*"

Two journalists came jogging down the

hall — the ones Jenny had called Derrick and Daniel.

"Where do you think you're going?" Clarissa said.

Derrick nodded at the door to 5-A. "We're covering Sterling . . . for the *Gazette.*" He held up his plastic photo ID, and Daniel did the same.

"I know who you are, but this is —"

"It's okay." Jenny King stepped into the hallway with her arms crossed and a clipboard against her chest. "I promised them a few minutes with the senator." She motioned to Derrick and Daniel. "Come in, gentlemen."

They passed into the room, and Jenny leaned toward Clarissa. "Senator Sterling insists the doors open at seven."

As Jenny slipped back into 5-A, Lieutenant Wolfski stepped out. He glanced at Shakespeare and squared up to Clarissa.

"My men found one of your guy's radios in the Sky Zone." His tone was low and serious. "No sign of your people yet."

"Where was the radio?" Shakespeare asked.

Wolfski continued looking at Clarissa. "In the small stairwell leading to the roof."

"These guys are in the building. You know that, don't you?" Shakespeare said.

"My men are still canvassing the Sky Zone." Wolfski continued to address Clarissa. He obviously didn't need or want Shakespeare's opinion.

"Sir, if I may . . ." Shakespeare waited for Wolfski to face him. Shakespeare didn't want to say the words he was thinking, that it was a mistake sending Lester and Sterling to the club level. So he spun it. "There are more exit points for the senator and Everett Lester down here."

Wolfski's eyes widened. "More exit points mean more *entry* points —"

"But entry points don't matter if the bad guys are *already in* the building." Shakespeare felt the heat rising in his face. "Two EventPros are missing. That's a fact. Until they're accounted for, don't you think this building should be cleared of all civilians?"

Wolfski stepped closer to Shakespeare, his boots pointing outward like a penguin's feet, his thick hands and big thumbs hooked on to his leather utility belt. "Mister" — he squinted at the ID badge hanging around Brian's neck — "Shakespeare." He smirked. "The fact that civilians are in the building was not our idea, but we're going to keep them safe. Let us finish our sweep in the Sky Zone and make an assessment at that time. Would that meet your approval?"

Smart aleck.

"It would," Shakespeare said. "As long as you postpone doors at least another fifteen minutes, to quarter past."

Wolfski blinked slowly. He had the wide, wet mouth of a slobbery bulldog and one of those five o'clock shadows that seemed always present, probably even right after he shaved.

"I'm about to discuss that with the senator," he said.

With a burst of static, Shakespeare's radio came to life. "This is Jack to Clarissa. Everett Lester and his party are safely in suite 213. I'm stationed outside the door. Over."

Clarissa's shoulders slumped in relief. "Ten-four. Over." She nodded to Shakespeare. "Okay. Get the senator and his party to suite 227 — ASAP. Keep me posted."

Shakespeare shot Wolfski one last glance and ducked into room 5-A.

Up on the plush club level, with its recessed lighting and expensive glass, chrome, and wood finish, a person could be fooled into thinking there was nothing at all going on at the arena that night.

Several of the familiar black-clad caterers hurried along the wide, cool concourse,

150

pushing silver food carts and talking on radios. The suite Jack had just opened for Everett Lester had been fully stocked with a line of hot entrees in silver warming trays, plus a variety of snacks and beverages.

Jack got out his phone to call Pam. Her cell rang and rang, and then her voice mail came on.

Jack shook the phone. What good were cell phones if people didn't answer them!

Now he was officially worried.

The only positive thing he had to cling to was the text she'd sent him earlier. He punched his messages and read it again.

I have a surprise for you!

Okay . . . whom else could he call to find out what on earth was going on?

Just then, his phone vibrated once.

A text message . . . from Pam!

His heart raced as he opened it.

What section are you in?

18

Trenton City, one day earlier

It was a brisk fall afternoon, and the red traffic light above Pamela's car in downtown Trenton City swayed in the wind. Leaves danced across the street, and people pinched their coats tight around their necks and pulled their hats and scarves close as they walked and jogged across the intersection.

She had gotten to work early that morning so she could break away in the afternoon to get to the bank. She phoned her mom to make sure the girls had made it home from the bus stop safely. Margaret said they were doing homework and she was ironing.

Before she hung up, Pamela said, "Now, Mom, I don't want you vegging out on that computer the whole time I'm gone." It was like having another child. Sometimes she wished they'd never taught her how to use the computer. "And be sure to unplug the iron when you're done with it."

The light changed and Pamela drove, resting a hand on her tummy, feeling the baby's elbow or a knee. Jack was going to be upset when he learned that she had discussed their financial situation with Margaret. She dreaded telling him. But it was a conversation she had already put off too long.

She wheeled the red Accord into the bank parking lot, feeling more alert and energetic than she had in days. *Bring on this baby,* she thought. Last night she'd slept better than she had in weeks, months maybe. Nine hours straight without waking. She attributed it to the chamomile tea Jack had prepared for her before bed. Of course, Shakespeare had suggested it, and Jack had made a special trip to buy some.

She entered the bank, got a deposit slip, and found herself standing at the desk, staring at the check her mother had written: *Pamela Crittendon, $5,000.*

Pamela's father had worked hard for that money, and the sad thing was, it wouldn't go far. She and Jack had burned through virtually all of their savings in the past year, and it wasn't as if they were eating out every night or buying new clothes at Nordstrom. They ate at home most of the time, and she shopped at secondhand stores for many of

153

the girls' clothes.

Both cars were paid off. But they had a mortgage and bills — and taxes were higher than Pamela could ever recall. Another good reason to vote for Martin Sterling. The dirty SUV she'd parked behind had featured a crooked bumper sticker: Sterling for President — Sterling for America! She hoped it was foreshadowing.

She got in line to make the deposit, thinking how down Jack had been. The financial stress was getting to him. Although he might think Pamela was disappointed in him, it wasn't true. She knew he was trying everything within his power to find a good job.

It was up to God.

Was she frustrated with God?

She thought about it for a moment and concluded maybe she was.

He could produce a job. On a silver platter. In a snap.

Why was he putting them through this?

Yet another trial by fire.

Like a battleship at war, their marriage had taken some jarring hits.

First it was the whole home-invasion nightmare with Granger Meade. Then her dad passing away. Then Jack and Derrick's frightening investigation of the crooks at Demler-Vargus. Now her mom was living with them, and all of the money they'd saved for weddings and college educations was gone. And her mom was struggling with dementia.

Frankly, it had been excruciating for Pamela to go from being a stay-at-home mom to a full-time career person. She gave 100 percent of herself at work and didn't have much energy or patience left by the time she got home.

She finished her transaction, put the receipt in her purse, dug for her keys — and felt a contraction.

"Pam?"

She looked up and felt her mouth drop open. "Jeanie?"

Her friend Jeanie Sorenson embraced her, then stepped back, holding Pamela's hands and looking wide-eyed at her tummy. "Look at you! I had no idea you were expecting!"

Pamela nodded. "One more month. And right now . . ." She paused with a hand on her lower back, concentrating on breathing through the pain. ". . . I'm having a Braxton-Hicks."

Jeanie's mouth and eyes were open wide. "Are you kidding me? You're having a contraction right now?"

Pamela nodded, trying to smile. "I'm sure it's Braxton-Hicks. I've been having them for the past week."

"So is it a girl or a boy?"

"Don't know!"

"That's right, you never wanted to know."

"Okay, okay, this is getting better. Getting better. Whew."

"Are you sure it's not the real thing?"

Pamela shook her head. "Not yet. But soon, I hope. I'm ready."

"Well, how is everything in your world, girl?"

Jeanie and Pamela had met in college and ended up sharing a house with two other girls their junior and senior years. Jeanie's husband was a dentist in Columbus, and they lived in one of the enormous nineteenth-century homes approaching the square in downtown Trenton City. Needless to say, Pamela did not mention their financial woes when catching her up to speed, but she did tell her she was back in the workforce.

"Why haven't we gotten together?" Jeanie said.

In truth, it was because Jack and Jeanie's husband, Quinton, never hit it off. Quinton was a prep schooler, Ivy Leaguer, and country clubber. Jack was a public schooler, attended a state university, and got along better with the guys at the paper than those in suits and high-rises. Otherwise, Pamela would have loved spending more time with Jeanie. They each had two children and a lot in common, including their faith.

"What have you been up to? You look fantastic," Pamela said.

Jeanie shook her shiny highlighted auburn hair over her shoulder and held up a red pouch. Pamela couldn't help but notice her heavy, expensive-looking bracelets, rings, and glossy french manicure.

Jeanie looked around the bank lobby and leaned in close. "I'm working with Martin Sterling. These are deposits. We've been supporting him for, oh gosh, almost two years. Right now it's just crazy."

"That is so funny. Jack just met him!"

"Really? Where?"

"He was . . ." Oops. She really didn't want Jeanie to know Jack was out of work. "He ran into him at the *Gazette* . . . when he was meeting a friend. Do you know Derrick Whittaker?"

"Sure! I mean, I don't know him as a friend, but he's covering Martin's campaign."

Oh, she and the senator were on a first-name basis . . . Perhaps Quinton was rubbing off on her. Pamela hoped not.

"He gave Jack an autographed picture to

give to my mom, and she freaked out. She's a huge fan."

"Are you guys going to the rally at the arena?"

Pamela deflated. "No, I wish we could . . ." Again, she was dodging truths that she really didn't want to share. "I thought about taking Mom and the girls, but" — she glanced at her huge tummy — "I don't want to be too far from home. Plus, it's a lot of walking."

"I'll take you! Quinton's out of town — teaching at some dental convention — so I'm taking the kids." Jeanie bounced and bubbled with enthusiasm. "I can pick you guys up. It's practically on the way!"

Pamela shook her head. "That is so nice of you, but no, it's too much to ask. Plus, really, I don't know if I'd be up to it." She rested a hand on her tummy, doing a circular motion, again feeling an elbow or a knee or a heel.

Jeanie's eyes narrowed, and she leaned in and gave Pamela a sneaky grin. "What if I told you Everett Lester's going to be there?" she whispered.

"What?" Pamela was floored and instantly taken back to the Everett Lester concert she and Jeanie attended together at Blossom Music Center, an outdoor amphitheater near Akron, not long after the bad-boy rocker had become a Christian.

"You're kidding me, right?"

Jeanie grinned ear to ear and shook her head.

"Why didn't I know about this?" Pamela said.

"We just found out! Sterling invited him a long time ago, but Everett said he couldn't come. He called just this morning and said he would be there. Sterling's PR people are scrambling. They're going to make a big announcement tomorrow."

"Oh, wow."

"Remember Blossom?"

"One of the best shows I've ever seen."

"We've *got* to go, Pam, for old time's sake. The kids'll love it. Your mom will love it. I'll probably be able to get us backstage to meet Martin. Who knows, maybe we'll get to meet Everett!"

Pamela had to laugh. The whole idea was crazy — but maybe a little crazy was what she needed right now. "Jeanie, I didn't tell you, but Jack lost his job. He works part-time at the arena. He's working the rally tomorrow night."

Jeanie's jaw dropped open and she gushed her apologies, but she kept it light. "That's all the more reason we should go. We'll surprise Jack. Heck, between my connections and Jack working there, we're sure to meet Everett!"

The two women giggled as if they were back in college.

19

Festival Arena, October 6

Shakespeare counted the number of people in the Sterling party for whom he and Chico were about to become responsible. Not including Derrick, Daniel, or Reese Jenkins, there were nine of them.

His cell phone vibrated, and he looked down to find a text from Sheena.

Breaking news on tv from arena. Copter overhead. Thousands mad outside cuz only some were let in. Whats going on? B careful.

He was grateful she still cared.

Maybe they could work this thing out after all. Maybe there was more he could do to be flexible, not to be such a know-it-all. Sheena had been a tried-and-true partner. And Brian knew deep down that he could be a self-righteous jerk at times.

He shot a quick text back.

Nothing happening yet. I'm guarding Sterling. Don't worry and thanks.

He took in a deep breath and walked to the front of the room.

Sterling was in an intense powwow with Wolfski, Clarissa, Jenkins, Jenny, and his three security guards. The senator circled his open hands like peddling a bike, then swept his arms like a referee calling a player out of bounds.

"Okay, folks." Shakespeare lifted both hands and waited for quiet. "I need your attention. It's been appointed to me and my partner, Chico, to escort you upstairs to the club level, where we have a nice suite prepared for you. I'm going to lead the way, and Chico will bring up the rear. So far *we're not aware* of any incidents in the building." He eyeballed Wolfski. "It's a bit crazy, with people wanting to get inside, but we can work with that."

Shakespeare knew very well that something was going down. But he had an assignment, and he was going to treat these people like happy kids on a field trip until he got it done.

"If anything should happen, please do *ex-*

actly as I say. Don't hesitate. Don't second-guess. Just follow orders. Okay? Let's move out."

Shakespeare gave Chico a thumbs-up, pushed open the door, and led the way down the long white hallway. Sterling, Clarissa, and Jenkins were arguing heatedly but quietly about whether there should be another delay in opening the doors.

Shakespeare's radio sounded. "This is Gordy Cavelli to base." The background noise almost drowned out his voice.

"Go, Gordy," Clarissa said.

"It's really bad up here on doors."

Shakespeare unplugged his headset so everyone could hear Gordy.

"The people outside were told six forty-five, then seven. They're furious. They're packed so deep and strong, it's like an ocean wall," Gordy shouted above the bedlam. "The people up front are getting smashed against the glass . . . They're pounding, screaming. We need to get more staff or police outside . . . Over."

"Open those doors before someone gets hurt!" Sterling yelled.

Shakespeare pressed on, leading the group into a plush reception area and a set of double elevators. Pushing the Up button and stopping to face the group, he knew full well they didn't have any more Event-Pros to station outside. Even if they did, it was too late. Only the police or SWAT or National Guard could get any order out there at this point.

"It's seven o'clock," Gordy called. "Are we opening or not? People are expecting to come in."

"I just got word, my men are almost done sweeping the Sky Zone," Wolfski told the group. "Probably two more minutes. My men on doors are confirming the chaos up there. We need more backup."

"Okay, this is not good." Gordy's radio shot static two, three, four times. "An Event-Pro opened a door to . . . Hold on. Oh boy. They're coming in!"

Static. Static.

Gordy again. "She opened her door to tell someone something, I don't know why, but . . . Oh, it's wide open! They're pouring in. They can't get it shut . . . Falling . . . Someone just fell . . . Oh my gosh. It's a stampede! Oh no . . . We're gonna need medics up here!"

20

Festival Arena, October 6

Pamela was relieved they were finally inside the arena where it was warmer, but something was definitely not right. The crowd outside was huge, and it had been chaotic trying to get inside when the doors opened at six thirty. In fact, in somewhat of a panic, ushers had shut the doors only moments after Pamela and the others had gotten through. They'd ducked in to get a glimpse of the stage and to take a quick look for Jack, and then they went back out into the concourse to buy the kids a treat.

Although there was an expected buzz in the air, it was not one of joyful anticipation. It was something else. The crowd was frenzied. There was a hint of hostility or defensiveness — as if something was happening behind the scenes, but no one knew what.

"What is going on?" Margaret said. "I

don't like this."

"Let's move over this way, out of the flow." Jeanie led them past an escalator that was being guarded by a white-haired female EventPro.

Pamela kept one hand tight around Rebecca and the other around Faye.

She could hear faint yelling toward the doors.

There was a sudden rush of cool air.

People were craning their necks and standing on their tiptoes, looking back toward the main lobby. A mass of people came toward them like a herd of cattle, just coming in out of the cold.

"This is craziness," said Jeanie, who was squeezing her son's and daughter's hands. In their free hands they clutched big soft pretzels.

Some of the people coming toward them were straightening their coats and brushing themselves off. Several were red faced, even crying.

What had gone on out there?

Pamela and Jeanie scooted Margaret and the children farther out of the way, past an ATM machine and between several kiosks.

"We need to find Jack." Pamela rubbed her tummy, already wishing they hadn't come. She'd just had a strong Braxton-

Hicks contraction. It was cold. It was dark. She and the girls were tired — and she was frightened. This had been a bad idea. But she had to stay calm for her mom and the girls. "He'll know what's going on."

"Check to see if you've heard back from him with his section," Margaret said.

Pamela dug in the outside pocket of her purse, pulled out the phone, and examined the screen. "Shoot, I missed a call from him."

"Can you call him?" Jeanie sounded panicked.

"I'm not supposed to. Let me text him again. We're okay. Everything's going to be fine."

"I'm not worried, Mommy," said Rebecca.

"Me, either," said Faye. "We're big girls. We're not worried."

Jeanie's children chimed in about how they weren't scared either, and Pamela told herself to relax.

She punched in a quick text message to Jack.

Surprise. We r here at arena! Jeanie drove us. I cdnt miss everett. What section are you in? Is something going on?

"Maybe we should just leave," Jeanie said.

"I mean, don't you guys feel like something's wrong?"

"I do," Margaret said, her arms crossed and hands buried in her armpits.

"Why, Mommy? Why are we going to leave?" said Jeanie's son, Jake.

"I'm not sure we're going to, son. Let's wait until we hear from Mr. Jack. He'll know what we should do."

Shakespeare eyed the Up elevator button, which was lit in orange, and checked his watch. This was what he'd feared. The elevator was taking way too long to arrive. There were no numbers to show what floor it was on, but he'd taken that elevator enough to know that something wasn't right.

Had the terrorists stopped it somehow?

He listened as Gordy described the bedlam unfolding in the main lobby. Although the SWAT team had managed to get the door closed again and locked, it wasn't before hundreds more had poured into the building. Several had fallen down at the entryway and were being treated by medics. One would be transported to the hospital with possible broken ribs, if they could get the ambulance anywhere near the building.

"What is taking so long? For crying out loud." Sterling rubbed his mouth with the back of his shaky wrist like an alcoholic struggling to avoid a glass of scotch.

Jenny patted his arm and whispered something, trying to calm him.

"This elevator's not working." Shakespeare nodded toward the stairwell.

"You think?" Sterling said.

"We're going to take the stairs," Shakespeare said. "Everyone, follow me in a single-file line with Chico last." He opened the door, shifted the weight of the backpack on his shoulder, and started up the concrete steps.

He just had to focus. His only job right now was to get the group safely to suite 227. Once that was done, he would have Chico keep an eye on Sterling's party while he found out what was really going on.

The only noise was the shuffling of everyone's shoes moving up the steps. They passed the door leading to the third floor without a word. The main concourse was on the next level, four, where all the chaos was. They needed to go all the way up to six to reach the club level and the suites, which were supposed to be blocked off to the general public.

"This is Tab, this is Tab." The nervous voice came over Shakespeare's headset, which he had plugged back in. "We've got reports of smoke in the concourse, sections 112 and 117. I'm on my way there now. Over."

Static.

It was starting.

They needed to evacuate the building.

But until he was given the order, Shakespeare would do what he was told and get his party up to six.

They made it to four, the main concourse.

"Hold up." He raised a hand, and everyone came to a halt at the landing in the stairwell. "Wait here. I'll be right back. I'm just gonna take a quick look."

He dashed to the metal door and peered through the vertical window.

The EventPro in the enclosed glass area stood facing the crowded concourse with his left hand outstretched high in the air and his radio pinned to his mouth. Shakespeare heard his frantic voice in his earpiece the exact second he saw the white smoke swirling in the concourse.

"We've got smoke at the double elevators outside section 105!" The staffer coughed and stuck his face in the crease of his arm, then to the radio again. "It's not fire . . . It's coming from a canister on the ground!" He buried his face again.

They had to get people out! *Out!*

Shakespeare looked back at Chico, raised a finger signaling for him to hold tight, opened the door, and hurried into the glass-enclosed area at the elevators. Three steps in, he knew from the odor and sting in his eyes that it was tear gas.

"Everyone . . . give me your attention, this instant." The loud, heavily accented male voice echoed over the PA system. "You will move *inside* the arena and be seated, immediately. I repeat, you will move *inside* the arena this instant, be seated, and you will *not* be hurt. If you attempt to leave the building, you will be shot. I repeat, do not leave the building or you will be executed."

Screams rang out, giving Shakespeare chills. He knew that couldn't possibly be true, because they couldn't have men at every exit. It was a scare tactic. But people would believe it. He grabbed the EventPro by the lapel of his windbreaker. "You need to open these doors and get people out!" He pulled the man to the glass doors leading outside and punched one of them open. "Keep going in and out for fresh air."

Shakespeare stepped into the cold night and dropped his backpack to the ground, taking deep breaths of clean air.

"Open all these doors!" he ordered the EventPro as he reached into the backpack, found his gas mask, and quickly put it on. Next he dug around, yanked out his .45, and racked it. Then he dashed inside to the double glass doors leading to the concourse, took a deep breath, and threw them open.

Horrific screams and sour, toxic smoke.

Children on the ground, crawling, screaming, burying their little faces in their arms. Parents covering them, dragging them away from the smoke. People running, slamming into one another.

"This way!" Shakespeare lifted the mask and yelled as loudly as he could. "This way! Outside! Outside!" He realized he probably looked like a terrorist with the gas mask and the waving gun.

He grabbed a woman in a yellow coat. "This way, outside!"

"My father . . ." She gasped and cried. "He's in there!" She ripped away from his grasp and disappeared into the smoke.

"Chico," he called into his mic. "It's Shakespeare. Continue on. Go ahead. I'll catch up." He didn't want to mention the suite in case the terrorists were listening.

"This way!" he shouted, grabbing people, pushing them into the enclosed glass area. "Outside . . . get outside!"

His mind whirled.

What else could he do? What were the terrorists' plans?

"Shakespeare, I want you with Sterling!" It was Clarissa, screaming into her radio. "That's an order. Right now, get back with Sterling! Do you read me? Over."

The other EventPro was spending more time outside, gasping for air, than he was in. But people were coming now. They were catching on that this was a safe exit. They were filing out now.

Good!

"Okay. This is Shakespeare." He clutched his radio. "I'll catch up with them now. Over."

He took a deep breath, removed the gas mask, and covered the EventPro's face with it momentarily. "Come on, man, do your best. Get people out."

Shakespeare took one last look into the concourse before ducking back into the stairwell.

That's when Jack's wife, Pamela, caught his eye.

Her stomach was the size of a medicine ball.

She was on her knees, screaming for help.

Leaning over her passed-out mother.

21

A new text message dinged on Jack's phone the instant he noticed the smoke rising up to the club level from the concourse below, along with the screams of terror. He read the text, hands shaking, trying to keep his composure.

Surprise. We r here at arena! Jeanie drove us. I cdnt miss everett. What section are you in? Is something going on?

No . . . no that can't be.
He read it again.
He looked up, scanned the landscape.
They are down there . . . in that smoke and chaos?
With trembling hands and no breath, he punched in Pam's number.
On his radio, Tab was yelling about smoke in different places on the concourse.
Pam's phone rang once, twice . . .

Dear God, where are they?

It rang and rang, then kicked over to voice mail.

His eyes stung from the biting smoke.

He hung up, coughing. He pressed the button on his radio to tell Clarissa he had to go find Pam, when another EventPro radioed in about smoke in section 105. Smoke from a canister.

Terrorists.

Tab radioed that people were being forced into the bowl.

Jack looked into Everett's suite. Everyone was on their feet, hands on heads, arms outstretched, on phones and radios, panicked. The boy, Cole, was leaning over the railing outside the suite, looking down on the arena below. Sid's eyes were enormous. He raised his shoulders as if to ask, *What do we do?*

As the foreign voice filled the arena, threatening to shoot anyone who attempted to leave, Jack took charge. "Everyone stay calm and stay right here!" he said. "Lock this door and do not leave. Do not leave until we know we can get you out safely. Stay away from that opening. Cole, get back, son."

Karen hurried over and brought him back inside.

"Get way inside here," Jack told them all. "Get behind furniture. We don't know who can see in." He motioned for Sid to step outside.

Everett, Gray, and others were all jabbering at once, firing questions, but Jack stepped out with Sid.

"What the heck is going on?" Wild-eyed, Sid closed the door behind him. "We don't get paid for this! We're not cops! We need to get out of here!"

Jack grabbed his thick shoulders and locked in on him, inches from his shiny nose. "Listen to me. I just found out my pregnant wife is in the building, and my kids. I need to go find them —"

Sid's mouth was agape. "Jack . . . you're leaving me in charge? I have no idea what to do. I've got a girlfriend too."

"My family's *here.* I've got to protect them. Lock yourself in. Call Clarissa and tell her what's going on. I'll have my radio. I'll do what I can . . ."

"But dude, you're bailing —"

"I'll help. Just let me find my wife and —"

All the lights in the concourse flickered like a giant spaceship suddenly losing power. Jack could hear the electricity whirring to a halt.

Everything slammed to black.

A red exit sign at the end of the hall was the only light.

Sid grabbed Jack's jacket and cussed in panic.

More screams of terror rose from below, from all around.

Emergency floodlights banged on loudly at various points in the concourse, like a monster's footsteps.

"Ladies and gentlemen, as you can see, we have control of the building." It was the same foreign-sounding voice over the PA. "Do not panic. Go into the arena and sit down. I repeat, sit down! Do not attempt to leave the building, or you and your families will be executed."

"This is Clarissa to all EventPros! Mr. Jenkins has ordered us to evacuate the building . . . I repeat —"

Now we evacuate.

Jack repeated the evacuation order to Sid, and the two men glared in the dark at the wet reflection in each other's eyes, waiting for more. Jack unplugged his earpiece and held the radio up on low volume so Sid could hear.

"Do not approach the main lobby." Clarissa's voice was strong but still reflected a tinge of uncertainty. "I repeat, stay away from the main lobby and find alternate exits. Get people outside. It *is* safe outside. The hostiles do not have anyone out there, as far as we know."

"Clarissa, I've got an EventPro leaving her post!" Tab called. "She's hightailing it!"

"There's nothing we can do about that! Remain calm. Do all you can to get guests out of the building. The exits and stairwells should be lit . . . Use your flashlights to direct people."

Bursts of static.

Up from the stairwell at the end of the hall came the roving beam of a flashlight. A tall guy was leading a pack of people. Their long shadows stretched toward Jack like spilled oil.

"Keep quiet," he whispered to Sid. "Stay still."

The flashlight shone past them, then settled on Jack and Sid.

"Jack!" came the voice. "It's Chico. Are we safe up here?"

The screams from below sounded like a torture chamber.

"Is Shakespeare with you?" Jack asked.

Chico hurried toward them, coughing. "He left us at the fourth floor. I think he's coming."

"I just found out my wife's here, and my kids. I've got to find them. You guys need to all stay together."

"You're not going to leave us?" snapped Jenny King as she stepped to the front of the group.

Now she wanted him around.

"Senator and everyone." Jack knocked at the door to Everett's suite. "You need to come in here and stay put. Chico and Sid will be here, and we will get you out as soon as possible."

Everett's manager, Gray, peered out and opened the door.

"Senator Sterling and his group are coming in." Jack opened the door and ushered them inside, at the same time flicking on his phone again to call Pam.

"It's too many people," Cole said.

Everett squeezed his son's shoulder, looked down at him, and shook his head. "Think about others, son," he said softly.

"We need to get the senator out of here." A bald security guard gripped Jack's elbow.

"For now, I think this is safest," Jack said. "Listen to the radio. Clarissa will know what to do."

"She said go for the exits," said the guard. "We've got drivers outside waiting."

Pam's phone was ringing.

Answer, please answer.

Jack was about to lose his mind. All he

could think about was getting to Pam and the girls. Margaret was probably with them too. And Jeanie and her kids? That would slow them down . . .

"Look," he said to the guard. "We're not sure where these hostiles are. Right now, you're safe here. That's all we know. I don't advise moving out with this large a group —"

"We don't have to take everyone — just take the senator."

Suddenly a male voice answered Pam's phone: "Jack?"

Jack paused, his mind spinning. "Who is this?"

"Shakespeare." A choir of chaos rang out in the background.

"Where's Pam, Brian? Where is she?"

"With me, bud. She's with me."

22

Eyes watering uncontrollably, Pamela clenched a clump of Shakespeare's jacket in one fist and held Faye's hand with the other. Flashlight in hand, Shakespeare led the way like a soldier racing through a smoky minefield, quickstepping, dodging dazed people, carrying Margaret in front of him like a load of firewood.

Rebecca, the brave little trouper, had taken charge of Jeanie's crying children because Jeanie was having difficulty breathing. Rebecca, too, held tight to the back of Shakespeare's jacket as they made their way through the surreal darkness into a restroom.

Faucets were running strong, and panicked voices filled the air. The glow of cellphone lights showed people washing out their wailing children's eyes in the sinks, elderly people lying on the floor with their heads buried in wet paper towels, families huddled together praying.

Shakespeare moved efficiently, working his way to a sink, propping Margaret over it and splashing her face with water repeatedly, then patting it with a bandana he whipped from his back pocket. She was nodding, coughing, insisting she was okay. He sat her down against a wall, then strapped his gas mask onto Jeanie's face and told her to sit next to Margaret. The children were next. He stuck their heads under the running water one at a time. Then he did the same for Pamela, who came up cold and trembling.

"Will the tear gas hurt the baby?"

Shakespeare dried her face with the front of his shirt. "I don't think so." He ducked his head under the running water, came up, and dried his face on his shirt. "You sure do pick weird times to go for a night out on the town. Aren't you due like any day now?"

She blurted a laugh amid tears and told him the due date wasn't for another month . . . but she couldn't help worry about the baby — and the recent contractions.

He filled a canteen with water, then came over and made sure they were all together. Kneeling over his backpack, he shone his light inside and began pulling things out and setting them on the floor around him: rope, spare phone, duct tape. He handed Pamela a metal apparatus the size of a Coke can. "Pass this around and have everyone breathe it in, deeply; hold this button while you do. It's mini oxygen. Just one big hit each."

"What are we going to do?" Jeanie said.

"Get you out of here." He strapped a black holster to his thigh, pulled a gun out from the back of his pants, and slipped it in. Then he wound a thick black utility belt around his waist, buckled it, and slipped another gun into its holster, adjacent to a compass, two grenades, and a large knife in a plastic sheath.

"Is it safe to leave?" Margaret asked. "He said anyone who does will —"

"Don't worry. I'll make sure." He got out a heavy-duty metal contraption, unfolded it once, twice, then locked it into one piece. Some sort of fancy rifle. He slammed a magazine into it, then ducked his head through its strap, which was lined with magazines.

"Mr. Brian, is my dad okay?" Rebecca asked.

Shakespeare nodded and held up a finger. He covered an ear and listened for a long time.

"This is Shakespeare." He lifted a micro-phone to his mouth. "Sorry. I got side-tracked — helping an elderly lady. Over." He winked at Margaret and listened.

"I don't know if I'm going to make it back up there —" He dropped his head, listened, then spoke. "What happened to the SWAT guys up front?"

Pamela saw him shake his head.

"Is it clear outside?" he asked. Then, "What about Charlie and Steve?" He rubbed the sweat from his forehead and breathed out heavily. "What about the SWAT guys who went after them?" He listened again, then looked up and stared at the children. "How many people are in the bowl — ballpark?"

Pamela didn't think there was any safer place to be than with Shakespeare. There wasn't a hint of hesitation in him. He was a rock, like the head of a command center. He'd told Jack on the phone where they were headed.

So why wasn't Jack there yet? She prayed nothing bad had happened to him.

"How many hostiles are there?" Shake-speare continued to talk on the radio. "What are they wearing?"

Pamela's stomach suddenly hardened, and the Braxton-Hicks contraction took her breath away.

"What is it?" Margaret sat up.

Pamela had accidentally shot her hand out and grabbed her mom's arm.

"Nothing . . . nothing. Sorry, Mom." She tried to catch her breath, released her hand, and rubbed her tummy. "I think the baby just shifted." The last thing they needed was for Margaret to start freaking out about Pamela going into labor.

But the contractions were coming closer together. She'd been calling them Braxton-Hicks. But she was beginning to wonder if these could possibly be the real thing.

Not now. Not now . . . please. This baby cannot come early.

"Ladies and gentlemen, your attention," said the voice over the PA. "You'll notice new guards at the doors around the venue. If you attempt to leave, they will shoot to kill. You will live if you make your way into the arena and sit down — now. If we are forced to come and retrieve you like dogs, we will view you as insurgents and you will be shot."

Pamela closed her eyes and forced away the fear, the voices, the crying, the disorder.

Be still, and know that I am God.

She allowed it to register.

Be still.

Let it lock in.

Know.

Let it release her.

I am God.

"Pam," Margaret whispered.

Pamela turned to face her.

"Don't worry." Her mom looked down, opened the right side of her coat, and revealed a small pink gun in some kind of shoulder-strap device. Then she closed her coat and winked. "You can get anything online these days."

23

By the time Derrick hung up with Zenia, she was crying and pleading with him to get out of the arena, to run. But it wasn't that easy anymore.

Derrick and Daniel had followed a frantic Jack to the restroom near section 105, where they met up with Shakespeare, Pam, and the rest of the group.

Shakespeare was on one knee with everyone surrounding him like players listening to a quarterback in a huddle. Jack and Pam were clinging to each other and the girls. Pam was clutching her stomach, wincing.

"The hostiles are wearing civilian clothes, and they're all shapes, sizes, and colors." Shakespeare's wrists were crossed and resting on a raised knee. His words were rapid and concise. "That's how they got so close to the SWAT guys at the front doors. They let off tear gas and got to them before they could get their masks on. I suspect they used tasers, too. Now they've got a bunch of hostages."

"What about Charlie and Steve?" Jack said.

"Still MIA. Same with the two SWAT guys who went up after them. I have a feeling the terrorists have set up some kind of base up top. In the Sky Zone."

"You've got guns." Daniel eyed Shakespeare's arsenal. "Can't we make a run for an exit?"

Shakespeare pursed his lips. "According to Tab, they've positioned one of their men at each bank of doors."

"How many are there?" Jack asked.

"Fifteen or twenty," Shakespeare said. "And now they're all wearing black stocking masks and carrying assault weapons."

"Did I hear right that there're two thousand people in the bowl?" Jack said.

"That's the estimate," Shakespeare said.

Pam had her head down and was making circular motions with both hands on her tummy. Rebecca and Faye had their little arms wrapped tight around Jack and Pam. Jeanie took a hit of the oxygen and passed it to Faye. Margaret had her arms around Jeanie's boy and girl.

Thank God Zenia isn't here, Derrick thought. "What do you think they're going to do?" he said.

"This is about Sterling," Shakespeare said.

"They're gonna kill him," Margaret blurted. "They know if he gets elected, they'll be rooted out and destroyed."

Static blasted from someone's radio.

Pop, pop . . . pop. The room broke out in screams and cries.

Derrick's chest almost collapsed.

That was gunfire.

"Quiet!" Shakespeare stood, hands in the air. "Quiet." He unplugged his headset so they could all hear.

"This is Clarissa." Her high-strung voice came over the radio. "The insurgents have cleared most of the concourse. They are sweeping restrooms. I repeat, they are sweeping all restrooms."

Muffled squeals arose from others in the dark restroom.

Derrick's heart hammered. *This is it. We could all die right here.*

Margaret was pressing hard on something in her lap. A gun! A pink and black gun, of all things.

Good for her.

She struggled a bit more, got it cocked, and clutched it with both hands, grinding her teeth as if she wasn't about to go down without one heck of a fight.

Jack held his mic to his mouth. "This is Jack. Me and Shakespeare are —"

Shakespeare chopped the air with his hand and mouthed *No!* He shook his head. "They're monitoring this," he whispered. "Don't give our twenty."

"Shakespeare . . ." Static. "This is Clarissa. Did you make it back to the senator? Over."

Shakespeare held up a hand and lifted his radio. "Clarissa, don't say any more about locations. They're monitoring this. Over."

A blurt of static. Shakespeare plugged his earpiece back in.

"Okay, everyone, we gotta move," he announced.

"Where do you think Clarissa is?" Jack said.

"Probably hunkered down in the command center, watching on monitors. They'll be searching for her."

"Where will we go?" Derrick said.

Shakespeare reached into his bag, pulled out a small gun, racked it, and handed it to Jack. "Listen, everyone."

The room fell silent, except for cries that had been reduced to whimpers.

"Turn your lights out," Shakespeare instructed. "Stay calm."

There was angry yelling down the concourse. Foreign voices. Getting closer.

"Listen," Shakespeare said. "They only have twenty people in this big house. They are stretched thin. Their leaders are probably in the bowl. I'm going to lead us out of here."

Choppy breathing, murmurs, and quiet crying sounded throughout the crowded room.

"We're going to make a left out the door and sprint for the food court — about forty yards," Shakespeare said. "There's a single door there that leads outside to a patio — the smoking area. Once outside, we'll go over a metal railing and drop down into the parking deck. I'm hoping they haven't seen that door and it's not blocked."

"What if it is?" someone asked in the dark.

"I'll take care of it," Shakespeare said.

The foreign voices outside shouted back and forth.

Possibly splitting up to check the different restrooms?

Shakespeare ripped a gun from his belt, racked it, and handed it to Derrick. Its bulk surprised him. Although he'd never discharged a gun before, he would not hesitate now.

Shakespeare yanked a lever on his rifle, metal locking against metal. He crossed to the door and turned around to the others. "When we get to the parking deck, sprint for the exit. Get as far away from this building as possible. Those of you with guns, hand them to me on your way out. I'll be coming back inside — but you'll be fine."

Derrick's countenance fell when he realized Shakespeare wouldn't be with them the entire journey. But he was a soldier. And that's what soldiers did.

Shakespeare's shoulders arched back, and he took in a deep breath.

"Here." Daniel handed him the gas mask.

"Thanks." He slipped it over his head and let the mask dangle at the back of his neck.

"Are we ready to take our freedom back?" he said.

Whispers of yes rose like a tide, sending chills down Derrick's back.

"Okay . . . let's roll."

24

Just before stepping into the concourse, Jack tugged Shakespeare's jacket. "How many shots do I have in here?" His heart thundered.

Shakespeare didn't even have to look at the gun. "Nine."

Jack bounced the heavy weapon in his hand, determined to do whatever he had to do to keep Pam and his family alive. He tried to picture the hostiles in his mind . . . to mentally prepare for them.

"What about me?" Derrick held up his weapon.

"Nine also," Shakespeare said.

Jack nodded at Derrick, whose face was resolute. Then he gathered Pam and the girls in his arms. "Father, put your angels around us. Get us out of here safely, we ask. In your name."

"Amen," Shakespeare said.

Pam looked up at Jack, holding back tears.

Besides all the uproar, he could tell she was uncomfortable, possibly in even more pain than she was letting on.

He touched her face. "It's gonna be okay, baby."

He turned to Rebecca and Faye, trying to sound upbeat. "Are you ready to *run,* girls? As fast as you can?"

"What about MawMaw?" Faye reached toward Margaret.

"I'll beat you there." Margaret pinched Faye's little nose. "I bet you a dollar."

"Okay . . ." Shakespeare held up one, two, three fingers. "Rolling!"

Jack grabbed Faye's hand. Margaret got Rebecca's.

Other people rushed in front of them.

Jack nodded for Margaret and Jeanie and her kids to go next.

They were off.

It was all rushing footsteps, no words.

Entering the cool concourse, Jack squinted in surprise at the police spotlights shining in from outside, lighting up portions of the smoky hall. No people were in sight! Shakespeare bent over and hauled toward the food court. Jack could almost feel the eyes and anticipation of the crowd of onlookers who must be gathered outside.

Copying Shakespeare, everyone in the

group, including the children, hunched over as they raced for their freedom, trying to make themselves as small as possible, invisible if they could.

Shakespeare waved dramatically for them to move it, move it, move it! Jack had never seen such animation and hope in his eyes. It was as if he was surprised that his ragtag underdog crew was having such success, so little opposition.

They were making it!

Margaret slowed . . . stopped.

"Mom, what is it?" Pam said.

"I . . ." She reached toward the ground.

Others bumped her, zigzagged around.

Jack spotted her pink gun on the carpet. "I'll get it, Mom. Keep going!" he ordered, realizing that was the first time he'd ever called her Mom.

He shook Faye's hand loose and snatched the gun, but Margaret hadn't gone. She stood with her hand out and mouth agape. He gave it to her, grabbed Faye's hand, and ran, urging Margaret to *move.*

"Andre! Over here, over here!" The voice came from a man running toward them, far left. Slender male. Black ski mask. Green cargo pants. Headset. Machine gun.

This was it! The enemy.

The sight ripped Jack's breath away.

"This way!" The insurgent glanced behind, waving. Within forty feet of Shakespeare, he yelled, "Hold it! Stop right now —"

Bam.

A flash and smoke from Shakespeare's rifle.

The hostile left the ground, flew backward, and bounced to the floor, apparently dead on impact.

"Keep moving!" Shakespeare waved them on with his rifle. "Almost there. *Move.*"

At the same split second, Jack spotted two more of the terrorists dashing toward them, one on the far left and one on the far right. The one on the left was yelling as he came, and Shakespeare was raising his rifle toward him. The one on the right wasn't yelling — he was aiming at their group.

"Go with Mommy." Jack pushed Rebecca and Faye ahead, stopped, lifted the gun with two hands, and took aim at midbody.

Bam.

The sound and kickback startled him, but only for an instant.

He'd missed.

The man was about to fire on the group.

Jack aimed and fired again. *Bam, bam, bam.*

The man dropped, and his machine gun

blistered an arc of smoke and bullets across the high ceiling.

Shakespeare put the other guy down. Then his eyes met Jack's, and they both nodded.

"Let's go!" Shakespeare said.

Everyone had hit the floor and now scrambled to their feet and ran.

Jack didn't think of what he'd just done. Instead, he pulled his family along, racing, trying to hurry them faster than they could go, looking back all the while.

Pop.

The sound of the single shot echoed in his chest.

Derrick fell, writhing.

"Keep going!" Shakespeare yelled.

Another shot rang out. No one went down.

Jack scanned 360 degrees but saw no one.

Shakespeare was on one knee, pointing his rifle upward toward a railing several stories above.

He fired three shots and turned to the group. "Go, go, go!" he shouted. "I've got you covered. *Move!*"

"Keep going, Pam. Kids, keep going!" Jack dropped to his knees over Derrick, whose face was contorted in pain. His bloody right hand was clutching his side.

The gun he'd been carrying was on the floor next to him. Jack grabbed it and stuck it in the back of his pants.

More gunfire exploded around them.

"Come on, man. Let's get you out of here." Jack took Derrick's other hand, stood, and hoisted him to his feet. Derrick grimaced. They were the last ones, except for Shakespeare. Everyone else had passed. "Come on!" Jack urged him on.

The hostiles were yelling back and forth.

Shakespeare remained planted like a statue of a war hero, exchanging fire with a growing number of insurgents above. "Move it, guys!" he yelled. "Get the others out. Go!"

As Jack and Derrick raced past him, Jack noticed Shakespeare's arm was covered in blood. The group was almost out of range of the hostiles, but not quite. Jack stopped, took aim, and fired two shots at one of the masked men above, but missed.

More were coming on the ground.

"Shakespeare." Jack pointed at one, two of them rounding the corner.

"Go, guys. I've got this!"

Derrick ran for it. Jack hesitated at first but then ran too. He got to the food court and spotted the group filing through a glass door leading to the patio.

"They're out!" Derrick said as they sprinted for it.

The door must've been clear, because the group was already on the smoking porch, climbing over the fence like desperate fleeing prisoners of war.

But no . . . there was a hostile sprawled out on the ground! Ski mask. Machine gun lying five feet from his bloody, bullet-riddled body.

Margaret stood over him, out of breath, the pink gun locked in front of her as she watched the backs of everyone in the group filing over the metal railing and down into the parking garage.

Jack's heart soared.

Never in his wildest dreams could he have imagined this — his fearful mother-in-law standing there like G.I. Jane, sacrificing herself for the lives of others.

Jack kissed her and gently pushed her outside. "Go."

Pam was still out there, holding her tummy with one hand and helping people over the railing with the other. Jack was surprised and annoyed that none of the men had helped her get over the fence. He rushed to her. "Go, Pam, *now.* Come on, girls!"

The gunfire continued in the concourse.

Jack prayed Shakespeare would make it out alive. What a rock he was.

He lifted Faye over the fence.

Daniel had gotten over and was shooting photos of the group from the parking garage as he backed away before finally turning and running. With blood soaking through his coat, Derrick helped others get their kids over the fence.

"Come with me, Faye!" Jeanie called from below, her son and daughter at her side.

Faye dashed to her as Jack lifted Rebecca over. She, too, hurried to Jeanie.

It sounded like a fireworks show in the concourse. No way Shakespeare could make it through that.

"Go, Jeanie!" Jack yelled. "Follow the exit signs. They'll lead you outside."

He turned to Pam. "You're next. Hurry."

"I don't think I can make it over. I'm hurting, Jack. I'm hurting bad."

He stuffed his gun in his pants, bent down, and swept her up, his arms behind her knees and shoulders.

"Stop! Stop right now!"

A deafening blast of machine-gun fire made Jack drop to the concrete. Pam screamed as he threw his body over hers. Debris and dust from ceiling tiles rained down on them.

Silence. Smoke. The smell of gunpowder.

Jack squinted at the parking level below them, beyond the railing. Thank God. Jeanie had taken all four of the kids, and they were out of sight.

Derrick was on his knees. So was Margaret, hands over her ears, her gun not in sight.

"Give us your weapons — now!" a voice screamed.

No one moved.

Another burst of gunfire.

Derrick took his gun from Jack, slid it toward the voices, and clutched his side.

Margaret's face was etched with fear. Jack nodded for her to give them her gun, but she didn't move. Jack got his gun out and set it on the floor.

"Come!" a different man ordered. "Come with us, now!"

Margaret must've holstered her gun beneath her coat. *Good.*

"To your feet. All of you!"

"Please." Jack faced the two masked men, who were breathing hard, eyes huge, machine guns leveled right at him. "My wife's pregnant . . . Please, just let her —"

"Silence!" one screamed.

The other motioned with his weapon. "Come. *Now.*"

25

After spraying the insurgents with almost a full clip of rapid-fire rifle rounds, Shakespeare had rolled and sprinted for the concession stand, slid over the counter, and dropped behind it — hoping he'd not been seen.

Burning up and bleeding profusely from a shot he'd taken in the left bicep, he reloaded the rifle and quietly set it aside. Wiping sweat from his eyes with his shirt, he caught his breath and peeked over the counter as two insurgents ordered Jack, Pam, Margaret, and Derrick from the terrace back into the building. He assumed they would be led into the bowl with everyone else.

Police spotlights shone brightly into the concourse, where smoke wafted in the air from the gun battle and tear gas. He debated whether to try to pick off the two men but realized he had to think about more than just his small group of friends; he had to think about the two thousand people inside the bowl.

He closed his eyes and sighed. At least they'd gotten almost the whole group out — especially Jack's girls. He would miss the two guns he'd given Jack and Derrick. He chuckled silently, almost certain Margaret still had the nine-millimeter pink Taurus she told him she'd ordered via the Internet. He just hoped they didn't find it on her.

"Your attention. Your attention, ladies and gentlemen," came a booming voice over the PA. "I am Shareek Zaher, head of the valiant band of brothers who have taken control of the Columbus Festival Arena."

Shakespeare presumed Zaher was speaking into a microphone onstage, in view of the crowd inside the bowl. "Everyone . . . sit down," Zaher said. "You may not leave the building. We have armed guards at every door. Take your seats right now . . . right where you are."

Avoiding the growing puddle of blood on the floor, Shakespeare took one last peek around the side of the counter, wincing from the pain deep in his arm. The men with the machine guns swung open several doors leading into the blackened arena and pushed Jack and the others inside. Shakespeare noticed a spot of blood on the carpet the size of a basketball where he'd opened fire.

Okay, he had to be smart now. Every second counted. Every move was critical.

There were holes in front and back of his arm, but he couldn't tell if the bullet had gone all the way through or if he'd been shot twice. He undid the holster on his thigh, snatched a towel from under the counter, put it on his wound, and yanked the holster strap with his teeth and hands as tightly as he could over the wounds. He'd had worse.

His mind flipped back to the Red Horse unit in Iraq. Scorching heat blanketed the sandy horizon in mirage-type fumes. He was in the third of four Humvees. A mangy black-and-brown dog crossed their path. The first vehicle stopped. There was a deafening explosion. Blood and smoke and shrapnel and body parts everywhere. He lost two of his best friends that day. And as far as he was concerned, Shareek Zaher was responsible.

Nothing was coming over the radio. He had to assume Clarissa, Tab, and the other EventPros had been overtaken. Either that or they'd realized the radios were being monitored and had gone dark. He wasn't about to speak and let the hostiles know he was still out there, although the ones who'd been shooting at him knew he'd disappeared.

His phone vibrated. A text from Sheena.

R u ok? News says terrorists in control. No one can get in. Gunshots heard inside. Tell me latest. B careful.

He punched in a quick note, sweat dripping from his face onto the screen.

Im ok and armed. They hv 2000 in bowl. They hv guns at all doors so no way out. Jack, pam, marg here. Kids got out. Ill b ok. Pray.

The power on his phone was down to 17 percent. *Not good.*

He dialed 911 and concisely told the operator his location and situation, then asked to be patched through to Hedgwick with Columbus PD. He crawled to the drink cabinet, grabbed two bottles of water, and went back to his spot.

"This is Officer Hedgwick. Go ahead."

"This is Brian Shakespeare." He spoke quietly, clearly. "I'm an usher at the arena, inside right now —"

"Shakespeare, we talked to the people you

got out. Good work. We've got the perimeter covered," Hedgwick said. "There's no way out for the hostiles. Where are you?"

That's exactly what scared Shakespeare — that there was no way out for them. That could only mean they intended to die.

"Food court." He looked up at the sign. "Behind the counter of the Buckeye Grille." He attached his Bluetooth to his ear, put his phone in his pocket, and told Hedgwick about Shareek Zaher and everything he knew about the situation.

"Someone said you have a rifle and you're a sharpshooter," Hedgwick said.

"That's right." Shakespeare unsnapped the metal scope from his utility belt and screwed it onto the rifle. "I'm going to try to work my way up to the Sky Zone. Find a spot up there where I can be helpful —"

"That might be good, but hold up —"

"Why? What's your plan?"

"Your intel changes the plan. I'm gonna need to call you right back," Hedgwick said.

"Text me first. By the way, the battery on my phone is low. So if you can't reach me . . ."

"You have an EventPros-issued radio, right?"

"Affirmative."

"Every ten minutes we're touching base

with Lieutenant Wolfski and Clarissa Dracone —"

"Wait, they're still active?"

"Roger. They're holed up with two more EventPros."

"Where?" Shakespeare opened a bottle of water and guzzled.

"First-aid room, mezzanine level," Hedgwick said. "One of them saw the hostiles check the room; then they moved in and set up shop there. It's pitch-black. No one's armed except Wolfski. Every ten minutes on the hour we're switching to a different radio frequency, counting by threes. So at 8:10 we'll be on channel fifteen. At 8:20, channel eighteen."

"What's the status on Wolfski's team?"

"Most of them got blindsided at the main entrance."

"I know, but where are they? If I could get to them —"

"They're not in the building. Nine were kicked out a side door at gunpoint," Hedgwick said.

Shakespeare deflated. "You're kidding me, right?"

"No. So that leaves Wolfski and two others —"

"Who got taken out up in the Sky Zone

— I know. Did they just throw them out too?"

"No, they're not out —"

"I was kidding." Shakespeare dropped his head, marveling at the incompetence of the supposed professionals. "Look, that's another reason I want to get up high, so I can figure out where everybody is. They've got two EventPros, too, you know, the ones the two SWAT guys went up to find. Maybe they're all inside with Zaher. Have you guys figured out how many hostiles there are?"

"Homeland is saying seventeen to eighteen."

"Seems like more."

Hedgwick continued to talk, but Shakespeare knew what he needed to do.

He was going up top.

He had to get a look into the bowl.

26

The pain. It took her breath away. Pamela squeezed Jack's hand — hard.

"What is it?" He leaned in close in the dark. "Are you okay?"

She shook her head.

She wasn't okay. The contractions were getting more painful, coming more often — almost constant.

This cannot be it.

Plenty of women had told her their third and fourth babies came much more quickly than their earlier ones. Even her labor with Faye had been much faster than with Rebecca.

No, Lord, this can't happen now. Please just let these contractions pass.

At least the girls were out safely. *Thank God for that.*

The men with the guns led them all the way down to the stage and shoved them into seats in the third row. A swarthy man calling himself Shareek Zaher stood on the stage, surrounded by three men with machine guns. All had on black masks and civilian street clothes.

Margaret helped Jack tighten his belt above Derrick's bloody wound. Derrick was slumped with his head back against the seat, mouth open, eyes half-closed. By the looks of his coat and shirt, he'd lost lots of blood.

"Go ahead, it's okay. You can do that." Zaher's loud voice boomed over the PA as he pointed to someone in the audience, a man holding his phone up, possibly taking a picture or recording a video. "Lights. It's time for lights. Bring them up!"

With that, one, two, three sections of lights came on at different locations, each with a loud, echoing slam. "That's enough. Hold it!" Zaher ordered. "You can video this, people." He waved his hand. "Go ahead. Video all you want. The American people need to see this."

Pamela's stomach turned. Zaher made the hair on the back of her neck stand on end. He wore baggy black pants, the cuffs of which were crumpled up at his worn leather boots, one untied. He moved loosely and proudly, like a puppet on strings, coming across like one of these nutcases who could be overly friendly, then turn on you like a horror movie.

What is he going to do? Slaughter people?

She tasted bile in her mouth.

The hostiles had moved everyone down around the stage. Two rows back, a woman sobbed uncontrollably. A man several seats over rocked forward and backward with his head down, praying. One man at their left had vomited twice. Parents who brought children engulfed them in their arms.

The way the arena was lit made the gray smoke seem to glow as it drifted in the stale air. Pamela's shoulders shot back as another contraction overtook her. She had to tell Jack. They had to get out of there — to a hospital.

She tugged his sleeve.

He leaned over.

"My contractions are hurting. They're coming . . . pretty often."

"How often?" he whispered.

She nodded. "Like, really often."

His head dropped, and a hand went to his forehead. After a moment, he reached over and put his hand on her hard stomach.

She wasn't about to tell him her water might've broken. She wasn't sure. It was earlier, just after they'd gotten into the arena. It had been just a trickle, and she'd assumed it was only urine.

"Dear Jesus, please . . . take the contractions away," Jack prayed. "Let the pain go away. Please . . . get us out of here safely; get everyone out." He squeezed her hand on and off as he prayed. "Let our baby be okay. Take care of the girls. God, come down and *devour* these terrorists. Turn their evil in on themselves —"

"Let me ask you a question." Zaher held the microphone to his mouth, his other hand high in the air, his machine gun dangling in front of him with its strap around his neck. "You people are here tonight to show your support, are you not, for United States presidential candidate Martin Sterling? Come, let's hear it for Senator Sterling!"

Silence.

People looked down, turned away, fighting back fears. Some buried their heads in their hands.

"Oh, I see . . ." He blurted a laugh. "Now you are not so certain about your candidate —"

"Sterling for America!" a male voice shouted.

Zaher stooped over, clanked the mic down, stood, pointed the machine gun, and blasted in the direction of the voice.

The shot echoed, and screams peeled

throughout the crowd.

He'd missed on purpose, with foam, fabric, concrete, and chair parts exploding in a crooked horizontal line of dust from the shots.

People were crying everywhere — men, women, and children. Jack's and Pamela's and Margaret's and Derrick's arms were now interlocked, squeezing tightly. Pamela barely breathed and could not stop shivering. Her mother was ghostly pale, but her face was like a stone, resolute and unflinching.

Zaher picked up the microphone and pointed to the voice. "See. That is you Americans. Proud and arrogant, yet cowards and infidels. Just like this man you adore, Martin Sterling." His gun still smoked as it hung in front of him. "You are all idolaters!"

Jack was squirming in his seat, looking all around, whispering with Derrick, who was clearly in pain. Margaret sat with her arms crossed, one hand inside her coat.

"Do you know what your candidate has said?" Zaher crossed to the front of the stage. "He said Americans should not accommodate Muslims in this country." He pointed an index finger in the air like a gun. "He called us parasites. He said that to allow the unrestricted immigration of Muslims in your land is cultural suicide. And you are all in agreement, are you not?"

Jack squeezed Pamela's arm tight and leaned close. "Have Margaret pass me the gun."

"The West is full of hostile unbelievers," Zaher said. "We're here to send a message tonight — one that will go down in the history of the West and in all of the world!" He spun around like a dancer. "Bring out our subjects!"

A large man in a black mask sauntered out of the shadows. He stopped, turned, and pointed his machine gun. Into the light, under gunpoint, came a towering SWAT guy who Jack whispered was Lieutenant Wolfski. His mouth was strapped with duct tape, hands tied behind him. He was followed by two more SWAT men. Then came Jack's coworkers. He whispered their names as they came into the light . . . Tab . . . Gordy . . . Clarissa — each bound in a similar manner.

Derrick's head dropped amid shrieks from the crowd. Jack pursed his lips and nodded impatiently for Pamela to get him Margaret's gun.

"Sit down, all of you!" Zaher pointed for the hostages to sit on the floor of the stage, and they did so fluidly, smoke drifting above them in the dim lights. "Do you know what we do to people like you and Martin Sterling?" He wagged his head toward the audience. "People who criticize Islam? Eh? Do you know?"

After some coaxing, Margaret carefully passed the gun to Pamela, looking at it longingly, as if she were giving up a childhood keepsake.

"We are about to *show you* what we do to infidels." Zaher laughed and began to turn in a circle, scanning the arena with his black eyes flashing. "Martin Sterling, where are you? It's time to come out. What do you Americans say? 'Come out, come out, wherever you are!' And I mean *now*!"

Pamela's heart was pumping so fast. She covered the gun with her arms and coat and passed it to Jack. He covered her trembling hands with his.

"Senator Sterling." Zaher closed his fingers into a fist, pounded his chest, and looked at his big watch. "You have precisely five minutes to make your way down to this stage." He pointed to a spot on the floor next to him. "And if you happen to be the coward I think you are and don't show up, we will begin killing people, one by one —"

Bedlam.

"And I want that Christian, too," Zaher

shouted over the pandemonium. "That infidel Everett Lester. You've got five minutes to get on this stage, rock star, and that goes for your wife and son, too. But no one else comes with you, or with the senator. I want the four of you — alone."

Jack held the gun low, between his legs, examining it. He grimaced as he slowly racked the slide, sending a bullet into the chamber just as the next contraction hit Pamela like a lightning bolt.

27

Shakespeare hadn't taken ten steps on the seemingly vacant club level when Zaher's loud voice demanded that Sterling and Everett get to the stage in five minutes.

It was 8:19.

He dashed down the half-lit corridor to suite 227, where Chico was supposed to have taken Sterling, and shone his flashlight through the glass. The room was empty. He eased the door open and ducked inside. The tables were lined with beverages and silver trays full of food, but nothing had been touched.

His phone vibrated, and he found a text from Hedgwick.

We have a plan. Call me.

Shakespeare's phone battery was down to 13 percent.

Zaher's voice continued to boom over the

PA: "And I want that Christian, too. That infidel Everett Lester. You've got five minutes to get on this stage . . ."

Shakespeare slung his rifle over his back, hit the floor, grimacing from the throbbing pain in his arm, and crawled like a commando to the terrace overlooking the bowl. He got his bearings, found the stage . . . *No!* Bound and sitting on the stage amid Zaher and his masked henchmen were Clarissa, Tab, Gordy, and the SWAT guys.

No sign of Jack or the others. They could be anywhere in the crowd.

He crawled back into the suite, slid to an interior wall, called Hedgwick, and told him Clarissa and company were now hostages.

"Okay, listen, we've got a plan, Brian. We want you to take out the hostile at the glass doors just outside section 115," Hedgwick said. "We think he's alone. We'll have an army of men ready to roll in —"

"Hold up," Shakespeare said. "Zaher just gave Sterling and Lester five minutes to turn themselves in, or he starts killing people." He looked at his watch. "We've got four minutes."

"Brian, go *now*! Section 115. Just get us in. We'll —"

"Are your men there? Are they ready *right now*?"

218

"They can be. Listen, by the time you get there —"

Shakespeare's chin slammed to his chest. He squeezed his sweating forehead. *Think . . . think.*

"If I can find Sterling and Lester," Shakespeare said, "I can go with them —"

"And do what? Listen to me, Brian. This is our best move. Tell me exactly where Zaher and his men are."

Shakespeare gave him the rundown.

"Okay, good. Now go!" Hedgwick said. "My men will be briefed and ready."

Yes, it made sense.

Shakespeare got to his feet, loaded a fresh magazine, and stood at the door for a second to plan his route. Around the corridor . . . to the stairwell . . . down to the main concourse . . . right a little ways to section 115.

His watch said he had three minutes till Sterling and Lester were expected onstage.

He cracked the door, checked both ways, and took off.

Everett was shivering with anxiety in anticipation of what he was about to do, but trying not to show it as he insisted for the fifth time that Karen and Cole were *not* coming with him to turn themselves in at the stage.

"We need to be together," Karen pleaded, close to tears. "He said all three of us. If we don't go, he'll kill you!"

"He might kill me anyway, Karen — and you. There's no way I'm taking you down there."

Senator Sterling's people were gathered around him, talking in hushed tones.

"Ev, I don't want you to go without us." She looked frantically about the suite. Cole's arms were wrapped tightly around her. "We could leave Cole here. How about that? Gray will watch him. That way —"

"No, Karen. You're staying. He needs you. I'll be okay."

"You need to make up your minds." Senator Sterling tapped his watch. "We need to move it." He took several steps toward the door as his people backed away from him.

"Sir, I insist we go with you as far as we can," said a bald body guard. The other two agreed.

"I will too," Jenny King said.

Everett's manager, Gray, offered to go with them as far as possible as well.

"Look, let's just do what the man asked." Sterling looked at Karen and Cole as if they should be going too. Then he panned the room. "There's no reason any of the rest of you should endanger your lives by leaving this suite. It's not you they want."

"Senator, I'm not taking my family down there," Everett said.

Surely he has to understand. Maybe he thinks I'll be jeopardizing our lives by not taking Karen and Cole.

Sterling turned his back. "Fine. In any case, we need to go."

Everett hugged Karen and Cole, the three of them locked in a surreal embrace, Karen's body trembling.

"Sir, I'm sorry, we are coming," said another security guard.

Sterling cursed and threw up a hand in disgust. "All right, but you heard the man. You're not going down to the stage."

"Everett or Senator, maybe you should take one of the bodyguards' guns," Gray said.

"No. They'll frisk us." Sterling leveled his gaze at Everett. "Ready?"

Suddenly the door opened, and Brian Shakespeare barged in, out of breath. He closed the door behind him. "How'd you guys end up in here?" he said.

"We changed suites," Jenny said. "The insurgents knew where we were."

Shakespeare nodded, catching his breath. "I'm on my way to let a pack of SWAT guys in." He examined Sterling, then Karen and

221

Cole, then Everett. "You going down?"

Everett answered. "Just the senator and me. His bodyguards will go with us as far as they can."

"Understood," Shakespeare said. "I'll cover you as long as I can. We'll get these SWAT guys in here ASAP." He checked his watch. "You guys get in the bowl and stall as long as you can. Talk to him. Agree with him. Cavalry's on the way."

With that, the confident Shakespeare burst out the door. "Let's go."

Everett turned to Karen and Cole and stared at them, drinking in their images, knowing he had to go, praying this wouldn't be the last time he ever saw them.

"It's time," Sterling said.

Everett heard him leave.

Chills engulfed him. Karen and Cole were sobbing.

Everett looked into the eyes of his wife and son and forced a smile. "It's gonna be okay."

But he didn't mean he was going to live.

He didn't mean it was all going to work out the way they wanted.

He meant, if this was his time to die, he would be going to heaven — and God would take care of them.

28

Shakespeare led the men quickly around the club-level corridor to the stairwell nearest section 115. Quietly they shuffled down the stairwell single file. Close behind him was one of Sterling's bodyguards, followed by Everett, then the bald bodyguard, then Sterling and the third of his men.

Many lives were depending on Shakespeare.

Not an unfamiliar feeling.

He and the bodyguards had their guns drawn. As they worked their way downward, Shakespeare mentally prepared to enter the concourse and respond instantly to any individuals they might encounter. The challenge was deciphering the good guys from the bad in a split second and not killing innocent people.

They got to the brown metal door leading to the concourse, and Shakespeare peered through the glass. Seeing no one, he turned to his group.

"I want the bodyguards to enter the concourse with me," he whispered. "Everett and Senator, you wait here till we signal for you. Once we do, get into the bowl quickly through the double doors and make your way to the stage."

He checked his watch. They had one minute.

Everett's head dropped. Shakespeare knew he was scared, but he was brave to go without his family.

Sterling peered at Shakespeare with an unusually cold stare. Instead of fear, anger and hatred blazed in his eyes. He really did loathe the terrorists and what they were doing to America.

"After we get Everett and the senator inside, I'd like you guys to come with me." Shakespeare nodded to the bodyguards. "We'll make sure Hedgwick and his team have a clear entry point."

He reached out to Everett and Sterling. "Remember, once you get to the stage, stall. Be agreeable. Tell them what they want to hear. The more you can make the clock tick, the better our chances."

They nodded. Everett was breathing hard.

Shakespeare took a deep breath and set his shoulders back. "Let's do it."

He gently pushed the door open and dashed to a wide white column. The bodyguards were with him like glue. Eighty yards to the left was a heavyset masked guard standing at a bank of doors.

"You guys stay here," Shakespeare told the bodyguards. "I'm going to that kiosk." He pointed toward a coffee station twenty feet to the right. "If it's clear, I'll give you the sign, and you wave them into the bowl."

Shakespeare made sure the hostile to his left wasn't looking, took off, and slid behind the kiosk. At the glass doors outside section 115, it was as Hedgwick had said — a lone masked insurgent meandering back and forth, head down.

Shakespeare signaled, and the bodyguards waved for Everett and Sterling to go. The two men walked rapidly to the double doors and entered the arena.

Okay, we got them in on time.

But Shakespeare was worried about a violent response from Zaher when he realized Everett hadn't brought Karen and Cole. All the more reason to hurry up and get SWAT into the building —

The glass case two feet from Shakespeare's head exploded, followed by more shots blistering all around him. He rolled left through broken glass, scrambled, and took cover within the entrance to a rest-room.

The shots had come from above.

The gunman on the far left sprinted toward them. One of the bodyguards popped out from behind the pillar, took a knee, and fired two shots.

The hostile dropped.

More rounds exploded all around Shakespeare, echoing loudly off the concrete and tile, bits of which rained down on him.

He crawled back into the restroom, scrambled to his feet, and sprinted to the other entrance thirty feet away. Peeking around the corner, he spotted four masked men — all pointing right at him. A blinding mass of gunfire tore the walls to shambles and sent him reeling back inside in a rush of heat and smoke.

He dashed back to the other entrance, knowing he couldn't stay in there a second longer or they'd have him. More gunfire rang out in the concourse. He peered around the corner to see the bald bodyguard down cold, bleeding badly, possibly dead. His colleagues were leaning around the pillar, squared off in a gun battle with the hostiles, whose machine-gun fire had shredded parts of the drywall column the bodyguards hid behind.

His phone vibrated.

He had to get out or he'd be trapped.

He checked around the corner. There were five masked men now, all blasting away at the bodyguards. He had to abort the plan to get those doors open.

It was Hedgwick on the phone; he'd have to wait.

Zaher's loud voice ranted over the PA, but Shakespeare couldn't make out what he was saying.

Where to?

He couldn't try to make it to the bowl, or they'd gun him down.

Up high.

Yes, he had to get back to the stairs.

He caught the attention of the bodyguard closest to him, who was sweating profusely and trembling under the hail of gunfire.

"Cover me!" Shakespeare yelled, pointing to the stairwell. "I'm going for the stairs."

The bodyguards dropped back behind the pillar, and the shooting came to a temporary halt. With their backs to the column, the bodyguards looked at each other, spoke, and wiped their faces. One changed clips. The other reached out tentatively to retrieve the dead colleague's weapon, but an onslaught of bullets sent him flinching back. He shook his head and said something to his partner.

They raised their guns at the same time, looked at Shakespeare, nodded, and then bent around the pillar, opening fire with all they had.

Shakespeare made a run for it.

29

"What time you got?" Derrick whispered. He was still pressing hard at the wound on his side.

Jack checked his watch. "It's time. 8:24. You gonna make it?"

Derrick nodded. They both scanned the bowl high and low, as did the other frightened faces around them.

"Five minutes . . . five minutes is up!" Zaher appeared from the shadows onstage, machine gun held high.

Pam's fingers dug into Jack's arm.

"Wait!" a voice called from high atop the steps on a side aisle. "We're here."

It was Senator Sterling, one flap of his dress shirt untucked, tie crooked. He looked down as he took each step, his hands in the air. "Take it easy."

He was followed by Everett Lester, who towered over Sterling with his hands in the air. Karen and Cole were not with him.

That took guts, Jack thought. *Zaher will be furious.*

"Aha." Zaher's voice projected loudly over the PA. "Hurry up. Make way for them . . . We haven't got all day."

Sterling and Everett got to the floor and zigzagged their way toward the stage.

"To the left," Zaher pointed. "Up the steps. Hurry along."

They disappeared in the darkness for what seemed like forever, then walked into the light onstage, squinting.

"Ladies and gentlemen, Senator Martin Sterling and recording artist Everett Lester!" Theatrically, Zaher swept a hand toward them as if introducing an act.

But the crowd did not applaud. Many of the hostages could be heard crying, speaking to one another in panicked voices.

"What's wrong?" Zaher walked to the front of the stage. "This is your man, is it not? This is who you want to run the great West, is it not? Where is all your loud, repugnant talk now? Senator . . ." He turned and crossed to Sterling, who stood with his shoulders back, next to Everett. "What's happened to your supporters? They seem to have lost a good deal of their enthusiasm." He laughed.

Sterling, with his hands behind his back,

said something and glared at Zaher.

Zaher ran over to him, comically, and held the mic to his mouth. "What did you say?"

"I said, they are not used to being coerced by bullies and terrorists." Sterling swallowed hard and looked straight ahead.

Zaher's head dropped, and so did his hand holding the mic. He bit his bottom lip, sneered, and flung the back of his hand across Sterling's face. The sound of the slap was sharp and crisp.

Everett looked down.

Sterling grimaced, then said something more. Zaher held the mic to his mouth again and told him to repeat it.

"Why don't you just let these people go?" Sterling nodded toward Clarissa and the others sitting on the stage. "Everyone else, too." He lifted his head toward the people in the bowl. "You can keep me. That's what you want, isn't it? To get rid of me before I get elected president and we put you and the rest of your psychotic friends out of business."

Zaher stuffed both hands on his waist and paced. Head dropped back, lips pursed, he looked up to the ceiling, at the hostages, at Sterling, at the crowd. The anticipation was sickening, and Jack feared the maniac might go ballistic and start executing people one by one.

Zaher crossed to Everett and Sterling and squared up directly in front of them. One of his henchman, a stocky oaf with dark skin showing behind the mask at his eyes and mouth, nodded and took several steps closer. The other hostile did the same, as if something was about to flare up.

"I thought I asked you to bring your wife and son." Zaher held the microphone with his elbow high in the air. "Did you not hear me, Mr. Lester?"

Everett's head lifted slowly. His face was red. He spoke, but not into the mic. All Jack could hear were the words, "I heard you . . ."

"Oh!" Zaher took an exaggerated step backward and stuck the mic to Everett's mouth. "Tell the people again . . ."

Everett hesitated. "I couldn't bring them. I didn't want them to be harmed."

"Oh, so you protect your family but don't care about any of these people." Zaher swept a hand toward the hostages on the stage. "Or them?" He did the same toward the people in the seats.

"Jack." Pam tugged at his arm, her face pale, her eyes sunken. She shook her head. "It's getting really bad. I need to get to the hospital."

Her mom leaned over Pam and reached out for Jack's arm. "We've got to do something, Jack. I'll ask if we can leave. I'm not afraid."

"Wait. Just wait!" Jack needed to think . . . *think.*

Zaher was still ranting. "That's the problem with you Christians. You are all talk, but you have no backbone. You cave in at the slightest threats. You are the ones who serve a false god!"

Jack could give Derrick the gun, stand, and tell Zaher he needed to get his wife to the hospital — that she was about to have a baby.

How would Zaher respond?

He could shoot Jack on the spot . . . He could do nothing . . . He could actually let them go —

"Ohhhh." Pam's entire body stiffened, her fingers digging into the armrests. Her neck was arched back, eyes shut tight. "Oh, oh, oh." Her head shot forward. "It's gonna come. Oh dear God, I can't believe this."

"Hold on, honey." Jack put a cool hand on her forehead. The heat of her skin alarmed him even more. Margaret's eyes were the size of quarters, and she looked as if she was about to stand up. "Don't do anything, Margaret. Let me handle this."

"If he doesn't want to let you go, Jack, I'll take her," Margaret said. "Tell him that."

Zaher's voice rose: "I need you to get your wife and your son down on this stage *right now!*"

Jack nudged Derrick, told him he had to make a move, and slipped the gun into his friend's hands.

"Dude." Derrick swallowed hard, looking faint. "Are you sure?"

"Look at her."

Pam was frozen, breathing in repeated short blows, trying to overcome the pain.

"The contractions are almost constant," Jack said.

"She's got to be close," Margaret whispered. "We've got to get her out of here."

Derrick nodded.

Jack was about to stand —

"What did you say?" Zaher whipped the mic to Everett's mouth.

Everett paused. "I won't do it. I'm sorry." He lowered his head.

"That's it!" Zaher whirled around like a madman, stopped with his legs spread wide, and shot both hands in the air toward the Sky Zone. "Lower them!"

Everyone looked up to the black rafters high above — and gasped.

Jack spotted a neon-orange jacket on the

catwalk to the left, and another to the far right. Men in masks knelt over each orange jacket, leaning, stretching, gently letting down as if they were lowering enormous fish back into water —

It was Charlie Clearwater! Dangling upside down, dropping toward the seats, held only by a rope that the men were feeding toward the ground. He was as still as a corpse, and his arms were crossed in front of him.

At the same time, across the arena, Steve Basheer dropped upside down toward the crowd. He, too, appeared alive but frozen, with his arms braced across his chest.

"Ho!" Zaher yelled.

Charlie's body jolted to a stop and swayed twelve feet above the crowd, which gasped in horror. Poor Charlie. His face was scarlet red from the blood rushing to it.

"Keep going on number two," Zaher ordered as Steve's body jerked and began zipping quickly toward the seats below.

"Halt!" Zaher shouted.

Steve's body bounced, then twisted in circles some twelve feet above another portion of the occupied seats.

"There's a bomb!" A man in the section of seats below pointed at Steve.

Pandemonium broke out in the bowl.

"Silence!" Zaher screamed.

Wrapped generously around Steve's stomach were layers of shiny black duct tape.

At his stomach, beneath the tape, was a pouch of what looked like sticks of dynamite taped together.

Sticking out from it were green, blue, and white wires.

And on top of all that was a small white box.

With red illuminated numbers.

Counting downward.

30

Shakespeare was winded by the time he made it up to the Sky Zone, and his injured arm was burning. Once through the door with the M14 drawn, he treaded slowly along the walkway that served as the very narrow upper rim overlooking the bowl of the arena.

"This is what happens, America, when you attempt to suppress us." Zaher's voice was muffled and distant. "When you embrace leaders who promote our extinction rather than brotherhood."

Shakespeare took a knee at what would be the end zone if it were a football field. He was about six stories up. This level was strictly for maintenance, and everything was black, from the walls and ceiling to the floors and railings. Black curtains blew like waves in the breeze.

He got his phone out to call Hedgwick, then stopped cold as he peered at the scene below. Those were orange jackets . . . coworkers . . . Charlie and Steve! Swinging by their ankles just above the occupied seats.

"Let this be a message to your fellow countrymen today." Zaher paced. "Do not try to stop our movement. We will take over the West. We will build our places of worship wherever we want, and we will move into your neighborhoods. We will enroll in your schools and practice Sharia and worship the only true god, Allah. And if you attempt to stop us . . ." He pointed to Steve, then Charlie. "This is what you will get. Fear. Terror. And ultimately, death."

The people below Steve and Charlie were cringing, arms and elbows covering their heads.

Shakespeare's stomach turned.

Almost frantically he hoisted the M14, peered through the scope, and found Charlie — and the apparatus. He scanned to Steve . . .

He jerked the gun down.

Dropped his head.

Calm . . . stay calm.

His phone vibrated. Hedgwick.

"Sorry," Shakespeare answered. "We took fire at 115. Had to abort. I'm in the Sky Zone. South end —"

"Everywhere we go, they stack men at the

doors. They must have eyes outside," Hedgwick said. "Did Sterling and Lester make it into the bowl on time?"

"Yeah, but hold up. Bad news."

"What?"

"They have two EventPros hanging upside down above the crowd, strapped with what look like explosives. They're hooked to one of four catwalks that crisscross up here in the Sky Zone."

Long pause.

"All right . . . I need specifics."

At that moment, something clamped Shakespeare's mouth. A hand!

He ripped the hostile's arm, flipped him, and slammed his neck to the floor, choking, choking, choking. The man's eyes grew enormous behind his black mask.

And he was out.

Shakespeare grabbed the man's machine gun and strapped it around his neck. Then he got the man's radio and headset and put it on with trembling hands. He found his phone.

"Hedgwick, you still there?"

"What the heck's going on?"

"Just got one of their radios." Shakespeare wiped the sweat from his eyes with his shirt. "Let me check it out, and I'll get back to you."

"What's your battery level?"

He checked it. "Eight percent."

"Tell me exactly where you see each hostile right now, and where the explosives are. I'm afraid I'm gonna lose you."

Shakespeare did so, then Hedgwick told him to find out anything he could about the bombs, whether they were set to go off at a certain time, or if Zaher had some kind of remote-control device.

"Listen, just in case I lose you. We're gonna storm the place. When you see us coming, I want you to try to take out Zaher. After that, I want you to get out on that catwalk as fast as you can and lower the two guys with the explosives — gently. Copy that?"

"Copy."

Just as he hung up, his phone vibrated with an incoming text from Sheena.

I'm worried. All over news. U ok? Love u.

The battery dropped to 7 percent. He wrote back:

I'm fine. Battery almost dead so last txt. Love u. Give kids hugs. C u soon.

Then he paused, and added two more lines.

We'll work things out. I promise.

And he meant it. There was junk in the world, downright evil and wrong and filth, but what he had in Sheena and the kids — that was true meaning and life. She'd been right. He'd gone way overboard. He needed to learn to live again, to simply deal with things as they came — as he was right now.

He hoped God would give him a second chance.

His closest shot at Zaher would be directly from the side of the arena. He peered through his scope and panned over that way. Two of five huge canister lights were on. Getting behind one of those bright boys would be perfect. For the bad guys, it would be like looking directly into a searchlight.

31

Derrick leaned forward, holding the gun below his knees, trying to stop shaking. Zenia must be worried stiff. But he had to put her out of his mind. He might be the only innocent civilian in the arena with a gun besides Shakespeare, and no one knew where he was. He had to stay sharp. Wait for the right moment. His head was woozy, and he just hoped he wouldn't pass out from the blood he'd lost.

"This is what we are going to do." Zaher jabbed Everett Lester with the microphone. "You must order your wife and boy down here this instant." He stepped to the center of the stage and spoke even louder. "And I need the rogue infidel by the name of Shakespeare to get down here *now,* or we begin executing people. You have been warned."

Zaher threw the mic by the cord over his shoulder, arched back, and blasted his machine gun toward the ceiling. Sparks flew from bullets hitting metal, and one large light exploded in a flash of orange smoke.

Once again screams rang out like sirens from every direction.

Derrick wanted to take Zaher out right then, but that would leave all the other insurgents free to open fire on him and the crowd.

Zaher crossed back to Everett and stuck the mic into his hands.

Jack elbowed Derrick. "I'm doing it," he whispered. "God have mercy." He stood and lifted a hand. "Sir," he called toward the stage.

Zaher spun around with an arm raised, pointing, scanning, finding Jack. "What is this?" he called without the mic. "What? Speak up."

Jack put his hands out toward Pam. "My wife is having a baby! She's in labor right now. I need to get her to a hospital. Please . . ."

"Come up here." Zaher waved. "Bring her."

Derrick's insides screamed. *No!*

Someone in the crowd called out, "Let her go."

"Yes!" someone else shouted.

"Please." Jack held up his hands innocently. "We just need to get to a hospital. If you want, my mother can take her. I can stay —"

"I said, get up here!"

Jack looked down at Pam, who shook her head in anguish. "No, please," she pleaded. "It's coming . . . The pain's so bad. Don't leave me."

Jack's jaw clenched, and he looked back at Zaher. "Please, just let her go. I don't have to go with her —"

"Let her go, you animals!" a male voice yelled.

"Let her go to the hospital!" another voice echoed.

The chanting began with several voices, then more joined in, and more, and it became a chant. "Let . . . her . . . go. Let . . . her . . . go." Deep. Loud. Resolute.

Chills ran down Derrick's arms as he joined in. "Let . . . her . . . go!"

Jack reached down for Pam's hand. "C'mon."

She wiggled to the front of her seat. Margaret stood and helped her get to her feet. Without another word they scooted out of the row amid the chanting.

"Silence." Zaher was barely heard. "Silence!"

The chanting was so loud, Zaher could

244

only muster a frustrated chuckle. His arms dropped to his sides, and he laughed, hesitantly looking around at his partners and slouching as if he didn't care. But his eyes burned with rage.

"Let . . . her . . . go . . ." Some in the crowd were standing, pumping their fists with angry scowls.

Zaher went over and took the microphone from Everett. Jack, Pam, and Margaret were a third of their way up the aisle.

"Okay, that's enough." Zaher said it softly amid the chanting. He pursed his lips and dropped his head back.

Derrick feared he was about to lose it.

"I said, *that's enough*!" He dropped the mic, lifted the machine gun, and blasted a horizontal line of fire twenty feet above the crowd, sweeping left to right, just missing one of the men swinging upside down.

Jack, Pam, and Margaret hit the ground, as did everyone else.

In a cloud of smoke, Zaher leaned down and picked up the mic where it lay on the floor among scattered bullet casings. "No one's leaving here till I say so. If you want me to end it all right now . . ." He reached into his coat and yanked out a small black box that looked like a TV remote. He held it high, waving it to one side of the crowd, then the other. "This little mechanism can bring this entire building down and blow up the entire city block. No one will survive. Sit down and shut up — *now!*"

Everyone was back in their seats and silent within seconds.

He called to a masked man standing armed about eight rows up from Jack. "Bring them back." Then he held a hand over his eyes and looked all around at the upper seats. "Brian Shakespeare, you have one minute to show your face. If you don't, bad things are going to happen to these people down here."

Zaher walked over to Everett. "And you still need to get your lovely wife and son down here." He handed the mic to Everett and patted Sterling on the shoulder. "Tell them to make it snappy. We don't have much time."

Zaher clasped his hands behind his back and walked away, as if taking a stroll in the park.

Jack, Pam, and Margaret arrived back at the seats under the guard's gunpoint. Pam winced as she sat, holding tightly to Jack's and Margaret's arms. Jack sighed as he sat, looking completely deflated.

"Karen and Cole, listen carefully." Everett's voice over the PA was deep and resolute. "No matter what, I want you to stay where you are safe. Whatever you do, *don't* come down here under any circumstances —"

Zaher spun around and lifted his gun toward Everett as the crowd erupted in a collective gasp.

32

Shakespeare had been aligning Zaher in his sights along the side of the arena, hidden perfectly behind an enormous silver canister light, when the ringleader called him out by name. It should have come as no surprise. The hostiles must have had access to Event-Pros radios from the start.

Down on the stage, Zaher had Everett on his knees with one arm locked around his neck and the other holding a gun to his temple. Zaher was wagging his head, yelling something that Shakespeare couldn't make out because the microphone was lying on the floor.

Shakespeare got his phone out. The battery had drained to 4 percent. He might not be able to complete the call, but he dialed Hedgwick anyway.

"This'll be my last call. Battery's gone. Zaher ordered me down to the stage or he starts killing people. I've got to go. We have a pregnant woman, Pam Crittendon, in the third row with my coworker Jack Crittendon. She's about to have a baby. They tried to get out, but Zaher wouldn't let them. Also, Everett Lester was told to make his wife and kid come down, but instead Lester told them over the PA to stay put. Zaher has fired several rounds into the ceiling and empty seats. What's your plan?"

Nothing.

"Hedgwick?"

The line was silent.

"Hedgwick, do you read?" He looked at the phone.

Black screen.

Battery dead.

He holstered the phone, not knowing how much Hedgwick had even heard.

Zaher shoved Everett face-first to the stage and grabbed the microphone. "Karen Lester? Cole Lester?" Zaher shouted. "If you don't get down here in two minutes, Daddy dies." He looked at his watch. "I'm counting."

This was insane.

How dare these men come in here, hold us hostage, and try to rip away our freedom — the freedom to go to the hospital to have a baby! On our own soil!

Shakespeare thought about dropping his

rope over the edge and rappelling down to them peacefully, but they'd probably think he was attacking and gun him down.

He leaned over the concrete ledge and peered down at the section of seats below, which was empty because the hostiles had forced everyone close to the stage.

What did he have to lose?

He quickly got the rope out of his backpack, looped one end through the trigger guard on his rifle, and tied a loose knot. Then he took off his ammo belt, rebuckled it, and tied it to the rope. Gently he began to lower the gun and ammo to the empty seats below, then let them down quickly, the rope zipping through his fingers. They hit the floor between two empty rows of seats, and he dropped the rope down with them.

Then he was off to turn himself in, hoping his presence would serve as a delaying tactic for Karen and Cole.

"She's in active labor." A woman had rushed to Pam's side, telling Jack she was a nurse and her name was Lucy.

Pam was now lying on the floor in the aisle, and Jack and Margaret knelt on either side of her.

"I'm guessing she's dilated. She should be in a hospital relaxing and focusing on her contractions."

"I need to shift," Pam moaned. "My back is killing me." She writhed and shifted onto her side.

"We need drinking water and cold compresses," Lucy said.

"Ohhh." Pam cried out and crossed her wrists over her chest. "Hoo, hoo, hoo . . ."

"That's another contraction." Lucy checked her watch. "That was three and a half minutes. She could have this baby soon."

Pam breathed, breathed, breathed through the pain, which was taking forever to subside.

Jack was beside himself. He had to get her out. But if he and Pam just headed out, would Zaher gun them down as his first victims?

"The contractions are getting longer," Lucy said. "You're doing good, Pam. So good. Just keep doing what you're doing. It's going to be okay."

The contraction subsided. Pam's shoulders slumped, and her whole body went limp. Jack wiped the sweat from her forehead.

"That was almost sixty seconds," Lucy said. "What do you want to do? You want to stay like you are or move around?"

Pam just shook her head.

"You need to relax now. Save your energy for the next one," Lucy said. "Try to breathe slow and easy, slow and easy. Deep breaths now . . . plenty of oxygen to your brain."

"It's not going away," Pam said. "It's like I'm cramping or like there's a charley horse in my stomach. Feel it, it's like a rock. My lower back . . . the pain won't let up." She talked in choppy blurts. "Do you think everything's okay? Is she turned the wrong way or something? It doesn't feel right. The pain's burning."

Lucy nodded. "Everything's fine. You're doing great, considering the circumstances."

On the stage, Zaher was sticking the mic in Sterling's face. "What did you say?"

The corner of Sterling's mouth was bleeding from where Zaher had backhanded him. The senator nodded toward Pam. "I said, why don't you at least show some human decency and let that lady go to the hospital to have her baby?"

Jack's heart thundered. All eyes turned to Pam.

"Do whatever you want to me. Just let her go," Sterling said. "Let them all go. Don't hurt these people; they've done nothing wrong."

"Except support you! And *fund* you! And

252

agree with whatever you say! They're your clones, Senator!"

"You want the sympathy of the American people? Let these folks go back to their homes. That'll do more to support your cause than taking innocent lives."

Suddenly Zaher's chin rose, and he craned his neck and cupped a hand over his eyes to block the lights. The crowd murmured. Everyone watched as a masked insurgent followed someone down the aisle, a machine gun pointed at his captive's back.

"Oh, look what we have here. Good. That was easy." Zaher checked his watch. "Now all we need is the rest of the Lester family and we'll have everyone together. Did you frisk him?"

The insurgent nodded.

Then Jack made out who the man was.

It was Shakespeare — their last hope — making his way to the stage unarmed, about to become just another useless hostage.

33

Pamela wanted to *hurt* Shareek Zaher.

Her mind was a blur. She was so scared and frustrated and in such intense pain, she thought for a hazy moment she might black out.

Lucy, her godsend, wiped her drenched face with a tissue and whispered to Jack and Margaret that the most recent contraction lasted a minute and a half. Pamela barely felt any letup between them. It all felt like one long, burning, painful nightmare.

"Calm . . . be calm, sweetie." Lucy patted her forehead.

Jack squeezed Pamela's hand, but she shook it away. *Stop! Why would you do that?*

"I'm just trying to keep you relaxed," he said. "You're shaking."

Duh, I'm shaking! Terrorists are about to blow us up, and I want to push this baby out right here on the floor of this godforsaken arena where you work part-time for nine dol-

lars an hour!

Zaher ordered Shakespeare to sit on the stage with the others. This was not good.

Where are the police? Why haven't they come?

Pamela was no midwife, but she bet she was close to being fully dilated. She had to go to the bathroom so badly. Or was it the baby, ready to come into this insane world?

"Ohhh." A searing pain knifed her lower back. "I've got to move. I've got to!"

"Okay, okay." Lucy guided her as she shifted through the pain onto all fours.

Jack and Margaret hovered over her, way too close. "Give me space," she said. They inched away, but not far enough. "More!"

Zaher was saying something to Everett, but she couldn't hear what. The crowd was gasping.

"Pam, what can I do?" Jack said.

She shook her head, which was buried in her arms on the floor, facedown. "Hospital" was all she could mumble.

The pain in her back and abdomen was so overpowering, her entire body hurt. But there was no escape.

"Breathe, Pam. Relax and breathe," Lucy said. "Let's take it one contraction at a time. You've been awesome so far."

Lucy didn't say she was an obstetrical

nurse, but she was clearly experienced. She probably had children of her own. But she was so extremely skinny — and pale. And she had several bruises on the inside of her right arm. In a fleeting moment, Pamela wondered if she was fighting some kind of illness or even cancer.

"Think how far you've come," Lucy whispered. "We're going to make it."

"How far am I?"

Lucy shook her head. "I'm not sure, but you're a champ."

Something had to happen. Or was she going to be forced to have the baby right there on —

"Ahhhh." The shooting cramp took her breath away, and it got worse . . . worse . . . *worse*!

She couldn't think.

Seemingly from a great distance away, Lucy was coaching her to breathe, but all Pamela was trying to do was keep her sanity.

"How long was that?" Jack said.

Who cares, Jack!

"Two minutes between contractions," Lucy said. "Give her space, Jack."

Suddenly Jack was gone. She was face-down, rubbing her forehead with her fists. Rubbing, rubbing, rubbing, as if she were scrubbing a dirty pan with steel wool.

"Take it easy," Lucy whispered, not touching her. "Breathe however you have to in order to get through it. That's it. Do what comes naturally."

There was a commotion.

People were starting to yell, screaming in anger.

"Look at her! She needs a hospital." It was Jack's voice.

Don't get shot, Jack. Don't get shot . . .

"It hurts so bad."

Lucy didn't hear her.

Pamela said it again.

Or did she?

All she knew for sure was that she was going out of her mind with the pain.

Derrick gripped Margaret's pink-and-black nine-millimeter Taurus a little tighter and inched it a little higher behind the seat in front of him as Jack argued with Zaher to let him get Pam to a hospital.

Everything was happening at once.

The crowd was chanting angrily to let Pam go. Shakespeare was whispering to the others seated onstage. Sterling was pleading to let the people go. The whole thing was reaching a boiling point.

"We're gonna walk out of here," Jack

stated to Zaher.

Derrick feared Zaher would snap.

"If Karen Lester doesn't get down here with that kid right now, the rock star *dies.*" Zaher had Everett's face pressed to the stage, gun to the back of his head. "And if you people don't *shut up,* and that includes you" — he pointed the remote control at Jack — "I will blow this place to pieces. Shut up right now!"

"Stop! Wait!" The crowd quieted when a woman's voice rang out from the top of the steps beyond the stage. "We're here!" It was Karen Lester. "Don't hurt him!" Clutching her son's hand. Holding her blonde hair behind her ear. Coming down the steps at gunpoint.

"No." Everett shook his head in torment, his shoulders lurching, unable to look up and see his family because Zaher still had the gun jammed to his head.

Just then one of the gunmen, a wide hulking guy with a toothpick in his mouth, stepped forward to get Zaher's attention and pointed at his own headset. Zaher dashed to him. The gunman put his head down and cupped his earpiece, listening intently.

Shakespeare made eye contact with Sterling.

Were they going to try something? But what? They had no weapons. Derrick breathed in enormously, eyeing the gun in his hands, mentally preparing to pick off as many of the terrorists as possible, should Shakespeare and Sterling make some kind of move.

The masked gunman explained something to Zaher, and they both turned toward the back of the stage, blocked the light from their eyes, and peered up to the top of the bowl. Two masked gunmen ran a quarter of the way down the steps, frantically waving their arms and machine guns.

Zaher turned back to Karen and Cole. "Stop where you are!" They had just reached the lower seats on the side of the bowl, near where red-faced Charlie Clearwater hung upside down with bombs strapped to his stomach.

Zaher quickstepped to the hostages onstage. "All of you, get over there with Lester's wife and boy — now! *Move!*" He pointed his gun toward Karen and Cole.

Everyone looked at one another, hesitating, except Everett, who scrambled to his feet and started toward his wife and son.

"Not you!" Zaher pointed the machine gun at Everett. "You stay."

Shakespeare quickly got to his feet and

took charge, leading the others into the dark shadows offstage and down the steps toward where Karen stood shivering, hugging Cole. Sterling slowly followed the group, making sure they were all accounted for.

"You're not going anywhere." Zaher bashed his machine gun into Sterling's gut, knocking the wind out of him.

"The rest of you get down there. Hurry!"

Zaher's two henchmen closed in on Sterling and Lester, and they made their way offstage. Zaher stopped in the light at the edge of the shadow. "Do not attempt to leave," he announced. "Stay where you are. And remember, America, this is just a taste of what is to come."

With that they disappeared into the shadows.

34

His heart pounding and his mind riffling through options, Shakespeare embraced Karen and Cole almost directly beneath Charlie, who was swaying upside down with the bomb. The frenzied crowd searched one another's faces with cautious hope rising in their fear-filled eyes.

"Where're they going? Where're they taking Everett?" Karen shook uncontrollably. "Can you follow them?"

"Let me think, just let me think." Shakespeare rested a hand on their backs and eyed the section where he'd lowered his rifle, about fifty yards away.

Zaher and his men were hurrying Sterling and Everett at gunpoint up the long aisle of steps leading to the main concourse. Several henchmen ran down to meet them and help them up the steps.

They must have had a plan to escape, but with all of the police outside, Shakespeare couldn't figure it out.

"Charlie, you okay?" he called up to his colleague, whose face was dark like a bruise.

Charlie didn't even attempt to see who was calling him. He was frozen, arms crossed over his chest. "I'm okay," he called. "Head's about to explode."

You could have used a different expression.

"Do you know anything about the bombs?" Shakespeare asked.

He slowly shook his head. "Just get me down."

"We will. Hang on."

Shakespeare scanned the seats near the stage. Jack and Derrick, Margaret and another lady surrounded Pam, who was still laid out in the aisle at the third row.

The hostiles who had been atop each set of steps were retreating into the concourse. All Shakespeare could figure was that Hedgwick's SWAT team was moving in, and Zaher's guys had gotten wind of it. His troops were pulling out, but by what exit? They were sure targets once they left the building.

Would the bombs go off any second?

Why hadn't they stayed? What kind of jihad was this?

Seeing the terrorists disappearing, people latched hands and began dashing in different directions, stopping, yelling, pointing, zigzagging. They all knew the bombs could go at any second. They had to get out. Some raced frantically for the steps leading up to the main concourse, while others forged into various large openings leading into the lower level of the arena.

"Everyone, go!" Shakespeare waved. "Follow any exit sign! Hurry!" He led Karen and Cole into the aisle. "You've got to get out of here."

"I can't go without Everett."

"Karen, I'm sorry. Get your son out. I'll do what I can. *Go.*"

Zaher and his gang had vanished into the main concourse.

The people in the seats below where Charlie and Steve hung cleared out like two rapidly expanding sinkholes until no one was left beneath them.

Shakespeare took off for Jack and Pam. Only Margaret and the skinny stranger remained with them. "How is she?" Shakespeare said.

"She doesn't think she can make it to a hospital," Jack said.

"We called. An ambulance is coming," Margaret said. "If they can get in here."

"You can't wait. You need to get her out of here." Shakespeare nodded toward Charlie. "Those things might go."

Jack nodded, suddenly looking resolute. "Okay, we've got to do this."

Pam began to protest —

"Good luck." Shakespeare took off for his rifle.

"Where're you going?" Jack called.

"After them."

"Wait!" Derrick held up Margaret's gun. "Here." He tossed it to him.

Shakespeare caught the pink weapon, gave a sly smile, and jammed it into his belt. "Thanks." He winked at Margaret and dashed away.

"Everybody, out, out, out!" he yelled. "Get out of the building."

He hit the steps and took them three at a time until he was three quarters of the way up. There. The coiled rope, rifle, and ammo lay on the ground between two rows of seats.

He ran to it and began loading up.

Shakespeare was not normally a praying man, but he knew it was going to take more than luck to save Everett Lester and presidential candidate Martin Sterling. He got fully locked and loaded and took off after them. With his first few strides, he whispered aloud, "Go with me, God."

Karen and Cole would be free, they would

be safe — that's all Everett clung to as he and Senator Sterling were shoved at gunpoint up the steps in the cold stairwell. Zaher led the pack of wolves, eight or nine of them, still in masks and breathing like gorillas as they climbed past level 5.

"ETA two minutes, two minutes." The voice came from behind.

Surely the building was crawling with police and SWAT by now.

Why hadn't the bombs blown?

"You okay?" Sterling said, out of breath.

"Yeah," Everett said.

"Sorry to get you into this —"

"Shut up!" Zaher yelled as the nose of a gun bashed the center of Everett's back. "Just shut your faces. We need quiet."

They were communicating with someone via radio.

They arrived at level 6 at a brown metal door. Zaher eased the door open, and the rest of them followed.

They passed through the doorway into blackness, and everyone slowed to adjust their eyes.

Whoa. They'd indeed reached the top of the arena. Only a skimpy black railing separated them from a six-story drop.

Whistles sounded from below, and militant voices shouted, "Go, go, go . . ." SWAT members chugged down virtually every set of steps in tight single-file lines like giant mechanical snakes slithering into the vast arena.

The seats had cleared.

No sign of Karen or Cole. *Thank God.*

The two men in orange jackets still swung above the seats, but a SWAT crew was hoisting ladders near them as people in astronaut-looking bomb suits stood by.

SWAT team members surrounded Jack and his wife, leading them out, possibly carrying her — Everett couldn't quite see. *Good. They'll get her to a hospital . . . They'll have their baby.*

"This way." Zaher knew right where he was going. "Silence." He had a flashlight now. They walked quickly and quietly against the wall. Zaher stopped and waved them into a nook off to the right. It was pitch-black except for the shaky beam of his flashlight. They made several tight turns.

"One minute. ETA one minute." It was the same voice as the man from before. It registered with Everett for the first time that this voice didn't sound foreign.

They hit a narrow set of black metal steps that rose into darkness.

Zaher grabbed the rail and started climbing.

Then he stopped and turned back to them.

Everett could only make out his small, watery eyes.

"Be watching for the others," Zaher whispered. "None of us who are alive must be left behind."

He hurried up the creaky steps.

A gun jabbed the spot on Everett's back that was already raw.

"Move, move."

He had no choice. He went up, up the wobbly stairs, higher than he'd expected, feeling for each step in the dark.

It was cold.

A breeze whipped in.

Night air and lights from outside.

They were heading for the roof.

35

Four SWAT guys carried Pam through the concourse, radioing to a waiting ambulance. Jack and Margaret followed hand in hand, passing dozens of SWAT members storming the building. Lucy trotted alongside Pam, reassuring her. Derrick was on his phone with his photographer, Daniel.

Finally they got to the lobby. All the doors were open, the wind was blowing in, glass was broken everywhere — and then they hit the cool night air. Hundreds of gawking people were roped off fifty yards away. Fire trucks, ambulances, and police vehicles were parked at every angle. The spotlights and red, blue, and orange flashing lights were blinding. Sirens seemed to be wailing from all directions.

Two paramedics spotted them, waved, and jogged toward them with a stretcher. Pam lurched in agony. The contractions all seemed like one now. And she didn't want anything to do with Jack — only Lucy could provide any form of instruction or encouragement. Where had she come from? Who had she been with? It was as if she were an angel sent specifically for them.

"Hey, I gotta meet Daniel." Derrick patted Jack's back. "You're in good hands."

Jack nodded and clasped his hand, then pulled him close and hugged him.

"Can you believe it?" Jack said.

"No, I can't. What a night. And it ain't over yet."

They loaded Pam into the ambulance.

"Now we just gotta pray those bombs don't go off while Lester and Sterling are still in there," Jack said.

Derrick nodded. "And the dudes they're strapped to. I'm afraid for them."

"I know."

"Your girls are covered, right?"

"Yeah, they're with our neighbors."

Rebecca and Faye were fine. He'd made a couple of quick calls earlier, arranging for the girls to stay with their neighbors, Tommy and Darlene, who didn't have children and were always thrilled to watch them.

Pam was already in the ambulance with the two paramedics, who were taking her blood pressure and getting her adjusted.

"We gotta go have this baby," Jack said.

"I know, and I got a story to cover."

"Be careful, dude," Jack said.

"I will. Text me when the baby comes."

"I will. Let me know what happens here."

Derrick slapped Jack's hand and took off.

"Mr. Crittendon." The female paramedic hopped out of the ambulance. "You can meet us at Mount Sinai Hospital. Do you know how to get there?"

Jack looked at Margaret and Lucy, then at Pam, who was staring up at the ceiling inside the ambulance.

"Can any of us ride with you? Is that an option? I'm just trying to figure out how to do this. Lucy, you're probably done here . . ."

Lucy looked at her watch and pressed her fingers to her forehead as if torn. "I want to see this through. How about if I meet you there?"

"Lucy." Pam lifted her head and squinted out at them. "Can you come?"

The EMT shook her head as if to say no, but Lucy spoke up.

"I'm an RN," she said. "I can help. I've been with her the whole night. I think she's really far along."

"We normally only take one passenger — up front," the paramedic said.

"Please." Jack held out a hand toward

Lucy. "She's been a lifesaver. Will you let her ride inside with Pam? I'll take her mom, and we'll meet you there."

"Gloria," the male paramedic called. "It's okay. Let her come. But we need to move out."

The female paramedic's shoulders dropped, and she reluctantly opened the door. Lucy scrambled in, and Jack peeked inside one last time. "Honey, I'll meet you at the hospital."

She nodded without looking at him. "Make sure the girls are okay."

"I will," Jack said. "Lucy, thank you. You're an angel."

Lucy nodded and smiled almost sadly as the paramedic closed the doors and hurried around to the driver's seat. "You can go straight to the emergency-room entrance, sir," she said to Jack.

"Okay." Jack grabbed Margaret's hand and glanced through the back window of the ambulance one last time.

While the male paramedic looked down, adjusting something next to Pam, Lucy leaned right over her, holding her hand, looking her in the eyes, talking to her like a sister or midwife.

"Okay, we better hustle." Jack led Margaret toward the parking deck, thoughts swirling about the fastest route to the hospital, Shakespeare's whereabouts, and the safety of Everett Lester and Martin Sterling.

"We're lucky to be alive," Margaret said.

Their eyes met, and Jack squeezed her fragile hand. He walked as fast as she could keep up.

"Well, no matter what else happens, it looks like you're about to have another baby," she said.

Jack knew he should be elated.

Elated they'd made it out alive. Elated his girls were safe. Elated his wife was in good hands, on the way to the hospital.

But instead, what dominated his thoughts was the cost of the ambulance, the emergency room, the meds — thousands more dollars in mounting bills he wouldn't be able to pay.

He hit the remote and opened the passenger door for Margaret, his chest feeling like a rigid metal cage within which his heart was about to explode from all the pressure.

36

When he hit the concourse level, Shake-speare was passed by an army of cops and SWAT guys blowing into the arena, dodging flustered people who were scurrying to the nearest exits — but there was no sign of Martin Sterling, Everett Lester, or Shareek Zaher and his henchmen.

Then it clicked.

They're going up.

He burst through the metal door leading back into the stairwell and charged up, up, up.

Why would they go to the Sky Zone?

He took as many steps at a time as he could, going up and around, up and around. Passing the fifth floor he tripped, bashing his knee, but he kept going, finally hitting the top floor completely out of breath. Breathing hard, rifle in his right arm, he eased the door open just inches, peering into darkness.

He could hear the police commandeering the arena below. He entered the Sky Zone slowly, eyes adjusting as he felt his way along the inside wall, away from the railing that encircled the very top of the arena.

He peered over the edge. Bomb-squad guys in astronaut-like gear were gently lowering Charlie to a stretcher. Others were in the process of getting Steve down. Why hadn't the bombs blown yet? Had the timers malfunctioned? Or did Zaher still intend to detonate them?

Shakespeare kept feeling his way along the wall until he came to an opening on the right. He got the Maglite off his belt, turned it on, and entered the blackness.

He felt cool air and assumed that was the norm up there — until he kept going around several tight turns and the air got colder, actually breezy.

Then everything hit him at once as the beam of his Maglite fell on the narrow metal steps leading up to a door — to the roof!

One foot on the steps, ready to ascend, he froze and listened, trying to separate the police clamor below from something he thought he heard above. He strained to listen, taking several tentative steps up the ladder.

The dull thumping noise filtered through

his ears and registered, suddenly, deeply, in the center of his chest —

Helicopter!

He doused the Maglite and raced up the steps, confirming in his mind that his weapons were locked and loaded, hoping he wasn't too late, that the chopper hadn't left.

Wind whipped near the top of the ladder, and the deafening noise from the chopper seemed to physically thump against his chest. He shook off the chill, took a deep breath, and eased his head out the opening. Sure enough, like a dream, forty yards away sat a rumbling UH-60 Black Hawk, a military chopper painted a dull black. A fractured line of dark figures, a dozen or more, snaked toward the long, intimidating aircraft, whose orange lights slowly pulsed on and off.

Sterling and Lester were under gunpoint halfway back in the line, with Zaher leading the way toward the large sliding door of the aircraft.

Shakespeare scanned the rooftop. His only option for cover was a large bank of heating and AC units about twenty yards to his right.

Zaher turned back around toward his men and yelled something. Several of them cupped their ears and jogged toward him, as if they couldn't hear. He got closer and said it again. Suddenly one of the men nodded and broke into a sprint directly toward Shakespeare.

For a second Shakespeare froze, wondering if he'd been seen. Then he dropped back down on the ladder, out of sight, sorting quickly through his options. He swung his rifle around his back, hurried down to the ground, and hid directly behind the ladder in the pitch-blackness.

As the hostile hit the top of the ladder, he was yelling into a radio headset. "Shareek thinks we're missing one . . . You're telling me he's dead? You're sure . . . Who? . . . Franco's with us on the roof, you idiot."

Halfway down the ladder the man stopped, just inches away from Shakespeare's face. "Are you *positive*? Because if we leave without someone, Zaher will *lynch* us."

"I'm positive." The voice came from around the dark corner. It was another masked figure, breathing hard, right there in the room with them. "I'm the last of us. Let's go."

Shakespeare froze, staring right at them in the dark, not breathing.

Not another word was spoken.

The two men hit the ladder and disappeared into the night.

Shakespeare climbed just behind them, determined to save Everett Lester and the man who might well be the next president of the United States.

Finally, Pamela caught her breath. Another nightmarish contraction had passed. Even though her face was full of sweat, she couldn't get warm jiggling around on that stretcher in the ambulance. Lucy was right there with her, patting her face, pulling up the thin blanket, coaching her through the burning contractions.

Marvin, the paramedic, said she was dilated nine centimeters. She couldn't believe how fast this baby was coming — and a month early.

Oh, God, let her be healthy.

"Breathe in deep, Pam," Lucy whispered. "Clear your head. You're doing so well. You're going to have this baby!"

Who was this Lucy? What kind of person just stepped up to help a total stranger like this?

Pamela felt badly about snapping at Jack, but she knew he would understand. They'd been through this twice before, so he knew to expect the worst during labor. She just hoped Shakespeare and everyone else at the arena made it out safely.

"Mrs. Crittendon, I'm going to set you up with an electronic fetal monitor." Marvin held up two white discs, each a little smaller than a deck of cards. "This measures your contractions, and this monitors the baby's heart rate. They simply attach to your stomach —"

"Oh . . . your hands are *freezing.*"

"I'm sorry about that." He continued settling the monitors right where he wanted them.

He examined the moving color graphs on a lunch-box-size computer he held in both hands, touching the screen, staring at various numbers.

"Are there any more blankets?" Pamela said.

Lucy, who was looking at her phone, leaned close to her. "We've used all Marvin has. We'll be at the hospital soon, and we'll get you a nice warm one, okay?"

Uh-oh.

She closed her eyes.

Turned within herself.

Another one was coming.

Focus.

"It's okay." Lucy must have seen her flinch. "Keep that good breathing going right through."

Pamela's eyes were glued on Lucy as the excruciating pain rose like a merciless beast. Rising, rising. Stronger. More powerful. Overcoming her . . .

She blocked everything out.

Just get through.

Would this ever end? Would she *live* through this?

Lucy's eyes closed. Her head moved back and forth slightly as if she was praying.

Good.

"Ohhhh." Pamela squirmed. It hurt so badly.

She felt Lucy squeeze her hand. That was okay. That was good.

But Marvin didn't lift his eyes from the monitor.

In fact, he squinted closer at the screen and actually readjusted the monitor on her belly with trembling hands — as if something was terribly wrong.

37

Everett's heart sparked with hope, and his adrenaline spiked. One of the attackers had dashed back to the ladder and disappeared into the arena. They would have to wait for him, giving police more time to get to the roof! He and Sterling exchanged glances and shuffled as slowly as they could.

But just seconds later the insurgent re-appeared, followed by a second. They trotted toward the group, waving at the helicopter, signaling that they were the last.

Everett knew if he set foot on that helicopter, things would only go from bad to worse. Somehow they were going to use Sterling and Everett as pawns, or examples, or human sacrifices. He shook off an image of being blindfolded and surrounded by hooded terrorists with machetes.

"Where's Folsom?" Zaher barked over the deep thud of the chopper.

The man who'd dashed back inside ran a

finger across his own neck. "Dead." He shook his head.

The second man nodded to confirm.

Zaher pursed his lips and stared at the ground. The line stopped moving, several of them bumping into each other. Everett looked at Sterling and then back to the door leading to the ladder.

A dark figure moved.

Everett looked away, not wanting to draw attention, but his senses revved with hope.

It had to be the police or SWAT.

He told himself to be ready to drop and roll — or flat out sprint.

Zaher yakked on his radio. The insurgents were restless, eyeing one another, turning their shoulders, scanning the rooftop — waiting for Zaher to order them onboard.

"Oh God, get us out of this," Everett said aloud beneath the blaring noise of the chopper. "Protect us. Bring fire down on these guys."

Nonchalantly he turned back toward the door and saw a man disappearing behind the large AC unit.

Everett's heart sank. It was the burly guy, Shakespeare, one of the security people from the arena. What could he possibly do?

With a sudden bounce in his step, Zaher swept an arm toward the helicopter. "Move it! Let's go."

As Everett looked back toward the AC unit, he saw the end of Shakespeare's throwing motion, then heard something hit the ground near him.

A silver metal canister . . . bouncing end over end . . . then rolling.

Everett dropped to the cold concrete and buried his face in the crook of his arm. Even with his eyes shut and face buried, his mind lit up with the flash from whatever Shakespeare had thrown.

Then the *boom.*

The ground shook.

Everett knew he had to move. This was his one shot.

He looked up and got to his knees as a white cloud rolled up into the night sky. Shakespeare waved frantically for Everett to come to him, so he took off as fast as he could, praying for God to give him wings.

Suddenly Shakespeare dropped to the ground with his rifle in front of him and, in a horrifying image, took dead aim at Everett.

When Everett saw the repeated flash of his gun, he slowed, expecting to be riddled with bullets. But nothing hit him. He kept going, every step feeling like ten yards, hearing the explosions, sensing a barrage of hot bullets skimming by him, almost tripping, then feeling like an invisible man, ever so close to freedom.

"Take cover!" Shakespeare yelled and continued firing on the hostiles, his rattling machine gun spitting lead and smoke.

Everett got safely behind the AC unit, caught his breath, and peered around the corner.

Four or five of the men were strewn dead or dying on the rooftop like black garbage bags blowing in the wind.

The others were manhandling Sterling into the copter and diving in themselves as it lifted off the roof. Zaher was among them.

Weapons flashed from the chopper, and gunfire burst all around Everett and Shakespeare with pings and sparks and holes torn in the AC unit.

The chopper lifted five, ten, fifteen yards off the concrete. They stopped firing.

It got higher.

As Shakespeare took aim again, SWAT guys finally popped onto the roof through the door like black ghosts — one, two, three, four, five . . . and kept coming. Each set up on one knee, took aim, and fired on the helicopter.

But it was lifting backward at an angle, quickly, quickly.

Their shots were not hitting.

Soon the bird was gone.
And so was Ohio senator Martin Sterling.

38

"You go ahead, Jack. I'll be there as soon as I can," Margaret said as she and Jack made their way from his car to the emergency room.

"I'm not going without you." Jack realized he should have dropped her off at the door. He had her by the arm, walking as fast as he could, but she was shuffling slowly.

"Please go." Margaret stopped and faced him. "I mean it. Pam needs you. I'll find you. I'm a big girl."

Jack didn't want to leave her. She was feeble, and her short-term memory wasn't great. But they were fifty feet from the sliding doors leading to the emergency room, and other people were coming and going. Help was all around if she needed it.

"Okay, I'll go," he said. "Ask for us when you get inside." He gave her a squeeze and ran for the entrance.

The waiting room was lined with blue

plastic chairs packed with people of all ages, races, and genders. A man and woman were in front of him at the desk.

"Excuse me." He approached to their left and put a hand on the counter. "I'm looking for Pamela Crittendon. She was just brought in — having a baby."

"And you are?" said the skinny, gum-chewing receptionist.

"Her husband. Jack Crittendon."

The short couple he'd interrupted gave him a frustrated look and mumbled something.

The receptionist pointed with the clipboard in her hand. "Go halfway down and hang a right. She's in surgery."

"Surgery? Don't you mean labor and delivery?"

"No, surgery, sir."

"Why, what's wrong?"

"She needed a C-section."

"C-section?" Jack was flabbergasted. He scanned the hallway for Margaret but didn't see her. He interrupted the woman at the desk again. "My mother-in-law, Margaret Wagner, is coming in. Will you let her know where we are?"

She closed her eyes and gave a nod. "I'll try my best."

"Thank you." He took off down the hallway, made a right, and found the swinging doors leading to surgery. An Authorized Personnel Only sign was posted on the door, but there was no one to ask, so Jack pushed open the door and walked in.

The large white room smelled like rubbing alcohol and bustled with activity. At the oval counter in the center, nurses in dark-blue scrubs were talking to doctors wearing white coats. A muted TV up in the corner showed the crowd and emergency vehicles outside the arena.

A male nurse with bright-orange hair, standing at the water cooler, noticed him. "I'm sorry, sir. This is hospital personnel only."

"My wife's here. Pamela Crittendon. She's having a C-section. I just got here."

The nurse finished his water, dropped the cup in the trash, and approached Jack. "She's in D, this way. I'm Freddie, by the way." He walked around the nurses' station.

Jack followed, worrying Margaret would never find them.

"The team that brought your wife in was on the ball." Freddie didn't look back as he walked silently in his yellow Nikes. "They noticed the baby's heart rate wasn't what it should be and called ahead so we'd be ready."

"What does that mean, about the heart rate? Is something wrong?"

"Probably nothing serious. The baby might have been experiencing some distress —"

That's an understatement.

"It's early. The baby's early by a month," Jack said.

"Okay, well, that's another reason it's good they got your wife right in. Best to get the baby out and get it cranked up. Is it a boy or girl?" The redhead smiled.

He didn't seem overly concerned, so Jack breathed a sigh of relief. "We don't know," he said.

"Okay, just wait here a sec." Freddie entered the scuffed double doors marked with a black *D.* Jack spotted a nurse with gloves and a mask on unfolding a light-blue blanket, and several other people walking about, but that was all he could see. None of them looked as if they were in any rush or as if anything serious was happening.

He didn't hear a baby crying.

Had they done the C-section yet?

He was so nervous he had chills.

"God, please, please take care of Pam and the baby," he whispered. "Let this go smoothly. Let them be fine . . ."

He looked back at the TV in the nurses'

station. It didn't look as if the bombs had exploded. He wondered how Shakespeare was and where on earth Zaher could have gone with Sterling and Lester. They had nowhere to go.

Suddenly Jack's mind rewound to the sulfury smell of gunpowder and the recoil of the gun in his hands and the masked man crumpling to the ground. Had the man died? Jack couldn't believe he might have committed murder.

On the way to the hospital he'd gotten a call from an agitated federal investigator who was beside himself that Jack and Margaret had left the arena before being interrogated. Jack explained they were in the middle of having a baby, and the man insisted they meet for an interview as early as possible the next day.

Jack scanned the busy room. There was no sign of Margaret yet. He hoped she wasn't lost.

How were he and Pam ever going to pay for all this?

But really, none of that mattered. All that mattered was that Pam and the baby were okay. If they had to take out a loan or borrow from Margaret, so be it. His heart sparked for a moment when he remembered the prospect of becoming an editor at the

Gazette. But just as quickly he deflated as it dawned on him that if anything happened to Martin Sterling, there would be no job for him at Derrick's paper.

One of the doors swung toward him.

Freddie came out, followed by a pale-faced doctor with a spotty, brown beard.

"Mr. Crittendon, this is Dr. Shapiro," Freddie said. "He did the C-section, and he's going to fill you in —"

"It's done? Where's the baby?" Jack looked beyond them toward the swinging doors. "Is it a boy or a girl?" He reached for the door.

Shapiro took a step in front of the door and shifted the white mask from his mouth to the top of his balding head. "It's a boy, Mr. Crittendon, and your wife is fine."

"I've got to take off." Freddie touched Jack's shoulder. "Congratulations."

"Thank you. Thank you very much."

"Mr. Crittendon." Shapiro snapped off his rubber gloves. "Your baby's one-minute Apgar was a three, which is quite low, so he's getting a little extra attention in progressive care right now."

Jack flushed. The baby had been whisked away from Pam? How normal was that?

"Is that like intensive care?" Jack said.

"A step down from ICU," Shapiro said.

Jack felt suddenly weak; his forehead broke out in sweat. "The Apgar is what again?" He'd heard of it when the girls were born, but it had never been an issue.

"It was a three out of ten."

"And what's the Apgar again?"

"It's a quick test done one minute after birth to determine how well the baby tolerated the delivery," Shapiro said soberly. He looked at his watch. "They will have done another at five minutes. We'll see how that went."

"Was he breathing okay? I mean, was he getting enough oxygen and everything?"

"He was having a little bit of difficulty. His extremities were a bit blue, and his response to stimulation and muscle tone were somewhat flat. But really, Mr. Crittendon, it's very early."

Flat?

All Jack could picture was a limp, white baby with something very wrong. He could hardly breathe. "Where is he now?"

"They will be doting on him in progressive care, I can assure you," Shapiro said. "Let's get you and Pamela into a private room and let you see your baby as soon as possible. How does that sound? In the meantime, go on in and see your wife." Shapiro stepped aside and lifted a hand toward the door.

"Is there any more you can tell me?" Jack pleaded. "Anything wrong that you're aware of?"

The doctor blinked and shook his head. "Not at this point. Just know that some babies take a bit longer to get used to the real world than others. He may've had some fluid in his lungs. They'll clear that out, give him oxygen if he needs it, maybe some physical stimulation to get his heart clicking at a healthy rate. We hope to see the five-minute Apgar rise significantly. Let's give it another look in a few minutes, shall we?"

But all that work sounded so *abnormal.*

Pam had gotten to hold Rebecca and Faye right after they were born. They had photos . . .

Okay, he needed to see Pam.

"Thank you, Doctor," he said. "Just please let us know as soon as possible."

"We will indeed."

"Where is progressive care?"

"It's just adjacent to us here." He pointed. "Your private room will be close to it."

"Okay. Thank you again."

They parted ways, and Jack went through the double doors.

"There you are," Pam said, lying on the operating table, shivering beneath a bunch of blankets. Her face was pale, but she'd put on lipstick. Her blonde hair was dark around the edges from sweat. Lucy sat in a chair pulled right up close to her. "Where's Mom?" Pam looked past him.

"She's coming." Although she should have been there by now. "I've been talking to Dr. Shapiro. How are you? Are you okay?"

"What did he say?" She held both arms out to him. "Is the baby okay? Just tell me he's okay, Jack. Right now. Tell me he's fine . . ."

39

Derrick cursed himself again for his blunder. Just minutes after he'd left the arena with Jack and Pam, he realized he had made a terrible mistake by walking out of the building — they would never allow him back in. Now he and Daniel were packed like sardines at a metal barricade along with every other journalist and cameraman in Ohio, and more from news sources across the nation, who were descending on the arena like vultures.

There was a chill in the air, and emergency spotlights lit up the night. Police were bustling around beyond the barricade, setting up a table and podium, running wires and cables and a gazillion microphones for the press conference that was supposed to have begun twenty minutes earlier.

The second Derrick had left Jack and Pam, a nearby paramedic flagged him down. She'd spotted the blood that had soaked through his shirt and insisted on treating him. The bullet had taken a small chunk of skin from his waist but had not lodged. The paramedic doused the wound with something that stung like alcohol, then bandaged and taped it nicely, but he was protecting it with his arm, afraid it was going to get nudged amid the elbowing crowd of reporters.

His phone vibrated — a text from Zenia. She was still on pins and needles, even though he'd assured her when he got out that he was fine. He wanted to call her, but he'd never be able to hear her in that crowd. And if he stepped aside to get away from the noise, he would lose his place. He shot her a quick reply and said he'd call as soon as he could.

Suddenly two doors opened at the front of the arena, which looked like a movie set with all the broken glass and smoke still wafting in the breezy night air. Electronic flashes fired like strobe lights. Large media lights popped on throughout the crowd, flooding the scene in blinding white.

A white-haired man in a dark, baggy suit led the way. Behind him came Lieutenant Wolfski, Phil Hedgwick, and Reese Jenkins. They filed up to the podium; the white-haired guy took center stage. Also coming through the glass doors — but stationing themselves well back from the podium — were Keefer O'Dell and Clarissa Dracone, who was white as a sheet.

"My name is Rufus Peek, special agent, FBI. I'm sorry to keep you waiting, but we needed to get our facts in order for you." Peek put on reading glasses, checked his notes, and introduced each of the men behind him. "Earlier today, Homeland Security learned of a possible terrorist threat here at Columbus Festival Arena. As you know, Ohio senator Martin Sterling was scheduled to appear for a campaign rally, along with recording artist Everett Lester —"

"Have Lester and Sterling been kidnapped?" yelled a reporter.

"Is Everett dead?" asked another.

"How many civilians are dead?"

"Tell us about the bombs!"

"If you will . . . if you will, *please.*" Peek held up both hands and patted the air. "I'm going to start from the beginning and get to where we are now, but you are going to have to be quiet. Please. This is difficult enough. I will give you all the information I have, but please don't bark out questions. I will not answer them.

"Before the show began, local police and

296

SWAT teams were called in because of the threat," Peek continued. "At that point, Homeland told arena officials there was a 38.8 percent chance the threat was real —"

"Why didn't they cancel right then?" a reporter shouted, and others chimed in.

"However" — Peek scowled — "due to traffic problems, only a small SWAT team was able to assemble inside the venue before the events started unfolding." Peek sighed and looked down at his notes. The special agent was thin, probably sixty-five, with sunken, red-ringed eyes and a hint of gray stubble on his gaunt face. He didn't look healthy and probably could well have done without a case of this magnitude so close to what was likely his approaching retirement.

"Doors were scheduled to open at six thirty p.m., but due to the threat, the opening was delayed. However, there was some confusion among arena staff, and the doors *did* open for a brief time, letting in hundreds of people before the doors were closed again."

Reporters shouted questions, and camera motors zinged. Peek held up a hand and bounced on his toes.

"At that time members of a terrorist group, led by a man calling himself Shareek Zaher, took over the main entrance of the arena by surprising and subduing SWAT forces. This was followed by the deployment of smoke bombs or tear gas at various points around the perimeter of the facility in an effort to get people inside to the seating and performance area.

"We believe Zaher had a team of some seventeen to twenty-one hostiles in the building and that they likely embedded themselves in the facility the night before, following a sporting event here." The crowd erupted, but he continued to speak above the noise. "All of the terrorists were masked and armed. They took over all entry points and the stage, eventually holding Senator Sterling and Everett Lester hostage, along with employees of the arena and its security company."

One reporter yelled a question about the bombs, another about Sterling's whereabouts. Peek frowned, took a deep breath, and moved forward with his statement.

"We do not know what the group's motives were," Peek said. "They obviously intended to stir up terror. They took two security people hostage, strapped them with fake bombs, and lowered them by rope, upside down, over the crowd from walkways that cross over the top of the arena —"

It was bedlam. Derrick could barely hear

Peek, but the agent kept going.

"Fortunately . . . fortunately, those two men are fine. A bomb squad got them down and took precautionary measures, but as I said, those bombs were bogus. They were a combination of wires, duct tape, and emergency road flares. Those employees are still being questioned. Now . . ."

Any delay, and the reporters were all over him.

Peek's hands shook as he turned over the top page of his notes.

"Thanks to the heroics of some very brave men and women, this situation turned out much better than it could have. Several arena and EventPros employees, as well as Senator Sterling's personal bodyguards, were able to take up arms and confront Zaher and his men, and nine of them died here tonight. I repeat, nine of the insurgents were killed by gunfire."

The questions came like a colony of bats . . .

"Who killed them?"

"Where did they get the weapons?"

"Where are Lester and Sterling now?"

"What about Lester's wife and son?"

"How many civilians are dead?"

Peek pursed his lips and shook his head. Then he began talking very softly so everyone had to shut up to hear.

"I'm going to finish telling you how things unfolded. Then I'm going to give you an injury report, if you'll let me talk." Peek peered out at the many faces of those hanging on his every word and licked his cracked lips. "Zaher and approximately twelve to sixteen men took the stairs to the roof, where a helicopter met them. They had Everett Lester and Senator Sterling with them at the time and were going to . . . abduct them."

Peek turned aside and coughed, then adjusted his glasses, looking down, waiting for the reporters to calm.

"One of the security staff members, whose name we are withholding right now — he is a former United States Marine — was able to get up to the roof. He used a flash-bang device and fired on the insurgents, killing four of them. The other five died earlier, inside the building."

Shakespeare. *That dude is a beast!*

"At that point Everett Lester was able to escape uninjured. I regret to report that Senator Sterling was taken hostage by Zaher and his remaining men. They left via helicopter. As we speak, we at the FBI, in partnership with state and local agencies, are bringing every force to bear to bring

Senator Sterling back alive and to bring these terrorists to justice."

Peek was pelted with a barrage of questions, but he took his notes in both hands and forged ahead. "I'm going to give you a report on injuries," he said. "Unfortunately, one of Senator Sterling's courageous bodyguards was killed in the line of duty. Two more of Senator Sterling's bodyguards were shot multiple times and are in guarded condition at Mount Sinai Hospital. Names are being withheld at this time. They played a key role in providing gunfire against the terrorists so that the former marine security staff member could continue his quest to save as many people as he could. That former marine, by the way, was wounded but is fine. We have a report that another gentleman, a member of the media, was hit by gunfire but is also going to be fine."

Derrick wondered how they even knew about his wound. No one had interviewed him.

Peek went on to tell about two SWAT team members who'd been knocked out and tied up in the Sky Zone, as well as the civilians who'd been hurt in the stampede when entering the building and were later treated for minor injuries and released.

"Now, if you'll be quiet, I am going to

turn it over to Lieutenant Ed Wolfski with Columbus SWAT . . ."

40

"Jack, you need to go find Mom," Pamela whispered. "She's never going to find us."

It had been at least thirty minutes since the C-section, and they'd just been moved to a private room. Jack was talking to his parents on his cell. Pamela's guardian angel, Lucy, had crept out to see if she could find out any more about the baby.

Jack ended the call and sighed. He squeezed the back of his neck and closed the blinds. "I'll look for her. I'm just . . . I don't want you to be alone. I'm worried about the baby. I mean, why haven't they brought him yet?"

"Lucy'll be back soon. I'm fine."

"How 'bout some juice or crushed ice? What can I get you?"

"Just find Mom. I'm worried about her."

They exchanged tentative smiles.

Pamela wasn't about to tell him how worried she was about the baby, whose little body and face had been alarmingly blue. And there'd been no crying, no grimacing. The little guy had been so sluggish. Jack would have freaked out. That was why God had sent Lucy in his place.

But even Lucy's steady brown eyes had widened at the sight of the baby. And among the nurses it had been all business — there'd been no laughter or joking around, no letting mom hold the newborn.

No.

None of that.

"Okay, you call my cell the second you hear anything." Jack set the hospital phone next to her on the bed and pulled the covers up tight around her neck. "It's all going to be okay, no matter what." He started to go. "I'll try to find you some hot tea. Does that sound good?"

She nodded, then was suddenly overcome by emotion. She lurched up and reached for him. Jack came back, and she hugged him and buried her head against his chest. She was certain he had no idea that low Apgar scores, especially after five minutes, could indicate cerebral palsy.

"It's okay, baby. It's gonna be okay," he said. He patted her back, about to go, but she held on — tightly.

"Pam, honey, we're gonna be fine." Jack

held her close. "Whatever comes, we'll manage, like we always do."

She hadn't felt this close to him in months. She knew he was worried about their financial situation, all the bills. Yet he was hanging in there. He was strong. She needed that. But the truth was . . .

Oh dear . . .

She wept as they held each other.

The baby's brain might be impaired, his muscle coordination forever out of sync.

And it was possibly *her* fault.

She couldn't look at Jack.

She'd kept it hidden, assuring herself it had been nothing — just a slip.

It was several months ago, stepping off the curb outside the nail salon; she'd twisted an ankle and gone down.

She'd laughed as she helped herself up and went on her way.

But that night, she'd googled "falls during pregnancy" and read all kinds of horror stories.

And now her face burned with the memory of it, the guilt.

"Oh my gosh." She sat up. "Jack, get me a trash can. I think I'm going to be sick."

41

Shakespeare was worn out after rehashing the night's events again, this time with FBI special agent Rufus Peek and three of his men, who'd just filed out of the FBI's makeshift interrogation room in the bowels of the arena.

The room was small and cold, with glossy, white cinder-block walls and dark-maroon carpet. There were two more just like it next door, where others were being questioned, everyone from Everett and Karen to Event-Pros and civilians. They'd also pulled Derrick back inside for questioning and were going to need to talk to Margaret, Jack, Pam, and Lucy as soon as possible.

Peek turned off the video cam, pulled his plastic chair close to Shakespeare's, and plunked down with a huff. The man was rail thin with a baggy white shirt that ballooned out the sides of his tight gray suspenders. Shakespeare wondered if he was fighting cancer or something; his face had a ghostly yellowish tone, and he had a pack of Camels stuffed in his shirt pocket.

"How's the arm?" Peek said.

"Fine." Shakespeare looked down at the clean white gauze and tape the EMTs had applied to his upper left bicep after cutting his sleeve away. "Better than I thought it'd be by now. Must be the Tylenol; they gave me a triple dose."

Peek shook his head. "It's a darn good thing you had that bag with you. What'd you call it?"

"Get Home Bag."

"You saved lives — a lot of lives."

"I can't believe we didn't have choppers up there," Shakespeare said. "We could have taken them all."

Peek raised his gray eyebrows. "Believe me, the press isn't going to let that die. There was a miscommunication between Wolfski and Hedgwick."

"To say the least."

"Fortunately there were two TV choppers nearby. One followed them a little ways, until they took gunfire. We'll find them."

"Which direction were they going?"

"East."

Shakespeare's phone vibrated, and he checked it. Sheena, wanting an update. That reminded him that he needed to contact Jack to see if they'd had the baby. Maybe something good could still come out of this day.

"What've you found out about the bad guys?" Shakespeare said.

"The corpses have been transported to Columbus Medical Center and officially pronounced dead." Peek checked his phone as he spoke. "Now the medical examiner determines cause of death. Once that's done we'll be able to find out who they were."

"Why the fake bombs?" Shakespeare couldn't get it out of his head.

Peek blew his nose into a white handkerchief, stuffed it into his pants pocket, and leaned forward, resting his elbows on his knees. "I have no idea, but the bottom line is they wanted Sterling out of the picture."

"Out of the race."

Peek nodded. "What the rest of it was, who knows? Who thinks like these people? We'll find out. We've got a team from Homeland down the hall, reviewing every photo and video taken by anyone who captured anything tonight. They're scouring every lead. Even just that one name you heard, Franco — that'll lead to something."

"Why would they want Everett Lester?"

Peek looked down and shook his head.

"Not sure. He wasn't their main objective."

Peek's phone buzzed. While he took the call, Shakespeare got his phone out and texted Jack.

Well do we have a baby yet?

"That was one of my men over at Mount Sinai Hospital," Peek said. "One of Sterling's bodyguards is out of ICU; he's gonna make it. The other's still touch and go." He stood, reached for his pack of smokes, and threw his head toward the door. "You want to get some fresh air?"

Shakespeare stood. "Sounds good." He needed a breath of cool night air — though he didn't know how fresh it would be with a Camel burning next to him. But he liked Peek and felt he'd built a rapport with him.

As they went through the door and down the hallway, Shakespeare thought about Sheena. Maybe tonight's events would show her he wasn't crazy. Regardless, she needed to be treated like a lady. He needed to give her more attention, more care. Maybe now they could find a happy medium. He needed to lighten up on the survivalist stuff. Jack had helped him see that it had become more than a hobby; it was an obsession. If he stopped doing everything right now, he would still be more prepared than 99 percent of Americans.

Peek led them around a corner and toward an exit he'd obviously frequented before. He acknowledged a tall officer standing at a side door. "We're catching some fresh air. Back in five."

Peek pushed his way outside, and Shakespeare followed.

Oddly, instead of making Shakespeare want to pursue more survivalist tactics, the night's attack had made him melancholy. It had been sobering. He'd stared his mortality in the face. He felt extremely humbled, as if he might want to clear the house of all that junk and live more simply, live for each moment with his family.

When this was over, he and Sheena were going to meet with Jack and Pam. That guy had something Shakespeare had never found in all his years of travel, reading, learning, or fighting in combat. It was peace. Contentment. Knowing that even when trials came, everything was ultimately going to be okay.

"Cigarette?" Peek extended the pack to Shakespeare.

Shakespeare shook his head. "Do I look like a smoker?"

"Never know." The old guy flipped a

Camel into the corner of his mouth, cupped his hands around a lighter to block the breeze, flicked it several times, and took an enormous drag, making the tip glow. He looked at it and sighed as he exhaled.

"This country's going to the dogs." Peek turned his back, took several steps, and stretched. "Can't imagine what it'll be like in ten years, five even. I won't be around for it, glad to say."

"You hanging up your badge?" Shakespeare took a seat on a bench next to the sidewalk.

"Later rather than sooner." Peek turned to face him. "I need to work as long as I can. Need the insurance. My wife's been sick."

Maybe that explained his gaunt appearance. Shakespeare felt bad for the guy, who was getting run ragged at work and probably at home, too.

"Sorry to hear that."

Peek sucked on that cigarette as if he were siphoning water from a hose. He exhaled through his nose and mouth as he spoke. "The day I dread is when these nut jobs start blowing themselves to pieces along with our citizens on buses and subways. You know. You see what's coming."

Suddenly Shakespeare was overcome by a

haunting homesick feeling, and he longed to be with Sheena and the children. "How much longer do you need me to stick around?" he said.

Peek held the Camel between the very tips of two fingers and checked his watch. "Once we start ID'ing these creeps and finding who they're associated with, we're gonna need you to pore over mug shots and video clips of suspects to find Zaher — or whoever he is — and the other hostiles at large."

"They all had masks on, you know. I told you that."

"Yes, but we have archives — tons of videos and images of the world's most notorious terrorists. You might recognize someone even by their mannerisms."

Peek stood, took one last giant drag on his cigarette, dropped it, and mashed it with his black shoe. "You ready to head back in?"

Did he think that cigarette butt was going to disintegrate?

"I'll be there in a minute." Shakespeare needed to talk to Sheena. "I've got a few calls to make."

"I'll see if there's some coffee around." Peek headed back toward the door.

Shakespeare's phone vibrated just as he was reaching for it. A text message from Jack.

It's a boy. Had c-section. There r complications. Please pray.

Whoa.
Complications?

Shakespeare was immediately transported back to when he and Sheena found out one of their two boys, Will, was diagnosed with autism. Then the same thing happened with their next one, Tyler. The anguish. The fear. The troubling powerlessness. It was something no one could ever understand or comprehend until they went through it.

Peek's phone rang as he was going back inside. He stopped, turned around, and took the call.

Shakespeare read the message from Jack again. Complications with the baby or with Pam?

He'd asked Shakespeare to pray.

Now that was a true friend. Jack knew Shakespeare wasn't some fanatic Christian, in church every time the doors opened, but he'd thought enough of him to request his prayers.

Peek covered one ear and clamped the phone to his head with the other. He glanced at Shakespeare, then back to the building, and barked a question.

"God . . ." Shakespeare looked up at the

night sky. "Whatever's wrong with the baby or Pam, please, let it all be okay," he whispered. "As I look up to you right this second, please look down on them and heal."

Peek clapped his phone shut, grabbed the door, and looked back at Shakespeare. "They found the chopper — Sterling's alive!"

42

Jack closed the door to Pam's hospital room and stood with his back to it, his hand still on the handle, trying to catch his breath and keep himself composed. Pam had just confessed she'd stumbled off a curb during her pregnancy but hadn't told him.

The nurses hadn't brought the baby back.

No doctors had returned.

His mind fizzled to gray.

Too much . . .

He needed to find something to eat, some fruit or protein — *and* his lost mother-in-law. Where could she possibly be?

He headed toward the nurses' station and slowed when he saw Lucy walking toward him. She was on her phone, and when they made eye contact she turned and walked to the wall, where she stopped with her back to him. Looking down as if trying to concentrate, she covered her free ear. "Stop. Just stop, okay? This is insane. I told you the truth." She lowered her voice. "No, don't. Don't. Please . . . I've told you . . . You're going to make a fool of yourself —"

Suddenly the conversation must've ended, because she lifted her head and just stood there with her back to Jack. The hand holding the phone dropped to her side. She set her narrow shoulders back, took in an audible breath, slipped the phone into her pocket, and turned around.

"Hey." She forced a smile.

Jack approached, trying to act as if he hadn't heard anything. "Hey," he said. "Everything okay?"

She nodded and took in another giant breath.

"You sure?"

Her sunken eyes closed, and she repeated the nod. "Yeah."

"What's happening? Did you find out anything?"

"They didn't let me see the baby," she said. "Dr. Shapiro is supposed to come talk to you and Pam."

"What's happening? Did they tell you anything?"

She looked down and rubbed her forehead, as if she was struggling with something. "They had to do some physical stimulation to get his heart beating at a healthy clip. He's on oxygen now. The doctor is going to come talk to you and Pam —"

Jack was suddenly sweating . . . light-headed.

"What was the second Apgar? Because the first was three, and that's 'critically low.' I looked it up on my phone." Jack's ears were ringing from the stress.

"The five-minute Apgar was a four." She stared at him, her head tilting as if she wanted to encourage him but had nothing good to offer.

"Four?" Jack said. "Seven to ten is normal. Is there something wrong? Did they say he's . . . he's . . . are there serious problems? Talk to me, Lucy."

He felt as if he were on a merry-go-round spinning out of control.

"Jack, they have him in progressive care. They are watching him very closely." She took his elbow and led him to a bench in the hallway. "Sit down. You're pale."

They sat. Lucy still had his elbow. He just stared at her, seeing little white dots float in and out of his vision.

"The second low Apgar does not mean he's going to have serious long-term health issues. It can't predict the baby's future health —"

"Cerebral palsy," Jack blurted. "I saw it online."

She shook her head emphatically. "Those are rare conditions. You're getting way ahead of yourself. Don't do that. This hospital has one of the best progressive-care units in the region. We're in good hands —"

"Pam just told me she fell. Did you know that? A few months ago. Off a curb. I read that a low Apgar could indicate that the infant's brain was hurt during pregnancy."

She ignored his words, dug in her purse, and handed him an apple. "Eat this and stop doing this to yourself. I just came from progressive care, and they assured me the baby's heart is going good, he's breathing okay —"

"With oxygen, you said . . ."

"I don't know the details!" Lucy said, losing her composure for the first time. "They wouldn't let me in to see him. We need to be calm and wait, and you need to be strong for Pam."

"All I know is that a lack of oxygen during birth is one of the causes of cerebral palsy. Also, if the baby's brain was hurt during the fall, that could affect his muscle coordination. From what I heard, he wasn't moving much when he came out, was he?

Tell me what he was like when he came out."

"No, Jack." She stood and slung her purse over her shoulder. "You need to eat that apple and find Pam's mom. That's all you need to do right now. One step at a time. We are not going to fret about things that haven't happened yet. I'll see you back at the room." She started to go, then turned back. "And when you get there, I hope you're in a better mind-set for Pam." She looked at her watch. "I'm not sure how much longer I can stay." She began to leave.

Jack took a deep breath and bit into the apple, feeling like a jerk. "Thanks for the apple," he called. Lucy waved but didn't look back. He needed to take her advice, pull it together.

He got up and headed for the elevator, figuring he would retrace his steps — go back down to the emergency room and even back to the parking lot, where he'd left Margaret, if he had to.

His baby boy was in progressive care. He felt as if he were dreaming, as if he hadn't slept in days. *What is this going to mean?* The poor kid could be in a wheelchair or in those metal walking braces his entire life. Jack imagined Rebecca and Faye dressing him, feeding him. Pam wouldn't be able to work; she'd need to be home with him. But that was impossible because they needed her insurance. She would have to keep working. He would need to be home with the boy.

He was so blasted mad. Why hadn't he landed a decent job by now? God saw what was happening. And here he was a part-time usher, of all things. He felt like a failure. How would they ever pay for this hospital stay? And the costs that lay beyond? It would require tens of thousands of dollars.

He wiped the sweat from his forehead as he got on the elevator, ignoring two nurses in light-blue scrubs who were also going down. He and Pam would never be able to retire. They would always be caregivers — the rest of their lives. He immediately felt selfish for thinking such a thing, but he was human. Didn't all couples look forward to rekindling the romance as empty nesters?

The elevator doors opened. He motioned for the nurses to go first, and he followed them into the bustling lobby. He walked around the circular information area, scanning the long, windowed room for Margaret. She'd been wearing a navy jacket and beige pants. People of all ages and ethnicities stood and sat and paced.

He walked over to a crowded seating area

to check the faces and make sure he hadn't missed her. A large TV mounted high in the corner broadcast Fox News and its live coverage outside the arena, where flashing lights lit up hundreds of people standing along a yellow line of tape, with law-enforcement personnel running to and fro. Jack read the text scrolling across the bottom of the screen:

. . . Ohio Sen. Martin Sterling and recording artist Everett Lester were abducted by terrorists and taken to the rooftop of Columbus Festival Arena . . . Lester was able to elude his captors, but Sen. Sterling was taken away via helicopter . . .

Derrick and Daniel were likely right in the thick of things, covering the unfolding story for the *Columbus Gazette.* Jack couldn't believe Sterling had been snatched, and he could only imagine what they might do to him.

If they did kill him, there would be no job for Jack at the *Gazette.* Another sickeningly selfish thought, Jack knew, but this was his reality — he *needed* a decent job.

He was about to leave when the words BREAKING NEWS appeared on the screen. He crossed to the TV until he was standing beneath it, so he could hear the anchorperson. "Fox reporters are working on some extraordinary breaking news in the terrorist attack at Columbus Festival Arena. Details in six minutes . . ."

Jack didn't have six minutes. He had to find Margaret and get back upstairs. He knew the direction of the emergency room and headed toward it, down a long, windowed hallway with a polished green tile floor.

He examined each person in the blue plastic chairs that lined the hall leading to the nurses' station. No Margaret. He got to the desk. The same skinny, gum-chewing receptionist was there. Great.

"Excuse me, I'm looking for my mother-in-law, Margaret —"

"She's over there." The woman nodded toward the far windows. "She keeps asking to see her husband. She thinks he's a patient."

Jack's countenance fell.

Margaret stood slightly hunched over, jacket over her shoulders, arms crossed as she stared into the night.

"I told her your wife was having a C-section." The receptionist shook her head. "It didn't seem to register with her. She insists we're keeping something from her about her husband's condition. She says he had a heart attack, and she wants to see him . . ."

43

Derrick flew over the hilly Ohio countryside, well above the speed limit. His heart pounded in his skull from the rush of being ahead of the other news agencies that were surely not far behind. He was being pushed forward by an adrenaline high, like a surfer who'd caught a monster wave and left the others bobbing in the wake.

Daniel rattled around in the backseat of the FJ Cruiser, his cameras and lenses spread out everywhere as he prepared for the biggest story of their lives — the biggest story in the world at the moment.

For the fifth or sixth time, as he concentrated on the country road unfurling before him in the night, Derrick replayed the call he'd received twenty minutes earlier from Senator Sterling's personal assistant.

"Derrick . . . Jenny King. Don't ask questions, I don't have time." She was distraught yet concise. "The senator is alive. I don't have details, but somehow he escaped."

"Where is he?"

"Seneca Falls. He flagged down a driver on I-24 right by Indian Lake. He called nine-one-one from the man's cell. He's wounded. I'm on my way."

"How bad is he hurt?"

"No idea. I've told you all I know. I wanted you to have it first."

That was it. She was gone.

Derrick pushed the gas pedal harder, hoping they would make it before police or paramedics whisked Sterling away.

"Are you ready?" He shot a glance back at Daniel, who was hunched over his equipment.

"Almost. How close are we?"

The blue glow of Indian Lake appeared on the GPS.

"Almost there. This is gonna be the shoot of your lifetime."

"And the story of yours."

Derrick squinted at the road ahead, thinking any minute he would see flashing lights and the car Sterling had flagged down.

He'd called Jack earlier and was troubled to hear of the baby's complications. That would add even more stress to the trials they were already facing. But Jack always had a way of taking things in stride. He'd even managed to laugh when he told how Pam's mom had wandered off in the hospital.

Jack's faith was special. He was the only person Derrick knew who actually lived as if this life was temporary, as if the real and important life was yet to come. Derrick had always assumed that someday in the future he would take his faith as seriously as Jack.

"There!" Daniel shouted from the back.

Derrick braked. A black-and-white squad car was parked sideways in the road up ahead, with its blue lights flashing. One officer was setting flares in the road while another had a flashlight out and was examining a dark pickup truck stopped just beyond the police car.

"There're more flashing lights through those trees," Daniel said. "Turn around — we'll find another way in."

Seeing no cars behind or ahead, Derrick did a U-turn into the grass and back onto the road.

"Just watch for any opening." Daniel leaned over the front seat.

They rode along slowly, and Derrick kept checking the rearview mirror to make sure the cops weren't coming after them.

"There." Daniel pointed. "Pull over."

Derrick pulled off into the weeds. They both looked to the right, where a patch of spindly trees and branches were backlit by flashing red and blue lights out in a clearing. There were no sirens.

"There are weeds matted down . . . keep going."

They bumped along off the side of the road.

"Ho!" Daniel said. "There."

Derrick's headlights lit up a path the width of a vehicle. He turned the SUV onto the path, and they rolled and rocked slowly through the spooky, sparsely wooded area. It was eerily silent except for the faint chirp of a police radio every few seconds. Up a slight hill the trees cleared, and they came to an open space the size of a football field.

"Turn off your lights, or they'll be all over us," Daniel said.

Derrick doused the lights, turned right, and rolled over the bumpy meadow off to the side of all the commotion.

"We got one fire truck . . . an ambulance . . . and only two cop cars," Daniel said. "Dang, we're early, dude. This is unreal."

Derrick's heart skipped a beat. "And a helicopter." He nodded toward the edge of the woods where a mammoth black chopper sat like a sleeping mechanical monster, blending in with the backdrop of thick woods behind it. Four other plain cars were parked at various angles nearby.

"Holy cow! Stop right here. I gotta shoot as much as I can before they throw us out. More law'll be here soon."

Derrick stopped and turned the car off.

Several people stood in a loose huddle about ten yards from the ambulance, whose lights were flashing and doors were closed. A spotlight popped on at one of the unmarked cars, and its beam of light zigzagged and finally fixed on the helicopter.

"I'm going," Daniel said. "I'll start shooting from here and work my way in."

"Hopefully Sterling's in the ambulance." Derrick opened his door, grabbed his pad, pen, and recorder, and got out. The pain from his side took his breath away.

"You okay?" Daniel said.

Derrick nodded. "I'll try to find Jenny. Good luck, dude."

"Good luck." Daniel scampered across the meadow with one mammoth camera hanging around his neck and his heavy bag of equipment over his shoulder.

Derrick tripped on the thick, knotty grass but caught his balance.

Police officers and firefighters hustled every whichway, shining powerful flashlights throughout the grassy area, around the chopper, and toward what Derrick guessed was another way out.

Two officers were unwinding yellow crime-scene tape and yelling back and forth about which area to cordon off first. Derrick heard a siren in the distance and moved at a faster clip through the thick grass.

"Hold it!" An officer he hadn't noticed broke toward him from the left, drawing his gun as he ran over the uneven pasture. "Stop right there! Hands high. Hands high!"

Derrick's heart lurched, and he jabbed his hands into the air, not dropping his things. "It's okay, I'm —"

"Hands stay high." The officer's gun was locked in front of him with both hands as he took long strides toward Derrick.

"I'm with the *Gazette*," Derrick blurted.

"Down on your face, now. Drop that stuff. Hands behind your back."

Derrick dropped to his knees and glanced back for Daniel but didn't see him.

"I cover Sterling for the *Gazette*. Is he still here?"

"Do what I said. Facedown. Hands behind your back. *Now!*"

44

Lucy and the nurses kept telling Pamela to get some sleep, but there was no way. She was worried about the baby and about her missing mom, and she still couldn't stop shivering, even though they'd brought her warm blankets.

"Eat more of this banana," Lucy said from the chair next to her bed. "You've got to keep your strength up."

Pamela took a piece.

Lucy gave her a napkin, then leaned her forward and puffed up her pillow.

"I can't believe we still haven't named him," Pamela said.

"Well, it hasn't exactly been your typical delivery," Lucy replied.

"We wanted to wait and see what the baby was like." Pamela drifted off for a second as she recalled how sluggish the baby had been, how bluish his little body was. Weeks ago she and Jack had narrowed boy names to Lukas, which meant *light,* and Andrew, which meant *brave.* She was sure one of the names would make sense soon enough.

There was a light knock, and the door to the room opened. It startled Lucy, who stood quickly.

"Hello, hello." Jack quietly led Margaret into the room. "Look who's here."

Margaret came toward Pamela's bed, shaking her head shyly, her eyes watering. "I'm sorry I wasn't here for you, sweetie. It was my fault."

"What happened to you?" Pamela said. "Did you get lost?"

Margaret started to answer, but Jack cut in. "She was down in the emergency room," he said. "It was confusing. You were in ER, then surgery, then you got moved up here . . ."

"Mom, I'm sorry," Pamela said. "Sit down. You must be hungry."

"I'm not hungry," Margaret said. "I guess I should've stayed with Jack in the first place. I've got to learn I can't do what I used to."

"Well, sit down now and relax."

Jack pulled a chair over for her, but she walked to the sink, poured herself a cup of ice water from the tan plastic pitcher, and just stood there, staring at the sink.

When her back was to them, Jack shot Pamela a wide-eyed wince, as if Margaret had done something embarrassing or even dangerous while they were apart.

Pamela let her head drop back onto the pillow and again tried to assure herself that they would get through this ordeal.

"Has the doctor been here?" Jack said.

She shook her head no.

"Have you had the news on at all?" he said.

She shook her head again. "I just wanted quiet."

He nodded. "It was on downstairs, and they said there was some kind of breaking news coming."

"Turn it on if you want," she said, but she wished he wouldn't.

Just then the door opened slightly, and Dr. Shapiro stuck his balding head in. "May I come in?"

Lucy stood suddenly.

"Yes." Jack shot to attention and went for the door. "Come in."

Dr. Shapiro entered quietly, examining each person. He carried a medical chart on a clipboard. Jack introduced him to Margaret, and they shook hands.

"We are all kidding around down there that the Crittendon baby doesn't have a name yet." Dr. Shapiro smiled. "Some of the nurses have started calling him Baby Critt."

That was supposed to be an icebreaker. Pamela gave a cordial chuckle. "Well, how is he, Doctor? What's going on?"

He folded his arms with the clipboard against his chest. "Well, I'm glad to tell you he's breathing fine on his own now, with a good strong heartbeat." He went up and down on his toes.

Pamela and Jack looked at each other and breathed a sigh of relief.

"His color is good, and his lungs are clear."

Dr. Shapiro had brown eyes that opened wide when he spoke, and he wore old-fashioned gold metal glasses.

"Why haven't they brought him to us yet?" Jack said.

The doctor opened his mouth, scratched a thick brown eyebrow with two fingers, and paused for several seconds. "He's still a bit sluggish . . ."

Sluggish. There was that word again.

"Is he still in progressive care?" Pamela's whole body was rigid.

The doctor took a deep breath and nodded. "Yes, he is."

"What's the problem, Doctor? Please, just

say," Jack said.

"If you will . . . let me explain."

Jack's shoulders slumped, and Pamela felt the wind go out of her sails. Margaret's forehead scrunched up with fret.

"We're still concerned with his muscle tone, his movement, his reaction when stimulated . . ."

No.

All Pamela could envision was her pale, lifeless baby — not moving, not crying, just lying there. She felt she might throw up again.

The color had drained from Jack's face.

"Right now we're doing tests that will tell us more about what's going on with his nervous system, if there's anything unusual. We're stimulating him a little bit and studying his responses —"

"Is there a chance he's disabled?" Jack said. "What are we looking at? What do you think it is?"

Jack was getting really intense, but Pamela couldn't say a word. She didn't think she was even breathing.

"I'm sorry. It's just too early to tell, but as I said, the tests —"

"Did the fall Pam took hurt him?" Jack interrupted.

Dr. Shapiro looked at Jack and then leveled his gaze at Pamela. "We're not certain there are *any* long-term problems at this point. He could come right around and be the loudest one in the nursery. We are working right now to pinpoint what's going on."

"Can we see him?" Margaret said. "Is he awake?"

"Yes, I'd like to feed him if I can," Pamela said.

"Don't worry about his feeding," Dr. Shapiro said. "He's getting plenty of nourishment —"

Lucy's sober expression hadn't changed the entire visit. "But I think she wants to encourage milk production, Doctor," she said, and Pamela gave her a grateful glance.

Dr. Shapiro looked at Pamela and nodded. "I understand. If you'd like, we can have a nurse help you pump until he's . . . until you can feed him. Let's do that. I'll tell —"

"Doctor, is he responding at all?" Jack's arms went out toward the physician in desperation. "I mean, we need to know what we're looking at here."

Margaret and Pamela stared intently. Lucy folded her arms and peeked at her watch.

Jack continued. "I know low Apgars can indicate cerebral palsy or —"

"He is responding, yes, to a degree. He

has been taking formula from a bottle. He's had at least one bowel movement."

"Oh, has he? Good." That relieved Pamela greatly. The more normal, the better. "Has he cried? I mean —"

"Look, can we see him?" Jack shook his head and threw up his hands. "We just need to see him, okay?"

But Pamela wasn't sure she was ready, mentally. She was scared. She wanted to see him when he was healthy and normal — not like this. *That is so wrong.* She *should* want to see him now, regardless. She didn't say anything.

"I'll tell you what," Dr. Shapiro said. "Give us another thirty minutes or so to wrap up the tests we're conducting, and we'll get him ready to see you. How does that sound?" He looked at Pamela. "And you can try to feed him then."

"Good. Okay." Jack sighed. "Thank you for all you're doing."

Jack walked him to the door, where Dr. Shapiro stopped and turned to Jack, looked him dead in the eyes, and said something with a somber expression, out of Pamela's earshot.

When he left and the door closed, Jack just stood there, staring at it for the longest time.

A dreadful, sour feeling twisted Pamela's gut, giving her the distinct impression that their lives were about to change — forever.

45

It was dark, damp, and getting cold. Derrick's face was in the wet grass, and his wound was burning like it was on fire. The cop gruffly cuffed his hands behind his back, got him up, retrieved his things, and pushed him up the slope toward the main activity near the helicopter and ambulance.

Police and firefighters were running around, calling out to one another. Sirens wailed, getting closer.

"Derrick?" Jenny King broke away from the people she was talking to and hurried over, one of her high heels catching in the thick grass. "My gosh, what's going on? Officer, I called him here. He's with the *Gazette.* He covers the senator —"

"I told him that," Derrick said.

The brash cop's wide face was set in stone. "Ma'am, we can't have the media trampling all over a live crime scene."

"He's the only one I called," she said.

"Uncuff him so he can do his job."

"I can't do that, Miss King. We're responsible —"

"Would you rather have Senator Sterling tell you?" she said.

The cop panned the grounds, shook his head, and eyed Derrick. "Lemme see your credentials."

"Around my neck." Derrick nodded down at his chest.

The cop dug inside his jacket and shone his flashlight on the plastic ID. Without a word he spun him around and uncuffed him.

"I don't want to hear a peep out of you," the officer said. "If you're any trouble, you'll spend the evening in my squad car. Here." He handed Derrick his pad and recorder.

Derrick took it and surveyed the situation.

"A thank-you would be in order," the officer said.

Derrick stared at him. "Thank you, Officer."

"Yes, thank you," Jenny said. "Oh, Officer, there will be one reporter coming from WSC-TV, James Jordan. I've promised him access, but that's all. I promise."

The officer's eyes burned into hers like lasers.

"I'm expecting him any minute. Give him access, please."

The cop twirled his little flashlight and stormed off.

Jenny squared up close to Derrick. He smelled coffee on her breath. "The senator's being treated in the ambulance. The hostiles landed the chopper here. Two vans were waiting; no plates."

She checked her small pad of notes. "When they were going from the chopper to the vans, the senator made some kind of move. I don't know the details yet; we'll find out. There was some turmoil between them, and he got free and ran toward I-24." She pointed toward the road Derrick and Daniel had come in on. "They shot him once in the leg. I'm not sure if he has any other injuries."

Jenny nodded toward a burly man in his midforties squatting near the ambulance, holding a Styrofoam cup in his large hands. "That gentleman stopped his pickup when he saw the senator. From there I don't know what happened — yet. Police have questioned him."

"Is Sterling going to make a statement here?" Derrick said.

"We'll see. If so, it'll be brief. He'll be anxious to see his family. We'll do a full press conference tomorrow morning if we can pull it together by then."

Derrick noticed Daniel just over the slope, hiding behind some brush. If the cops saw him there, he'd get them both kicked out. "Jenny, my cameraman's out there." He nodded in Daniel's direction. "Can he come over with me? I don't want to cause any more commotion."

"Derrick, really?" She was annoyed. "You should've told me he was here when we were talking to Officer Grumpy."

Two police cars with blue strobe lights bounced onto the grounds from the far entrance. As they came to a stop, their sirens bleeped to a halt.

"He'd better stick close to you. Tell him no flash. You make me mad, Whittaker."

"Thanks, Jenny." Derrick texted Daniel to come over.

"That's Rufus Peek, FBI special agent in charge," Jenny said.

Derrick recognized the gaunt man from the press conference. He was talking on his phone while telling some cops where to tape off the area and others where to erect tarps and wind blocks. "The rest of you, stay back, stay back." Peek waved his free arm in disgust. "This is all evidence. All of it. Get back. Way back. No one but my investigators in there."

"And you know Hedgwick and Wolfski." Jenny pointed toward the police captain and SWAT chief, who were deep in conversation. Derrick was surprised Peek had even let them in after the way they'd botched the arena event.

Jenny's phone played a funky ring tone. She dug for it, pulled out the pearl-white case, and examined the screen. "I've got to take this. Behave yourselves. Don't make me sorry I called you."

Derrick thanked her again as Daniel approached timidly, like a kid lurking around at a party full of adults.

"Don't use your flash. I'm gonna talk to this guy." Derrick nodded toward Sterling's rescuer, who was still squatting. "Sterling flagged him down for help. Get some shots of him if you can, but be subtle. He doesn't look much like the photogenic type."

Derrick felt this guy would respond better to a pad and pen, so he put the tape recorder in his pocket and approached. "Hey there."

The man barely moved, but his dark eyes shifted upward.

"I'm Derrick Whittaker with the *Gazette*. I understand Senator Sterling flagged you down over here on I-24. Can you tell me about it?"

The man's bottom lip was bulging with snuff. He worked his jaw as if he were chewing taffy, then leaned over the cup and let a long line of spit sink to the cup. "I told the police everything." He wiped his beard with the back of his wrist.

"I could get it from their report, but probably not till tomorrow," Derrick said. "Which way were you going on I-24?"

Without looking up, the man pointed to the right.

"Okay, so you were heading east, and then what happened? Had you seen the helicopter?"

The big man pursed his lips and shook his head. "I didn't see nothin' till he come runnin' out the woods. He caught my eye from the side. I thought it was a deer; there's a lot of them out here. Then he come right out onto the road. You can see my skid marks. I almost hit him."

Derrick looked back out to his truck, where more flashing lights and detectives had arrived, then jotted down some notes.

"What happened then?"

The driver looked down and spit into the cup again. "He was panicked. Said people was after him. He'd been shot, was limpin' pretty bad. I put the truck in park, grabbed my gun, and told him to get down on my side."

"You had a gun with you in the truck?"

"Always."

"What kind?"

"Mossberg 500 pump-action with a fifteen-inch barrel. Twelve gauge."

"A shotgun?" Derrick wrote as fast as he could. It was dark, and his pad was damp, and he wondered if he would even be able to read what he wrote in good light.

"Yeah. By then I'd recognized him —"

"That he was . . ."

"The senator. Martin Sterling. I got out, pushed him down on my side of the truck, and started firin'. My truck's big, ya know, so we had plenty of cover."

"Were they firing at you?"

"At first, but they changed their tune when they heard me blasting back at 'em. I took three shots, and they was good as gone. Cops took my gun, though. That aggravates me."

"Could you see what they did next?"

"They took off out the other side in a couple big vehicles. I couldn't see what kind they was."

"Then what?"

"Cops showed up. Two of 'em seized my truck, my shotgun. Two others brung me up

344

here. You think they'll take my truck?"

"They'll definitely need to look at it closely, probably in daylight. They might have to keep it awhile."

"Of all the . . . I'm supposed to start a new job out in West Jefferson tomorrow."

"What do you do?" Derrick said.

"Welder."

"You live here?"

"Now I do. Spent most of my life in Heath. Typical Ohio country boy."

"What's your name?"

"Ed Scarborough." He spelled the last name for Derrick and gave his age, forty-two.

"Let me ask you, what transpired between the time the bad guys drove away and the cops got here?" Derrick said. "What did you and Sterling do? What was said?"

"Well, we had a look at his wound," Scarborough said. "I tied it off with a clean rag I had in the truck."

"Was there just one wound?"

"Yep."

"And what did he have to say?"

"Not much. He was just about out of juice. I thought he might pass out. Like I said, cops got here lickety-split."

Just then, Derrick noticed Jenny King drop her phone in her bag and head for the back of the ambulance at a good clip. With her was the WSC-TV camera guy, who must've showed up while Derrick was interviewing Scarborough. Special Agent Peek was headed in the same direction, as were Hedgwick and Wolfski.

This was it.

He and the TV guy had a worldwide exclusive.

Derrick's heartbeat surged. He wished Jack could be there.

He thanked Scarborough and signaled for Daniel to get to the back of the ambulance and be ready to shoot.

More sirens were coming from every direction.

The police were stopping cars at both entry points now.

Derrick got out his recorder as he made his way over, his hands trembling as he checked the settings.

Jenny fixed her lipstick, then spruced her hair.

The fact that Sterling — this hard-nosed, fiery presidential hopeful — had survived, had beaten his assailants, generated an electricity in the air the likes of which Derrick had never experienced before.

The door latch sounded.

All heads turned.
And the ambulance doors opened . . .

46

Jack had pulled the blinds and stood staring out the window of Pam's hospital room at the sparsely lit parking lot, the cars, the people coming and going. Most of them were probably worried, hurting, grieving; a few happy — those who'd had successful surgeries and healthy babies. But for the most part, he thought, hospitals weren't the happiest places to be. In fact, no one wanted to be there, except perhaps the doctors and nurses who made their livelihoods there.

In the window's reflection he watched as Pam sat up in bed and Lucy and Margaret spoke quietly, one on each side of her, eating sandwiches he'd picked up in the café. He had no appetite but sipped weak coffee from a dinky Styrofoam cup. He and Pam had just hung up with Rebecca and Faye, who'd stayed up late watching a movie at Tommy and Darlene's house. Thank God they were safe.

What would he and Pam be up against in the days ahead? The years ahead?

Before Dr. Shapiro left the room, he whispered to Jack that he and Pam should prepare themselves mentally for anything. Jack hadn't shared the physician's comment with Pam.

What if down the hall in that progressive-care unit lay a baby boy with special needs? How would they ever manage? Would they need to build ramps and widen doorways, have a special hospital bed and a full-time nurse? Would the child be able to feed himself, bathe, get dressed, walk? What about all the doctors' visits and physical therapy?

How would they pay for it all?

Jack's face burned.

Why did it always come back to *money*?

It infuriated him.

Why hadn't God provided a job for him? It had been almost an entire year!

He needed that editorial position at the *Gazette* desperately.

His stomach churned. The apple Lucy gave him was all he'd eaten in a long time, but he didn't want to eat. He felt like starving himself — whatever it took to understand God's purpose in all of this.

He needed some air — fresh air. On his

way he would find a TV and get the status on Sterling.

"Jack, don't you think you and Pam need to decide on a name?" Margaret said.

He turned around to find all three women staring at him. Pam rolled her eyes without a word.

"I think we're going to wait till we see him, Mom," Jack said. "Right, honey? I mean, who knows, we might want to name him something totally different."

"Oh, but I thought Andrew would be good," Margaret said. "He's been a brave baby so far, to make it through all the tests and the whole thing at the arena."

"That's true. But I think we still want to see him first," Jack said. "Did they say we need to name him within a certain time?"

"Well, they've got to do the paperwork —" Margaret started.

"They can wait," Pam said. "Mom, we'll get to that." She patted her mom's hand.

"You're doing pretty well, aren't you?" Margaret squeezed her hand.

Pam nodded. "I'm feeling okay."

"You know, when I had you, they gave me ether. I wasn't the same for days," Margaret said. "Can you believe that?"

"Ether?" Jack said. "The solvent? No wonder Pam turned out the way she did."

Lucy and Pam chuckled, but Margaret frowned.

"I don't think that's funny, Jack." She shifted in her chair.

"Oh come on, Mom, you know I'm just teasing," Jack said.

"Well, I don't find it humorous."

"Mom, lighten up," Pam said. "We need to laugh. That was a pretty good one."

Jack's phone vibrated. He glanced at the caller ID and answered. "Hey, Brian."

"How's the baby?" Shakespeare said.

"We don't know." Jack caught him up to speed.

"You stay on top of those doctors. Don't let them give you the runaround."

"We will." Jack walked into the hallway. "What's the latest on Sterling?"

"What's the last you heard?"

"That they'd taken him, but I saw there was breaking news — I haven't had time to follow up."

Jack wandered down the hall, bracing himself for the bad news that Sterling had been found dead.

"He escaped."

Shakespeare's words hit Jack like a shot of adrenaline.

"The chopper landed in Seneca Falls. Some vans met them. Somehow Sterling got away. Flagged down a car. He got shot, but from what I hear, he's gonna make it. Don't hold me to that; it's secondhand."

"No way! Where is he now?" Jack's spirit soared.

"Not sure. So maybe you'll get that job after all. Wouldn't that be somethin'?"

"Oh, man. You know it." Jack laughed. He turned back to the room and noticed a slender man in street clothes checking the name on the door to Pam's room. "Hey, I gotta go. Can you give me an update when you know more? Call or text me."

"Roger that. Remember, stay on those doctors. Get answers."

"Will do."

"Hey, and you and Pam are gonna meet with Sheena and me when this is all over, right?"

"Absolutely."

Jack slipped the phone into his pocket and headed toward the room. The man was pushing the door open.

Jack's heart lurched. "Excuse me," he called.

The man leaned back into the hallway and stared at Jack but said nothing, his eyes open wide from behind gold-rimmed glasses that sat halfway down his long nose.

"Can I help you?"

The man waited until Jack got to him. "I'm looking for Lucy," he said.

"Oh, hey," Jack said, relieved. He reached out to shake the man's large, bony hand. "I'm Jack, Pam's husband. You must be Lucy's husband."

The man's brown eyes moved mechanically up and down Jack. "That's right. Victor. Dr. Victor Gambrell. Is Lucy here?"

"Yes, of course. She's been a total godsend."

"I'm sure." Victor nodded and began to enter.

"Hold up." Jack reached for the door handle. "Listen, if you don't mind, my wife's in there, and her mother. Lucy probably told you we just had a baby."

Victor looked at the door handle and back at Jack. "She told me. I've been worried with all that happened at the rally. Is that where you met Lucy for the first time?"

The question threw Jack. It sounded like an interrogation.

"Yeah. Pam started going into labor while we were in the arena. Lucy came to help. She rode with her in the ambulance. She's been amazing."

"Uh-huh." Victor took in a deep breath and set his shoulders back. "Look, if you don't want me to go in, can you tell her I'm here?"

"Sure." Jack got a really bad vibe as he squeezed past Victor to enter the room. "Just a second."

Jack entered the room.

"What'd Shakespeare have to say?" Pam said.

"Sterling's alive. He escaped. He got shot, but they think he's gonna make it."

The women squealed and began asking questions.

"We'll turn the TV on in a minute, but first — Lucy, your husband's here." Jack motioned toward the door.

She shot to her feet, wide-eyed. "Victor? Here?"

In the whole time they'd known Lucy, through all of the trauma at the arena and hospital, Jack hadn't seen her rattled — until that moment.

"Yeah, he's right outside," Jack said.

Her head dropped. She searched the floor, then the room, as if she was suddenly confused.

"Lucy?" Pam said.

Margaret stood and put a hand around her shoulder. "What is it, dear?"

"Nothing, nothing." She snapped out of the fog and gave a chuckle. "It's been a long day. I'm . . . He'll want me to get home. I have to work tomorrow."

The newspaperman in Jack immediately took over. He glanced at the bruises on her arm, her rail-thin frame, her pronounced hip bones protruding beneath her shirt. "Were you expecting him?"

Lucy looked at Jack and froze. Her face was ghostly white — even more so than normal.

"Yeah," she managed. "Yeah . . . I told him I'd pretty much done all I could do. He'll take me back to the arena for my car. Or we'll just wait till tomorrow to get it; it's probably still crazy over there." She scanned the room and crossed to a chair where her purse was hanging. She took the strap with trembling hands and threw it over her shoulder.

"What is taking so long?" Victor barged into the room, muttering, and headed for Lucy like a magnet, not looking at the others. "What's all this business about a presidential rally? I know you. I'm not about to fall for your tricks . . ."

Jack froze in shock, unable to think or move.

Victor's narrow jaw clenched, and he grabbed Lucy by the upper part of her arm. She winced but said nothing. "You'll have

355

to excuse us." He began muscling her toward the door, and she didn't retaliate in the least. "We have a lot of talking to do, don't we, dear?"

Silent alarms clanged in Jack's head.

He had to intervene.

The horror on Margaret's and Pam's faces confirmed something was terribly amiss.

"Let's just hold it a second." Jack stepped directly in front of Victor, blocking the way to the door. "Lucy, what's going on?"

Victor's eyes burned with rage. He formed a claw with his free hand and pounded Jack's chest with all five bony fingers, pressing them hard, pushing him back. "Oh, you do not want to do that, Mr. Crittendon. No, sir."

47

A gust of wind kicked up and raindrops began to fall as the ambulance doors opened. A short, bleached-blonde paramedic wearing navy scrubs and blue surgical gloves jumped out of the back. She nodded to the group with a half smile, then squinted and covered her eyes as the TV guy flipped on his obnoxiously bright camera light.

"Is he going to want that?" Peek said to Jenny King, nodding at the light.

She nodded. "It's okay. We're good. This is going to be quick."

A stocky Hispanic paramedic hopped out next, wearing the same garb, right down to the plastic gloves. He kept his head down and didn't make eye contact with anyone except his female partner. They glanced at each other, nodded, and leaned into the back of the ambulance.

The anticipation was at a fever pitch as

they bumped the stretcher out. On it sat Martin Sterling, wearing a somber expression. He still had on his white dress shirt, which was spotted with blood and dirt. It was unbuttoned to the chest. His tie was loose, and his sleeves were rolled up. His legs were covered with blankets.

The drizzle came harder and was lit up by the cameraman's neon light. Derrick had chills. The paramedics got the stretcher stabilized on the uneven ground and stood on either side of the senator. The woman whispered something to him, to which he nodded.

It was extraordinarily quiet, when this type of scene would usually have been chaotic, with an onslaught of questions from reporters. But since there were only two of them, both present at the invitation of Jenny King, Derrick felt he should simply let the senator say what he was going to say and then possibly ask questions, if it seemed appropriate.

"That rain feels good, doesn't it?" Sterling dropped his head back and opened his mouth, to a smattering of laughter. After a moment he evened his gaze at the faces around him, only a dozen or so people in all.

"I am a lucky man." He paused and nodded, seemingly taken aback with emotion. "Columbus is a lucky city tonight."

There were nods and yeses all around as the rain came harder, tapping at the police ponchos and umbrellas popping up.

"This event . . . what happened tonight at Columbus Festival Arena, is what I have been warning the American people about." Again, an emotional pause. "If this isn't a wake-up call, I sure as heck don't know what is. Let me just say, it was only thanks to the courage and sacrifice of some remarkably brave individuals — US citizens — that there was not much more death, destruction, and bloodshed in our fair city tonight. Thank God. I will be recognizing those people in the days ahead."

Derrick was getting antsy, wondering if Sterling was going to say anything about how he had escaped. That's what his readers would want to know.

"How could this happen on American soil? In the land of the free?" Sterling looked directly into the camera. "You want to know how? Ask your president! Ask him about the protocols and agencies and intelligence he has *slashed*. Ask him about the Homeland initiatives and security forces he has *cut*."

Sterling dropped his head and combed a

hand through his drenched, messy hair. After about fifteen seconds he looked up.

"The United States of America *must* awaken from its slumber. We used to be the most powerful force in the world, but not anymore — not under this administration. No matter what this president says, he has let us down. And we're going to change all that next November.

"We don't have to put up with this unbridled hatred and terror. We shouldn't have to be afraid to go to a campaign rally or a concert or a ball game. We can snuff these terrorists out." Sterling shook a fist, and the veins in his neck protruded. "But it must become our number one priority and not some bottom-of-the-list agenda item we continue to butcher so we can spend more on giving handouts to people who are too lazy to go out and work —"

He ran out of breath, and the Hispanic paramedic put a hand on his shoulder and whispered something.

Sterling looked down, listened, and nodded.

"Okay, okay," he said. "This isn't the time for all this. You don't want me to get all worked up and have a stroke now, do you?"

A few people chuckled. "I'll talk more tomorrow." He looked at Jenny. "We'll be having a press conference."

"That's right," Jenny said. "I'll get that out as soon as we finalize a place and time." She extended a hand toward the senator. "What else would you like to say right now?"

Sterling sighed. "Uh, look . . . this is not about me. It's about America. As for my condition, I'm going to be fine. I was shot in the back of the leg. These good people assure me I'll be up and about in no time — on crutches, of course." His words were concise and matter-of-fact, as if he truly didn't want to talk about it. "I don't know if we want to get into a lot more detail than that."

Jenny raised her eyebrows, nodding at Sterling and bouncing on her toes as if encouraging him to wrap up.

Derrick couldn't help himself. "Sir, how did you get away from the terrorists?" he said. "Is that when you got shot?"

Jenny glared at him. The TV guy took several steps toward Sterling. The blonde paramedic whispered something to him.

"Without getting into a lot of detail," Sterling said, "because these good people need to get me to the hospital, yes, the wound to my leg came as I was getting away."

"Can you tell us what happened — when

the helicopter landed?" the TV guy said.

Good. At least Derrick wasn't the only one asking questions.

"We landed. They had vans waiting. I believed once I got in one of those, my chances would diminish a hundredfold. So I figured it was worth taking a gamble out here in this field."

It was raining hard now. Derrick pulled his sleeve over his tape recorder and only hoped it wasn't getting damaged by the rain.

"What happened was . . ." Sterling shook his head and chuckled because his voice was getting drowned out by the volume of the downpour. He spoke louder. "On the way from the helicopter to the vans I moved slowly on purpose, letting the guy in front of me get ahead." He held up his left elbow and patted it. "I took out the armed guy behind me with this elbow to his face — and I ran. It was dark. I thought they'd have a hard time hitting me."

"But they did hit you?" Derrick said.

Sterling smiled and nodded. "I fell down . . . twice, actually — the ground's so uneven. The second time, one of them hit me with a shot to the thigh. I mean, it was like the Fourth of July. They unleashed all the firepower they had. I didn't think I was going to make it, but I kept going. Had to.

Thank God I ran into Mr. Scarborough over here." He motioned toward the driver of the pickup, who was standing between two police officers. "I'll talk more about Ed and the other brave men and women tomorrow."

He looked at Jenny. She gave him one distinct nod and went into motion. "Okay, get him out of here," she told the paramedics. "I will contact all of you with details about tomorrow morning's press conference. Thank you all. Go get dry!"

48

"Oh my gosh, Jack!" Pamela squirmed as Lucy's husband shoved him. "What on earth?"

Jack took the shove, but his legs locked and his jaw clenched. She knew that look. He was about to explode.

"Jack, not in here," Pamela said. "Please!"

It felt like a slow-motion dream. Could it be a dream? The arena attack. The baby's problems. Now this? Could it be that she was sleeping in her own bed at home and this was all a nightmare? She prayed it was.

"What's going on, Lucy?" Margaret said. "What's this about? You talk to us."

No, it wasn't a dream. Even her mother was onto it.

"Never mind." Victor pointed at Margaret, then swung the finger around to the rest of them. "Never mind. We're going."

"Lucy, are you okay to go with him?" Jack said.

Lucy nodded quickly, blinking. She'd changed from a confident, outgoing health-care professional to a blubbering, inhibited slave. The transformation was incredible.

"It's not okay, Jack," Margaret blurted. "Look at her. Lucy, talk to us."

"You be quiet!" Victor clenched Lucy's arm and began to walk, but Jack got in his path again.

"Just cool it, Victor. Just cool it." Jack's breathing was exaggerated, his whole body rigid. "Let's just be calm and talk through this."

"What are you saying?" Victor squinted in disgust. "We don't even know you."

"We know Lucy. She's our friend. And we're gonna do what's best for her."

Pamela could not believe this was happening.

"Look, we're leaving," Victor announced. "None of this is any of your business."

"You made it our business when you came in here," Margaret said. "What are you, one of those wife abusers?"

No, Mom, don't do that!

"Lucy, you speak up," Margaret said. "We can help you, but not after you leave here."

"This is ridiculous," Victor said. "It's the middle of the night. My wife was involved in a terrorist attack. She served as your personal nurse for the past five hours. And now we're going home." He straightened the pen in the breast pocket of his blue-and-white-checked short-sleeved shirt.

The room fell silent. "And as for your doubts about my character," he said, "I'll have you know I'm one of the most re-spected mechanical engineers in the state —"

"Then you should know better than to bust in here like some savage," Margaret said. "It's obvious Lucy's frightened. Now why don't you leave?"

Margaret crossed to the phone and picked up the receiver. "Just go. You go, alone. Leave us with Lucy for a few minutes — or I'll call security right now."

Victor's eyes burned into Margaret. He looked like a caged animal, with his brown beard stubble and fiery eyes, which moved from Margaret to Pamela and Jack, and then settled on Lucy.

"I'm gonna be at the end of the hall." He spoke with his mouth closed like a ventrilo-quist, as if they weren't going to hear him. "Don't you dare keep me waiting more than five minutes. And, by golly . . . ." Then he stared at her, his eyes darting back and forth as if he was trying to convey something more — a harsh warning.

"Go on." Margaret held up the receiver. "Leave us alone."

He huffed and stalked out of the room, and the rest of them breathed a collective sigh of relief.

Lucy's shoulders jumped, and she began to cry. Margaret hung up the phone and embraced her.

"Come here," Pamela said from the bed.

Margaret took Lucy to the bed, and they plunked down next to Pamela.

Jack looked at his watch. They still hadn't brought the baby.

This was insane.

"Most of the time he's fine, a gentleman — I promise you." Lucy shook her head. "Other times it's like walking on eggshells. He has temper issues. I've pleaded with him to get counseling or see a doctor —"

"How long?" Margaret said. "Has he always been like this?"

Lucy nodded, then dropped her head.

"It was subtle at first. But slowly I started realizing what he was like. We'd try to talk about something serious, like money, and he'd fly off the handle. I gave it right back to him at first, until things got violent."

"Has he hurt you?" Jack said.

"Not like battery or anything, but grab-bing my shoulders and wrists. Pushing. Pinning me to walls. Yelling in my face."

"That is not okay, Lucy!" Pamela said. "You can't be with him until that changes."

"She's right," Margaret said.

"Did you know he was coming here?" Jack said.

Lucy shook her head. "I told him where I was and what had happened, that I was fine after the attack and helping you. But when he's like this, he gets jealous; he invents all kinds of things in his mind. He tracks my cell phone with GPS."

"Oh brother, a real wing nut," Margaret said.

"Mom, that's not necessary," Pamela said.

"He came here because he suspected something," Lucy said. "That I was meeting a doctor or . . . whatever. Who knows?"

Pamela and Jack exchanged a look of concern.

"It's okay," Lucy said. "I've got to go."

Margaret started to argue, but Lucy stood. "No, you have enough on your minds." She rubbed her nose with a tissue. "The fact that you saw him and confirmed that I need to get help — that's good, that's enough. I will. I will get help. I promise you." She looped her purse over her shoulder and started to go.

Pamela felt completely overwhelmed.

Margaret craned her neck toward Pamela as if to urge her to invite Lucy to stay with them. And she would do that, except for the fact that Margaret was already living in their small house, plus the new baby would be coming home — and who knew what challenges that would bring?

"Lucy, wait," Jack said. "You could stay with us."

She shook her head, walked to the bed, and squeezed Pamela's hand. "I'll come by first thing in the morning to see how you are and to see that baby. Maybe by then you'll have a name for him." She managed a smile and was off.

"Oh, Jack." Pamela sighed. "That poor thing."

"I don't know about this." Margaret shook her head. "Letting her go home with that lunatic."

Jack headed for the door. "I'll be right back."

"Where're you going?" Pamela said.

"Just to make sure he knows we're watching him. Then I'll check on the baby. It's been too long. We've got to find out what's going on. This is nuts."

49

One of Senator Sterling's bodyguards, Kennedy Cline, had been killed as he bravely provided gunfire that allowed Brian Shakespeare to continue on his rescue mission that night. Two other bodyguards — Tim Dokens and Robert Ocee — had been shot up badly. Now Tim was in fair condition and Robert was in intensive care at Mount Sinai Hospital. Everett Lester was there to console them and their families.

The extent to which his rock stardom empowered him to bring joy and comfort to others, simply by showing up, never ceased to amaze Everett. Ever since he'd become a Christian and walked away from his heavy-metal heyday, he'd taken advantage of as many opportunities as possible to bring light and meaning to other people's lives.

That's why he had dragged Karen and Cole with him in the middle of the night to Mount Sinai, even after the lengthy interview process with detectives at the arena following the terrorist attack. They'd been in the limo on the way to their hotel when Everett got the idea to visit those who'd been injured.

"Excuse me, Mr. Lester." A nurse named Tammy approached in the dark waiting area. "Tim Dokens says he is ready to see you for a minute, if you still want to."

"Absolutely." Everett followed her through one set of double doors, then another, down a short hallway to Tim's room.

"You can go on in," she said. "I think about five minutes would be good. He's still very weak."

"Okay, thank you." Everett stopped outside the door. Karen and Cole had gone to another floor to visit several people who'd been trampled in the stampede at the entrance of the arena. Everett knocked and walked in quietly.

Tim was on his back in bed, which was tilted up slightly. Tubes ran from his nose and mouth. There was a large white bandage on the side of his neck, and the rest of his body was covered with a sheet and blanket. His arms, which rested atop the blanket, were nicked with cuts and scratches and were covered with all kinds of needles, tubes, and white tape.

A light from over the sink cast a bluish glow over the bed.

Tim turned his head toward Everett and smiled.

"Tim, how are you doing, man?" Everett walked around the bed and stood next to him.

Tim raised his right hand a few inches, then dropped it. "I'm okay. Nice of you to come." He spoke in a low, unhurried tone. "I'm a big fan."

"Thank you. That's awesome." Everett rested a hand on his shoulder. "I hear you are one heck of a brave man."

Tim turned his head and eyed a chair in the corner. "Have a seat."

Everett dragged the chair next to the bed and sat on the edge of it. "How are you feeling?"

Tim clenched his jaw, and his nostrils flared. "Mad." He swallowed hard. "One of our men died tonight. This shouldn't happen in America."

"I know. It still doesn't seem real," Everett said.

"This is why I applied to work on Sterling's detail in the first place."

Everett wondered if he would want to continue working with Sterling, who was probably America's most obvious terrorist target.

"So much more is going on than the American people know," Tim said. "This is the tip of the iceberg."

Everett wondered how much more Tim knew, Sterling knew, the government knew. It was a sick and scary world in which to live, in which to bring up a child — like Cole.

"Do you know how Robert Ocee is? My partner?" Tim asked.

Everett could tell by the strain in his voice that Tim was extremely worn out.

"From what I understand, he was in surgery for a long time. They're monitoring him closely."

"He was hit bad." Tim's eyes welled up with tears. "He lost a lot of blood."

"What about you? That's a pretty big bandage on your neck."

"I got hit there." Tim's eyes flicked down to his chest. "And I think they said I took three more. But they missed the important parts. I'm gonna be fine."

"You're courageous, Tim. I appreciate what you did. So do the American people. And so does Senator Sterling."

"I can't believe he's alive."

"It's a miracle," Everett said.

Tim squirmed and made a sour face.

Everett stood and found the remote for the bed. "You want this tilted up more?"

"Yeah, please."

Everett pushed the button, making the bed rise. His phone vibrated. He checked it and saw Karen's name. "Excuse me a sec, Tim, this is my wife. I'm gonna need to shove off soon."

He walked over to the small hallway by the door. "Hey, honey. What's up?"

"Hey. We got to see three people. They're all gonna be fine. I'm so glad we came. How'd you do?"

"Good. I'm with Tim now, one of Sterling's security people. He got shot like four times, but he's good. Really strong. Amazing."

Tim gave a half smile and shrugged.

"Oh wow, that's incredible." Karen paused. "Why did I call you? I'm so tired . . . Oh yeah. You're not gonna believe this. Remember Jack, the security guy from the arena whose wife's pregnant?"

"The one you gave the flowers to?"

"Yeah. He's here! I just saw him a second ago. I wonder if they had their baby."

"On a night like tonight, I guess anything could happen," Everett said. "Where are you, anyway?"

"Second floor. There's a waiting area right around the corner from the nurses' station. Where're you?"

"Fourth floor. I'll come down in a minute, okay?"

Everett walked back into the main room. Tim had turned on the TV to a news station broadcasting live from the arena; the volume was muted.

"Okay, Tim, I'm going to take off. It's been a pleasure meeting you," Everett said.

"Something's bugging me." Tim stared at the TV. "Do me a favor, will you?"

"Sure."

"Hand me my phone. It's in the inside pocket of my jacket, hanging in the closet."

"Okay." Everett went to the closet. "But you better get some rest." He felt around in the black suit coat and found the phone.

"Thanks." Tim grimaced and with one hand thumbed through his contacts. "I need to talk to the investigator who came in earlier."

"Why? What's up?"

"One of their shooters . . . his eyes." Tim shook his head, as if shaking away cobwebs.

But Zaher and his men all wore masks. What was Tim thinking? There was no way he could have recognized any of them. He was running on empty, probably still in shock and definitely in need of sleep.

Everett told him that again.

"I just want to see if there's any more surveillance video," Tim said. "It's probably nothing . . ."

50

Jack stood waiting forever at the dimly lit nurses' station — trying with everything in him to keep his cool. *You're tired . . . hungry . . . stressed . . . Be calm.* But he was so frustrated! No one seemed to know anything about the baby. That section of the hospital was quiet as a morgue, as if they were running a skeleton shift. They'd been trying to track down Dr. Shapiro for twenty minutes, to no avail.

Jack stretched and paced, remaining close to the nurses' station.

The whole thing with Lucy was messed up. Victor may have been a reputable engineer, but he appeared to be one sick individual. Jack felt terrible for letting Lucy leave with him. But what could he do? His baby boy was in progressive care. He couldn't leave Pam, and he certainly couldn't leave her mother.

He had entered the hallway in time to get

one last glimpse of Victor leading Lucy to the elevator, one arm locked awkwardly around her shoulder. As he stood there now, Jack vowed to follow up with her once this ordeal had passed.

A nurse showed up behind the counter, and Jack approached. "Were you able to find Dr. Shapiro?"

She looked up and stared blankly at him for several seconds before speaking. "We're still looking," she said. "I'm sorry. We'll let you know."

Jack started to speak, but she talked louder. "Why don't you try to get some rest, Mr. Crittendon? We know where to find you."

"I'm not resting until I find out what's going on with our baby," Jack said. "I'm not leaving here till I see the doctor and see my baby. That's it. Now, please, get the doctor for me. Or just tell me where he is, and I'll go to him."

The nurse forced a smile and a nod, then snatched a manila folder from the desk and took off.

Oh great. *That's how you respond? Really?*

He was tempted to just go back there and find the baby, but he knew he couldn't do that. He was at the mercy of these people, who had all seemed to have checked out for the night.

His phone vibrated, and he picked up.

"What's the latest?" Derrick asked.

Jack told him they'd gotten nowhere and filled him in briefly on the episode with Lucy and Victor. Then Derrick told him about the encounter with Sterling out in the field at Seneca Falls.

"Heading back to the office now," Derrick said. "Got at least two stories to write. Then I'm gonna try to sneak home and get a few hours of sleep."

"Sterling's press conference will be on every station. That's national news. And you're right in the thick of it. I love it."

"Hey, and you're about to become an editor for us! You realize that, don't you? Sterling's ratings are soaring. I'm telling you, man, this is gonna push him over the top. He wins, I get the Washington beat, the chick comes off the news desk, you take her place."

I hope you're right, Derrick. I pray you're right.

Jack's head dropped, and he closed his eyes. The thought did feel good. "I know," he said. "I need that job so badly."

"Hey, I was thinking Z and I could come over before the press conference. Maybe bring you guys some coffee and dough-nuts?"

"Dude, that's nice of you, but not knowing the baby's status, we're still up in the air. You know what I mean?"

"Gotcha. Well, just let me know when you know."

"Nurse Ratched" reappeared just then at the nurses' station, hunched over, shuffling paperwork, trying to look busy.

"Excuse me." Jack approached the desk. "Any word on Dr. Shapiro?"

She put both hands on the desk, sighed, and looked at him. "I'm afraid he's left for the night."

Woooosh.

Jack's face was on fire. "What did you say?"

"He will be in first thing in the —"

"He was doing tests! On the nervous system. Cognitive tests. He said they would bring the baby to us an hour ago!"

"I'm sorry, Mr. Crittendon. Please, if you'll give me a few minutes, I will do my best to —"

"How could he just go home in the middle of this? I haven't even seen our baby."

"Mr. Crittendon, please —"

"And you weren't even going to tell me he'd left? What kind of operation is this?

Who's in charge of my baby right now? What doctor?"

"I can assure you, your baby is resting comfortably, Mr. Crittendon. There's nothing more that can be done tonight."

"I want to talk to whoever's in charge, right now — your supervisor."

Her face got sour, and she picked up the phone and punched some numbers. Then she spun around, crossed her arms, and sat her wide behind on the edge of the desk.

Jack heard her announcement for the supervisor over the PA system. She hung up and went back to shuffling file folders.

"I want to see my baby. Please, can I do that?"

"Mr. Crittendon, my supervisor will be here as soon as possible. I'm going to have you address that with her."

As she launched into a recital of some rote hospital policy, Jack felt the presence of someone coming up behind him. That was all he needed — to be whisked away by hospital security.

The nurse's eyes suddenly widened, and her speech slowed as she stared past Jack at whoever had stepped up behind him.

Jack turned around to find Everett Lester and his wife and son standing there.

"Hey, Jack." Everett's eyes shifted from

Jack to the nurse and back.

"Everett Lester." The nurse scanned the nurses' station to see who else might be around. "Oh my gosh, I can't believe this!"

Everett nodded toward her with a slight smile, then squared up with Jack. "Sorry. I overheard some of that. What's happening? You had your baby?"

Jack gave a nervous laugh. "Glad to see you all in one piece."

"Let's go over here." Everett crossed some ten feet from the nurses' station, and Jack explained what had transpired. His heart warmed as Everett, Karen, and Cole encircled him closely, listening with deep concern.

"So you haven't even seen the little guy yet?" Everett said.

Jack shook his head and sighed. Everett patted him on the shoulder.

"It's been a long day for you," Karen said.

"For all of us." Jack looked at each one of them and asked what they were doing at the hospital. Karen explained, and as she did, Everett quietly made his way over to Nurse Ratched.

"You wouldn't believe how brave those people were who got trampled," Cole said. "One was just a kid my age, a girl. She has a cast on her leg — pink."

"She actually broke her leg in two places," Karen said. "It's amazing no civilians got killed — besides the one bodyguard."

At six foot two or more, Everett towered over Nurse Ratched, who stared up at him with dreamy eyes and mouth agape.

Karen nodded toward Everett and kidded, "He makes friends wherever he goes."

Jack chuckled. "Making friends with her would be a true feat."

Karen smiled. "Where is your wife's room?"

"Just down the hall and around the corner."

"I suppose we'll need to get her some new flowers. I'm assuming the ones I gave you didn't make it."

He thought of the beautiful bouquet sitting back in room 5-A at the arena. "No, they didn't."

"Do you think she would be up for a visit?"

Jack's heart soared. "Oh, would she ever."

Karen looked over at Everett. "Hey honey, you ready?" she said.

Everett turned from Nurse Ratched to face them.

"I think we should stop by to meet Jack's wife before we head out," Karen said.

"Sounds good," Everett said. "But first,

how about if Jack gets to say hello to his son . . ."

51

Shakespeare rubbed his eyes, leaned back in the chair, stretched, and . . . "Ouch. Oh, man . . ." He kept forgetting about the wound.

Prichard, the young FBI investigator who'd been appointed to him when Peek left, glanced over, then got back to whatever he was doing on his glowing laptop.

"I've about had it," Shakespeare told him. "None of these guys is Zaher."

"We have a lot more to look at," said the investigator. He looked like a kid with his messy dark hair and retro black glasses.

"Is there any way I could go home and get some rest? Do more of this tomorrow?" Something was pulling at Shakespeare to get home, to be with Sheena. He was hot and uncomfortable, a little on the shaky side from not having eaten much.

The kid loosened his thin black tie, looked at his watch, and locked his fingers behind his head. "Special Agent Peek wanted me to have you get through all of those."

"I know, but I'm beat, I'm in pain, and I don't know how much good I'm doing you right now. Comprende?"

Prichard looked at his watch again, then pecked out some sort of message on his phone. "I'm checking with Agent Peek. Please just keep going for now, if you will."

"What else is going on?" Shakespeare said. "Do you guys have any significant leads? Have they ID'd bodies?"

"I can't say, sir. That's all strictly confidential."

Shakespeare rolled his eyes, thinking they probably had nothing. He needed some fresh air, if nothing else.

There was commotion in the hallway. A group of agents passed by, all talking at once. Special Agent Peek ducked in. "Well?" He looked at Prichard, then Shakespeare.

"Needle in a haystack." Shakespeare threw up his hands. "I mean, really, almost all of these guys could be Zaher, or none of them. The masks make it impossible to ID —"

"The idea is to narrow it down," Peek interrupted. "Just flag the ones that *could* be him."

"I've flagged dozens just because I didn't want to be negligent," Shakespeare said.

"But even the obese guys I didn't flag could be him, if they went on *Biggest Loser* or something since these photos were taken."

Peek dropped his head.

"Sir." Prichard stood, one flap of his shirt coming loose at his skinny waist. "Did you get my text?"

"Yes, I got your text, Prichard," Peek said. "What you have yet to get through your thick skull is that I do not text. I take calls. I call people. It's old-fashioned, but that's what I do. That's what I will always do. You should know that by now. You want me, you pick up the phone and call me."

Shakespeare smirked.

"Can Mr. Shakespeare go home and get some rest?" Prichard said.

"Yes he can." Peek pointed at Shakespeare but pretended to talk to Prichard. "But I want him back here at the crack of dawn to finish what we started."

Shakespeare stood and crossed to the door. "Thank you, boys." His whole body was sore. The pain in his arm was deep and annoying. He was hot. Needed to find a water fountain and maybe something to snack on for the drive home.

"You should be proud, Mr. Shakespeare." Peek got serious on him. "What you did here tonight was . . . well, valiant, to say the least. I would only hope I would have done the same."

Shakespeare slowed at the door.

Suddenly the pungent smell of gunfire and the sharp sting of smoke in his eyes from earlier that night came flooding back. He tried to focus on the carpet, but it was blurry and seemed ten feet away.

He placed a hand on the doorway to steady himself.

His head whirled.

From the corner of his eye, he noticed Prichard and Peek moving toward him.

"Are you all right? . . . Mr. Shakespeare?"

Prichard's words were the last thing he remembered before hitting the floor.

52

Nothing else mattered to Jack now except seeing his baby boy. Everett Lester had pulled the strings to get Jack back into the progressive-care unit, and Nurse Ratched walked in front of him now, leading the way.

The hallway was quiet and dimly lit. Nurse Ratched's white Nikes didn't make a sound.

Jack's heart ticked like a fast clock. He adjusted the light-blue germ mask she'd stuffed in his hand.

He was anxious about the unknown — the baby's true condition.

Let him be fine, Lord, please. Let him be fine.

He had to block out the bad stuff — Shapiro's disappearance, the nurse's inexcusable bedside manner.

She turned several corners, passed two rooms, and entered another with light-green walls. Just inside the doorway, she folded her arms around a clipboard and spoke without making eye contact. "Let's do about five minutes. And please don't disturb him. Can you find your way back?"

"Yes. Thank you." Jack walked past a clipboard hanging on the door that read: Baby Crittendon (male). The nurse disappeared, probably going back to make goo-goo eyes at Everett Lester.

The tiny bed, only two feet by three feet, was raised waist high and looked as if it was suspended in midair. It was flanked by colorful computer screens stacked three high on the right and some kind of monitors stacked ten high on the left. A small white box resembling a microwave, with lights and numbers, hung at the head of the bed, and directly overhead was a large, rectangular-shaped light with a red lens.

There were many wires and tubes. Some led directly to the baby, who lay sleeping, half-covered by light-green sheets and a blanket.

"Hey, my man," Jack whispered.

The baby was sound asleep on his back, facing right. Jack gently touched his warm head and thin reddish-brown hair. White plastic patches the size of quarters were attached to the infant's chest in several places, with wires leading to various monitors. His little right arm, which was up by his mouth, had a white splint on it, with several caps attached to his fingers.

"Oh, you little trouper," Jack said. "You've been through so much, haven't you?"

He leaned in close. The baby's eyelashes were long, like his mom's. His nose and mouth were tiny. He seemed very much at peace.

Jack lifted the sheet and blanket. There were several more monitor patches and wires adjoined to the baby's legs and sides. His body was small compared to the girls' when they were newborns; of course, neither of them had been born a month early. Jack gently rested a hand on the little guy's tummy.

"Excuse me?"

Startled, Jack turned to see a short African American nurse standing there.

"Sir, we don't allow visitors back here. Are you Mr. Crittendon?"

"Yes, yes, I am. I hadn't gotten to see him yet."

She came right over. "I'm sorry about that, but we can't have you back here. It's just not safe for any of the little ones we're caring for." She waved him toward the door and began walking toward it herself. "Let's head back up front together, and you can tell me how you got back here."

Perhaps this was the supervisor Nurse Ratched had paged.

"Dr. Shapiro assured us they would bring the baby to our room, but that was a long time ago." Jack stopped short of the door and squared up with her. "We haven't gotten any answers."

"I'm afraid Dr. Shapiro has left for the night. It must've been some sort of emergency. I apologize."

"He was supposed to give us an update on the tests. My wife was going to feed the baby. Shapiro left us hanging."

"May I ask, did you just wander back here on your own?"

"No, not exactly. A nurse let me come back. I don't want to get her in trouble. Look, we still don't know what's wrong with our baby. No one's told us anything. We've gotten no answers. Can you help us?"

"If you'll just follow me, sir, I'll do my best." She continued to force him out of the room without actually touching him. "Please, come along now."

Jack took one last glimpse at the baby and followed her out the door and back to the nurses' station, where Nurse Ratched was around the front of the desk, speaking animatedly with Everett and Karen. Cole was curled up on a couch near the elevators, asleep.

"Is this the nurse who let you go back?" His guide gestured toward Nurse Ratched.

Jack nodded.

"Nancy. Can I speak with you a moment?" She led Nurse Ratched back around the corner, out of sight.

Jack described the baby to Everett and Karen, and the African American nurse was back within two minutes.

"Okay, I'm sorry about that, folks. My name is Trevinia Alexander. I'm the supervisor on duty for the night. I am very sorry for all the trouble you've had."

The other nurse didn't return.

"I have your baby's file here." Trevinia went through one page after another. "I'm familiar with this. I went over it with Dr. Shapiro earlier this evening." She continued to scan, reading here and there. Then she let the chart drop to her side and addressed Jack.

"We think your baby suffered some sort of hemorrhage to the brain."

No . . . don't say that. Please . . .

"But it's too early to make a diagnosis," she continued, the volume of her voice fading. "We have several more tests to do."

When Pam fell . . .

"The good news is, he's in the best of hands here," Trevinia said. "He's eating. His vitals are steady. He's sleeping a lot, which is normal, but when he's awake, he's somewhat lethargic."

There's that word again.

Jack's mind reeled.

His forehead was covered in sweat.

He felt Everett's hand squeeze the top of his shoulder, but he couldn't move — or speak. His mind had seared to white.

Karen took in a deep breath and set her shoulders back with both hands in the prayer position in front of her mouth. Her eyes were filling with tears.

It was as if Jack had slipped out of his body.

Hovering there.

Not accepting it.

No!

Rebelling against it — *all of it.* The unemployment, the attack, the troubles with Pam, the debt, and now this: this terrible trouble that lay ahead for them, for their baby, for the boy whom they had yet to give a name.

53

It was the middle of the night, and the puddle-filled parking lot at the *Gazette* was overflowing with cars. Derrick was forced to create a space for his FJ Cruiser at the end of an aisle. He and Daniel hustled in through the steady rain to find the hallways packed with staff; all hands were on deck.

When he entered the newsroom, it was bright, loud, and buzzing with electricity. He stood there stunned for a moment, taking it all in. Almost instantly, several reporters and editors converged on him, knowing he'd just returned from the outskirts of town where the Ohio senator had escaped from his captors.

It wasn't until that moment that the enormity of the terrorist attack and the Sterling abduction hit Derrick as reality. Until then, it had all been like a dream — the screams and terror and gunfire at the smoke-filled arena; racing around the dark hilly roads of central Ohio; squabbling with the cop in the wet field in Seneca Falls.

A hand squeezed his shoulder from behind. "How fast can you have the first piece?" It was Buck Stevens, who never worked at night. The others smothered Derrick with congratulations and questions.

"Everybody quiet!" Buck motioned for the colleagues to give Derrick room. "He can tell us all about it over a drink later, but right now he needs to write. Okay? So back off and let the guy do his job. Where's Daniel?"

Derrick was still in a daze, staring out at the bustling newsroom. "I think he stopped at the john."

"Okay, how fast can you have the first story?" Buck repeated. "We want the very latest in the a.m. edition."

Derrick eyeballed him. "With a cup of coffee, I can crank it out in forty-five — maybe thirty."

"What do you take in it?" Buck was on his way.

"Black. Hold up, Buck. One more thing."

Buck stopped and craned his neck at Derrick, who took advantage of the moment.

"Remember my buddy, Jack?"

Buck shook his head, waved a hand, and kept going. "It's a no-brainer. Sterling's a shoo-in," he called. "We'll get your buddy on board, don't you worry."

Derrick gave a thumbs-up and headed for his desk, thinking that was the best news he'd heard all day.

Everett, Karen, and Cole watched Jack walk the long hallway and round the corner that would lead him back to his wife's room. Everett felt bad for him because he was going to have to tell Pam that the doctor had left for the night and that the baby had likely suffered some sort of brain hemorrhage.

Everett and Karen were going to wait a few minutes for a text from Jack, to see whether Pam was up for a visit.

"Dad, can we go back to the hotel?" Cole's shoulders drooped, and he wandered like a zombie. "I'm so tired. I just want to crash."

All three of them were looking pale and worn out.

"I know you're tired, buddy. Just hang in there a little bit longer. Mr. Jack and his wife are going through a rough time, so if we can do a little something to encourage them, we want to do that."

Cole dropped his head back and closed his eyes.

"Come here, baby." Karen sat down and patted the leather bench. "Sit here with me for a minute. You can go back to sleep if you want."

Cole took her up on it and within seconds was sprawled out with his head resting in her lap.

"Man, this floor's deserted," Everett said.

"The emergency room was packed," Karen said softly.

"The fourth floor was crazy too." Everett scanned the area. "I'm gonna wander around for a minute."

"Wander around?" Karen squinted. Then her face went cold, and she glared at him. "Everett Lester. Don't you dare get us in trouble."

She knows me too well.

"Don't worry. I'll be right back."

Seeing no one at the nurses' station, he snatched a germ mask from behind the counter and slipped around the corner. Karen protested in a desperate whisper, but Everett kept going toward a short hallway of rooms, slipping the mask over his nose and mouth, searching for the name Crittendon on each door.

He entered the quiet room and approached the baby, who was asleep on his back, with many wires attached.

Everett gently rested the fingers of his right hand on the baby's head, noting how soft his straight reddish hair was. He and Karen hadn't been able to have babies. They had been in the process of trying to adopt an infant when Cole came up for adoption at age nine — and changed their lives.

"Father in heaven, you're a miracle worker," he whispered. "You healed the lame and blind. You raised the dead. Now you're right here. As I touch this precious boy, please, open the floodgates of heaven. Unleash your healing power. In the name of Jesus Christ —"

"Amen . . . Now you need to get straight out of here."

He turned.

Trevinia Alexander stood with her hands clasped in front of her, eyebrows raised.

"Thank you." Everett crossed to the door and tiptoed out.

"Thank *you* . . . We need all the help we can get around here."

54

Shakespeare phased in and out during the bumpy ambulance ride. At one point he took inventory of his condition. His arm was still killing him, but the rest of his body seemed okay. Except for his throat. It was terribly parched, which he determined was the result of the icy oxygen mask strapped too tightly to his face.

Normally he would fight such a thing and insist he didn't need any help.

But not this time. He was just too tired. Too zapped of all energy to put up any kind of fight.

So he rested.

In fact, he slept . . .

But now he was awake again, wide-awake with an IV stuck in his wrist, sitting half upright in a cold hospital bed with sheets that felt like plastic.

The guy behind the curtain on the other side of the hospital room was coughing his lungs out. It was driving Shakespeare crazy. Why on earth didn't they give him something?

"You need to drink some water or something," Shakespeare called toward the white curtain that went from ceiling to floor, hanging from a metal track.

The man only coughed louder, to the point of retching.

Suddenly a pale little doctor in a white coat appeared with a clipboard under one arm, rubbing his hands with antiseptic he'd pumped from a device on the wall. "Good evening, Mr. Shakespeare. I'm Dr. Theodore Brogden. How are you feeling?"

"Fine. A little tired. But pretty good."

"Sit up for me and take deep breaths." Brogden probed Shakespeare's big chest with cold fingers, placing his stethoscope in various places. He had a large nose and smelled strongly of cologne. "Is that the deepest you can breathe?"

"No." Shakespeare concentrated and took in some really deep breaths. "What's the problem, Ted?"

The doctor paused. "Do you remember blacking out?"

"I got light-headed. I think I was just hungry or dehydrated or something."

"That's possible. You needed nourishment. When's the last time you ate?"

Shakespeare thought about it. "Lunch. I was gonna have dinner on my break, but . . . well, we never got around to breaks."

"Yes, your wife told me you were working at the arena this evening."

"You talked to Sheena?"

"Yes. She's on her way."

"Oh shoot, that's not necessary. What on earth is she going to do with the kids? Darn it, Ted. I should call her and tell her not to come." He started to go for his phone, but the doctor told him to wait; he wasn't finished.

The man on the other side of the curtain was coughing to death.

"Did you have any chest discomfort or upper body pain before you passed out?" Brogden asked, scratching the curly black hair that sprang from the sides of his head.

Shakespeare thought about it. "No."

"Stomach pain? Shortness of breath?"

"No."

"Anxiety. Nervousness?"

Shakespeare chuckled. "Anxiety . . . a little, I'd say."

"Do you drink an excessive amount of alcohol?"

"No."

"Are you on any medications?"

"No. Well, just fish oil for cholesterol."

There was a knock at the door, and Sheena entered, wearing sweats, a black baseball cap, and a sympathetic frown.

"Who's watching the kids?" Shakespeare said, then realized that wasn't a very kind greeting when she'd come to be with him. "Sorry. Hi, honey."

"Mandy," she said. "What's going on? How are you?"

Mandy was their twentysomething neighbor who still lived at home, didn't work, and mooched off her parents. All she did as far as Shakespeare could see was tweet, text, and talk on her phone.

"I'm fine. You didn't have to come," Shakespeare said.

The doctor introduced himself. "His blood sugar plummeted," he said. "It's possible he may have some form of hypoglycemia."

"Seriously?" Sheena said.

The doctor pursed his lips. "Too early to tell. We've got his blood sugar climbing back up to normal. I'm going to keep him for the night, however."

"Oh sheesh," Shakespeare protested. "You're gonna have to give that guy something for his cough, or neither of us is gonna get any sleep."

Sheena glared at him.

"If everything looks good in the morning, we'll send you home," said Dr. Brogden. "But I want you to see your personal physician first thing in the morning to get to the bottom of this. It is nothing to flirt with."

"We'll get him in tomorrow," Sheena said. "Thank you very much, Doctor."

The physician marked something on his chart and started to leave.

"Can I walk around, Ted?" Shakespeare asked. "I mean, this sugar you're feeding me is getting me hyped up. I've got to move."

Sheena shook her head.

The doctor faced him. "That's fine. Just be careful with the IV. That'll probably come out within another hour or two. Your nurse will be checking it."

"Great. Thanks," Shakespeare said. "And Doc, please, give that guy some cough syrup or something on your way out, will you?"

"We'll see what we can do." He was gone.

Sheena and Shakespeare stared at each other.

She stood with her arms crossed, purse over her shoulder, hair up under the cap. "Are you all right?" she said.

He nodded, relieved to be reunited with her after the attack. "Come here."

She approached slowly, arms still crossed. "Closer," he said.

She got within two feet and stopped. He reached out and drew her into his arms. They remained still like that for some time.

"I owe you an apology," he finally managed. "For a lot of things."

She was quiet in his big arms. They hadn't held each other in so long.

"I'm gonna change," he said. "You deserve better than I've been giving you."

Slowly, ever so slowly, she rested her head on his shoulder.

As far as Shakespeare was concerned, that was a start.

A good start.

55

"Help me up — please." Pamela grimaced as Jack and Margaret raised her up to the edge of the hospital bed. Jack had delivered the news about the baby possibly having a brain hemorrhage, and the room had fallen silent for the past five minutes, except for Margaret's sniffles.

"Where're you going?" Jack said as Pamela stood, leaning her weight on his shoulder and Margaret's.

"Bathroom," she said.

She didn't want to talk about the baby.

She needed to be alone.

They walked with her, slowly.

Her legs were stiff, and the pain in her abdomen from the C-section was sharp and deep.

She heard Jack's phone go off.

"I'll be okay," she said. "Leave me alone for a minute."

"Are you sure?" Margaret said.

"Yes, Mom — I'm sure."

She immediately regretted how nasty that sounded.

"By the way, I talked to the nurse. She's going to bring a breast pump in a little while," Margaret said.

Pamela didn't respond. She got into the bathroom, closed the door, and gingerly made her way to the sink.

There was a tap at the door. "Did you hear me?" her mother called.

"Yes, Mom! That will be delightful," she jested.

Pamela leaned over the sink on her forearms and peered into the mirror. Her blonde hair was frizzy and wild, as if she'd just ridden a hundred miles in a convertible. Her brown eyes seemed almost black and were sunken into her head.

What a hot mess.

She ran cold water, splashed her face four or five times, and patted dry with a spongy towel that didn't seem to absorb any water.

With a great deal of pain, she eased her way onto the toilet.

Ouch. Oh . . . She was sore everywhere, from the chest down.

Once she got into a semicomfortable position, she just sat there and stared at the floor — remembering the fall.

She'd gotten her nails done in a glossy bright orange that day.

Coming out of the salon, she'd stepped off the curb and fallen.

It hadn't even been that jarring!

Okay, forget it. It happened. It's in the past. She leaned forward and rocked. *What if he is . . . does have special needs? We keep going. There's no choice.*

I keep working, and Jack watches the baby.

Or he gets the job at the Gazette, *and I come home.*

We face it. We deal with it. We cope.

She thought of their older friends who were empty nesters and how much fun they all said it was to be romantic couples on their own again. She thought of the people she knew who had children with special needs — how much time, energy, and money it required of them. It drained the very life out of them and aged them by twenty years overnight.

And so that was going to be their lot?

Would it draw her and Jack closer or drive an even bigger wedge between them?

There was another knock at the door, and she replied as nicely as she could muster, knowing it would be her mom.

"It's me. Can I open?" Jack said.

"Yeah."

The door opened a crack, and he popped his head in. "You okay?"

She nodded wearily.

"You're not gonna believe it," he said. "That was Shakespeare. He blacked out at the arena. He's here! An ambulance brought him to the ER. Says he's fine. They think it might be hypoglycemia. His blood sugar bottomed out."

"Great, we can have a party," she said numbly.

"Sheena's here too, for a while. She might go back home. He's staying the night."

When he seemed to realize she didn't have a whole lot to say about his big news, he focused in on her. "Are you sore?"

She took a deep breath and nodded.

"Are you up on your pain relievers?"

"Yes."

"What else can I do for you?" he said.

"I'm a little hungry. Maybe some fruit?"

"Your mom has bananas and apples."

"Apple sounds good."

Knowing Shakespeare, he might pop in any minute.

"Would you get me my makeup bag?" she said. "It's out there somewhere."

Jack disappeared and returned with the small pink bag.

"Maybe I should get a shower?" she said.

Before he could say anything, she made up her mind. "Nah. I'll wait till morning. Go on. Skedaddle. I'll be right out."

"Okay . . . are you gonna be up for a little surprise in a minute?"

She deflated. "What kind of surprise, Jack? Really?"

"A visitor." He stared at her like a wide-eyed kid.

Her heart suddenly leaped. "The baby!"

He frowned and shook his head. "No. Not yet."

"Jack, not Shakespeare and Sheena — I'm not up for that."

He shook his head with a smile. "Nope. You're gonna like this. Just get yourself prettied up."

"Jack!" she protested, but he'd left.

That made her mad.

There was no visitor she wanted to see, except her baby.

She dug into the makeup bag, found her brush, and began working on her hair. Who could it be? Not his parents. They lived in Florida and didn't travel far from home anymore.

She found her lipstick. Maybe Derrick and Zenia? That she could live with, but not for more than a few minutes. She was dead tired and hoped Jack would take her mom home for the night so she could get some sleep.

There was a tap at the door. "Honey, you ready?" Jack said.

Honestly? She was kind of annoyed at him for railroading this visit with whoever it was. Instead of answering him, she checked herself in the mirror one last time, figuring a lady could only look so good in a light-gray hospital gown, then slowly entered the room. Whoever it was would just have to get over her glamorous appearance.

Standing there tan and larger than life — in *her* hospital room — with curly dark hair and incredibly rugged-looking beard stubble, was rock legend Everett Lester.

Pamela stopped. Her face flushed.

Her breath was gone.

Someone was behind him — his wife, Karen, and their son. She probably knew more about them than they knew about themselves!

Realizing her mouth was open three inches, she shut it and crossed her arms, thinking how homely she looked and how she could kill Jack for not preparing her better.

"Hi, Pam. We're not going to stay long; we know you've had a long day." Everett smiled brilliantly and reached out his hand, engulfing hers. "I'm Everett Lester, and this is my wife, Karen, and our son, Cole."

Everett wore several thick leather bracelets, and she immediately noticed the black, swirling tattoos on his forearms — tattoos she had seen a million times in magazines like *People*, and which she knew from media reports he wasn't proud of.

Pamela looked at him, at them, at Jack, at Margaret, and back at him. She tried to speak but almost began crying instead. Margaret *was* crying, with her hands locked together in front of her mouth and her eyes welling over with tears.

Pamela wanted to say, "How do you do? It's such an incredible pleasure to meet you," but nothing came. They must have realized she was shell-shocked.

"These are for you." Karen stepped forward with a colorful summer bouquet. "There's a funny story behind them."

Jack laughed and spoke up excitedly, looking like a kid who'd just downed a giant energy drink. "We met backstage at the arena. When they heard you were about to have a baby, Karen wanted me to bring you the dozen roses Everett had given her. Obviously, they got left behind."

"I would have gotten you roses, but they didn't have any in the gift shop," Karen said.

Pamela finally found her voice. "I know all about the roses, what a big part they played in your past! This is incredible. Thank you for coming. I . . . I'm . . . in shock."

They all laughed, and Margaret blubbered even more.

Karen said something about the baby, but Pamela was enraptured with Everett, who was absolutely mesmerizing. To think that this was the legendary metal front man who'd performed before sellout crowds on famous stages around the world, standing in her hospital room! No matter what the future held with the baby, this moment, *right this second,* was special, and Pamela was determined to celebrate it.

"Pam, did you hear that, honey?" Jack said.

She snapped out of it with an idiotic chuckle. "I'm sorry. I . . . I just . . . No, I didn't."

"I just wondered how you're feeling," Karen said. "You've been through quite an ordeal."

"Oh gosh, I know. I was stupid for even going to the rally. But when I heard you were going to be there, that close to home" — Pamela looked at Everett — "I just couldn't miss it."

Everett and Karen looked at each other and smiled.

"That was the scariest thing I've ever been through," Karen said.

"Me, too," said Cole.

Karen put her arm around the boy and squeezed him. Everett rubbed the top of his head.

"I know, buddy, it was bad. But we made it, didn't we? God took care of us. Thanks to people like Mr. Jack here, not too many people got hurt — except the one security guard who died."

"And except the bad guys," Cole said. "They got what was coming to 'em."

"That's right, except the bad guys," Everett said.

A reverent silence fell over the room.

"We should go." Everett looked at Karen, who nodded.

"Thank you so much for coming, and for the flowers," Pamela said. "I'll never forget this."

"Truly, this was special," Jack said.

"I'm going to put these in this spare pitcher for now." Karen gently placed the flowers in the plastic container and filled it with water.

"Mr. Lester?" Margaret spoke up, her voice cracking. "I was wondering if I could have your autograph?"

"Most certainly." Everett went into motion.

"I was thinking you could sign this bulletin thingy." She dug in her purse and pulled out the program from the night's campaign rally.

"Oh, now, that'll be a keeper," Jack said.

Margaret finally produced a pen, and Everett signed with a confident, looping stroke.

"Now I'm not gonna see this pop up on eBay or Craigslist, am I?"

They all laughed.

"Not a chance!" Margaret beamed and reached out for the autographed program as if it were a gleaming diamond pendant.

Cole whispered something to his mom and buried his head in her chest.

"Okay," Karen said. "Well, good evening to you all, and best of luck with the new baby."

Pamela made sure she got a hug from Everett, who smelled as delightful as he looked.

As they began to file out, there was a knock, and the door opened.

"Mr. and Mrs. Crittendon?"

"Trevinia," Jack said. "Come in."

The pretty supervisor Jack had mentioned

popped her head in. "Oh my goodness, you have a full house."

"Is everything okay?" Pamela's heart kicked up a notch, and she determined right then that this had been the most stressful day of her life. "What is it?"

"Well . . ." Trevinia shot a knowing smile at Everett. "It just so happens that I have a hungry little fellow right outside with me. Do you think you're up for a feeding?"

56

"What's going on?" Jack panicked and hurried into the hallway to see the baby. "Is he okay to be out of progressive care?" The baby was on his back, awake, swaddled in a soft pastel-striped blanket.

"It's okay, Mr. Crittendon. You won't believe it," Trevinia said. "I took it upon myself to call Dr. Shapiro. He asked me to convey his deepest apologies. His father-in-law had a seizure this evening. That's why he had to dash off."

Jack felt as if he'd just dropped a hundred-pound sack of flour from his shoulders.

He didn't know whether to pick up the baby or not. The little guy was awake, his big brown eyes staring up at him.

Cole was leaning over the edge of the baby cart, gently rubbing the baby's tiny face with the back of his fingers. "He looks like a strong little guy," he said. Everett and Karen leaned down to admire the infant, both touching his snug-fitting white knit cap and his swaddled body. Then Everett put his arm around Cole, and they said their goodnights.

"I'm going to get your recordings, Mr. Lester," Trevinia called to Everett. "That's for sure! You sold me tonight."

Everett smiled and winked at her, as if they shared a secret.

"Bring him here, Jack," Pam called from the room.

Trevinia wheeled the baby the rest of the way into the room. With the greatest of care, Jack bent over and gathered up his first and only son and gently rested him close against his chest.

"Dr. Shapiro had me read him the baby's latest vitals and instructed me to get him right down here to you," Trevinia said.

"Oh my stars." Margaret came close to the baby, patting his little back. "Oh, what a beauty. He's got your nose and mouth, Pamela."

Jack held the little guy out in front of him, and they made eye contact. The baby was very still, his shiny brown eyes inspecting every inch of Jack's face.

Margaret moved the knit cap up slightly, and they all examined his thin reddish hair.

"How does he seem?" Pam said. "Bring

him here, honey."

"He seems good." Jack lowered the baby into Pam's waiting arms, uncertain whether he was lethargic or completely normal.

"He's hungry," Margaret said.

That was all they needed — an announcer.

Pam scooted around a bit, adjusted her gown, and began feeding the little guy. At first she winced, but soon she was feeding him as naturally as if she'd already done so a dozen times.

"That's it. That's it," Margaret said. "Look at him go to town."

Jack couldn't take the running commentary from his mother-in-law. He walked to the window and checked his phone. Nothing new.

He shot a text message to Shakespeare, asking how he was doing. Once the baby left, Jack would try to sneak down to see him.

He imagined the excitement and stress in the newsroom at the *Gazette* as Derrick pounded out his stories on the night's dramatic events.

He wanted to turn on the news to catch the latest about the attack and the pursuit of the terrorists, but it was no time for that. Margaret was sitting on the edge of the bed, inspecting the baby from head to toe, and

Pam was staring down at him, stroking his hair.

"My goodness, this boy has a grip like a vise," Margaret said as the baby squeezed her thumb in his tiny fist. "He's eating like a champ."

The thought of bringing up another child in this crazy world nagged at Jack as he watched the peaceful exchange between his precious wife and baby. Children were abducted and abused every day. Mass shootings at schools and businesses were becoming sickeningly commonplace. Why those troubled souls didn't simply take their own lives was beyond Jack. It was sick, sick, sick. He couldn't fathom how the families of those victims coped, especially those without God.

And now terrorist attacks, right in their own backyard.

What can you do?

Trust.

Simple trust in God. That was it. Hope for the best.

And realize . . . this is not all there is. This is not our ultimate destination.

"Jack." Pam spoke softly, bringing him out of his daze.

He turned from the window and went to her. She was finished nursing.

"Yeah, sweetie."

"What about Everett . . . for a name?"

Pam glanced at him and looked back down at the baby. Margaret raised her eyebrows at Jack.

"Everett Crittendon," Jack said, contemplatively. "Everett Crittendon . . ."

"I like it," Margaret said. "It's very masculine."

"What does it mean, Jack?"

He got out his phone and did a search.

"What do you think, baby?" Pam shook her head close to the baby's face. "Do you like the name Everett? Huh?"

"Okay, let's see, it's Old English and it means . . . Wow, get this. Strong, brave, hearty!" Jack laughed.

"That's it!" Margaret bounced on the bed as she turned to face Pam and the baby. "Everett Crittendon."

"What do you think, Everett?" Pam tapped the baby's nose. "Do you like that name? Are you gonna be strong and brave? I think you are. I think you already are."

"Says it means 'strong as a boar.'" Jack chuckled and moved Margaret over so he could nestle up with Pam and the baby.

"You know what would make the *perfect* middle name?" Margaret stood and pinned her fists to her waist.

Jack only hoped she didn't see his eyes roll.

"Benjamin," she exclaimed. "Everett Benjamin Crittendon!"

It was Pam's father's name.

"Oh, Pam, your father would be so thrilled . . ."

Gee, no pressure.

57

Shakespeare could care less that all he was wearing was a wispy hospital gown, his boxers underneath, and the black flip-flops Sheena had brought from home. He had never been big on what other people thought. That was a hang-up for some people, but not him. He checked to make sure the nurses weren't watching, took Sheena by the hand, and quickly led her out to the parking lot.

He sensed she was pleased he had offered to escort her to the car by the way she stayed so close that she bumped up against him several times as they walked. He literally couldn't remember the last time they'd shown any affection. It felt good. No, it felt *great.*

The only problem was that he'd promised he was going to make some big changes, and that was dicey, because if he didn't follow through this time, she would leave him for sure. He knew her, and she meant business. She had been more than patient for a long time, but the girl from Cleveland had some serious moxie. If and when it came time, she would walk out the door and never even consider looking back.

He planned to clear out most of the survivalist junk he'd accumulated, which had become a stupid obsession. But could he do it? He realized he might still not be thinking clearly. After all, he'd just survived a traumatic assault, it was the middle of the night, he hadn't eaten properly in half a day, and he was dog tired yet jittery awake from all the glucose.

He just hoped he didn't change his mind once things got back to normal — whatever that was.

"Okay." Sheena stopped and squared up to him off to the side of the automatic glass doors leading to the parking lot. "Now you go up and get back on that IV. Get some sleep."

Shakespeare took her hands in his. "How far out are you parked?"

"Not far." She looked out at the rows of cars.

"I'll watch till you get in."

"Why are you being so nice?" She squinted up at him with a suspicious smile.

He examined her blue eyes, her glowing face, her sexy smile. Jack had once told him that he believed it was up to husbands to bring out the very best in their wives. Shakespeare had denied that — until now. And suddenly he realized he had failed at it, miserably, for a long time.

"What?" She looked up at him. "What's wrong?"

He shook his head and peered into her eyes, hoping he wasn't too late. "I am sorry . . ." His eyes brimmed with a tidal wave of emotions — regret, selfishness, time wasted.

She shook her head and wiped away a tear that streaked down his face, but she said nothing.

Then her own tears welled up.

He locked her in his arms.

Close.

So close.

"I hope I'm not too late," he whispered.

Still she didn't speak.

He wanted her to say he wasn't too late, that she accepted his apology.

But she just stood there, very still in his arms.

He'd taken her for granted for so long.

Too long.

Too much neglect.

He pulled back and looked at her, and she at him. Their faces were wet. They both wiped their eyes and cheeks with their hands.

"What would you say if I told you I wanted to go to church?" he said.

Her eyebrows arched, and she looked at him with a casual half smile.

"Jack's church," he said.

She paused and blinked. "I'd do that. I'll try anything once."

He nodded and brought her close. "Okay then." He rested his hands on her back. Through his touch he hoped she would know that he still treasured her, that this was the start of making up for lost time.

Lots of lost time.

58

The hospital was dimly lit and quiet — peaceful even. Jack was sore and dragging; his ears were still ringing from the gunfire at the arena. He found a restroom on his way to see Shakespeare, and he stopped to splash some hot water on his face. He patted dry with paper towels and leaned on the sink.

The baby was fine, he told himself. The little guy had eaten well, gripped their fingers, examined their faces with those innocent, searching eyes.

Had he seemed lethargic?

He told himself no, that the baby was completely healthy.

But he had seemed somewhat . . . tranquil.

"Oh, God." He stared down at the sink. "Please, please let him be okay. He's in your hands. It's not up to me —"

There was a knock, and the door swung open. In came a hunched-over Hispanic woman wheeling a metal bucket and mop. "Oops." She began to back out. "Sorry about that."

Jack chuckled and assured her it was okay as he excused himself and went to find Shakespeare's room.

"There's usually no one in here this time of night," the lady called.

He waved. There was a lady breaking her back to make ends meet. On an hourly wage it would be practically impossible. Jack knew this all too well and hoped again for the job at the *Gazette* to come through.

He got confused at first and took a wrong turn but then back-pedaled and found the numbers leading to Shakespeare's room.

Fifteen feet from the door he heard the roommate Shakespeare had described, hacking away as if he'd just staggered out of a coal mine after thirty years.

Jack knocked, but no one heard. He crept in.

The bony old gentleman was sitting on the edge of his chair in a gray gown, looking down, leaning on his knees with clear tubes coming out his nose, wheezing as a green oxygen tank rumbled loudly on the floor between his legs.

Jack tiptoed past him, around the curtain, as Shakespeare had instructed.

"Aha, you made it past my astute security guard." Shakespeare was upright in bed, IV attached to one wrist, heavy white gauze and tape on the other arm. The TV was on Fox News. There was a half-eaten plate of fruit in his lap.

"Hey, man." Jack approached, and they shook hands and gave a slight embrace.

"Good news about the baby." Shakespeare took a bite of banana.

"Yeah." Jack pulled up a chair. "It's still a little hard to tell at this point. We'll see."

"If it was bad, you'd know by now. How did he seem?" Shakespeare bit into a peach and made a slurping sound, then wiped his chin and mouth with a napkin.

"Good. I mean, if I didn't know any better, I would say he's just a quiet little guy."

"It'll be fine." Shakespeare waved. "Did you come up with a name yet?"

Jack gave a lazy nod. "We're leaning toward Everett."

"Everett Crittendon? What kind of name is that? What's wrong with Brian Crittendon? Now that has some punch to it."

They laughed, and Shakespeare explained that Sheena had come and gone, but things were looking up between them.

"I'm taking your advice. I'm gonna win her back," Shakespeare said. "Gonna romance her like when we were dating."

Jack looked down and shook his head. "I need to take my own advice. Pam and I haven't been out in a long time."

He was too embarrassed to mention that they couldn't afford it.

While Shakespeare told of his plans to turn over a new leaf and clear out his survivalist stash, Jack eyed the TV in the upper corner of the room. The volume was low. There was a shaky video clip, shot earlier, of Everett and Karen Lester leaving a back door of the arena with Cole. They were shielding their faces, being guided by bodyguards, dozens of electronic flashes igniting.

"Are you listening to me?" Shakespeare said.

"Yeah, I am, but I don't get it. I would've thought tonight would have sent you completely off the grid," Jack said.

"That's just it. Tonight showed me something. It woke me up. Anything can happen, any minute — to end things. I don't know . . ." Shakespeare shook his head and stared at Jack with an unusually somber face. "I've been preparing physically, but the rest of my life's been in shambles. Me and Sheena, the kids, things that matter."

Jack was floored, in a good way.

"I saw evil tonight, Jack." Shakespeare

closed his eyes and shook his head. "I've seen it before, but . . . I don't know. Something shook me tonight. I want to be closer to God. That's what I need."

Shakespeare had killed men that night. The man Jack shot was probably dead. It was sickening and humbling.

"Dude, that's what I need too," Jack said.

"I told Sheena I'm going to church with you."

Jack felt his eyes bulge.

"She said she'd come."

"You got a deal." Jack kept his voice calm, not wanting to sound as excited as he was. By now he knew how to handle Shakespeare, and in this instance cool and nonchalant was the way to play it.

It was quiet between them for a few minutes.

"Sounds like my neighbor finally found some cough medicine," Shakespeare said. "Are you staying here tonight?"

"I would, but Pam's mom's here. I'm not sure."

"You'll probably want to take her home."

"We'll see. They're supposed to bring the baby back in a few hours. I'd like to be here."

Shakespeare turned the TV volume up with the remote. "This thing's a fiasco."

431

"What's the latest?"

"By now they must've ID'd some of the bodies, but they're not releasing anything," Shakespeare said. "They're not saying anything about where the getaway vans went. One guy posted a video on YouTube of what he says is one of the vans. He claims they split up, went separate directions. Who knows if that's legit? More's coming in from civilians than from the media. The flares used for the fake dynamite were purchased in Columbus, but they haven't said who bought them."

The video on the TV replayed segments of the news conference led earlier by special agent Rufus Peek.

"The good news is that the second bodyguard got moved out of intensive care, so it looks like they're both gonna make it," Shakespeare said.

"Oh, man, that's good."

"I know. Oh, listen to this." Shakespeare turned it up. "You see your buddy?"

"Who? Oh yeah." There was Derrick, holding a tape recorder up as Senator Sterling spoke from a stretcher at the back of an ambulance. A light rain was falling, lit by a TV spotlight. Sterling's handler, Jenny King, was nearby, along with Peek, Hedgwick, Wolfski, paramedics, and others.

Jack and Shakespeare listened intently as the station played various pertinent segments of Sterling's talk before he was whisked to the hospital.

"He's not here, is he?" It just dawned on Jack that the senator could be at Mount Sinai Hospital.

"No, he's probably at one of the other ones. They were trying to keep it hush-hush. I also heard he might not have even gone to a hospital; they might've treated him and taken him to another location to meet his wife. His house is swarming with media — they showed it."

The video of Sterling cut off, and the word *Live* popped onto the screen. "We interrupt this footage to take you live to Columbus Festival Arena, where special agent Rufus Peek is speaking about the latest on the terrorist attack," said the female Fox broadcaster.

"Good evening," Peek said, his gaunt face washed out by the white media lights and barrage of electronic flashes. "Although we are still early in our investigation, our findings are leading us to believe that the terrorists involved in the attack tonight are homegrown, possibly even citizens of the United States."

The crowd around Peek erupted, so much

so that the camera shook. Shouts and yelling and questions came from every direction. Peek lowered his head, paused, then held up a shaky hand and leaned toward the dozens of microphones. "We are releasing two new photographs of the man calling himself Shareek Zaher."

The camera cut to side-by-side photos of Zaher, just as Jack remembered him. "These are good-quality photographs, taken by civilians in the arena this evening. Obviously, we are on the lookout for this man. He is armed and dangerous. If you see him, do not confront him, but call the number on your screen."

A toll-free number came up. "A five-million-dollar reward is being offered to anyone who can provide us with information leading to the capture of this man," Peek said. "Next we have two more photographs, also fairly close-up shots and of good quality. These two men worked closely with Zaher this evening."

Again the screen split in two.

Jack didn't recognize the guy on the right.

He zeroed in on the heavy man on the left . . . and everything stopped.

Something slammed in his stomach.

Everything froze.

The large man had been onstage with Zaher that night — but that wasn't all.

Jack's mind freewheeled — like a runaway fishing reel.

It wasn't a physical thing but a mental thing.

A sudden knowledge.

An awareness.

A fact.

He was on his feet.

Peek was talking.

Shakespeare said something.

Jack approached the TV, focusing on the man's masked face, his mouth. And suddenly all the sound in the room — the TV, Shakespeare, the man coughing, his loud oxygen tank — all sucked away.

Shakespeare spoke again, but Jack wasn't even there anymore.

His ears thundered with the pounding of his pulse as he stepped closer to the TV.

All he could do was stare, stare, stare at the toothpick in the man's mouth.

The toothpick . . . the man he'd seen somewhere before that night. Somewhere a terrorist never should have been.

59

"Yo, Jack!" Shakespeare said for a third time. "What's with you?"

Jack finally turned around, his mouth agape, his face ashen.

"Sheesh. You look like you're gonna be sick," Shakespeare said. "What gives?"

He shook his head. "Nothing." Slowly he backed away from the TV. "I should get back to Pam."

"Wait a second. What did you see? You saw something." Shakespeare nodded at the TV.

Jack's eyes searched the room, and he ran a hand through his hair.

"Talk to me," Shakespeare said.

Instead Jack went to the window, leaned on the ledge, and stared into the darkness.

"Obviously something just happened," Shakespeare said.

"I'm just thinking . . . about the baby." He didn't turn around.

Shakespeare wasn't sure what just transpired. They'd been watching the press conference. Photos of some of the terrorists had come up. Jack popped up like a jack-in-the-box and totally spaced.

Shakespeare muted the TV. "Hey, bud . . ."

Jack turned around, leaned back on the window ledge, and crossed his arms. "It's just a lot. I think I'm just overwhelmed. All this stuff happening at once — the attack, the baby. I've never shot anyone before. That guy's probably dead."

Okay. Now Shakespeare was getting it. He recalled with clarity the first insurgent he'd ever gunned down. Their eyes had met for milliseconds from sixty feet. Whoever was quickest and got off the most accurate shot would live. When Shakespeare's first blast hit his target, the man's whole body spun as if he'd been struck by a car. His feet left the ground. Blood spit from his chest like an exploding water balloon. He was probably dead before he hit the dust.

"Listen, I hear you. I know it may not feel like it, but you did the right thing," Shakespeare assured him. "You saved lives by putting him down, Jack. These people . . . they're evil to the core. They hate us, our freedom, our liberty — all we stand for. We have to defend ourselves. This is our land,

and you defended it. You were a hero to-night. You were a soldier. Do you hear me? It's no different than war."

Jack's head dropped, and he sighed.

"Sit down, man. I've been through what you have. I can relate," Shakespeare said. "Just take a load off and relax for a few minutes."

Jack raised his hands and let them drop. "I can't. I appreciate it, man." He walked to the bed. "I've got to get back to Pam, decide what we're doing for the night." He patted Shakespeare on the shoulder and headed toward the curtain, looking totally distracted.

"Don't let this get to you, man. Trust me. You did the right thing."

Jack stopped at the curtain and turned to face Shakespeare. He was about to say something. His eyes shifted to the wall, then the floor.

"What?" Shakespeare said.

Jack's mouth sealed closed, and there was a long pause. He shrugged and shook his head as if he'd come to a conclusion about something. "I'm just tired, that's all. My mind's going in a hundred different directions. I need some shut-eye. I'll see you in the morning."

They said good night, and Jack disappeared through the curtain.

But something nagged at Shakespeare.

He examined the muted TV.

Something more had been bothering Jack than the man he'd shot . . .

60

Pamela lay awake in her hospital bed. The only light was the fluorescent one casting a dreary yellow glow from behind and above her head. Her mom was asleep in the chair next to her, covered in a thin navy blanket. The TV was off. It was quiet. Pamela's stomach churned. She couldn't stop worrying.

Before Margaret fell asleep, she was struggling with memory issues, asking when Jack would return from work, asking how long they had to stay in this "hotel." As if things weren't difficult enough, her mom's dementia was worsening.

For about the sixth time, Pamela attempted to concentrate as she read the words in red that, over the years, had been underlined and highlighted in her worn Bible: *Peace I leave with you; my peace I give you. I do not give to you as the world gives. Do not let your hearts be troubled and do not be afraid.*

She rested her head on the pillow and closed her eyes, trying to relax her neck, shoulders, arms, legs. *This too shall pass.* It's what her dad used to say. He'd had an easy manner that could diffuse even her mother's fits of paranoia. Pamela wished he could be there now. He would know what to do about their financial situation. He would assure her that everything would work out with the baby. But he was gone.

She told herself he was in heaven, just as she told herself the baby was okay, but she didn't know for sure. Her dad had been a good man, a great husband and father, but he'd never had very much to say about God. They had attended church when Pamela was growing up, but it had been more out of tradition or obligation than anything. At least her father had never rejected Christ. Knowing that, she hoped to see him again one day in heaven.

Margaret stirred in her chair and shifted positions, pulling the blanket up close beneath her chin.

There were several light taps at the door. She heard it open. Jack entered quietly, adjusting his eyes. She held up a finger to her lips.

He moved smoothly across the room and

441

kissed her on the forehead. "How are you?" he whispered.

"Anxious to see my baby again. How's Shakespeare?" She, too, whispered.

"I couldn't tell anything was wrong."

"Sounds like Shakespeare. Was Sheena there?"

"Earlier, but she went home. They're gonna come to church."

Pamela's head tilted. "You're kidding me."

He shook his head but showed no emotion.

"You look so tired." She stroked his cheek, which was now filled with beard stubble.

"I am." He sighed. "We need to decide what we're doing, where we're sleeping." He nodded at Margaret.

"You should grow a beard," Pamela whispered, still exploring his face. "It would be handsome. Mr. Lumberjack."

He gave a forced smile. "What do you say? You want me to take her home and come back? Should I stay there? Do you want us both to stay here?"

Pamela dropped her hand from his face. "What's wrong?"

He stared at her for what seemed like twenty seconds. "I'm tired, that's all."

"We all are. Gee whiz. Can't we have a nice minute together?"

"Sorry, honey. I've got a lot on my mind. I know you do too." He rested a hand on her shoulder. His mind was definitely someplace else — probably fretting about the same things she was: the baby, the bills, a job, her mother.

Margaret suddenly snored loudly, paused, then snorted and lifted her head. She examined Pamela, then Jack, but said nothing — just looked at them.

"Hi, Mom. You had a good little catnap," Pamela said.

Margaret's eyes darted from the sink to the window and back at them. "I must be in the wrong room. I'm sorry." She rose quickly, tossed the blanket in the chair, and slipped into her shoes. "I apologize."

Pamela's heart rate quickened as she anticipated her mother's latest accidental charade. "Mom, you're fine." She spoke as casually as possible. "Sit back down and rest. We're deciding what you guys are gonna do for the night."

As if she wasn't listening, Margaret crossed to the phone on the table by the bed, picked it up, listened, and punched a number.

"Who are you calling, Mom?" Jack asked.

"The front desk. They gave me the wrong room. Don't worry. I'll be out of your hair in a minute. Let me gather my things and get the bellboy —"

"Do something," Pamela urged Jack. "It's worse at night."

Jack went over and gently took the phone. "Mom, let's go back home, okay?" He gently patted her back and set the phone down. "Wouldn't you like to sleep in your own bed tonight? It's been a long day. Come on. I'll take us home. We'll get the girls in bed."

"Oh, darn it." She wrestled herself away from Jack's hands and walked away with her head down. "I was thinking we were . . . Just, just go back to what you were doing. I'm sorry. Blast it. My memory's going."

Margaret shook her head and muttered, obviously angry at herself for slipping into dementia land again.

"Mom, have some cranberry juice. There's fruit and crackers over there too."

"Okay, okay, enough, Pam," she said. "You don't have to baby me. We all recognize what's happening to me. No need to dance around it."

Pamela turned away quickly, fighting back tears.

This whole thing is a mess. Just a mess! It's too much . . . too much to handle.

Jack urged Margaret to get her things

together.

"I am not going anywhere. I'm staying right here," Margaret said. "If you want to sleep in here with Pam, that's fine. I'll go find a bench in the waiting room, but I want to be close."

There was a long pause.

"What are you doing?" Margaret said.

"Getting your things. We're going home," Jack said sternly. "Pam needs her sleep. She's not going to get it if we're here. Come on, Mom. We're all tired. This is the best thing. Besides, I don't want to have to ask Tommy and Darlene to keep the girls overnight."

Pamela flipped over, wincing as she did. Her mom pouted as she gathered her knitting, a book, her glasses, and some other things.

"I'll be fine, Mom," Pamela said, relieved they were going, relieved the girls would be home in their own beds. "Thanks, Jack."

He came over, kissed her, and gave a gloomy good-bye.

Margaret wasn't any better, shuffling for the door with her head down, only managing a weak wave.

Okay, be that way.

There was nothing more Pamela could do. Nothing.

She was giving up for the day . . . and drifting off before the door closed behind them.

61

By the time Jack navigated the rainy Ohio freeways and got Margaret situated back home, then retrieved sleepy Rebecca and Faye from the Sweeneys' house next door, his whole body was depleted. His neck felt as if it had metal rods in it from the stress, and the headache behind his ears was excruciating.

But it was no time to rest. There was something he desperately needed to do.

Standing at the kitchen sink, he took three aspirin and threw back half a glass of water. Then he grabbed an apple and headed for the computer in the den, where he logged on and went straight to Fox News. Sure enough, the photos they'd shown earlier of Zaher topped the headlines. Jack's heart ticked like a rabbit's as he skimmed the article, scrolled down, skimmed, scrolled down — and *there* . . . there he was.

That's him.

That's got to be him.

Jack's hand trembled as he moved the mouse and clicked the photo he and Shakespeare had seen earlier on TV — of the dark-skinned man with the mask . . . the thick neck . . . the toothpick tucked like a fixture in the corner of his mouth.

Dear God . . . that's him.

It was a very clear shot, especially for one taken by a citizen, probably on a cell phone.

He enlarged the photo — and froze.

Staring.

Barely breathing.

Recalling the family joke, how Jack never forgot a face. He could meet someone once in passing and recognize the person months later at a quick glance.

He was virtually positive this was the same man he'd seen with Derrick that day at —

"Who's that?" Margaret's voice startled him.

The apple dropped out of his hand and rolled across the desk.

"Gee whiz, Mom. A little notice might be good next time. Maybe a knock?"

"Sorry, honey." She stood there in her robe and slippers, hair up, rubbing her hands with lotion, nodding at the computer. "He was one of the men onstage, wasn't he?"

"Yeah."

"What are you doing? You need sleep."

He picked up the apple and reduced the size of the photo on the screen to regular size.

"I can't sleep yet. Too wired."

"Me, neither. I can't stop thinking about the baby."

That, too, Jack thought, taking a deep breath, feeling the pressure of it all.

"Maybe you should take a sleeping pill or something," Margaret said. "You know, Ben used to take them once in a while." She snickered. "He called them 'blue bombs.' "

Jack stood. "I'll be fine. I'm about to go up. I just want to read the latest." He ushered her toward the door. "You gonna be okay?"

She used to drink herself to sleep. He was glad those days were behind her.

Margaret took the hint and wandered toward the steps in the foyer. He walked with her. "I'm fine." She stopped and turned to face him. "You know, I don't feel any remorse for what I did tonight." She shook her head as if replaying the moment when she was forced to gun down one of the terrorists as innocent people fled the arena. "It was us or them . . ."

Jack suddenly felt a bond with Margaret

449

he'd never experienced before. "I know. I know exactly what you mean." Once again he pictured the man he shot, spinning, exploding, dropping. "It doesn't seem real."

There was a long, quiet pause.

"God will forgive us, won't he, Jack?"

He thought about it. "He knew the circumstances we were in. It was like a war. We had to do what we did. So, yes, I believe he will forgive us."

"I feel sorry for the girls, to have to grow up in this nutty world," she said. "I'll tell you what, Martin Sterling won the presidency tonight. This is exactly what he's been warning us about. Anyone who was on the fence post before tonight is in his camp now."

Margaret's words made Jack anxious to get back into the den and figure out what he was going to do about his hunch.

"Next November can't come soon enough. We need him." She turned to go, then stopped and turned back around. "Thank you for having me here all these months, Jack. I know it hasn't been easy."

"We're glad you're here. We wouldn't want you anyplace else."

"Well, it's been good for me, to be with Pam and the girls . . . and you, of course."

They both laughed quietly.

She patted his arm and started up the stairs, watching each step while reminding him not to stay up much longer, and that they had to meet with the federal investigator sometime the next day.

He returned to his chair in the dark room, in front of the bright screen.

The reduced-size photo of the masked man was crystal clear.

The toothpick was what did it.

That was the giveaway.

If he hadn't had that in his mouth during the attack — and in that photo — Jack probably wouldn't have recognized him as one of the men in Martin Sterling's entourage the day they'd met at the *Gazette,* the day of Jack's interview.

But the toothpick got Jack's attention, especially the way it was buried in the corner of the guy's mouth as if it were part of him.

And the toothpick led up to the watery black eyes, set wide apart, just like the eyes behind the mask in the photo he stared at now. Just like the man who had been with Sterling when Derrick introduced them in the newsroom.

And if that was true, it meant the man worked for the Ohio senator.

Preposterous.

But in the back of his mind, Jack had always felt Sterling was somewhat of a wild card. He was unconventional. A renegade. That was turning out to be the understatement of the century.

If that was the case, it meant Sterling — the independent would-be candidate for president of the United States — had *staged* the terrorist attack at the arena.

Why?

To *prove* to the American people that the threat of terror on US soil was real and dangerous and terrifying and imminent — and that if they wanted to avoid such horrors in the future, they'd darn well better put him on the ballot and cast their vote for the candidate who'd built his entire platform on squelching terrorists.

Martin Sterling.

Jack buried his head in his hands.

If he was right, he had to tell . . . he had to say something — to Derrick, to Rufus Peek of the FBI, or Hedgwick with the Columbus PD.

He glanced at the masked man and backed his chair away from the desk, sticking his elbows on his knees, leaning over, thinking and rocking, thinking and rocking.

Hadn't anyone else noticed the man? Put two and two together? Said anything?

What was he waiting for?

Why wasn't he reaching for the phone to call the authorities?

And then it hit him — like a sobering, ghastly lightning bolt tossed by the Devil himself.

Jack wanted the job at the *Gazette.*

If he contacted the authorities, Sterling would go down.

The job would go away.

It was going on a year that Jack had been out of work. He *needed* the job. Their lives depended on it.

He stood and crossed his arms and paced. He turned on the overhead fan and wiped the sweat from his forehead. All he could think about was the tidal wave of bills they were facing, and the baby's future expenses. If he got the job at the *Gazette,* he'd finally have a solid, regular paycheck again, and insurance —

Where was his faith?

You don't even know the baby has problems.

What was he even thinking?

You can't do that.

But people had done worse. Staying silent wouldn't actually be doing anything wrong. Besides, the FBI would certainly realize what was going on, wouldn't they?

You've been dealt a rotten hand. You need

this job. You deserve it.

He left the den, walked through the dark house to the back door, and went out onto the screen porch. A steady rain fell. A cool breeze blew.

He just couldn't fathom that Martin Sterling could have masterminded the attack. It was insane. If Jack told authorities what he suspected, they would certainly check it out. If he turned out to be wrong, no harm would be done. If he was right, it would set the world on its ear.

And the job at the *Gazette* would be gone.

He sat down in one of the rockers. A cool mist of rain blew in on him.

You know you can't orchestrate your own destiny.

The second you cover this thing up is the second you will not *get that job . . . and other things will go wrong.*

You know from experience that God will be faithful to you if you trust him and do the right thing. He'll bless. He's proven it a million times.

Jack sat there. The mist from the rain felt like God's prompting, God's presence.

He got out his phone. If he was going to alert the authorities, Shakespeare would know the best protocol.

He punched the number.

It rang twice.

"Aw, you miss me that much already?" Shakespeare answered.

"Hey, yeah. Funny. Listen, I need to talk to you. This is serious."

"Hit me."

Jack quickly explained his suspicions. It was a relief just to get it off his chest. When he finished, the other end of the line was silent.

"You there?" Jack said.

More silence.

"Brian?"

"Yeah," Shakespeare said. "I'm here."

"Well?"

Long pause.

"We need to contact Rufus Peek. Right now."

62

Derrick hung up the phone on his desk, took a deep breath, and looked out at the bustling newsroom. Buck Stevens had just told him that all systems were go for a special morning edition of the *Columbus Gazette* focusing almost entirely on the attack at the arena.

Now he was really under the gun, but he couldn't recall a more exciting moment in his career as a journalist. He wished Jack could be in on it. They'd once shared side-by-side cubicles at the *Trenton City Dispatch*. He knew his friend missed reporting with a passion — and needed the regular paycheck. But Derrick took solace in knowing they would be working together again soon, especially since Martin Sterling's run for president looked so promising.

He skimmed the story he'd written about the night's events at the arena, stopped and thought for a second, then continued where he'd left off.

Derrick was firing on all cylinders, clicking away at his keyboard in a steady flow when his cell phone rang.

Jack.

He thought about sending him to voice mail but decided to take it and make it quick.

"Hey, what's up?" Derrick answered.

"Hey. Listen, I need to give you a heads-up on something," Jack said.

"Okay. Talk fast. I'm on deadline."

"Well, take a breather. This'll impact what you're doing."

Derrick clicked Save, pushed back from the computer, and grabbed his mug. "Okay, I'm going for coffee."

It felt good to stretch.

"Remember the day I came to the newsroom for the interview with Buck Stevens, and I saw you? You were with Martin Sterling and his entourage?"

"Yeah." Derrick weaved in and out of people standing about the busy newsroom.

"There was a big guy in Sterling's security detail, dark skinned, quiet — huge guy."

"Yeah, I know the one."

"Toothpick."

"Yeah, yeah."

"Do you know his name?"

"No. Why?" Derrick excused himself as he squeezed between two guys and filled his coffee mug.

"Do you know if he and Sterling are tight?"

"No idea. I've only seen him once or twice. He's like a fill-in." Derrick headed back through the crowd. "What's this about, dude?"

"I think I recognized him at the arena attack — wearing a mask. One of Zaher's men."

Derrick stopped. Hot coffee splashed from his cup onto his hand. "Ouch." He shook it off. "That's impossible."

"I know it sounds nuts, but I recognized him in the picture they're posting all over the place. He's got a toothpick, just like the day I was in the newsroom."

"Jack, c'mon."

But Derrick knew Jack never forgot a face. And he knew the photo of the hostile; it was everywhere.

Jack had to be wrong. "Hold on." Derrick's heart thundered as he hurried back to his desk so he could pull up the photo.

"What's happening?" Jack said.

"I'm heading to my computer to check it out. There's no way, dude."

But he knew there was a way.

"I might be wrong, but Shakespeare put me in touch with Rufus Peek. He was especially interested. You know why?"

Derrick slid into his chair, closed his story, and called up the latest news on CNN. He found the photo of the guy and immediately saw the resemblance, but this was one shot in a million. "I got it up. I see what you're saying about the similarity, but . . . there is no way . . ."

"Listen to me, Derrick. Just listen. Peek thinks these guys are homegrown."

"I heard that, and we got it in the story, but most of it's speculation at this point."

"No, it isn't. Shakespeare's in tight with Peek. Peek told him the guy who bought the flares for the fake bombs is an American citizen. Born and raised in Chillicothe."

"Chillicothe, Ohio?" Derrick felt as if he were on the edge of a cliff, waiting to be pushed off.

"One and the same," Jack said.

Derrick's mind reeled. This new information was a can of worms. If he dared to follow up on what Jack was saying, he would be working all night and would never make his deadlines.

"You there?" Jack said.

"Yeah —"

"That's not all," Jack said. "That guy you

interviewed tonight out in the field, the loner who helped Sterling, Ed somebody?"

"Scarborough. Ed Scarborough." Derrick was slipping into a daze, his suspicions and blood pressure mounting with each word out of Jack's mouth.

"His spending habits changed dramatically two months ago. They think he received an influx of cash — a lot of it."

Suddenly the story Derrick had written was old news. He swallowed hard and sat there in a fog. If that was true, it meant Senator Sterling had hired Ed Scarborough to corroborate the story about his heroic escape.

This was a bomb.

Jack wasn't finished. "He bought new tires and wheels for his pickup, new hunting gear, fancy deer stand, a two-thousand-dollar gun safe. They're searching his place as we speak."

Derrick was light-headed, his mind fuzzy. He stared at the photograph of the masked man with the toothpick, recalling his various conversations and interviews with Martin Sterling. Could Sterling be *that* nuts? To put all those citizens in harm's way? To let people die?

Deep inside, Derrick had always thought there was something brazen about the senator, but this . . .

"That's all we got right now," Jack said. "What's the deal on Sterling's press conference in the morning — do you know yet?"

Derrick was sweating profusely, almost gasping for breath. He wiped his forehead with his shirtsleeve. He needed to get with his editor.

"Derrick?"

"Yeah . . ."

"I know it's a lot to take in."

"Sterling's gonna be at Mount Sinai at eight sharp to visit the people hurt in the attack." Derrick's voice had fallen to a monotone. It took all he had to keep going. "He's scheduled to do a press conference on the steps outside the hospital right after, around nine."

"I assume you'll be there," Jack said.

Derrick started in motion toward Buck Stevens's office. "I'll be there — if I still have a job."

63

Pamela's phone buzzed next to her on the bed. She opened her eyes from a deep sleep. The hospital room was dark now, except for light from around the edges of the door and her phone, which glowed next to her.

She squinted at the screen. A text from Jack.

Hey if you're still up call me.

She let the phone drop at her side and stretched. The aftermath of the C-section left her with a gnawing pain in her abdomen. She would ask for something to take the edge off when the nurse returned.

She was anxious to see the baby again — and ready to feed him.

Everett Crittendon.

Yes, she liked the ring of it.

She was wide-awake now and determined that no matter what issues the baby faced, they would deal with it. They would play the hand they were dealt, as her dad used to say. If she had to continue working full-time, with Jack at home, so be it. If they had to take out loans, it was only money.

Her thoughts turned to frail Lucy, her guardian angel that night, and to her menacing husband, Victor, who she just knew was explosively dangerous. What had happened when they had walked to their car, rode home, gone inside? Pamela shuddered at the thought of any more physical harm coming to Lucy. The mental anguish alone had to be unbearable.

"God, please help Lucy right now," Pamela whispered. "Protect her. Be her shield. Her defense. Her comforter."

At least Lucy had agreed to seek help. That had to be one of the reasons God had brought them together that night, so Pamela and Jack and Margaret could confirm to her — through sober, unbiased counsel — that she needed outside intervention, sooner rather than later.

She patted for her phone, found it, and pressed Jack's number.

"Hey, babe," he answered. "How are you?"

"I'm good. How are the girls?"

"Fine. Sound asleep. Darlene had them in their nightgowns. They were falling asleep on that big couch of theirs, watching *The Lion King.* Tommy was asleep right next to them."

Pamela giggled.

"They barely said a word; slipped right into their beds," Jack said.

"Good. What about Mom?"

"It's crazy. She was fine, absolutely fine. No sign of dementia. We had a good conversation. She's in her room now. I think she's reading. Did you sleep?"

"Oh gosh, yeah. I crashed. Now I'm wide-awake."

"Are you ready for the latest time bomb?"

"Oh no. What now?"

When he told her he thought he recognized the masked man as having been part of Sterling's security detail, all Pamela could do was shake her head. She knew Jack was right. He never forgot a face — ever.

Jack told her that his tip was just one more in a series of similar clues that were surfacing and leading Peek to believe these were homegrown terrorists — and possibly not even terrorists at all. Quite possibly, they were murderous thugs hired by the independent candidate to wreak havoc and, in turn, send people rushing desperately to put him on the ballot and in the White House next November to save them from their fears.

There was so much dishonesty in politics anymore, it didn't take Pamela ten seconds to believe that Martin Sterling could have masterminded the terrorist plot at the arena.

But to allow American citizens to be thrust into harm's way? He had to be insane.

"The last I heard, Peek may wait till the press conference in the morning to arrest Sterling. They're hoping that by waiting they can draw the toothpick guy out, and as many others as possible who might've been in on the attack."

"How do you know all this?"

"Shakespeare and Peek hit it off. It's all top secret."

There was a knock at Pamela's door. "Hold on, Jack," she said, then called for whoever it was to come in.

"Who is it?" Jack said.

"Whoever it is, I'm sorry, you're going to need to turn a light on," Pamela called.

The overhead light flicked on.

Pam squinted.

Dr. Shapiro?

Yes, it was Dr. Shapiro, awkwardly holding the door open with one hand and wheeling the baby into the room on a cart with the other.

"Pam, what's going on? Who is it?" Jack said.

"Hold on, Jack."

"Mrs. Crittendon, I know it's late." He bumped the cart into the room and rolled it right over to the bed. Little Everett was swaddled with his knit cap on and eyes open wide.

"Jack, it's the baby — and Dr. Shapiro. I'll call you back."

"Shapiro's back? Good. Hurry up. Let me know what's going on."

She assured him she would, then hung up.

The doctor parked the cart, gently lifted the baby out, and placed him in Pamela's waiting arms. "Your baby's going to be fine."

She looked at the doctor's confident smile, then at tiny Everett, who was searching her eyes with his — and she burst into tears.

The doctor smiled. "I need to apologize for leaving in the middle of everything. I'm very sorry. It was an emergency. My father-in-law had a seizure this evening. I dropped everything to get to him."

"Oh my, I'm so sorry," Pamela said. "Is he okay?"

"He's going to be fine, yes, thank you."

Pamela was so relieved. She helped the little guy find his nourishment and settled back against the pillows.

"Anyway, the nurses told me you and your husband were concerned, and rightfully so.

I left you in the lurch. So I wanted to get back here and look at the results of our most recent tests. As it turns out, I think Everett here is just a super mellow little fellow. But he is completely fine."

Dr. Shapiro continued explaining, but Pamela was lost in a flood of tears and praise.

64

With his phone on the bathroom counter, Jack brushed his teeth, then threw on some pajama shorts and a T-shirt. He tossed the covers back and climbed into bed, wide-awake, propping up several pillows behind him.

He was anxious to hear from Pam and was so cold he was practically shivering.

Why had Dr. Shapiro returned to the hospital at that time of night? Was he bringing good news — or bad?

The bedroom was intensely quiet and lonely without Pam.

A spy novel sat next to him, which he had put there thinking it would get his mind off things, but he was in no mood to crack it. He pointed the remote at the TV and checked the news on CNN, but they kept playing the same segments over and over again. He turned it off, dropped his head back on the pillows, and closed his eyes.

At least the girls were asleep in their own beds; that was a good feeling. At last check, Margaret's light was still on in her room down the hall. The way she had been in and out with her dementia, he wondered about her future and how long she could stay with them without needing additional help.

His phone buzzed.

This is it . . . news on the baby.

But no, it wasn't. It was a text from Shakespeare.

Just hung up with Peek. They r gathering more evidence. Arrest likely at 9 am press conf. Come to my room at 7:45. R u still here? Latest on baby?

Jack quickly texted him with the latest and agreed to meet him at the hospital at 7:45, which was only a few hours away. He hit Send, and while the text was transmitting, his phone rang.

He checked the screen. *Pamela.*

"Hey, babe, what's going on?" He took a deep breath.

Just then Margaret appeared in the doorway.

"He's okay, honey. He's fine!" Pam gushed. "He's going to be just fine."

Jack ripped out of bed and reached out

for Margaret.

By the time she got to him, he was crying.

They embraced.

Pam continued talking.

Jack held the phone up so Margaret could hear.

They both listened and squeezed each other, laughing with delight.

In his hospital gown and flip-flops, Shakespeare handed the old man beyond the curtain a plastic glass filled with ice water. The man had been coughing a blue streak. With a trembling hand and watery, yellow eyes, he nodded and took the glass but didn't drink.

"Drink some," Shakespeare said. "You need to wet your pipes."

When he tried, the old gentleman's hand shook so badly that the water spilled all over the floor and onto his gown. None made it to his mouth.

"Gee whiz." Shakespeare grabbed a towel and wiped him off, then dried the floor.

The poor guy shook his head and lowered his eyes in defeat, then turned back to the oxygen machine that sat on the floor between his bony knees. He appeared to have no hope or strength.

Shakespeare found a straw back on his

side of the room, dropped it in the glass of water, and held it up to the man's mouth.

The man craned his neck and stared up at Shakespeare for a moment, then found the straw with a shaking hand, put it in his bone-dry mouth, and drank until half the water was gone.

Even that simple action winded the man. He caught his breath and said a feeble thanks.

Shakespeare nodded, set the glass by him, and went through the curtain to his side of the room. He sat down in the chair by his bed. The poor old guy appeared to have no family or friends to visit him.

Shakespeare wondered who would visit him if he were on his deathbed. Who would come to his funeral? Shakespeare had worked so hard at isolating himself and his family that they barely had any relationships outside their own little tribe. Many of his family ties had been severed, because all of his relatives thought he was a survivalist nutcase.

Something was happening inside Shakespeare. He wanted to help people.

He'd once been like that. Outgoing. Caring.

When had he changed? When had he managed to turn so insanely inward?

He'd denied it until now.

But it had been when his son Will was born — with special needs. Then Tyler. Back-to-back children who were not "normal" by the world's standards.

Elbows on his knees, Shakespeare buried his head in his hands.

You allowed them to be born like that, he thought. *And I've hated you for it.*

So he'd rebelled — against authority, against evil, against society.

Without admitting it, he had been spitting in the face of God.

But now — in that stuffy, smelly hospital room — a light was arising. It was shining with something good and pure and bright. It was telling him it was time for a change. He wasn't sure what it all meant, but he knew he wanted to be closer to God. And he knew he wanted to make up for lost time with Sheena and the kids. And he knew he wanted to invest in other people, like Jack and Pam . . . and needy people, like the old man beyond the curtain.

His cell phone chirped with a new text message.

He wiped his eyes and took in a deep breath and stretched.

He liked what he was feeling.

It was a gratefulness he'd never experienced before.

He got up and crossed to his phone and examined the screen.

The text from Jack read:

Baby FINE ! ! ! Official name: Everett BRIAN Crittendon. C u at 7:45.

He read it again.

And he stared at the baby's middle name.

BRIAN.

My name.

And he bent over.

And he cried.

And he laughed.

And he let everything pour out that he'd held in for so long.

65

Pamela could tell by the dull light around the edge of the window curtain in her hospital room that it was almost dawn. Excitedly she did what she'd done half a dozen times in the night, leaning over the side of her bed and shining the light from her cell phone onto the baby as he slept. He really was a mellow little guy and a good sleeper.

With a little coaxing, Dr. Shapiro had let her keep the baby in the cart next to her. Pamela hadn't slept well, but she didn't care. The baby was fine. That was all that mattered. She was so happy, so relieved.

She'd thought about Lucy through the night and had prayed for her — for her protection, for a good future. She'd thought of Jack and how lucky she was to be married to such a man of faith. He'd risked the promise of the job at the *Gazette* to blow the whistle on Sterling's bodyguard. She trusted it was for the best.

It was all so surreal.

She lifted herself up, ignoring the pain in her abdomen, and slipped out of bed. She opened the curtain several inches, just enough so she could see her way around. She went over to Everett's little bed and leaned over him. His eyes were open.

"Good morning, baby . . . Good morning, sunshine."

When his eyes found hers, his whole body flinched.

"You recognize Mommy? You recognize me?" She reached in and scooped him up. "Are you hungry? Yes, sir. I bet you are. I bet . . ."

Carrying him gently in her arms, she hit the remote to raise the back of the bed and settled back to feed him.

He was going to be a good boy, a gentleman, just like his dad.

"You're gonna be brave and strong." Pamela ran her fingers across his little forehead and rubbed his silky hair. "And you're hearty. Yes, you're a hearty little eater."

Her phone buzzed on the bed next to her.

It was still so early.

It was a text message — from Lucy.

Pamela's heart raced as she read.

How are you and baby? Let me know when you can. I won't be able to make it this morning. Will explain later. I'm fine.
Lucy

Pamela looked at the time the text was sent: 6:57 a.m., just a minute ago.

She quickly dialed Lucy's number and waited as it rang.

"Hello," Lucy whispered.

"Lucy? It's Pamela. I got your text."

"Hey, I didn't mean to wake you. I'm gonna be busy later and knew I wouldn't be able to contact you —"

"Is everything okay?" Pamela held her breath.

"Yes . . . yes. Everything's fine, thanks to you and Jack — and your mom. I'm safe, Pam. I'm finally safe." Lucy began to cry softly.

"What happened, Lucy? Do you want to talk about it?"

"This was the last time, thanks to you guys," she said, choking back sobs. "The last time . . ."

Pamela waited.

But Lucy continued to whimper.

"Where are you?" Pamela finally asked.

"He shook me . . . going to the car. He was furious — for no reason. We got home, and I knew what was coming. I knew you were right. I got the car keys. He swung at me, at my head. I ducked and I . . . My adrenaline was pumping so hard. I ran at him with all my might. He hit the wall . . . a sculpture on the wall. It was this big metal thing. He was bleeding. I ran! I ran to the car. He was down. I might've hurt him really badly."

"Where are you right now?" Pamela said.

"I'm safe. I'm safe, thank God. I can't believe it. I'm finally going to be free. I went to the police. I told them. They were going to get him. I'm at a safe house for . . . for battered women."

Pamela sighed.

She closed her eyes and squeezed the baby. "Thank God, Lucy. Thank God."

"I don't know if they got him . . . how he is . . . I don't care. I never want to see him again. I'm never going back. And it's thanks to you. Last night happened for a reason."

"For lots of reasons," Pamela said in a daze.

God had sent Lucy for her, in her time of trial. Yet, somehow, they had helped each other. And now Lucy was going to be okay. She was going to be safe from harm. She was going to have a future.

"I can't believe it," Pamela said. "You're free."

"When they brought me here in the middle of the night, I slept, Pam. For the first time in months, I slept so deeply — like a baby."

There was a long silence.

"Speaking of babies," Lucy said. "How is our little guy?"

66

The first crack of dawn was quickly changing the look of the newsroom at the *Gazette.* Derrick watched as the massive room seemed to shift from having a dim, almost romantic appeal to being stark white, with every mark on the wall and stain on the carpet visible and ugly.

He usually wasn't there that time of day, because he and most of the reporters worked afternoons and nights. But because of the extraordinary events brought on by the terrorist attack, the newsroom was packed with weary reporters and editors who'd worked frantically all night on the stories and photos that would fill the morning edition.

Male and female reporters sat and stood, chatted and sipped coffee to pass the time, waiting for Senator Sterling's press conference. Derrick chuckled to himself, thinking they looked like the engineers at NASA headquarters, anxiously awaiting a lunar landing or shuttle launch.

He sat at his computer, leaning on his knees, recapping the night's events.

After he'd hung up with Jack hours earlier, he'd made a slew of calls, confirming that a man named Jody Johnson, twenty-eight, of Chillicothe, had purchased a large quantity of emergency flares from a store in Lancaster, Ohio. These were eventually used to build the fake bombs that had been strapped to the two EventPros staffers. Johnson was now in FBI custody.

Derrick had also been able to confirm that Ed Scarborough, the guy who just happened to be driving by Seneca Falls when Martin Sterling was fleeing his captors, had indeed come into some serious cash two months earlier. Derrick phoned his house in the wee hours of the morning to question him further, but his elderly mother claimed Scarborough had left town to attend to a sick relative. She also said the FBI had been there looking for him.

Derrick had pounded out three stories about the attack. Other reporters had chipped in more. And they had a bunch of Daniel's photographs slated to run on a special six-page spread.

He checked his watch. It was almost time

for them to head over to Mount Sinai Hospital, where Sterling was scheduled to visit those who'd been injured in the attack, then hold his press conference. The morning edition of the *Gazette* wouldn't roll off the presses until just after his visit to the hospital. As far as Derrick knew, the Sterling camp wasn't aware that their candidate was a prime suspect in the attack.

The phone on his desk rang.

"Derrick Whittaker."

"Hey man, it's Daniel. Come to my computer."

"Dude, we gotta get going."

"I know. Just come." Daniel hung up.

Derrick huffed, grabbed his stuff, and hurried through the newsroom. He turned a corner and headed for the photography department, where he spotted Daniel standing at a large iMac, waiting for him.

"We gotta roll, man," Derrick said as he approached.

"Just look at this." Daniel pointed to several photographs he had enlarged on the screen. "It was the day of Sterling's photo shoot, here in the studio."

Derrick examined the photographs. Sterling wasn't in them, but Jenny King and several of his entourage were pictured, casually standing around a black stool and white curtain backdrop, not realizing they were being photographed.

"I was testing my light meter. You see him?" Daniel pointed to the large, dark-skinned man, toothpick embedded in the corner of his mouth.

"I sure do." Derrick got chills. "That's him."

"I thought so. The FBI got copies of all my photos last night, but I didn't think of these till this morning." Daniel closed out the photos and opened his email. "I'm gonna shoot these to Rufus Peek real quick. Then we can take off."

"Good idea. Maybe we can run them tomorrow — if he turns out to be who we think he is."

Derrick drove them across town in his FJ Cruiser. As they came within about four city blocks of Mount Sinai Hospital, they began seeing the people.

"Oh my gosh," Daniel said.

Clusters of men, women, and children trudged toward the hospital, laughing and talking, resembling crowds filing into a major-league baseball stadium. Several of them carried American flags. Many carried signs.

Derrick read one aloud: Sterling — American Hero.

Daniel read another: Vote to Stop Terror: Vote Sterling.

"They don't have a clue," Derrick said.

But their support made Derrick question once again whether Martin Sterling could really be guilty of orchestrating such an outlandish plot.

"Wait . . . listen." Daniel rolled down his window.

A group of them were chanting. Derrick listened until he could make out what they were yelling: "Protect the US, Sterling for president! Protect the US, Sterling for president!"

"I think you better find the first availablc," Daniel said.

"You got that right." Derrick swung down a side street, searching for a parking place. His phone rang.

"This is Derrick."

"Derrick. Jenny King. Are you at the hospital yet?" She sounded frazzled.

"We're close."

"We're postponing the senator's visit with the people injured in the attack." She was practically yelling over the crowd. "It's a security issue. We can't . . . we don't have the control and coverage we need. We'll go on with the press conference at nine. I'm trying to get the word out. Pass it on, will you?"

Derrick spotted a small parking space and put his blinker on. "I will," he said. "Can you get me and Daniel up close?"

"We've got a press section, but . . ." She stopped and called to someone else. Then she came back. "This is nuts. If you want a spot, you better get here. I'll do what I can." She hung up.

Derrick set the phone down and began backing into the spot.

"Whoa!" Daniel said.

Derrick stopped in the middle of his maneuver.

Two . . . three . . . four . . . five enormous camouflage trucks rumbled past on the cross street in front of them.

"What the heck?" Daniel said. "We better hurry!"

Derrick's phone buzzed. He finished backing into the spot, pulled forward, and jerked to a stop. The car was crooked and not close to the curb, but it would have to do.

He checked his phone. It was a text from their editor:

Governor has issued state of emergency for Columbus. He's called in Ohio National Guard for public safety. B careful.

67

Jack was relieved Shakespeare was with him. Shakespeare would know what to do if all hell broke loose, which Jack felt it might, as they stood amid the growing crowd in front of Mount Sinai Hospital.

Minutes ago the Ohio National Guard roared in with their massive trucks, slowing but not stopping for pedestrians, who laughed nervously and scurried out of the way. Some forty to fifty soldiers filed out of various vehicles in precise lines and hustled up the hospital steps, forming a line in the shape of a half moon around the back of Sterling's podium, which was set up at the bottom of the steps beyond the facility's front doors.

Jenny King was there, dressed in a beige pantsuit, pacing with her brown high heels and big walkie-talkie, along with several other Sterling handlers who skittishly awaited her commands.

485

Shakespeare had gotten wind that the governor had called in the Guard to keep the peace at the event, knowing there would be a mix of Sterling supporters and protestors — and potential terrorist threats. The soldiers were in camouflage gear from their boots to their helmets. They carried machine guns and clear bulletproof shields. Columbus police were out in full force as well, some on foot and some on horseback. So far Jack had seen no sign of Wolfski and his SWAT team.

More people filed in from all directions. Most of the thousands in attendance, including a handful of families with strollers and small children, were there to support the independent presidential hopeful. But there were packs of protestors throughout, waving signs and shouting into megaphones in opposition of Sterling and his "hate" tactics.

"I just got a text from Derrick. They're making their way up here," Jack told Shakespeare, as they stood some thirty feet from the podium.

"Good luck with that," Shakespeare said as he scanned the landscape like a secret-service agent.

Sterling was due onstage any minute.

"See the guys in the black suits?" Shakespeare nodded to one twenty feet to the right of the podium and another twenty-five feet to the left. They wore sunglasses and earpieces with wires that ran down into their jackets.

"Yeah."

"They're FBI — Peek's guys."

"I haven't seen him. Have you?" Jack said.

"He's here somewhere. Look around, there's more of them. I've counted seven."

Jack stood on his tiptoes, craned around, and spotted three . . . four . . . five . . . six.

"Here he comes now." Shakespeare nodded toward the front doors of the hospital.

Rufus Peek walked out with several other dark suits behind him. They settled to the side of the top steps, just beyond the human wall of National Guardsmen.

The chanting to Jack's right grew louder. It was a large group of protestors yelling, "Stop the profiling." One of their signs read Keep America Free and featured Sterling's face with a red slash through it. Another read Vote Sterling = INSANITY!

News crews camped in a long, sloppy line along the front of the podium, with cameras, recorders, and video equipment — ready to rock and roll.

Jack surveyed the crowd once more. He spotted Derrick and waved to get his attention. Daniel was right behind him. Derrick saw him and weaved in and out of bystanders in his direction.

When he finally got there, he was out of breath. "I can't believe this!" he said, shaking hands with Jack and Shakespeare.

"We gotta get closer." Daniel bumped into Derrick from behind as he fooled with his camera.

"Okay, let's keep going. See you boys." Derrick headed into the mass of people, and Daniel followed.

Jack heard the chirps of a siren in the distance and tried to figure out which way it was coming from. Then a patrol car from the Columbus PD pulled down Washington Boulevard with its lights flashing, followed by another. Two black SUVs followed, with two more flashing patrol cars behind them.

Jack's heart thundered. To think that he was partly responsible for blowing the whistle on one of the most popular men in America, a man who was on his way to becoming president of the United States — it blew his mind.

The procession of vehicles stopped at the curb along the front of the hospital. Jack noticed Derrick and Daniel shouting back and forth with Jenny King, who finally made some reporters move over to make room for them. They were within ten feet of the podium. The menagerie of media people was chomping at the bit, inching forward with their equipment, as Jenny and the others ran across the line, literally pushing them back to keep them in their places.

Jack looked up at the large hospital and noticed people in many of the windows, staring down on the historic scene unfolding at street level.

"This is it," Shakespeare said, as the doors of the first SUV swung open.

68

Shakespeare was on his toes, eyes glued to the first black SUV.

Two men in suits got out of the front of the vehicle.

The crowd went crazy. People pushed in tighter, forcing Shakespeare and Jack forward three, four, five steps.

"Are either of those the toothpick guy?" Shakespeare said.

"Negative," Jack said.

One of them opened a back door. The other came around, reached in, and retrieved a pair of silver crutches. Then, almost larger than life, Martin Sterling shimmied out of the back of the SUV and hopped onto the waiting crutches.

People screamed so loudly, Shakespeare covered his ears momentarily. Rolls of toilet paper sailed through the air. Flags waved. People pushed forward, wanting to get closer. One little boy nearby screamed in panic; his father scooped him up with a look of alarm etched on his face.

The Ohio senator wore a dark-blue suit and red tie. His entire left leg was in a white cast, which had been decorated with a bright drawing of an American flag. Like a movie star on the red carpet, he stood there waving and smiling for about a minute. Then, suddenly stone-faced, he set his shoulders back and saluted with animation.

Foghorns blasted from amid the sea of people. American flags of all sizes waved above people's heads. Hundreds of red-white-and-blue signs jumped up and down above the crowd; most of them read Sterling for President — Sterling for America!

As the senator leaned forward on the crutches and began making his way toward the podium, the crowd's roar became deafening.

Shakespeare and Jack looked at each other in amazement. Sterling's popularity was over the top.

Maybe Jack was wrong.

He *wanted* Jack to be wrong. He wanted to cheer for Sterling.

But all of the other evidence was pointing directly at him.

Shakespeare noticed that the back windows of the second SUV had rolled down, but he couldn't see who was inside.

Several of Peek's agents in the crowd held binoculars to their faces, watching Sterling and his team. When he got to the podium, the press crept in closer and closer. Derrick and Daniel were literally at his feet.

"That's far enough," Sterling said as he handed the crutches to one of Jenny's helpers and gripped the podium, one hand on each side. "Thank you. Thanks for the support . . ."

The thunderous applause was so loud that it drowned out the senator's voice.

His mouth sealed shut, he squinted and raised a hand with fingers splayed, firmly motioning for everyone to quiet down. Before they did, he launched forward, boldly, with no notes in front of him.

"What is terror?" His voice boomed, and the volume of the crowd dialed down. "I repeat, what — is — terror? I'll tell you what it is — it is *intense fear.* That is what a number of us experienced firsthand last night right here in the heartland of America, at Columbus Festival Arena."

Angry screams and boos rang out. More foghorns. And yelling from the opposition for peace.

"Let me tell you something. Hey, you . . ." Sterling pointed to an obnoxious protester with a megaphone who was perched atop the shoulders of a tall bearded guy wearing a red bandana. "It's people like you who are *ruining* this country. And you know what? It's about time someone stands up and calls a spade a spade; enough of this 'politically correct' garbage. It's about time anti-Americans like you got run out of this country on a rail. You don't deserve to be here. You don't understand the blood and sacrifice it took to make this country free."

Absolute bedlam.

"Let me talk. Let me talk," Sterling called. "I appreciate your applause, but please just be quiet. It's what I have to say that the American people need to hear. I'm not here to be a superstar. I'm here to make a difference for this great country. Now, what happened last night is something no more Americans should ever have to experience — *ever again*!"

People were pressing in so hard that Shakespeare and Jack couldn't keep their places; they were being forced every which-way. Another child screamed amid the frenzy. This was no place for a child, Shakespeare thought.

"Terrorists *hate* the liberties we enjoy in these great United States. They're jealous. They're full of hatred. They're evil to the core. I look at our current president in utter disbelief. Don't you get it, Mr. President? There are people who are out to *destroy* our freedom and our way of life. Life as we know it. Coming and going freely. Working and playing where we want. Worshipping when and where we want. Going to the park, the mall, the ball game — with no fear!"

Everything was getting tighter, more ramped up, more chaotic. The media people inched in, and so did the Guardsmen. The crowd forged in as well, everyone attempting to get as close as possible to their new-found American hero.

"If we leave it up to the current president, soon — very soon — there will be suicide bombers exploding themselves on our buses and subways, in our malls and stadiums. I promise you that! Why? Because he is actually *reducing* the amount we spend on national defense and homeland security. Our securities and defenses are crumbling around us. I will *quadruple* those budgets and make US security my number one priority. It's time for that . . ."

A door on the far side of the second black SUV opened, and a man got out.

"That's him, getting out now!" Jack said.

He was wide and thick. Dark skin.

Shakespeare couldn't tell if he had a toothpick; he was too far away.

But it was he. He buttoned his coat over his large, hard belly and began walking slowly toward Sterling with the other security guy.

Peek saw him too. He lifted his wrist to his mouth and spoke into his radio.

The wheels were turning.

This thing was coming down right now.

"Based on the conversations I overheard among the terrorists last night," Sterling continued, "those thugs were going to make me some kind of sacrificial lamb, live on the Internet, to show what happens to those of us who have the guts to fight them. Well, you know what? It backfired. Now they've got a tiger by the tail."

Amid the deafening noise of the crowd, the large man and his partner made their way to within ten feet of Sterling, stopped, and clasped their hands in front of them.

The FBI men in dark suits were tightening their circle around the podium.

"FBI's closing in," Shakespeare said.

Up on his toes, Jack looked around.

"This is about to get interesting," Shakespeare said.

The FBI agents inched in — closer, closer.

Peek did the same, slowly.

The crowd wasn't going to like it.

Peek lifted his wrist and spoke; then he and his men suddenly walked freely toward Sterling, toward the large man, no longer trying to hide their actions.

Sterling stopped in midsentence and peered back at Peek, who was walking toward him as if he was taking a brisk walk in the park. Peek's men had broken free of the crowd and were moving in at the same clip.

Sterling's bodyguards exchanged anxious glances.

The big guy unbuttoned his jacket . . . going for his gun?

Agents closed in.

Wait . . .

Smoke.

Rising thick gray smoke to the right.

People screamed and pushed away from it in a maddening rush.

Bang-bang-bang-bang!

Shakespeare jumped and yanked Jack to the ground.

"Don't panic. I think it's firecrackers," Shakespeare yelled over the chaos. "Probably a smoke bomb. Sit tight."

But the crowd thought it was gunshots.

Order was lost.

There was screaming and shoving.

A stampede.

Shakespeare ripped a gun from a holster at his ankle and racked the slide.

69

The smoke . . . It was burning Derrick's eyes so badly . . . all he could do was cling to the pavement, as if he were on the floor of a fast merry-go-round. He could barely see through the tears. Someone stepped on his leg.

The explosions . . . gunfire?

Bodies bashed against him as people fled. Even reporters were running.

He forced himself to peer through watery eyes. The FBI had Sterling; they were cuffing him! But as they were, Peek and another agent — and even Sterling — looked at Derrick in horror, their eyes and mouths wide open, their hands extended toward him —

"Derrick, look out!" Daniel screamed.

It was too late.

Derrick was snatched from the ground like a rag doll.

He got a glimpse . . . dark skin . . . toothpick!

The man's thick arm locked around Derrick's throat like a machine.

Derrick's feet left the ground and he swung around.

The metal nose of a gun smashed his temple.

The man's sweat flung onto Derrick, but he said nothing — just continued to pivot in every direction, frantically seeking a way out.

Derrick knew there was none.

People were scurrying in every direction, screaming.

The only ones left had guns drawn on them: Peck and his agents, the National Guardsmen . . .

Derrick might die.

Little had he known when he got up that morning that this day might be his last.

He would never see Zenia again.

He spun again, and there was Shakespeare, legs spread and arms locked in front of him, pointing a big black gun right at them. Jack and Daniel were on the ground nearby with their hands outstretched toward Derrick, as if trying to calm the maniac holding the gun to his head.

The abductor shifted again, grunting, but still without a word.

And really, nothing needed to be said.

The situation was obvious.

The man wanted out — didn't want to be caught, taken in.

He would probably rather die . . . and he certainly didn't care about Derrick.

A massive wave of heat rolled over Derrick.

So this was it.

"Drop the gun. Let him go," Peek called.

The man jerked toward Peek —

BAM.

The abductor's body jolted.

Everything went silent . . . slow motion.

A mist hit Derrick's face. *Blood.*

The arm around his neck released.

Derrick fell away . . . rolled.

BAM.

Like an elephant hit by poisonous darts, the massive abductor crumpled to the pavement.

Derrick looked up.

Shakespeare's gun was still smoking.

70

The Crittendons' home, eight days later

Sheena beamed as she sat on Shakespeare's lap with her arm around his neck. They had showed up at church that morning, so Jack and Pam invited the whole family over for pizza afterward. The children were playing ball tag in the backyard beneath a menacing afternoon sky, and the adults were bundled up on the back porch.

"You read today's paper?" Shakespeare said.

"Not yet," Jack said.

"Only the ads," Margaret said.

"Sterling says he still wants to be on the ticket."

They all chuckled.

"That would be good." Margaret wiped her mouth with a napkin, her hands trembling slightly. "He can conduct his campaign from the prison exercise yard."

"He's really got issues, doesn't he?" Pam

501

said. "It's amazing he got as far as he did."

"Nixon on steroids," Sheena said. "He insists he was doing what was best for the country. Stands behind everything that happened. Claims no one was supposed to get hurt. Are you serious?"

"Think of the planning that went into it," Jack said. "I can't believe he got all those guys to go along with him."

"Oh, I can." Shakespeare took an enormous bite of pizza. "There're plenty of screwballs out there. That'll never change."

"I read they were all headed out of the country. Every one of them had a boarding pass," Margaret said. "They were changing their appearance, then all heading their separate ways."

"They've all been captured, right?" Pam said.

"Got the last one yesterday," Shakespeare said.

"Did he really think he'd get away with it — with all of those people involved?" Pam said.

"You gotta understand his mind-set," Shakespeare said. "He really thought his plan was righteous — like an investment in America. He said the lives lost were a small price to pay —"

"To get him into office," Margaret said.

"Exactly, to get him into office," Shakespeare said. "That's how much he believes the threat of terror is imminent. I don't think he's far off base on that point."

"Oh, I've got to show you all something." Margaret stood and went inside.

"Brrr, it feels like winter out here." Pam crossed her arms and pulled her sweater tight at her neck.

"Pretty roses." Sheena nodded at a vase filled with a dozen yellow roses sitting at the center of the picnic table. "Did Jack get you those?"

Pam shook her head and smiled bashfully. "Believe it or not, those came from Everett Lester."

"No way!" Sheena said.

"Yep . . . well, they're from Karen, too." She giggled. "Anyway, they have this thing about roses. So when they heard we named the baby Everett, they sent these. Yellow means friendship."

"That is so cool," Sheena said.

"Hey, so we're on for Tuesday night, right?" Jack looked at Shakespeare, then Sheena.

They both nodded and smiled. "He got us the book already," Sheena said.

"I already read the first chapter. Can't you tell?" Shakespeare said.

They laughed. The book was about enhancing marriages. Jack was looking forward to going through it with Pam — and Sheena and Shakespeare.

It was quiet except for the wind and the children's laughter outside. Just a really nice moment between two couples who had been through a heck of a lot.

Jack interlocked his fingers with Pam's. He was so thankful at that moment. Thankful Shakespeare and Sheena had come to church. Thankful he and Pam were back on track. Thankful the baby was healthy.

Things were going to work out.

He would still have his job at the arena, when it opened back up. Pam still had her job — and insurance.

"Okay, here we go." Margaret made her way back outside, carrying a big brown box. "Look what showed up in the mail yesterday." She set the box on a bench and pointed at Shakespeare. "Remember how you told us we need to have a meeting place outside somewhere, in case of a fire or emergency?"

"Yeah, but I told you, you need to have a way down from the second floor to get to the meeting spot."

"Aha!" Margaret snapped her fingers and reached into the box. "Voilà!" She hoisted out a rope ladder designed to roll out of an upper-story window. "I got three of these babies — one for each of the girls' rooms, and one for yours."

"What about your room?" Jack said.

"Well, I won't be here forever. And I can go out one of the girls' rooms if I have to."

"Margaret, you don't want to move to that assisted-living place, do you?" Shakespeare said. "You're fine right here. These guys need you. And we like having you around."

Pam and Jack looked at each other and smiled, unsure about where that road would lead.

"Okay, okay, enough of the sentimental stuff," Margaret said. "Everybody close your eyes. I've got one more thing to show you. You're gonna love this."

Jack closed his eyes and assumed everyone else did too. He could hear Margaret digging around in the box.

"Wait just one second," she said.

They waited.

"The suspense is killing me," Shakespeare said.

In a muffled voice she said, "Okay, you can look!"

They all opened their eyes, and frail Margaret was standing there with an enormous pink gas mask strapped to her face.

Everyone howled.

Margaret took off the mask and laughed with them.

A cold breeze whipped in.

"Hey, it's starting to rain. Should we call the kids in?" Pam said.

"Absolutely not. They're having a blast," Shakespeare said. "And they're all gonna sleep like babies tonight."

"Speaking of babies, when do we get to see the little guy?" Sheena said.

Jack's phone buzzed.

"He takes long naps," Pam said. "He's like Jack. Gotta have his Sunday nap."

"Oh really? I hope we're not keeping you up, Jack," Shakespeare jested.

Jack got up and dug his phone out of his pocket. "Actually, I'm enjoying myself very much." He looked at the phone but didn't recognize the number.

"Hello, this is Jack."

"Jack, this is Buck Stevens from the *Gazette*. I hate to bother you on Sunday."

Jack stopped breathing for a second. He shot Pam an excited look and stepped into the house. "No bother at all, Mr. Stevens. What can I do for you?"

"Well, I'm in kind of a pinch."

"Okay." Jack walked to the kitchen and leaned on the counter, barely breathing.

"The city editor I told you about who was looking to get back onto a beat . . . Well, she got back onto a beat all right. At another paper." Buck chuckled. "She's moving to Cincinnati."

Jack lowered his head, knowing what was coming, knowing his God was intimate and loving and faithful.

"So that leaves me with a gaping hole on my city desk."

Tears welled up in Jack's eyes. "I see."

"I'm calling to see if you'd like to become the newest city editor at the *Gazette.* If there's any way you could, I'd like you to start tomorrow. If you were to come in around ten, we could talk about salary and benefits. I know it's short notice, but I also know you've been looking pretty hard."

Jack had to gather himself.

God blew him away.

He took several very deep breaths. Very deep.

"Jack? Are you there?"

"Yes, sir . . . I'm here." He cleared his throat. "I would be honored to be your new city editor."

"Oh, that is fantastic. Shall we say ten tomorrow?"

"Absolutely! Ten tomorrow, it is. Ten sharp."

■ ■ ■ ■

AFTER
WORDS

. . . A LITTLE MORE . . .

When a delightful concert comes to an
end, the orchestra might offer an encore.
When a fine meal comes to an end, it's
always nice to savor a bit of dessert.
When a great story comes to an end, we
think you may want to linger.
And so, we offer . . .

AfterWords — just a little something more
after you have finished a David C Cook
novel.

We invite you to stay awhile in the story.
Thanks for reading!

Turn the page for . . .

• DISCUSSION QUESTIONS

SKY ZONE:
DISCUSSION QUESTIONS

1. Do you know any "survivalists" like Brian Shakespeare? Should people prepare for widespread emergencies? How much preparation is too much? Discuss.

2. Discuss how your faith influences the extent to which you prepare for such emergencies.

3. When Jack, Shakespeare, and the rest of the EventPros staff were given the opportunity to go home before the event began at Columbus Festival Arena, should they have left? Why or why not? Would *you* have left?

4. Financial troubles deeply affected Jack and Pam's relationship in the book. How have financial circumstances impacted your life, marriage, family? Did you learn anything from Jack and Pam's story that

might help you in this area?

5. Who was your favorite character in *Sky Zone,* and why? Least favorite?

6. Did you have suspicions early on about who might be behind the terrorist attack at the arena? Discuss.

7. Pam sure did go through a lot in this book! Put yourself in her shoes for a moment and describe what would have been the most difficult part of this ordeal. How would *you* have dealt with it?

8. The fear of terrorism is a very real and growing problem in our society. Do you worry about acts of terror in your daily life? What are your biggest fears — and how do you overcome them?

9. This is the third book in The Crittendon Files. Did you read all of them? Which was your favorite, and why? Would you like to see more books in this series?

10. Did you recognize any of the characters in *Sky Zone* from Creston's earlier novels? Fun fact: Everett and Karen Lester were the main characters in Creston's first two

thrillers, *Dark Star: Confessions of a Rock Idol* and *Full Tilt.* You can find out more about those and all of Creston's books at CrestonMapes.com.

11. Did you know that Creston enjoys engaging with readers and book clubs both in person and via Skype and Face-Time? To find out more, contact Creston through his website: CrestonMapes.com.

Dear Reader,

Since my first novel was published back in 2005, many of you have been with me on this journey every step of the way. Others have joined in somewhere along the line and have gone back to read all six of my thrillers. To each of you, I want to take a moment to say thank you!

Being an author is a solitary job. For me, it is extremely hard work that comes with hours upon hours of organizing, research, deep concentration, and soul searching. So, when I hear from readers like you, it really makes my day. And the generous way in which you have shared my books with so many people — those in prisons, neighborhoods, drug rehab facilities, and book clubs — really makes it all worthwhile.

As you may know by now, I enjoy connecting with my readers, so don't hesitate to reach out via my website, Twitter, and Facebook:

www.CrestonMapes.com

www.Twitter.com/CrestonMapes

www.Facebook.com/Creston.Mapes

The most powerful things you can do to help me continue writing tension-filled thrillers are to share my books with your friends and to post reviews about them on Amazon and Goodreads.

Thank you again for being along for the ride.

Best regards,
Creston Mapes